L ruse

Adele Hope

Published by Adele Hope, 2024.

This is a work of fiction. Similarities to real people, places, or events are entirely coincidental.

DARK FUSE

First edition. November 11, 2024.

Copyright © 2024 Adele Hope.

ISBN: 979-8224519736

Written by Adele Hope.

Chapter 1: Smoke and Shadows

The air smells like burned wood and the bitter tang of chemicals, thick and acrid in my lungs. My boots hit the pavement with a quiet thud, the kind that doesn't match the chaos around me. The fire crackles, roars, and snaps like an angry beast, eager to consume everything in its path. The warehouse, once a vibrant hub of whatever people use warehouses for, now stands reduced to a jagged skeleton of metal and charred rubble. It looks almost poetic, in a way—how something so heavy and solid could collapse into ash so effortlessly.

I raise my camera, snapping a few wide shots of the scene, the smoke swirling in thick columns above the wreckage. I'm not here to mourn the building. I'm here to tell the story. The one that's still unfolding, as the firemen dart about, hoses blasting water that hisses in protest as it hits the flames. The sirens are finally fading, but the heat? The heat is unrelenting, as if the fire is trying to make some kind of statement, an explosive punctuation to a sentence no one's yet deciphered.

I'm about to make my way over to a group of witnesses, their faces smeared with soot and their voices shaky from the trauma, when a shout splits the air. It's sharp, commanding, unmistakable.

"Hey, you! Get back!"

I freeze, instinctively lifting my chin as I turn toward the voice, already knowing who it is. Even before I spot him, I know. It's impossible not to. The man's voice is like gravel being ground under the weight of a moving truck, rough and unyielding. And then there he is, striding toward me with the kind of confidence that could only come from wearing fire-resistant gear and carrying the weight of a hundred blazing structures on his shoulders.

Evan Stark. The firefighter who never saw a woman he couldn't intimidate, or so he liked to think. With his thick dark hair tousled from the heat, his jawline carved like granite, and those eyes—those damn eyes that could freeze you in place with a single glance—he's the last person I wanted to run into tonight. I didn't need this. I had a story to write, and I sure as hell didn't need him messing it up with his broad shoulders and narrow mind.

"I said, back off!" He's right there now, the smell of smoke clinging to his clothes like an old lover's perfume, a reminder that he's seen things—worse things than most people could even begin to imagine.

I tilt my head, not moving an inch. "You're barking up the wrong tree, Stark," I mutter under my breath, but loud enough for him to hear. "I'm here for a story, not a kiss."

His lips twist into something between a smirk and a snarl, and I can practically feel the heat of his gaze as it burns into me. He crosses his arms, standing tall and imposing, like he thinks he's the boss of me. I hate that. I hate how people—especially him—tend to think they can order me around just because I'm holding a camera. "This is a crime scene," he says, his voice dropping into a low growl that rumbles in his chest. "I'm telling you, stay out of the way."

I force myself to meet his eyes, daring him to look away first. His hands are still steady, no sign of nerves, no sign of the chaos around us affecting him. It's like he was born for this—sacrificing his soul to battle flames, to save strangers, to carry the weight of everything that burns.

But I'm not afraid. I've covered disasters before—fires, floods, all of it. I've been in the trenches with people who are used to seeing death and destruction every day. And none of that compares to the feeling of someone trying to tell me what to do. Especially not someone like him.

"I'm not here for your permission," I say coolly, keeping my voice steady even though I want to punch him right in his perfectly chiseled jaw. "And I'm not here to stand behind you while you pretend you've got this whole situation under control. I'm here for the story."

His eyes narrow, a flicker of irritation crossing his face, but he doesn't back down. Instead, he leans in, lowering his voice so it's just for me. "You think you're here for a story? This is more than you're bargaining for, sweetheart. Get out of here while you still can."

A part of me wants to heed his warning. A smaller, more sensible part of me. But the stubborn streak, the one that never lets me walk away from a challenge, especially one I haven't won yet, pushes that part down like a beachball in a swimming pool. I refuse to let him intimidate me, especially not when I've got a job to do.

"I'll decide when it's time to go," I shoot back, my voice firm, unshakable.

Evan doesn't respond right away. Instead, he stares at me for what feels like an eternity. I know what he's thinking: he's trying to figure out what kind of woman would stand in front of a fire, practically daring it to burn her alive. And I know the answer. The kind of woman who refuses to let anyone dictate her fate, even if it's a man with the power to save lives with a snap of his fingers.

Finally, he lets out a breath, like he's deciding whether or not to argue further, and then he does the one thing I didn't expect. He steps back, just slightly, as if giving me the tiniest sliver of space to breathe. But it's not enough to make me think I've won. Not by a long shot.

"You're pushing your luck," he warns, his tone lowering to a near whisper as the wind picks up, stirring the edges of the smoke that are drifting past us.

"I've been known to do that," I reply, just as quietly, with a smile that I know will drive him crazy.

The heat from the fire beats down on us, but somehow, the tension between Evan and me feels hotter, sharper. He stands there, his posture a solid wall of resolve, a man who's used to being right, who's used to giving orders that people follow without question. I'm not sure if it's the smoke in my lungs or his arrogant little smirk, but I'm about to give him an answer he won't forget.

Instead, I fold my arms over my chest, matching his stance. "I'm not going anywhere," I say, my tone light, almost playful, but laced with steel. The kind of steel that makes people stop, look, and realize they might have underestimated me. I've spent my entire career getting where I am by pushing back, by questioning, by not letting anyone decide what I can and can't do.

He shifts slightly, like he's recalculating, and for a moment, I think we might be at a stalemate. But then, he surprises me.

"Suit yourself," he says with a shrug, turning his back on me and marching back to his team. There's something oddly satisfying about the way he dismisses me, as if he's already made his decision about me. It's almost like he's telling me I'm just a blip on his radar, something he can ignore.

And maybe, just maybe, it's the way he walks—so damn sure of himself—that makes me want to prove him wrong. There's a quiet arrogance about him, but beneath it, something else flickers. Something... darker. Maybe I've been watching too many crime dramas, but I can't shake the feeling that this fire isn't as simple as it seems. It isn't just some random disaster waiting to be written off.

I follow at a distance, my boots crunching against the gravel, each step a little more reluctant than the last. I hate how much I want to keep him in my sights, how much I want to know what's really going on under that stoic exterior. But, like every damn man who thinks he can walk through life with an effortless swagger, Evan Stark is impossible to ignore.

At the edge of the fire's perimeter, the sounds of radio static and urgent orders fill the air. Evan is kneeling down by the edge of the warehouse ruins, his brow furrowed, his mouth set in a tight line as he talks to a colleague. His words are clipped, but I catch just enough to understand that something's not right.

"It wasn't an accident," he says. "No way. This wasn't just some faulty wiring."

I freeze, my pulse picking up speed. I knew it. Something about the way the flames spread, how they didn't seem to follow any natural pattern, had bugged me since I arrived. The warehouse wasn't the only thing in that neighborhood, and the fire had spread far too quickly. I could smell it in the air now—the tang of something more deliberate than a simple mishap.

Evan turns to look at me as if he senses my presence, his gaze sharp. "I said stay back," he grates, but there's an edge to his voice now, like he's suddenly aware that I might be more than just a nuisance.

I lift my chin, refusing to shrink under the weight of his glare. "You're not the only one here trying to get the story, Stark." My voice carries, loud and steady, to make sure everyone in earshot knows that I'm not about to be bullied off the scene.

For a moment, he says nothing. He just stands there, looking at me, like he's debating whether or not to tell me to go home again. But instead, something in his eyes shifts. He's not quite relenting, but there's a flicker of something else—recognition, maybe. It's as if, for a split second, we're not adversaries anymore, just two people caught in the same tangled mess.

And then, before I can read too much into it, he speaks again, but this time it's different. There's a subtle change in his tone, something almost resigned. "This fire," he begins, his voice quieter now, "was started intentionally. Whoever did this, they knew what they were doing."

I narrow my eyes. "So it wasn't just some freak accident? Someone actually set this fire on purpose?" I can't believe it—except I can, because the details are starting to line up. Fires don't just happen like this.

"Yeah," he replies, rubbing his hand over his face, his exhaustion showing more now than it did before. "But it's not just about the fire. There's something off. We can't just put it out and move on. Whoever did this is still out there."

The air around us feels heavier now, thick with unspoken truths, the kind of truths that no one wants to deal with but that linger, pressing down on everyone involved. Evan's eyes flicker over to me again, and this time, I notice something else in them—something more than just frustration, more than the usual disdain for anyone who doesn't wear a uniform.

I can't help but feel a little surge of victory. I'm in. Not just for the story, but for whatever's coming next.

"You're not just a firefighter, are you?" I say, the question slipping out before I can stop it. I'm already regretting it—already wishing I had kept my mouth shut, but there's something about him that pulls at my curiosity. "You're onto something, aren't you?"

For a moment, he doesn't answer. His jaw tightens, his hand resting on his hip, and I can tell that whatever he's dealing with—whatever he's not saying—is a hell of a lot bigger than a simple arson investigation.

He finally looks at me, his expression unreadable, his lips pulling into a wry smile. "You're too smart for your own good, you know that?"

And just like that, I know I've gotten under his skin. Maybe not in the way I'd hoped, but in a way that tells me we're not done yet. Not by a long shot.

There's a moment, just before the words fall from my lips, when I can see the invisible line I've just crossed. Evan's eyes narrow, his posture shifting into something almost predatory, like he's decided I'm worth the trouble after all. I don't know if I'm a puzzle to him or just a distraction, but whatever it is, I've got his attention. That's dangerous. I've spent years honing the art of blending into the background, of disappearing behind a camera and a notebook, never really the center of anything. And now, here I am—splashed across the front of his world like an oil stain on a silk shirt.

"You've got this wrong," he says, voice a low rumble, almost like he's trying to talk himself into believing it. "You don't know anything about this fire. Hell, you don't know anything about what's really going on here."

I feel the weight of his words like a challenge. I know he's right about one thing: I don't know everything. I'm just piecing together a puzzle from the fragments that have landed at my feet. But I'm damn good at it. "So, why don't you fill me in, then?" I say, forcing my voice to stay steady despite the spark of irritation crawling up my spine.

He runs a hand through his hair, looking over at the wreckage again, his face twisted in thought. The fire is subdued now, the massive billows of smoke turning into a thick haze. But there's something in the way the flames have burned that doesn't sit right with me. It's too controlled, too... deliberate. The heat is too concentrated in some places, the spreading pattern too perfect. I've seen arson before. This isn't the chaos of an accident; it's the art of someone who knew exactly what they were doing.

"You really think this was an accident?" Evan says it like he's talking to a child, and for a moment, I almost want to snap back at him. But then the truth hits me, cold and hard.

"No," I reply, the word slipping from my mouth like it was always meant to be there. "I don't."

For a moment, there's only silence between us, the crackle of still-burning embers the only sound. It feels like something else is happening—something unspoken between us, like we're both aware of the weight of what we've just admitted.

Evan glances at me, his expression unreadable, before his gaze shifts past me, scanning the crowd of bystanders still huddled at the edge of the scene. It's like he's pulling away again, retreating into whatever mask he wears when he's trying to shield himself from the reality of what's really going on.

"You don't get it," he says, his voice a little quieter now. "This isn't just about a fire. This is bigger. And whoever did this... they're still out there."

The air around us seems to freeze. I've covered enough stories to know when someone's telling you they've just scratched the surface of something much worse. But the way Evan says it—so matter-of-factly, like he's seen the worst of it and doesn't have the time to explain it to anyone who isn't already in on the secret—makes my blood run cold.

I take a deep breath, trying to steady myself, but the unease in my chest refuses to be soothed. "Whoever did this... you think they've done it before?"

He doesn't answer immediately, just stares into the smoke, his jaw tense. And I get it. He doesn't want to admit how bad things might really be. He's a man of action, not words. But it's there, hanging between us—something darker than the fire, something that doesn't belong to this neighborhood, this town, or anyone who should be here.

"I don't know," Evan says, finally. He doesn't look at me when he speaks. "But if they have, I'm betting they won't stop here."

The weight of his words hits me like a ton of bricks. I hadn't considered that—hadn't let myself think beyond the fire and the immediate aftermath. But now? Now I realize just how deep this could go. This isn't just about reporting a fire, about finding out who started it and why. This is about something much bigger—something that could unravel the fabric of this entire neighborhood.

"Then we need to find them," I say, the words tumbling out before I can stop them. The certainty in my voice surprises even me, but it's there. It's real.

Evan finally turns to face me, his eyes piercing and intense. "You don't understand, do you? This isn't just about tracking down some random criminal. Whoever did this—whatever they're after—it's not just fire they're playing with. They're playing with something much worse. Something you won't be able to just write away in your little stories."

I bristle at the way he talks about my work. It's the same way every man has ever talked about it, dismissing it as if there's some kind of secret hierarchy where my words can't possibly mean anything unless they're wrapped in a uniform or a badge.

But this time, for some reason, I let it slide. I know he's not talking down to me. He's trying to warn me, to keep me safe from something he knows is coming. And that, in its own twisted way, makes me feel more alive than I've ever felt before.

"I don't need your protection, Stark," I say, meeting his gaze with all the fire I can muster. "What I need is the truth. And you're not the only one who can find it."

He doesn't respond immediately. There's something in his eyes, something guarded, like he's trying to make up his mind about me all over again. I don't know what he sees when he looks at me—whether it's admiration, irritation, or something else entirely—but whatever it is, it's enough to make him hesitate before he turns away.

"You don't know what you're getting yourself into," he says, his voice low and strained.

And with that, I realize—I might not. But that's never stopped me before. And it won't stop me now.

Just then, a distant scream pierces the air. It's sharp, frantic, and full of terror. Both of us freeze, heads snapping in the direction of the sound.

"Stay here," Evan orders, already moving toward the source of the scream.

But I don't stay. I follow him. Because whatever is happening now, it's about to get a whole lot worse.

Chapter 2: Sparks in the Ashes

The sun had barely begun to stretch its pale fingers over the city when I stepped into the chill of the morning air, the hum of a new day already filling the streets. I hadn't expected Evan to be waiting for me. He stood by the cracked pavement just outside the newsroom, arms crossed tight enough that his sleeves barely reached his wrists, his posture stiff, shoulders tense, like a man holding onto something far more fragile than pride. His usual sharp jawline seemed sharper today, his lips pressed into a line so thin I wondered if he was physically biting back words.

His eyes caught mine the moment I walked out the door, an accusation hanging between us before any words were exchanged. I half-expected him to lash out, something loud, something volatile to match the anger that had been simmering under his skin last night. But instead, he just stood there, waiting, looking at me like I'd done something more than ask a few pointed questions. Like I'd just planted a knife in his chest and was now wondering why he wasn't bleeding.

"Last night," he started, his voice low, each syllable measured like he was holding back a storm. "What you asked—it's reckless. You've put my team at risk."

I sighed, but the frustration clung to me, sharp and unforgiving. "You think I'm the one putting people at risk?"

Evan's eyes darkened, a flash of something deeper flickering behind them—something I couldn't quite place. Maybe it was guilt. Or maybe it was fear. He didn't say anything, though, just took a step closer, his boots scraping the concrete with a sharp edge.

"You've seen the fires, right?" he asked, his voice barely above a whisper now. "Whoever's setting them? They won't hesitate to burn down a journalist if they think it'll keep their secrets safe." His eyes locked onto mine, and I felt the weight of his words settle over me like a thick fog. "You don't understand how dangerous this is."

Dangerous? I'd been chasing dangerous stories for years. Some of the people I'd gone after had more blood on their hands than I cared to count. So, yeah, I understood danger. But what I didn't understand was Evan. This wasn't the way he usually spoke to me. He didn't speak to me like this, with that edge of something unspoken, like I was both an ally and a threat. And I couldn't quite decide if I was annoyed or... intrigued.

I raised an eyebrow, forcing a grin, trying to push past the uncertainty gnawing at me. "Are you trying to protect me? Or are you trying to scare me off?"

Evan's expression faltered, just for a moment, but it was enough to make me second-guess everything. The tough, stony exterior cracked, and something else slid through—a fleeting vulnerability, like a crack in the facade that threatened to widen. Then, just as quickly, he was back to being the distant, frustratingly unreadable man I had been trying to figure out for weeks.

"Look, it's not about protecting you," he snapped, though his voice was quieter now. "It's about keeping your head on straight. You're not the first journalist to try to dig into something they don't understand. And most of them end up regretting it."

I didn't know whether to be offended or impressed. The challenge in his words was undeniable, but it didn't scare me. It only fueled something else inside me, something sharp and focused. Evan had always been a puzzle—an intriguing, frustrating puzzle. And now, it felt like he was daring me to solve him, to get beneath that icy veneer of his and see what was really driving him.

"And if I decide not to listen?" I asked, folding my arms across my chest, meeting his gaze head-on.

"Then you'll be doing more than risking your career," he said, his tone suddenly colder, the anger flaring back. "You'll be putting your life on the line for a story that might not be worth it."

There it was again—the warning. But it wasn't just a warning. There was something more layered underneath it, something unspoken. I could feel the tension in the air between us, thick enough to cut with a knife. He was still standing there, close enough that I could feel the heat radiating off him, but it wasn't the heat of anger anymore. It was something else. Something... personal.

"You're not the first person to tell me that," I said, with a small laugh that didn't quite reach my eyes. "But I'm not going to stop digging just because someone tells me to. Not when I know there's something bigger behind these fires. Something more than what they want me to see."

Evan's gaze darkened, his jaw tightening as if he wanted to say more but couldn't bring himself to. He opened his mouth, then closed it again, his chest rising and falling with the kind of breath that spoke of frustration too thick to vocalize.

"Then I guess," he said slowly, his voice suddenly softer than before, "you're not as easily scared off as I thought."

I wanted to laugh. He still didn't get it, did he? The adrenaline, the chase—it was in my blood. He couldn't scare me off with words. But I could see that he wasn't so easily convinced of that. The more he stood there, the more I realized he wasn't just trying to protect me. No, there was something else going on beneath the surface. Something deeper.

And now, for better or worse, I was in this mess with him. Too deep to turn back, and maybe, just maybe, I didn't want to.

Evan was right about one thing, though—whoever was behind these fires didn't want anyone poking around. And that fact alone made me more determined than ever to find out who they were—and why they were willing to burn everything down to keep their secrets buried.

Evan didn't leave after our conversation. He didn't storm off in a huff like I half-expected, or give me the icy silence I was starting to get used to. Instead, he stayed right there, watching me as I walked towards the newsroom doors like he was waiting for me to crack, for me to suddenly drop everything and ask for help.

That wouldn't happen. Not with me. Not when the story was this close to burning through my fingers.

I paused just inside the glass doors, casting a quick glance back at him. He was still standing in the same spot, his arms now folded, his posture more rigid than before, but his eyes... they were watching me like I was the only thing in the world worth paying attention to. I felt an unexpected twist of something—guilt, maybe?—creep into my chest, but I shook it off. There was a story here, something huge, something that could make my career, and I wasn't going to let some overprotective, brooding man derail it.

The door clicked shut behind me, but I couldn't shake the feeling of being followed. Maybe it was his presence, so heavy in the air, like smoke lingering long after the fire's been put out.

I made my way up to my desk, greeted by the low murmur of a newsroom that was already buzzing with the usual chaos of deadlines, phone calls, and the incessant clacking of keyboards. There was a certain rhythm to it—the sort of hum that you could almost get lost in if you weren't careful. I pulled my chair out and sat down, but even as I began scanning through the emails, the usual monotony of the morning didn't settle me. Instead, I felt restless, like I was standing at the edge of something dangerous and exciting, and every instinct told me to jump.

"How's the fire story going?" Lila, the photojournalist, leaned over the partition between our desks, her eyes sharp but playful.

She was always on the hunt for a good story, always the first one to get her hands dirty in the field.

I gave her a tight-lipped smile, not ready to share much. "It's still burning," I said, my voice casual, but I knew she could read the undertones in it. Lila had that gift, that ability to see through the surface and into the chaos beneath.

She raised an eyebrow, leaning in closer. "You're not gonna let it go, are you?"

I shook my head. "Not when there's something more to it."

"Just don't get yourself hurt. Or worse," she added with a warning glint in her eye. "We need you around here."

I didn't answer her right away. Instead, I turned my attention to the latest updates on the fire investigation. The authorities were still calling it arson, but they didn't have much to go on. They had their usual list of suspects—disgruntled employees, people with insurance money to gain—but none of it sat right with me. There was something... off about the whole thing, something I couldn't quite put my finger on.

I was about to dive deeper into the reports when my phone buzzed on the desk. A message from Evan. I hesitated for a second before unlocking it.

"Meet me. You need to hear this."

I swallowed, my fingers tightening around the phone. A part of me wanted to ignore it—wanted to bury myself in work, to pretend like he wasn't still sitting there in the back of my mind, stirring something that wasn't quite curiosity but something far more dangerous.

I could feel my pulse quicken as I typed a response.

"Where?"

His reply came quickly.

"Bunker down in the old factory. No one will find us there."

My brow furrowed. The old factory? The place had been abandoned for years, a half-rotted shell of what it once was, filled with broken windows and rusted beams. There was no reason for him to be there unless—

Unless he had something to show me.

I didn't like the sound of it, but I wasn't about to back out now. I grabbed my coat from the back of my chair, shoved my phone into my pocket, and stood up.

"Where are you going?" Lila's voice rang out as I made my way to the door.

"I'll be back," I said over my shoulder, not waiting for her to ask more questions.

The city was still waking up when I stepped outside, the streets damp from last night's rain, a slight fog hanging in the air. It had a strange quality to it—an eerie sort of quiet that felt heavier than usual. As I crossed the street to my car, I glanced back toward the newsroom, the lights inside glowing in sharp contrast to the gray morning. I wasn't sure if I was doing the right thing. Hell, I didn't even know if I should be meeting Evan in some decrepit factory, but the pull of the story was too strong to ignore.

The drive was quick, but by the time I reached the factory, the unease that had started in my chest had blossomed into full-blown tension. The factory loomed before me, a silhouette against the soft light of the rising sun, its windows dark and its door hanging loosely on its hinges. I hesitated for a moment, wondering if this was some kind of trap. But then I saw Evan—just a shadow at first, standing just inside the door, waiting for me.

I parked and stepped out of the car, my boots crunching on the gravel as I approached him. He didn't move as I got closer, his eyes narrowed in the dim light, but there was something about the way he stood there that sent a shiver down my spine.

"Here?" I asked, keeping my voice steady, though inside, I was anything but calm.

He didn't answer right away. Instead, he turned and walked further into the factory, the faint echo of his footsteps ringing in the silence.

I followed him without another word, the air thick with anticipation. There was no going back now.

The floor of the old factory creaked beneath my boots as I followed Evan deeper into the shadows, each step echoing off the crumbling walls. The air inside was thick with the scent of mildew and rust, a feeling of decay that wrapped around me like an unwelcome embrace. The sunlight filtered through the broken windows in thin, streaked beams, casting pale slivers of light across the dusty floor, making the place feel more like a forgotten tomb than a place of business.

"Why here?" I asked, my voice sounding too loud in the oppressive silence. "Why not somewhere safer? Somewhere we don't look like we're planning to get murdered?"

Evan didn't answer immediately. Instead, he paused in front of an old, weathered workbench, the wood scarred with years of neglect. He ran a hand along the edge, his fingers brushing lightly over the grain as if it held some kind of secret he couldn't share.

"Because it's the one place no one will come looking," he finally muttered, his voice low and edged with something that could have been worry—or perhaps fear.

I leaned against the frame of the door, watching him carefully, but his attention was fixed on the floor, on a set of old files and scattered papers. The silence between us stretched long, and I could feel the weight of it, like a stone pressing down on my chest. Something was off. The Evan I knew—the one who was always so damn confident, so in control—had disappeared. In his place stood a man who looked like he was carrying a burden too heavy to bear.

"So, what's the big reveal?" I pushed, trying to break through the wall he was putting up. "You call me all the way out here, dragging me through a ghost town of a factory, and you still haven't told me what's going on."

He turned to me, his gaze flicking to mine for just a second before dropping again, as if the weight of his words was something he didn't want to face. "I don't want you involved," he said, his voice low and tight, like he was trying to hold something back. "I shouldn't have brought you here. But you're already in too deep."

I let out a sharp laugh, the sound of it cutting through the stillness of the factory like a knife. "You think I'm going to back off just because you say so? If anything, this is only making me more determined to find out what the hell's going on."

Evan's jaw tightened, the muscle in his cheek twitching as he clenched his teeth. "This isn't a game. You have no idea what you're dealing with." He stepped closer, his expression darkening. "There are people involved in this who would burn the entire city down just to keep their secrets. They won't hesitate to make sure you disappear if you start digging too deep."

I stared at him, the edge of his words sinking in. There was more going on here than I realized. This wasn't just about some arsonist setting fires for kicks. This was bigger. Much bigger.

"Who are these people?" I asked, my voice softer now, less challenging, more... curious. "Why are you so scared?"

Evan's eyes narrowed, and he took a step back, as if my question had startled him. "You don't want to know," he said sharply. "Trust me."

I could feel the air between us thicken, the tension crawling under my skin, until it became almost unbearable. There was something he wasn't telling me, something that was eating away at him, and the more he held it back, the more desperate I became to uncover it. I wasn't going to walk away from this. Not now.

The old factory had become a maze of shadowed corners and forgotten debris, the silence pressing in from all sides as I followed Evan through the winding passageways. We reached the far end of the building, where a large, rusted door stood half ajar. He didn't hesitate before pushing it open, revealing a small, dimly lit room beyond.

Inside, there were crates stacked high, covered in dust and cobwebs, and in the far corner, a metal filing cabinet that looked like it hadn't been touched in years. Evan crossed the room quickly, his footsteps barely making a sound on the worn concrete floor, and began rifling through the top drawer of the cabinet.

I stood back, watching him carefully. There was a sense of urgency in his movements now, something almost frantic in the way he fumbled through the papers, pulling them out and skimming through them, his brow furrowed in concentration.

Finally, he stopped, pulling out a thick folder with a frayed edge. He turned to face me, his face pale in the dim light. "This is what you're looking for," he said, holding the folder out toward me.

I hesitated, my fingers brushing against the edge of the folder, but I didn't take it right away. Instead, I looked up at him, studying the look on his face. He was sweating now, his eyes darting around the room like he expected someone to burst through the door at any moment.

"You're not telling me everything," I said, my voice steady, even though my heart was racing. "What are you so afraid of?"

Evan's eyes darkened, and for a moment, I saw something in them that made my stomach tighten. Something dark and dangerous, like a storm that was just starting to brew.

"You need to leave," he said abruptly, his voice low and harsh. "Now."

I opened my mouth to protest, but before I could say anything, the sound of footsteps echoed from the hallway outside the room. My heart skipped a beat.

Someone else was here.

I turned toward the door just as the sound of a door crashing open echoed through the building, followed by a voice. A voice I recognized.

"Looking for something?"

Before I could react, the door slammed shut behind me, and the world seemed to freeze.

Chapter 3: Beneath the Flames

The air was thick with the acrid scent of burnt wood and the pungent sting of gasoline. I stepped over the charred remains of what used to be a quaint little bakery, a place where the warm scent of fresh bread used to drift into the street, tempting passersby with promises of sweetness and warmth. Now, all that remained was a skeleton of scorched brick and blackened beams, the remains of something once full of life. My camera clicked again, capturing the haunting aftermath. I knew the scene would make the front page, but it wasn't just the destruction that drew me in—it was the certainty in my gut that this wasn't an accident.

There was a rhythm to the way fires like this started. A pattern, one I couldn't ignore. And as I squatted to adjust the lens, focusing on a particular spot where the flames had licked the walls a little too eagerly, I felt the hair on the back of my neck stand on end. It wasn't just the fire; it was something more.

My hand stilled as I heard a sharp intake of breath behind me. I didn't need to look to know who it was. The scent of cedarwood and smoke preceded him. Evan had that effect—like a gust of wind on a summer day, unpredictable but never unwelcome. I didn't turn around. There was something about him that made me want to avoid his gaze, as if I already knew how this encounter would unfold.

"You shouldn't be here," Evan said, his voice low, clipped. He didn't need to tell me that; I knew the dangers of being on a scene like this, especially one involving fire. But there was something in his tone, something that spoke more of worry than authority, and it made me pause, just for a moment.

"I've got my reasons," I muttered, not bothering to meet his eyes. I knew he'd never approve of me being here. To Evan, everything was a risk, and everyone else was a liability. It was his job to keep people safe, but I didn't need him hovering over me, questioning my decisions.

He took a few steps closer, his boots crunching against the gravel, and then he was standing next to me, close enough that I could feel the warmth radiating off him, despite the cold morning air. His presence was a weight I hadn't anticipated, one that pressed on my chest in a way that made it hard to breathe.

"Are you trying to get yourself killed?" His eyes flickered from my camera to the burning remains of the building, his jaw tight with something I couldn't quite decipher. Maybe it was frustration, maybe concern. Either way, it felt too personal for a man who barely knew me.

"Someone has to figure out what's going on," I replied, meeting his gaze for the first time. His expression was unreadable, a mask of authority and restraint. I couldn't help but wonder if he was hiding something, something I wasn't supposed to see.

He hesitated for a moment, his lips pressing into a thin line, and I could feel the tension in the space between us, as thick and suffocating as the smoke hanging in the air. It wasn't the first time we'd crossed paths, but something about this moment felt different. There was an electricity in the air, a spark of recognition, but also a deep, unspoken warning. His eyes softened, just for a second, and I could tell he was weighing something—something that would change everything between us if he decided to say it aloud.

"I don't want you involved in this," he said, his voice barely above a whisper.

His words hung in the air, suspended between us like a fragile thread. It wasn't a request, not exactly, but it wasn't an order either. It was something more—a plea wrapped in the weight of years of experience. I could see it in the way he shifted his stance, as if bracing himself for my response, but I wasn't sure what he expected me to say.

"You think I'm just going to walk away?" I raised an eyebrow, unable to stop the dry humor from creeping into my voice.

Evan's lips twitched, and for a moment, I caught a glimpse of the man behind the uniform—the one who had spent years putting out fires, not just the literal ones, but the kind that left scars in places you couldn't see. He wasn't just concerned for my safety. He was afraid of what might happen if I started asking the right questions.

"I think you're stubborn," he said, his tone softening just enough that I almost missed it. "And you have no idea what you're getting into."

I didn't argue with him, but I didn't back down either. There was too much at stake. The fire was no accident. I could feel it in my bones, in the way the scorch marks seemed to form patterns, almost deliberate. This wasn't the work of a random arsonist; someone was setting these fires on purpose. And I was the only one who seemed to see it.

"You can't stop me from asking questions," I said, taking a step back and adjusting the strap on my camera. "I'll be careful. But I'm not walking away."

Evan stared at me for a long moment, as if trying to read me, to figure out whether I was truly as stubborn as he thought. Maybe I was, but that didn't change the fact that I had a job to do. And if I was going to do it, I needed to understand everything about these fires. Even if it meant crossing a line I hadn't yet seen.

He exhaled sharply, a sound filled with frustration, but also something else—resignation. "I just don't want you to get hurt."

The words, simple and raw, cut through the tension like a knife. And in that moment, I realized that Evan's worry wasn't just about the fires. It was about me.

Something was happening here, something neither of us had expected.

The flames had long been extinguished, but the scar they left on the town seemed as fresh as ever. I could see the way the burnt edges of the building seemed to hold onto the memories of its life, stubbornly clinging to the traces of what it once was. It was almost as if the fire had stolen a piece of history—a chapter that would never be written again. The heat still lingered in the air, the kind that clung to your skin like an unwanted lover's touch, a reminder of what had happened and what might be coming next.

I was crouched near the remnants of the bakery, my camera snapping away as I worked to capture the heartache frozen in time. The scene was raw, unsettling, and I had to get every angle, every scar that the fire had left behind. This wasn't just about documenting another tragedy; this was about understanding it. I wasn't one to shy away from discomfort, not when it was the key to uncovering the truth.

And then he was there again, like a shadow that never quite left. Evan.

"You're still here?" His voice had that edge to it, the kind that warned me I wasn't supposed to be doing this. But I didn't need his permission, not now, not with so many unanswered questions hanging in the air like smoke.

I didn't look up right away, not wanting to give him the satisfaction of knowing how much his presence affected me. Instead, I adjusted the lens of my camera, trying to ignore the way his footsteps grew louder, as if he was trying to make his presence felt, trying to dominate the space I was claiming for myself.

"Someone has to do the dirty work," I said, flicking a glance at him through my peripheral vision. He wasn't standing too far behind me, and I could feel the weight of his gaze on my back. If I were the sort of person who allowed others to influence my decisions, I might have taken a step back, but I wasn't.

"You think this is something you should be involved in?" The question was sharp, loaded with a frustration I didn't want to acknowledge. Evan's voice was a contradiction—a mix of command and uncertainty. He wasn't just angry anymore. He was anxious, like there was something much bigger than the fire at play, and I was about to fall right into it.

I pressed the shutter once more, capturing the fading light that hung in the air like a fading memory. "What I think is that something isn't right here. I can feel it."

Evan didn't answer right away, his eyes scanning the ruins of the building, looking for something I couldn't see. I knew it then—he was hiding something. I could sense it in the way his jaw clenched, the way his hands stayed tight at his sides as if they were itching to do something but couldn't.

"Look," he said after a long pause, his voice lower now, almost tired, like he had already played out this conversation a hundred times in his head. "This isn't a game. You don't know what you're walking into."

I turned to face him, finally meeting his eyes, and I saw it—the flicker of something underneath the surface. He wasn't just trying to protect me; he was trying to protect something else. Something he didn't want me to see.

"Then tell me," I said, my voice firm despite the surge of doubt that threatened to creep in. "Tell me what's really going on. You're hiding something, Evan. I can feel it."

His eyes darted to the ground for a moment, as if he couldn't bear to meet my gaze any longer. I could see the struggle in his face, the way his lips pressed together as if he was fighting against a truth that didn't want to be buried any longer.

"It's not just a fire," he muttered finally, his words laced with the kind of tension that set my nerves on edge. "These aren't accidents, and you're playing with fire if you keep poking around."

I froze at his words, the camera dangling from my fingers as the full weight of what he was saying sank in. I had known it deep down, but hearing it from him made it real in a way I wasn't quite prepared for.

"Then what is it?" I asked, my voice quieter now, as if the mere act of speaking too loudly might make this whole thing implode. "Who's doing this, and why?"

He shook his head, a quick, sharp motion. "I can't tell you that."

The air between us thickened, the space growing smaller with every second that ticked by. My mind raced, the pieces of the puzzle swirling around in my head, refusing to lock into place. There was something he wasn't saying, something that he couldn't—something that made this all more dangerous than I'd realized.

"You want me to just walk away, don't you?" I said, a bitter laugh escaping before I could stop it. "You think that's going to solve anything?"

"I'm trying to protect you," he said, his voice tight with frustration.

"From what?" I shot back, stepping a little closer to him. "From the truth?"

The anger in his eyes flared for a moment, but it was quickly smothered, replaced by something far more complicated—something that had nothing to do with the fire. His gaze softened, almost imperceptibly, and for a second, I saw something else in him. Regret, maybe. Or guilt. But before I could get too caught up in trying to decipher it, he looked away.

"I didn't want you involved," he repeated, his words softer now, almost like a plea. "Not like this."

I took a deep breath, steadying myself against the tension that seemed to radiate off him. There was something about this whole situation that didn't add up, and no matter how much he tried to keep me in the dark, I wasn't going to let it go.

"Then it's a good thing I'm not the type to back down," I said, a wry smile tugging at the corner of my lips.

His lips twitched, as if the corners of his mouth wanted to curve upward but didn't quite dare. He was on the edge, I could tell. One word, one moment, and this whole thing would unravel. The fire was just the beginning. And whatever was lurking beneath the ashes was going to burn a lot hotter.

The moment his words sank in, I felt an electric jolt between us, as if the very ground beneath us had shifted. I hadn't realized how badly I needed him to give me something—to open up, to let me into whatever world he was desperately trying to keep me out of. But Evan wasn't the type to let his walls down easily. He had that much down to an art, like a fortress with a drawbridge permanently raised.

I could tell by the way his eyes flitted away from mine, how his jaw tightened again, that he was battling something—something far deeper than just a concern for my safety. And maybe, just maybe, I'd finally found the crack in his armor. But no matter how much I wanted him to speak, to tell me what he was hiding, he wasn't budging.

"I'm not backing down," I said again, my voice even, as though my resolve had somehow seeped into the ground beneath me, rooting me in place.

His gaze shifted, narrowing slightly as though calculating the consequences of my stubbornness. He let out a slow, controlled breath, as if he had already come to terms with the fact that I wouldn't leave until I had answers. There was something almost reluctantly appreciative in the way he looked at me, as if, despite everything, he respected the fire I had in me.

"You don't get it," he muttered, looking back at the blackened remnants of the bakery, his tone filled with a kind of weary resignation. "You think you're just dealing with arson, but this is bigger than that. There's something... more going on. People don't just set fires for no reason."

I felt the air grow colder, the weight of his words hitting me with an unexpected force. There was something layered underneath the simple statement, a quiet urgency that I couldn't quite grasp. What was he really trying to say? What was he keeping from me?

"So what's the deal, then?" I pressed, unable to hide the edge of impatience creeping into my voice. "What aren't you telling me, Evan?"

His eyes darted around, almost nervously, like he was trying to figure out how much of the truth I could handle without completely unraveling. And in that moment, I knew—he was afraid. Afraid of what might happen if I knew too much.

"Some things are better left alone," he said finally, his voice tight. "Some people will do whatever it takes to keep things quiet. And you don't want to get caught in the crossfire."

My pulse quickened, the words sending a ripple of unease through me. The stakes were higher than I'd imagined. This wasn't just about me getting caught up in a fire. It was about a much darker force at work, something he wasn't willing—or able—to explain. Not yet, anyway.

I took a step forward, not because I was braver than I felt, but because I was desperate for the truth. "Who's behind this, Evan? Who's really pulling the strings?"

His silence was deafening. For a moment, I thought maybe he wouldn't answer at all, that I had finally pushed him too far. But then, just when I thought I might never get an answer, his lips parted, and the words came out in a harsh whisper.

"You're already involved, whether you know it or not."

My heart skipped, a sudden tension rushing through my veins. What did he mean by that? How could I already be involved in something that felt so out of my reach?

Before I could ask him to elaborate, the shrill ring of his phone cut through the air like a blade. Evan cursed under his breath, glancing at the screen, then back at me with a resigned look that spoke volumes.

"Wait here," he commanded, his voice firm and insistent. "Don't move."

I nodded, though I had no intention of staying put for long. He walked a few steps away, speaking low and urgent into the phone, the tension in his posture unmistakable. I couldn't make out the words, but the way his shoulders tensed and his brow furrowed told me everything I needed to know. Something was happening, and it wasn't just about this fire. The world around me felt suddenly smaller, the air too thin, as if the walls were closing in.

I tried to shake the feeling off, to focus on what I could control. My camera. The scene. The missing pieces of the puzzle. But as I turned to take a few more shots of the wreckage, I heard a faint noise behind me—footsteps, soft but deliberate. Someone was approaching, but not from Evan's direction.

I spun around, my heart leaping into my throat as I caught sight of the figure emerging from the shadows, just beyond the remains of the bakery. A man, tall and imposing, his silhouette cutting a sharp line against the faint glow of the afternoon light. He was too calm, too purposeful in his approach, and something about him sent a chill down my spine.

I didn't recognize him, but there was something about his presence that felt too familiar, too calculated, like a thread being pulled tighter around me. His eyes—dark and unreadable—locked onto mine as he closed the distance.

Before I could make a move, before I could even process the danger in the air, I saw Evan glance over his shoulder, his eyes widening in alarm. He shouted something, but it was too late. The man was already too close.

"Get away from her!" Evan's voice rang out, laced with authority.

The figure didn't flinch. Didn't even slow down.

And then everything went black.

Chapter 4: A Heat That Burns

I didn't know what it was about fire that seemed to crackle in the air long after it had been put out, but I could feel it now, sitting in the stale silence of my cramped office, the faint smell of burned wood still clinging to the back of my throat. Each file I opened, each photograph of charred remnants, sent a shiver through my spine, a flicker of a thought that maybe I wasn't looking at random incidents. Maybe I wasn't just chasing smoke.

The cases had been all too similar: abandoned properties, uninhabited for years, but now, for some reason, their time had come. It was almost as if someone had planned them, their timing too precise to be anything but deliberate. And every fire, every building that went up in flames, was always miles apart, but somehow tied to the same mystery—an underground network, or something even darker. I didn't know which direction this was heading, but the walls of my small apartment felt too close, as if the fire wasn't just contained in the photos anymore. It had seeped into my space, my thoughts.

Then came the knock.

It wasn't the kind of knock that invited a visitor, nor was it the kind that demanded attention. It was somewhere in between, the sort of knock that makes you hesitate before answering, like a shadow slipping through the curtains when you're not looking. I knew who it was before I even opened the door. The way he stood outside, tall and rigid, was enough to make my pulse hitch. Evan.

He had that way of filling up a doorway, like the weight of his presence always tried to press in, forcing people to notice him. I couldn't help but notice the familiar irritation in his eyes, the kind that only came from someone who knew how to play the game of patience but would rather do anything else. He was exactly what I didn't need right now, but somehow, he had a way of making his appearance feel inevitable, like he'd been waiting for this moment all along.

"You're digging into something dangerous," he said, his voice low, a warning wrapped in steel. His gaze flicked briefly to the mess of papers on my desk, as if he could sense that the pattern I was finding had grown beyond coincidence.

I didn't answer immediately, just stood there, staring at him with narrowed eyes. His jaw clenched, and I couldn't tell if he was holding himself back from saying something else or if he was just waiting for me to back down. Neither of us spoke for a long beat, the tension between us hanging thick, suffocating in its own right.

"You don't get it, do you?" I said, finally breaking the silence. I wasn't sure why my voice sounded so sharp, so defiant, but it did. "This isn't just about the fires. Something's bigger than that. It's… it's like they're trying to erase something, something old. I think these buildings are part of a map, a network."

He raised an eyebrow, the closest he would come to admitting I wasn't entirely wrong. "A map to what?"

"That's what I'm trying to figure out." I waved a hand in the air, my frustration spilling over. "But I can't do it alone."

He tilted his head, regarding me for a long moment. A mix of curiosity and disdain passed through his eyes, like he was weighing the decision to trust me with this mess. But Evan had his own secrets, I knew that much, and whatever this was—it wasn't just mine to solve. "I think I can help," he said after a long pause, his words tentative, like he was testing the waters. "But we need to make a deal."

I crossed my arms, wary. "I'm not interested in any deals. You have your own agenda."

A faint smile touched his lips, one that didn't quite reach his eyes. "I'm not here for you, not exactly. But what you're chasing? It's dangerous. You're poking a hornet's nest, and if you keep digging, you might not get out unscathed. I'm offering you a truce—information in exchange for protection."

Protection. The word hung in the air like a promise, but one I didn't quite trust. Evan was someone who could protect people, that much was clear. But the protection he offered always came with a price, one I hadn't been willing to pay. Not yet.

"You don't get to decide what I do," I said, my voice steady despite the small flicker of unease in my stomach. "I'm not some rookie who needs babysitting."

"I know," he replied smoothly, his gaze flickering over my face in a way that felt both too intimate and far too calculating. "But even rookies know when they're in over their heads."

I wanted to argue, to throw him out, to send him on his way. But a part of me—one that I couldn't quite suppress—knew he was right. I was in deep. Deeper than I'd anticipated, and I couldn't keep pretending I had all the answers.

"I'm listening," I said, lowering my arms. The truce felt like a dangerous gamble, but I wasn't sure I had much of a choice anymore.

His smile widened, but it didn't soften the look in his eyes. "We'll start with your network. You're onto something, but you're missing pieces. You won't get the full picture alone."

"Then what's your angle?" I asked, unwilling to trust his sudden offer so easily.

Evan stepped closer, his shadow filling my small office like it was threatening to overtake the light. "My angle?" He leaned in, his breath warm against my cheek. "I'm not the one you should be worried about."

And just like that, the air between us shifted again, the tension becoming something more. Something I didn't fully understand. But whatever this was, whatever game we were playing—it was only just beginning.

I didn't trust him. Not one bit. But in that moment, I knew I didn't have much of a choice. Evan, with his too-sharp gaze and the effortless way he slipped into my life like he'd always belonged there, wasn't someone who could be easily dismissed. As much as I wanted to slam the door in his face, I could feel the pull of the situation growing tighter around me, and I wasn't sure how much longer I could stay untangled.

"Fine," I said, exhaling sharply. "You want a truce, you've got one. But this doesn't mean we're friends." I stared at him, trying to hold his gaze, but the heat in his eyes made it feel like I was looking into the sun.

Evan's lips quirked into that same infuriating, knowing smile that made me want to both slap and kiss him in the same breath. "Never said we were. I think you and I both know that's not going to happen."

I resisted the urge to roll my eyes. He had a way of being so infuriatingly smug, like he already knew everything about me. I wasn't sure if I hated that about him or if it made me just a little... curious.

He leaned against the doorframe, crossing his arms in that way that made everything about his posture seem deliberate, like he was testing my patience without even trying. "Let's start with the basics. You're after a network targeting abandoned properties. What exactly makes you think there's a connection between them?"

I wasn't in the mood for small talk, but something about the way he asked made me stop. Evan might have been the last person I'd want to confide in, but he wasn't entirely wrong. This wasn't something I could keep to myself forever. My instincts told me that the pattern was more than just a series of unlucky fires. There was something hidden beneath it—something old, something dangerous.

"It's the buildings," I said slowly, running a hand through my hair. "They weren't just left to burn. It's like someone's using them as beacons, setting them ablaze to send a message. But what's the message? That's what I'm trying to figure out."

Evan's brow furrowed as he stepped into the room, the air around us charged with something unspoken, an awareness that neither of us could ignore. His presence filled the space like a storm gathering strength, and I didn't want to acknowledge how it rattled me.

"So you think this is more than arson," he said, his voice low, cautious. "But why would someone want to send a message with abandoned properties?"

I hesitated, unsure if I should tell him everything I suspected. Part of me wanted to keep the details to myself, to keep the mystery between us, but the idea of running in circles on my own was wearing thin. "It's not just the buildings," I said, my voice quieter now. "It's the locations. They follow a specific pattern, one that's tied to some old mapping system I don't understand. I think it's deliberate, but I'm not sure why."

Evan considered this, his gaze narrowing as he thought it over. "And you're telling me this because..."

"Because I need help," I said, biting back the frustration that threatened to spill out. "But it's not like I trust you. So you'll have to earn that."

He nodded, almost to himself, like he already knew the path this conversation would take. "Fair enough," he said, voice thick with something that felt like both amusement and caution. "But you're right about one thing. You're in over your head. And if you keep pushing, someone will notice."

The air in the room crackled again, but this time, it wasn't just the tension between us. It was something darker, something that felt like a premonition of things to come. I'd been in dangerous situations before, but nothing had felt as inevitable as this. Evan's presence was like a warning sign, flashing bright and insistent, but I couldn't ignore the fact that we were in this together, whether I liked it or not.

"What makes you think I'm in over my head?" I asked, narrowing my eyes, watching for any signs of weakness in his usual confident demeanor.

His lips twisted in a half-smile, the kind that didn't quite reach his eyes. "Because you're not looking at the big picture. You're focused on the fires, but you're missing the forest for the trees. This isn't just about setting buildings on fire, it's about something much bigger."

The weight of his words hung in the air, heavy and ominous. I couldn't shake the feeling that I was only just scratching the surface of something that went far beyond a few suspicious fires. And whatever it was, Evan seemed to know more than he was letting on.

I didn't want to admit it, but the truth was, I needed him. Not just because he had access to information I didn't, but because his presence here, even in all its frustrating, irritating glory, was somehow grounding me. Even though he seemed like a man who thrived in chaos, I had the distinct feeling that chaos was following us now. And maybe—just maybe—he was the only one who knew how to navigate it.

"So, what's the plan?" I asked, my voice more resigned than I cared to admit.

Evan's eyes gleamed with something I couldn't name, something dark and dangerous that sent a chill crawling down my spine. "First, we find out who's behind these fires," he said, his voice like gravel. "Then we make sure they don't get away with it."

"And what's your role in all of this?" I asked, my gaze steady, defiant.

He stepped closer, close enough that I could smell the faint trace of his cologne—woodsy, sharp, and entirely too close for comfort. "My role?" He grinned, that wicked, unreadable grin of his. "To make sure you don't get yourself killed in the process."

I thought I understood Evan. Thought I had him figured out, like a puzzle with just enough missing pieces to leave room for some mystery but not enough to make him unbearable. But that night, as the air crackled with the intensity between us, I realized how little I truly knew. The protectiveness in his gaze wasn't a courtesy—it was a command, like he was willing me to play along with something he wasn't yet ready to explain. And I hated that I couldn't walk away from it.

His words lingered in the space between us, echoing off the walls of my small, dimly lit apartment. I didn't get the sense that he was trying to be comforting. If anything, he seemed amused by my frustration, like I was the one who was out of my depth. But he hadn't seen what I had seen, hadn't felt the urgency crawling beneath the surface of each report I sifted through. Maybe he didn't care about the bigger picture. Maybe he had his own agenda.

"Well, you're not making this easy," I muttered, trying to sound casual, but my voice betrayed me, coming out sharper than I intended. I turned away, pacing across the small room, my shoes scraping against the wood floor. The walls felt too close, like they were pressing in on me, suffocating me with every step I took.

Evan didn't follow me, just stood there in his usual unnerving stillness. It was like he was waiting for me to crack, to give him something, anything to make this partnership feel less... forced. I wasn't sure if that annoyed me more than the fact that he was right: I was in over my head. And the longer I stayed tangled in this mess, the harder it would be to get out.

"Let's just get one thing straight," I said, stopping in front of the window, looking out at the dim cityscape. "This isn't a favor you're doing me. I'm not some damsel in distress that needs rescuing. I'm in this for the long haul."

Evan's laughter came, low and dangerous, cutting through the tension like a knife. "I never said you were, but you're not in this alone anymore. Whether you like it or not."

I let that sink in for a second before turning back to him. "Fine. So, what's next? How do we take this 'dangerous network' down?"

His eyes gleamed with something unspoken, and for the briefest moment, I caught a flicker of something I couldn't quite place. Regret? Guilt? Maybe it was nothing, or maybe it was everything. He didn't answer me right away, just studied me like I was a problem he was still trying to solve.

"You'll need to be more careful," he said finally. His voice was quieter now, as though he was letting his guard down just enough to offer a sliver of sincerity. "They won't hesitate to target anyone who gets too close. You're playing with fire, and not the kind you're used to."

I stared at him, the weight of his words sinking in. But that wasn't enough to shake me, not yet. I had my own fire to deal with, my own demons to face.

"I've been playing with fire for months," I replied coolly, taking a step toward him. "And I'm still standing. So don't think you're the only one who knows how to navigate danger."

Evan's gaze flickered with something I couldn't identify, but it wasn't the usual coldness. There was an understanding there, just a crack in the wall he kept built around himself. He sighed, running a hand through his hair, and for a moment, I saw the slightest crack in his armor.

"Just don't say I didn't warn you," he muttered under his breath, almost like he was talking to himself.

But I was done with half-answers, with cryptic warnings. I needed facts, not whispers of caution. "Where do we start?" I asked again, firmer this time.

He looked at me, his eyes narrowing as though he was debating whether to trust me with what he knew. And I could feel the shift in the air, the moment where our little agreement morphed into something else. He wasn't just playing the role of protector anymore; he was pulling me into something much deeper. Something I wasn't sure I wanted to be part of. But there was no backing out now.

"Follow the money," he said, his voice low. "It all leads back to one place. And if we're lucky, we might be able to cut the head off the snake before it gets worse."

"Lucky?" I snorted, my skepticism plain. "Is that your idea of optimism?"

Evan didn't smile, didn't even acknowledge my sarcasm. "In our line of work, luck is just another word for survival."

"Great," I muttered, leaning back against the desk. "So, we're gambling on survival. What's the plan after that? Do we hope it all falls into place?"

His eyes met mine, and for the first time in this entire absurd exchange, I saw something close to a smirk. "You really think I'd leave it to chance?"

I opened my mouth to respond, but then I heard it. A muffled sound, faint but distinct. A knock. Not just any knock—a rhythm, deliberate, calculated, like someone who knew exactly when to strike.

I froze, my heart skipping a beat. Evan's eyes darted toward the door, his expression shifting into something unreadable. A second knock, louder this time, followed by a rustling of footsteps outside. Someone was here. And they weren't waiting for an invitation.

"Stay back," Evan hissed, stepping closer to me, his body blocking mine from the door.

I was too stunned to respond, too focused on the sound of the footsteps now retreating down the hall. And then it hit me—this wasn't a coincidence. This wasn't just someone passing by. This was someone who knew exactly where we were, exactly what we were doing.

Before I could react, the door flung open, and a figure stepped into the room—someone I didn't recognize, someone with eyes that burned with the same intensity I'd seen in Evan's but much darker.

And just like that, the world I thought I understood spun out of control.

Chapter 5: Ignition

The smoke in the air is thick, clinging to my skin like a second coat, sour and suffocating. I can taste it—burnt wood, chemicals, the metallic bite of danger. It swirls around us, wrapping the world in a haze of gray, a fog so dense it's like the city itself is holding its breath. Evan moves ahead of me, his movements steady, purposeful, and I can't decide if I want to keep up or retreat into the safe distance where I can pretend I don't see what's happening. His back is a fortress, and every time he turns to check on me, I can see the edges of something sharper, something darker in his eyes, like a man who's had too much of this kind of night.

"Stay close," he murmurs, voice low and rough, the kind of voice that makes me want to listen, not out of fear, but because it holds some unspoken promise of understanding.

We make our way deeper into the abandoned church, the smell of burning insulation growing stronger, more immediate. The floor is slick beneath my boots, not from rain, but from the water that's been sprayed in vain, trying to tame a fire that's too stubborn, too angry. The walls tremble under the force of it, the beams overhead groaning, as if they, too, are aware of the weight of what's happening here. There's no sign of the fire truck, no hint of any other firefighters yet. Just Evan, me, and the wailing sirens growing distant in the background.

I can feel the tension crawling up my spine, the quiet kind that coils around your ribs and refuses to let go. It's strange, how quickly I've learned to recognize the difference between a story that's just another headline and one that gets under your skin. This one, this fire, it's not just a job for Evan. It's personal. It's a fight. And he's fighting it with every breath he takes.

"There," Evan says suddenly, his voice cutting through the fog of my thoughts. His hand grips my arm, pulling me to a stop just as I almost walk into a gaping hole in the floor.

I follow his gaze, heart racing, and I see her—a young girl, no older than ten, her tiny form curled up in the corner by the altar. Her clothes are singed, her hair a wild mess of smoke and soot, but her eyes—those eyes are wide, full of panic, and trust.

Evan steps forward like he's done this a hundred times. His movements are almost mechanical, practiced, like he's been trained to run into danger, not away from it. He crouches down, hands steady as he reaches out, but there's a softness to him now, a tenderness that catches me off guard. He speaks to her in a tone that's too calm for the chaos around us.

"Hey there," he says, his voice low, soothing. "We're getting you out of here, alright? I need you to be brave for me just a little longer. Can you do that?"

The girl nods, her lips trembling, but she doesn't cry out, doesn't pull away. Her trust is complete, unspoken, and for a moment, I feel a flash of something sharp in my chest—envy, maybe, or admiration. I don't know how he does it, this ability to calm a frightened child in the middle of hell.

I step back as Evan picks the girl up with careful precision, cradling her in his arms as though she weighs no more than a doll. His body is a shield, and I'm struck by the image of him—like a hero in a book, like something out of a dream that doesn't quite belong to this world. I watch them, both of them, as he moves effortlessly toward the exit. The girl is nestled against his chest, her head resting on his shoulder, her small hands clutching the edges of his coat. And for the first time, I see Evan not as a firefighter, not as the man who keeps this city safe, but as something—someone—who could have easily been a character in my own life. Something real. Something to be admired.

The flames roar behind us, and the floor creaks again, threatening to give way. The church is crumbling around us, but Evan's focus never wavers. He keeps moving, steady and sure, each step pulling him closer to the safety of the street. I don't even notice that I've started following them until the smoke becomes too thick, and I'm forced to catch my breath in the same air that's choking us both.

"Keep up, Charlotte," he calls over his shoulder, his voice still that calm, commanding tone I can't seem to get used to. But there's something different in the way he says it now. Something softer, as though he's actually paying attention to me. He looks back at me, his eyes flickering with a brief, unexpected flash of something I can't quite read.

"I'm right behind you," I manage, forcing my legs to move even though they feel like they've turned to stone. My mind is still spinning, still caught on the way he carried her, the way he didn't hesitate for a second, even when every instinct must have been screaming at him to run.

I don't know what it is about that moment, that split second of raw vulnerability where I realize how much he's put on the line. He doesn't just save people; he becomes part of their story, too. And I'm starting to wonder what my own story is—what part I'm supposed to play in his.

We emerge from the church's shadows, the cold night air slapping at my face, and I realize that for all my fears about writing something too sensational, this—this is the story I've been waiting for. Not just the fire, not just the girl he saved. It's the moment I see the man beneath the uniform. And in that moment, I'm not sure whether I want to write about it or live it.

I try to shake off the image of him, the girl in his arms, the raw urgency in his movements. I can't. It's stuck to me like the smoke that clings to my hair, and no matter how hard I try to scrub it out, it's there, swirling in the back of my mind, a whisper I can't ignore.

We're standing in the street now, the fire trucks pulling up, lights flashing like a dream too surreal to be real. I watch the paramedics take over, stepping in to check the girl's vitals, but all I can see is Evan, standing a few feet away, running a hand through his damp hair, his eyes scanning the scene like he's still searching for something. I know that look—it's the look of someone who's been carrying the weight of the world for so long, they forget what it's like to put it down.

"Evan," I say, stepping toward him, unsure of whether I want to ask or if I'm just drawn to him. "Are you okay?"

He turns to face me, his expression unreadable for a moment before a faint smile tugs at the corner of his lips. It's not a happy smile, but it's not entirely resigned either. It's a smile that says, I've been through worse.

"Yeah, I'm fine," he says, voice rough, the words sounding more like a default than truth.

I want to push further, but there's something in his posture that tells me not to. It's like he's already sealed himself off, the fire not the only thing that's burned him tonight. So, instead, I nod, biting my lip, feeling that all-too-familiar flutter of hesitation in my chest. The kind of hesitation that comes from wanting to reach out and say something more, but not knowing how.

"I've got to check on the rest of the crew," he adds, his eyes flicking back to the fire trucks, where the other firefighters are starting to unload gear, their movements as rehearsed as if this is just another day at the office.

"Of course," I say, even though I don't want him to leave. It's strange how quickly I've gotten used to his presence, like the moment we stepped into that building, everything else faded away. But I know better than to say that out loud. I've spent enough time in the company of people who hide their emotions behind walls to understand when someone's shutting down.

He turns away without another word, his figure swallowed by the bustling chaos around us. I watch him go, a dull ache blooming in my chest, the kind that's familiar but never any less uncomfortable. It's not like I'm unused to being around intense situations, but this—this feels different.

I exhale sharply, pushing the feeling away, when I feel a tap on my shoulder. I spin around, startled, and find myself face to face with a firefighter I don't recognize. He's tall, broad-shouldered, with eyes that have seen too many nights like this one. His uniform's covered in grime, his face marked with the strain of a long shift, but there's something in his gaze that's warm, a curiosity mixed with a bit of skepticism.

"You with him?" he asks, his tone blunt but not unkind.

"With who?" I ask, confused for a second.

"Evan," he says, his lips curving into a half-smile. "The guy who saved that little girl. Are you one of his... friends?" He emphasizes the word like it holds some secret meaning, like I should understand it.

I blink, a little thrown by the question. "I'm... just someone he brought along tonight," I say, trying to keep it vague. After all, I'm not sure where exactly I fall in the hierarchy of people in Evan's life. I mean, I'm not a reporter—though I'm starting to think I'm walking a fine line between documenting his life and living it.

The firefighter gives me a knowing look, one that says he's seen this before, but he doesn't press the issue. Instead, he nods and holds out his hand.

"Damon," he says, his grip firm but not overpowering. "You're lucky you didn't get caught up in the fire. It was a close call."

I glance over at the smoldering church, now a blackened skeleton of what it once was, and nod. "Yeah, well... you don't exactly think about danger when you're following someone who looks like they've done this a hundred times," I say, offering him a wry smile.

Damon laughs, and there's something about it that feels easy, like it belongs here in the middle of the chaos. "You're not wrong. Evan doesn't mess around when it comes to rescues. We all give him shit for it, but at the end of the day, he's the one who gets things done."

The casual mention of Evan's name, the easy respect Damon holds for him, lingers in the air, and I feel a pang of something—maybe it's jealousy, or maybe it's something more complicated than that.

I realize I don't really know Evan, not like that. I've seen him at work, seen him in the firehouse, but it's never been like this. We've never shared a moment like the one in that church, never had the kind of connection that would tie us to the other people who know him, who've worked alongside him for years. It makes me wonder what kind of life he has outside of the uniform, outside of the fires, and whether there's any space for someone like me in it.

Damon's voice pulls me out of my thoughts. "He's not much for small talk," he says, as if reading my mind. "But if you ever want to know more about him, you could always stick around. He's one of the good ones."

I watch Evan from across the street as he talks to a couple of the other firefighters, his face hard, his shoulders tight, but there's something there—something I can't quite place, something that makes my curiosity burn hotter than the fire we just left behind.

The night drags on, and the air feels heavy, thick with the weight of something unspoken. I watch as the paramedics finish up with the girl, slipping her onto a stretcher and rolling her toward the ambulance. They're moving efficiently, but there's a quiet reverence in their motions, a recognition of the fact that she should never have been in this position in the first place.

Evan, however, doesn't linger. He's back in the thick of things, giving orders, helping coordinate with the other crew members as they assess the damage. I want to follow him, to get closer and maybe make sense of the puzzle pieces in my mind that just don't quite fit. But something holds me back, a voice that tells me I'm not supposed to be here—not in this world, not yet, not in this way.

Damon's still standing by me, hands tucked into the pockets of his jacket. He's watching Evan too, his eyes narrowing slightly as if trying to decipher a secret written only on Evan's back.

"He doesn't let anyone in," Damon says quietly, like he's letting me in on some truth. "Not really. He's got his walls, you know?"

I nod, but the truth of it stings. I knew that. I've seen it in the way Evan isolates himself when the calls are over, when the adrenaline has worn off, and the normal world comes back into focus. He doesn't look for people to lean on. He doesn't ask for help.

"He's the one everyone looks to," Damon continues, his tone a mix of admiration and something else—maybe frustration. "When things go wrong, when the shit hits the fan, they turn to him. It's like he's the anchor. But I'm telling you, Charlotte... not even an anchor can hold forever."

I look at Damon, his face drawn with a tired kind of wisdom. He's not trying to get me to pity Evan, but I can't help it. I've seen enough to know that Evan's carrying something, something heavy, and he's carrying it alone. I wonder if he even knows how to ask for help anymore.

"Is it always like this?" I ask, my voice quieter than I intend. "The weight of it all?"

Damon shrugs, his gaze flicking back to Evan. "It doesn't get easier, if that's what you mean. But you find a way to live with it.

Some days, you just get through. Other days... well, that's when you see the cracks."

I open my mouth to respond, but a siren cuts through the air, louder now, as the fire engine pulls away with a deafening roar. The street seems to vibrate with the sound, the noise so invasive that it fills every corner of my mind. For a split second, it feels like everything is on the edge of something—like the world is waiting for something big to happen.

I turn to look at Evan, but he's already walking away from the crew, his expression closed off, as though the fire has left him with nothing but emptiness. The distance between us feels vast, a chasm that no amount of small talk or idle chatter can bridge. But as I watch him, I feel something shift. Maybe it's the exhaustion in his posture, or the lines of stress around his eyes that make him seem older than he is, but whatever it is, it pulls me closer to him, without even meaning to.

I take a step forward, but Damon grabs my arm, holding me back just enough to make me pause.

"Don't," he warns softly, his grip firm but not unkind. "Let him come to you. He always does, but on his terms, not anyone else's."

I open my mouth to argue, to ask why I should just sit back and wait, but Damon's eyes stop me. There's something there, a quiet plea that tells me he's seen too much of this, too much of the people who get too close to the fire and end up burned in ways they never expected.

"Trust me," he says, his voice low, "if you want to be a part of his life, you'll have to give him space to let you in. He won't take it any other way."

I'm not sure I believe him. Part of me wants to push past Damon's words, to walk straight up to Evan and demand that he stop hiding behind his walls. But the other part of me— the part that's been watching from the sidelines—knows there's truth in what Damon says. And maybe, just maybe, that's the part of me that's afraid of what might happen if I don't listen.

But I don't have time to contemplate it further. I glance back toward Evan and see him turn toward me, his gaze piercing through the distance. His expression is unreadable, but there's something in the way he holds himself now—something that makes the air between us crackle with unspoken tension.

For a moment, the noise of the city fades away, and everything seems to slow down, just enough to let me catch my breath. He's walking toward me now, and I can't look away. I don't know what he's going to say, what he's going to do, but something tells me I won't be able to ignore it.

When he's close enough, he stops, just a few feet away, and for a moment, neither of us speaks. The tension hangs between us like a storm cloud, charged with energy but unwilling to release.

Then he breaks the silence, his voice rough and unexpected.

"You're still here," he says, as though it's a question.

I nod, unsure of how to answer, unsure of what he even means. But the words come before I can stop them.

"I'm not going anywhere," I say, my voice steady, though my heart is pounding.

And for just a moment, I think I see a flicker of something in his eyes—something soft, something real. But before I can grasp it, before I can decipher it, the world shifts again.

A sudden shout breaks through the air, and I turn to see a man stumbling out of the shadows, his face twisted with panic. He's looking straight at us, his eyes wide with something close to terror.

"Fire!" he shouts, his voice hoarse. "It's not over! The fire's still burning!"

And just like that, everything changes.

Chapter 6: Playing with Fire

The diner was one of those places where time slowed down to the rhythm of sizzling grease and the clink of silverware. The neon sign outside buzzed faintly in the cold night air, casting an eerie glow over the parking lot, while the low hum of conversations filled the space inside. It smelled like grilled onions, fries too crispy to resist, and coffee that had been brewed at the crack of dawn and somehow kept its warmth despite being far past its prime.

Evan slid into the booth across from me with a quiet sigh, his jacket still damp from the rain that had fallen like an afterthought earlier. The faint glow from the overhead lights caught the lines on his face, shadows deepening around his eyes, as if the world had handed him more than his share of tragedies. He had been silent for the last ten minutes, his eyes fixed on the laminated menu like it held the answers to questions neither of us had asked.

I wasn't in much of a mood for food, but the coffee here always seemed to pull something out of me, some unspoken craving for connection. And I needed that more than anything right now. I let my fingers circle the edge of my cup, keeping my gaze on the chipped ceramic, not sure if I was avoiding his eyes or trying to calm the war in my head. There were so many things I wanted to say, and yet I knew some of them could never leave my lips. The words might burn more than the fire I had just seen.

"So," I said, my voice barely rising above a whisper. "How many times has it been? A case like tonight's."

Evan didn't answer immediately, his eyes flicking up at me for just a fraction of a second before dropping again to the table, tracing the patterns on the vinyl. His hands were tense, fingertips tapping a rhythm of their own, the smallest tremor betraying his calm exterior. It was a sound I knew all too well—the quiet hum of a soul who had seen too much, too many moments where everything had turned to ash, and he hadn't been able to stop it.

"Too many," he finally muttered, like the admission had weight. "You start to wonder if you missed something—anything. A sign, a detail, a moment where you could've stepped in before the world caught fire."

His words were measured, but the weight in his tone was enough to pull me in. I was still staring at the cup in my hands, feeling the heat of the ceramic seep into my palms. There was a strange comfort in how he said it, like he was asking me, silently, to understand. To not judge him.

I closed my eyes, knowing the ghosts would find me if I stayed silent too long. My past had always been one of shadows, the kind that crept into your skin without permission, marked you in places you couldn't see. Sometimes I thought I could outrun it with my camera, or my notepad, but those things were just distractions. Bandages that wouldn't hold when the wound was too deep.

"I get it," I said, the words slipping out before I could stop them. "You think if you just... did something different, everything would've turned out better. That it was your fault."

He didn't say anything, but there was a sharpness in his eyes when they flicked to mine, something almost painful, like the words I'd spoken had been a needle to the skin of a wound he hadn't let anyone touch. I knew I had hit something, but I wasn't sure if it was something I wanted to dig into.

"So, what do you do with that?" I asked, the question hanging in the air, too heavy for any polite small talk. "When you carry around that kind of weight."

Evan leaned back in the booth, letting his hands fall to his lap as if the answer to my question had weight too. He exhaled, a long breath that seemed to pull him back into the real world, away from whatever memories had been playing behind his eyes.

"You keep going," he said simply, as if the solution was the easiest thing in the world. "You find a way to keep going."

I nodded, feeling the sting of recognition twist in my chest. It was the same thing I'd told myself every morning for years. Keep moving. Don't stop. Don't let the past catch up to you.

"Is that all?" I asked, my voice soft, teasing a little, though I wasn't sure if I believed what I was saying. "I mean, it sounds simple, but I'm guessing there's more to it."

A small, humorless smile flickered at the corners of his lips. For a moment, he seemed like a different person, someone who didn't carry the weight of a thousand unsaid things. But that moment passed, and the mask settled back into place.

"I guess you figure out what's worth saving," he said after a beat. "And then you protect it. Because if you don't—who will?"

I felt something warm, something fierce, stir in my chest at his words. The vulnerability that had slipped into the space between us felt almost sacred, as if we were both offering pieces of ourselves we had long since buried, trusting the other wouldn't break them.

I didn't know what to say to that, so I just took another sip of my coffee, letting the bitterness fill the silence between us. The hum of the diner, the scrape of forks against plates, and the soft clatter of the bell as the door swung open and shut filled the space, but for the first time in a long while, it felt like we were just two people, sharing a moment of fragile honesty.

It was easy to let the words hang there, suspended in the air like smoke that would eventually dissipate. But in that moment, I felt an unspoken promise between us, something I wasn't sure I was ready to acknowledge. It wasn't just about the fires we fought or the pasts we carried; it was about the quiet, fleeting things—the ones that could burn you faster than anything else.

The coffee began to grow cold between us, and I knew it was time to shift the conversation, or at least, to stop staring at my reflection in the dark mug. The steam from it had long since evaporated, leaving only the bitter memory of something that had once been warm.

"So," I said, breaking the silence with a jolt of humor I didn't entirely feel but thought might be the best way to avoid any more serious confessions. "Do you always make life-and-death decisions over a cup of diner coffee?"

Evan's lips quirked at the corners. I could see him fighting a smile, the corners of his mouth twitching. He didn't look at me directly, but there was something in his eyes that softened ever so slightly. "I find it easier than being surrounded by sirens and flashing lights."

I snorted. "Fair point. Nothing says calm like the smell of stale grease and the music of a jukebox that's stuck on repeat."

"Yeah, nothing like a healthy dose of existential dread with a side of fries," he added, leaning back in the booth, his hand coming up to rub at his jaw, his fingers grazing the stubble there. His voice dropped, like he was trying to turn the words into something more playful than they felt.

"But," I pushed, my own curiosity growing, "does it work? The whole 'keep moving forward' thing? You know, when everything feels like it's on fire?"

The way he looked at me then was enough to make the air between us feel heavier, as if I'd dropped something that wasn't meant to be picked up. His expression went from light to guarded in the span of a breath. For a moment, I regretted the question. It had been too much, too soon.

"Sometimes," Evan said, his voice quieter now. "You don't get to choose when it burns, but you do get to decide if you're going to let it turn you to ash."

I wasn't sure if he was speaking in riddles or if he had actually said something profound. Either way, his words stuck with me.

Maybe it was his vulnerability finally showing, or maybe it was just the way he was letting me in when, clearly, he hadn't meant to. Either way, I didn't want to backpedal. Not now.

"I don't know," I said, leaning forward, my own voice quieter now. "I've tried the whole 'keep moving' thing. But eventually you run out of places to go, right? You can't outrun everything forever."

Evan let out a slow breath, like my words had caught him off guard in the best way possible. His eyes flicked up to meet mine, and there was something raw in them, like he hadn't expected me to understand—or maybe like he hadn't expected to let me.

"Running's overrated," he muttered. "Eventually, the past catches up with you, and you either stand and face it or you let it break you."

A silence fell between us, heavy and thick, the kind of silence that isn't uncomfortable, but rather full of things left unsaid. My hand closed around the cold coffee mug again, the porcelain colder against my fingers this time. I stared into it, like it held all the answers I wasn't ready to hear.

"And what happens when standing doesn't feel like enough?" I asked, my voice surprisingly steady considering the tremor in my chest. "What happens when standing feels like you're just waiting for the next thing to tear you down?"

Evan's gaze softened just a touch, a fleeting moment where I felt like he truly saw me. His lips parted, like he was going to say something, but he stopped himself. He had the words, but for the first time tonight, he hesitated. He took another breath, and when he spoke, his voice was careful, almost deliberate.

"I don't know," he said quietly, "But I think you keep standing anyway. Even when you're waiting for the world to fall apart."

There was something about the way he said it that made the weight of the words impossible to ignore. It was almost as if he were speaking to both of us, and not just me. Like he was trying to convince himself just as much as he was trying to convince me.

I gave a small, tight-lipped smile, trying to make light of it. "You're really into motivational speeches, huh? Should I start taking notes? Get a 'Keep standing' mantra or something?"

Evan chuckled, the sound deep and warm, like it was long overdue. "Maybe," he said with a smirk. "But only if you're up for it. I have more where that came from."

"I'm sure you do," I teased, though a part of me appreciated how effortless it felt to joke about it. Sometimes, it felt like the only way to avoid the unspoken truths lying between us.

But still, the tension hung in the air. It wasn't the kind that could be dismissed with a joke or a smile. The longer we sat there, the more I felt it shift between us—something unresolved, something we both knew was hanging over our heads. The connection between us was undeniable, but neither of us seemed ready to face it directly.

As I stirred the cold coffee absentmindedly, I realized that we weren't just talking about the weight of our pasts anymore. We were standing on the edge of something else, something I wasn't sure I could define. Maybe it was the promise of something that wasn't tied to tragedy or loss. Maybe it was something that could be different—something I hadn't yet allowed myself to believe in.

And for the first time in what felt like a lifetime, I wondered if standing here, in the silence that followed, was the first step in figuring it out.

He cleared his throat, his voice returning to its usual gravelly tone. "We're both carrying a lot, huh?"

"That's one way to put it," I said, the words tinged with a humor that wasn't entirely lighthearted. "But I think you're right. We're standing."

And maybe, just maybe, that was enough. For now.

The minutes stretched on as the last of the diner's patrons began to file out, leaving the space quieter than before. The clatter of dishes had all but ceased, replaced by the muted sound of the jukebox, which seemed to be playing a song it had been stuck on for hours. Evan leaned forward now, his elbows resting on the table, his eyes searching mine like he was about to ask a question that might undo everything we'd built in the last hour.

I wasn't ready for it, but I knew it was coming. There was always a point where the walls you'd both worked so hard to break down came crashing back in, forcing the truth to surface. The silence was thick with anticipation, like two forces tugging in opposite directions, unwilling to let go.

"You don't have to tell me," Evan began, his voice lower now, tinged with an edge I hadn't heard before. "But I can tell that something's eating at you. You're not as good at hiding it as you think."

I blinked, his words landing like a stone thrown into a still pond. It wasn't the question that caught me off guard—it was the quiet intensity with which he asked it. There was no judgment, no pity. Just an openness that almost felt like a dare, asking me to lay down whatever armor I had left.

"What do you want me to say?" I asked, my voice barely above a whisper, more to myself than to him. The question was one I'd danced around for too long, and I was starting to wonder if it was time to let it spill out, even if it hurt.

He didn't answer right away, just watched me, letting the question linger. There was something in his eyes that shifted, like he was waiting for me to make up my mind, to decide if I could trust him with the truth.

"I don't know," I said finally, my fingers curling tightly around the edge of the mug. "I guess... I guess I never learned how to stop hiding."

Evan's gaze softened, the sharpness in his expression dulling just enough to let a sliver of vulnerability show. "You don't have to hide from me, you know."

I let out a short, humorless laugh, shaking my head. "That's easy for you to say. You're not the one who's been running from their past for years."

His brow furrowed at my words, but there was no accusation in his eyes—just understanding. It was strange, this ability he had to make me feel like maybe, just maybe, I didn't have to carry the weight of everything by myself.

"I'm not asking you to let it go," he said slowly, his voice steady but with a layer of something almost raw underneath. "But maybe it's time to stop running. You don't have to do it alone."

I froze, the weight of his words sinking deep. How could he ask me to stop running when I wasn't sure what I was running from—or worse, what would happen if I stopped?

"I don't even know what that means," I confessed, almost ashamed by the admission. The words came out like an apology I wasn't sure I owed, but they were out there now, and I couldn't take them back.

For a long moment, Evan didn't say anything. He just sat there, his expression unreadable, the quiet between us stretching out until I started to wonder if maybe this conversation was one we weren't meant to finish. But then, as if he had made a decision, his voice broke the silence.

"You don't have to know right now," he said softly, his eyes unwavering. "But maybe you'll figure it out, piece by piece. Sometimes you don't have to understand the whole thing at once. You just have to take one step forward, even if it's small."

I wanted to respond, to say something that would cut through the tension that had built up, but the words stuck in my throat. Maybe he was right. Maybe I didn't have to have it all figured out in this moment. Maybe it was enough to admit that I was tired—tired of pretending like I had all the answers, tired of keeping my walls intact for fear that if they came down, everything would crumble.

I opened my mouth to speak, but the sound of the diner door swinging open interrupted me. A blast of cold air rushed in, carrying with it the unmistakable scent of rain. The door slammed shut again, and the sound seemed to echo in the quiet room.

I turned instinctively, my eyes narrowing as I scanned the entrance. There was a man standing there, dripping wet, his shoulders hunched as if he were trying to avoid being noticed. But something about him made the hairs on the back of my neck stand up. He wasn't the type of person you could ignore, even in a place like this.

Evan noticed it too. His eyes flicked to the man, then back to me, a silent question hanging in the air. I could see the shift in his posture, a subtle change that told me everything I needed to know. He was already on alert, even if his expression remained unreadable.

I wasn't sure why, but something in me stirred, the familiar pull of intuition telling me that this wasn't just an ordinary late-night diner visit. There was something off about the way the man was standing there, looking around like he was waiting for someone—or worse, expecting something.

Before I could say anything, the man's gaze landed on us. His eyes were dark, calculating, and for a moment, I could have sworn I saw something flash behind them—recognition, maybe, or something much more dangerous.

The air in the diner felt heavier now, charged with a tension I couldn't shake. I wasn't sure how I knew it, but I could feel the shift in the room. This wasn't just a coincidence. Whatever was about to happen, it was going to change everything.

And then, without warning, the man started to move toward our booth.

Chapter 7: Smoke and Mirrors

The smell of burning paper, wood, and old ink wafts through the air, clinging to everything—clothes, skin, even thoughts. I hadn't even known I was holding my breath until the silence cracked. The fire's aftermath isn't just the smoldering remains of books; it's the loss of a place that had been a sanctuary for so many. Now, nothing but charred fragments of paper and broken dreams. That bookstore had been a patch of warmth in an otherwise cold world—a haven where time didn't race by, where every customer was a character, and each book on the shelf whispered a secret.

Evan's fingers had tightened around mine as we stood at the foot of the ashes, the glow from the smoldering embers casting a soft, eerie light across his face. He wasn't the kind of man to show emotion unless it was deliberate, but today, his jaw was tight, his eyes dark, like a storm was brewing beneath the calm surface.

"I told you," he muttered, voice low, as though the words themselves might ignite something more dangerous than just a fire. "Someone's doing this on purpose. This is no accident."

I should've listened when he first said it—when he raised the possibility that someone might be systematically erasing parts of our city's history, one beloved landmark at a time. But my mind didn't want to go there, didn't want to imagine that anyone could be so cruel. But standing there, looking at the crumbling remnants of pages that would never turn again, I realized Evan might have been right.

"I'll look into it," I said, more to convince myself than him.

"Stop," he snapped, his voice sharper than usual. "You're not getting involved in this. It's too dangerous."

I glanced over at him, taking in the tense lines of his face, the way his eyes darted around like there might be someone—something—lurking in the shadows, waiting to strike. I knew this side of him. It was the side that came out when he was scared, when his protectiveness kicked in. And, damn him, it made my heart ache. I wanted to give him the reassurance he was asking for, tell him I'd let this one go, that I'd drop it and let the authorities take over. But I wasn't like that. Not anymore.

"I'm already involved," I said firmly, pulling my hand from his, eyes meeting his in a silent challenge. "This won't stop until someone gets to the bottom of it. And I'm not the kind of person who walks away."

Evan's mouth tightened, his gaze darkening further, but there was a flicker of something—something I couldn't quite place—in his eyes. It wasn't fear anymore; it was... frustration. As if the very idea that I wouldn't heed his warning was a betrayal, though he would never say it aloud. He didn't need to. I could feel it in the tension between us.

"Don't say I didn't warn you," he muttered, his voice barely a whisper, before turning away and walking toward his car.

I stayed for a moment longer, taking in the empty, hollow space where the bookstore had once stood. The place that had smelled like fresh coffee and old paper, the place where a young couple had once whispered their first "I love you" between the stacks, the place that had held a thousand lives in a thousand pages. Now, just a pile of ash and memories.

I'd have to dig deeper. There was no turning back now.

The first note came two days later, folded neatly and placed under my front door like it was a carefully constructed piece of origami. I had been expecting it. In fact, I'd been almost waiting for it, as if some invisible force had already prepared me for what was coming. Still, it rattled me. My hands trembled as I unfolded the note, and the words jumped out at me in crisp black ink:

Stop looking into it. Or next time, it'll be you.

I stared at the message for a long moment, my mind spinning, trying to make sense of it. There were no hints, no signatures, nothing to give me any clues as to who might be behind it. But the implication was clear. Someone knew exactly what I was doing—and they didn't want me to keep digging.

I wanted to ignore it. I wanted to crumple the paper and pretend it didn't exist, to walk away from this whole mess. But something inside me, something I couldn't explain, refused to let it go. The words had landed like a blow to my gut, and now I couldn't breathe without feeling the weight of them pressing down on me. I was scared, but I was also... angry.

I went straight to Evan's place, determined to tell him what had happened, to show him the note and get his take on it. But when I arrived, I found him pacing in his living room, his face a mask of frustration. It wasn't the way he usually carried himself. He was more poised, more controlled, but today, something had set him off.

"I'm not going to stop," I said before he could even open his mouth. My voice was firmer than I intended, but the words felt like they belonged there.

Evan's eyes met mine, and for the first time, I saw something flicker across his face—something between fear and fury. He opened his mouth, then closed it again, as if he wasn't sure what to say.

"You don't understand what you're dealing with," he said finally, his voice quiet but intense. "These fires aren't random. And you don't want to be the next target."

"I'm already a target," I shot back. "The note's already here. What difference does it make?"

His gaze hardened. "I don't want to see you get hurt."

But I'd already made my decision. "You're not the only one who's scared, Evan. But this is bigger than both of us. It's bigger than just a few fires. Someone is trying to erase everything this city stands for, and I won't stand by and let it happen."

He stared at me for a long moment, his jaw clenched tight. Then, with a deep breath, he nodded. "You're stubborn as hell, you know that?"

"Someone's got to be," I said, my voice softening just enough to show him that, yes, I understood his concern. But there was no turning back now.

And as the evening stretched on, with the shadows in the room growing longer, I knew it wasn't just the fires that had ignited something in me. It was the knowledge that I was walking down a path that could end in more than just destruction. It could end in something far worse. But I wasn't going to stop. I couldn't.

The sky was bruised, swirling with shades of violet and dark gray, as if the world itself was bruised from the weight of the fires. I stood in front of the small coffee shop that had become my unofficial office. It was warm inside, a scent of roasted beans masking the chill in the air. But despite the comfort, there was no escaping the gnawing sensation in my chest. The note, folded neatly in my coat pocket, felt heavier than it had when I first read it. Each step I took seemed to be echoing in my ears, reminding me of what I was up against, the unseen eyes tracking my every move.

I'd told Evan I was going to keep pushing forward, but I could see the hesitation in his eyes when I left him standing there. I hadn't just walked away from him—I'd walked away from something else, too: the safety of ignorance. Sometimes, I wished I could've ignored the voice inside me, that insistent whisper that told me I couldn't turn my back. But there it was, pushing me forward, even when I didn't know where I was going.

The bell over the coffee shop door jingled as I walked inside, and I gave a small wave to the barista, who was more of a friend now than just a person who made my coffee. There was something about her that made the world seem a little less heavy, like she could take the worst day and turn it into something worth remembering. She gave me a knowing smile, the kind you offer someone who's had too many bad days and still hasn't given up.

"Rough morning?" she asked as she began to make my usual—black coffee, no nonsense.

I could tell she wasn't expecting a casual answer. The look in my eyes must have been a clue. "You could say that," I muttered, sliding into my regular spot at the corner of the counter. The notebook I'd been scribbling in for weeks sat open in front of me. Notes. Observations. A thousand half-baked theories that kept bouncing around in my head like lost marbles. None of them had amounted to anything concrete.

"Any luck with your investigation?" she asked, carefully setting the steaming mug in front of me, her eyes scanning my face like she was trying to piece together the puzzle of who I was that day.

I opened my mouth to say something, but then I froze. My eyes locked onto the piece of paper that had slid under the door moments ago, unnoticed until now. The handwriting was similar. Same clean, deliberate strokes that sent a chill racing down my spine.

You're not done yet.

I read the note quickly, then slipped it into the back of my notebook. I didn't want to think about it. Didn't want to admit that the person watching me had just stepped up their game. Someone out there knew exactly what I was doing, and they were taking it personally. I wasn't scared—at least, not in the way you'd expect. Fear wasn't the word for it. This was more like the feeling you get when you realize you're the last one at the party and all the lights have gone out.

"No luck yet," I said, trying to keep my voice steady, but I felt like every word was an effort, like I was holding onto a thread that was about to snap.

"Don't let them get to you," she said softly. "Whoever 'they' are."

I almost laughed at the absurdity of it. But I didn't. Instead, I found myself glancing around the room, my eyes scanning the patrons with suspicion. I was starting to think that everyone was involved in some way. Maybe the barista. Maybe the man sitting across from me with the newspaper. Maybe it was the woman I'd passed in the parking lot earlier. In a world where nothing was what it seemed, it was hard to trust anyone, even the people who'd been kind to me.

The bell above the door jingled again, and I turned, expecting another customer. But it was Evan.

His face was unreadable, his movements tight as he strode toward me, his eyes flicking over my shoulder before he sat down across from me. He didn't say anything at first, just watched me with that same intensity, like he was trying to figure out which part of me was real and which part was just a mask.

"I know you got the second note," he said quietly, his voice low enough that only I could hear him.

"Then you know what I'm going to do about it," I replied, meeting his gaze with the same determination. There was no backing down now, not after everything.

He leaned forward, his elbows resting on the table. "This isn't just about some bookshop, you know. These fires—whoever's behind them—they're trying to erase everything. And you're digging into something they don't want exposed."

"Then maybe I'll expose it," I shot back, almost too quickly. The words tasted bitter, like I was daring the world to prove me wrong.

Evan's jaw tightened. "You're playing with fire, and you don't even realize it."

"I know exactly what I'm doing," I said, my heart pounding in my chest as the words spilled out of me. "And I'm not going to stop."

He didn't respond right away. His gaze softened, just for a second, but in that fleeting moment, I saw something else in his eyes—something beyond the frustration. It was concern. For me, maybe. Or maybe for both of us.

"You need to be careful," he said, and for the first time, his voice wasn't harsh. It was almost gentle. But it didn't change anything. The decision had already been made.

"You don't get to tell me that," I said, my tone softer than I meant it to be.

Evan didn't answer right away, instead folding his arms across his chest and staring at me with a look that could've been carved from stone. "Fine. But when this blows up in your face, don't say I didn't warn you."

I smiled, but it wasn't the kind of smile that could make the air lighter. It was the kind of smile you give when you're drowning, but trying to look like you're still swimming.

"I won't. But if I do blow up, you'll be right here, won't you? Watching the whole thing burn down?"

The silence between us stretched long, heavy, and then finally, he broke it with a low sigh. "You're impossible."

"I know," I said, my voice laced with humor, though inside, the storm was gathering. "But you love me for it."

His lips twitched in the faintest of smiles. "I'm starting to think it's the other way around."

I let that sink in for a moment, leaning back in my chair and sipping my coffee. Despite everything, the world felt a little quieter, a little more bearable. But I couldn't forget the note that was tucked away in my notebook, the invisible threat that hovered just beyond the edge of my vision. Someone was out there. Watching. Waiting. And this time, they weren't just playing games.

The city hummed beneath the weight of its secrets, each one more suffocating than the last. I couldn't shake the feeling that everything I touched was slowly disintegrating, turning to ash in my hands, like that bookstore. It had been a place of refuge, of stories untold, of quiet voices sharing space in the background of life. And now, all that was left were memories clinging to the walls of a burned-out husk. I could almost hear the books whispering to me, urging me to keep going, even as the danger closed in.

Evan hadn't come by that night, and I didn't expect him to. There was something between us now, a distance I wasn't sure how to bridge. It wasn't just about the investigation. It was the way he looked at me, like I'd betrayed him without even meaning to. But the truth was, I wasn't sure who I had betrayed. Not him. Not myself. Just... something.

The wind rattled the window, and I shifted uncomfortably in my chair. The note from earlier still sat, hidden beneath the pile of papers on my desk. I hadn't dared to look at it again, not yet, but it lingered, like an itch that couldn't be scratched. A threat was a threat, no matter how neatly it was folded or how carefully it was written. Someone out there wanted me to stop. And for the first time, I didn't just want to keep going—I needed to.

I glanced at the clock. Late again. It always seemed to be late when I got lost in this city's tangled web of history and deceit. Every lead, every scrap of information, only led to more questions. The detective in me—a part of me I hadn't known was there until all this started—was starting to unravel, piece by piece, every thread I pulled at. I couldn't let go now. Not with everything on the line.

There was a knock on the door, sharp and insistent, and before I could even rise from my chair, Evan stepped into the room. His eyes were dark, his posture rigid. He wasn't here for small talk, I could tell.

"Got another note," I said before he could speak.

He glanced at the closed door, then back at me, his expression unreadable. "You didn't listen, did you?"

"Never have," I replied with a wry smile, but even I knew it wasn't funny. It was more of a defense mechanism, one that had started to crack beneath the weight of everything.

Evan didn't smile. "This isn't some game. You're not playing detective here. People are getting hurt, and you're making it worse by getting involved."

"And if I don't?" I countered, standing up now, my hands clenching into fists at my sides. "What happens then? We let them burn everything down? Watch our city turn into ashes while we sit around and wait for someone else to do something?"

"Someone else has already done something," he said, his voice growing tense. "That's the problem. You think you can stop this? You think you're invincible?"

I took a step toward him, my eyes narrowing. "What's the alternative? Pretend like I don't care? Let you be the one to do all the dirty work while I hide behind my desk?"

He didn't flinch, though I could see the frustration building in him. "You're not the only one who cares, okay? But you can't do this alone. You shouldn't be doing it at all."

The words stung. There was something in his voice—something raw—that made me pause, made me think twice for the first time since this whole mess started.

I wanted to push back, tell him he was wrong, that he didn't understand. But deep down, I knew he wasn't wrong. He was just scared. And so was I. This wasn't some abstract problem anymore. It was real. And it had found me.

"I can't back down, Evan," I said quietly, my voice softer now, the defiance still there but tempered with something else. "If I don't do this, then what? I don't know how to let this go."

He stared at me for a long time, his face a mask of conflicting emotions. He didn't want me involved. I knew that. But the thing was, I didn't want to be involved either. Not in the way I was now. This wasn't just about solving a case anymore. It was about survival.

Finally, he sighed, running a hand through his hair. "This isn't going to end well."

"Maybe it already has," I muttered, unable to stop the bitterness that seeped into my voice.

Evan didn't answer. Instead, he took a step closer to me, his eyes searching mine. "I can't stop you. But I can keep you safe."

"You?" I scoffed, my heart pounding. "You think you can protect me from whatever this is?"

His face hardened. "I'll try. But I need you to be smart. No more lone wolf stuff. No more going off on your own."

"I'm not some damsel, Evan," I snapped. "I'm not going to sit around and wait for a hero."

He looked at me, his expression softening just for a second. "I'm not trying to be your hero. But I can't lose you in this. I won't."

The weight of his words hung between us like an anchor, threatening to drag us both under. And for a moment, the world outside seemed to fade away, as if time itself had stopped.

But it was broken by the sound of a car engine revving outside. We both turned toward the window, but by the time I had moved to look, the car had already sped away, its taillights fading into the night.

"You see that?" I asked, my pulse quickening.

Evan was already moving toward the door. "Get your coat."

"Why?"

"Because whoever's been watching you doesn't like being watched."

Before I could respond, the sound of footsteps on the stairs echoed in the hall. Rapid, urgent, like someone in a hurry.

The door burst open, and a man I didn't recognize stood in the doorway, his eyes wide with panic.

"They know," he said, his voice trembling. "They know everything. And they're coming for you."

Chapter 8: A Blazing Revelation

The night air had an edge to it, biting, just enough to make the hairs on the back of my neck stand up as I stood in the shadow of the crumbling hotel. The tip had been vague, like they always were: a whisper in the wind, a message passed from one crooked hand to the next. But my instincts told me it was the place. The old hotel was like a half-forgotten relic, abandoned for years, its sagging windows staring out like hollow eyes. The perfect target.

I checked the camera strap, adjusting it over my shoulder. My hands shook, a mix of adrenaline and uncertainty. There was something eerily quiet about the night, the usual hum of the city muted, as if the streets themselves knew something was about to unfold. My breath caught in the chill, swirling in the air before me, dissipating as quickly as it came.

This was my job—find the story, follow the trail, and capture it all. I wasn't one for surprises, especially the dangerous kind. But as I moved closer to the hotel's rusting doors, an unsettling feeling slithered up my spine. It wasn't just the decrepit structure or the fact that I was trespassing in the middle of the night. No, something was different this time. There was a pulse to the air, something heavy, waiting.

I crouched near a broken window, peering inside. The flickering light from a distant streetlamp barely reached the abandoned lobby. The walls were adorned with peeling wallpaper, the floor littered with debris. Not a soul in sight. But something... something was off. It was too quiet.

I pulled out my camera, lifting it to my eye, clicking the shutter as I captured the shadows and the decay. It was the perfect shot—haunting and unsettling in its desolation. But as I lowered the camera, I felt a presence, a shift in the air that was too sudden to be explained away by nerves.

A shadow stretched out beside me, and before I could react, a hand was on my arm, pulling me back, away from the window. My heart lurched, the sound of the blood pounding in my ears almost deafening. I spun around, ready to lash out, but there he was.

Evan.

Of course.

His eyes were wild, focused, as if he had known exactly where I would be, exactly when I'd be there. "What the hell are you doing here?" he hissed, his grip tightening for a moment before he let go.

I wanted to scream at him, to demand why he was following me—again—but his urgent look stopped me. There was something in the air, something electric.

I glanced back at the building, my gaze darting to the flickering light on the upper floors. It wasn't just the quiet that had unsettled me. It was him. His sudden appearance. The fact that I had no idea how long he'd been lurking behind me. It was like he knew exactly what I was doing here.

"Are you alone?" he asked, his voice low, tight.

I nodded, still trying to make sense of what was happening. "What do you know about this place?"

He scanned the hotel, his jaw tightening. "More than I want to." His eyes met mine for a split second, and then he was moving, pulling me away from the window. "Get back. Now."

I didn't argue. He moved with such authority, the kind of confidence that could only come from someone who had seen things go wrong in ways that made ordinary people's nightmares look tame. I followed him into the shadows, my heart racing. The air around us was charged, thick with tension.

Then, just as we rounded the corner, it happened. The explosion rocked the ground beneath us.

I was thrown forward, the world a blur of light and sound. It felt like the sky itself had cracked open. My ears rang, and for a moment, I thought I might lose my balance completely. But then Evan was there, grabbing me, pulling me down, shielding me with his body. His muscles tensed beneath me, his warmth a stark contrast to the cold night air.

The blast sent a wave of heat over us, and I could feel the force of it through every inch of my body. The shockwave knocked the breath from my lungs, leaving me gasping. We hit the ground, hard, his body cushioning mine as debris rained down around us, and the world seemed to implode in on itself.

I couldn't hear anything for a few seconds. My heart hammered in my chest, and I struggled to breathe, struggling to make sense of what had just happened. Through the haze of smoke and dust, Evan's face appeared above me, his eyes dark and focused, scanning for any immediate danger.

"You okay?" His voice was rough, urgent. I nodded, my throat tight.

He pulled me into a sitting position, his hand on my shoulder steadying me. We were in the middle of an absolute warzone, the hotel in flames behind us. The heat of the fire licked at the air, but I barely felt it now.

I was shaken, my mind reeling. We had barely escaped, and yet, I couldn't tear my gaze away from him. My pulse didn't settle. His body had protected mine—like a shield—and for a moment, I was uncomfortably aware of how close we were. How close we'd always been.

"Thank you," I managed, my voice hoarse. I couldn't look away from his face, and the weight of everything that had just happened pressed down on me like a vice. His proximity made everything feel sharper, more real.

Evan didn't respond right away. Instead, he just nodded, his hand still on my arm as if he were keeping me tethered to reality.

Then, finally, he spoke, his voice barely a whisper against the sound of the burning building.

"You shouldn't have come here alone."

The smoke was thick, swirling around us like a ghost that refused to let go. The air felt suffocating, the heat from the flames licking at my skin, but I barely noticed it. My head was still spinning, my heartbeat thundering in my ears, and the only thing I could focus on was the steady pressure of Evan's hand on my arm, pulling me further into the shadows.

"Stay low," he muttered, his breath warm against my ear as he guided me through the debris-strewn alley. I didn't need telling twice. My knees felt weak, like they might give way at any moment, but I held myself steady. There was something about his presence that made me want to listen, to follow, as if I didn't trust myself without him there.

I glanced back at the hotel, now a roaring inferno behind us, flames dancing like angry spirits. The building that had been so still, so haunting just moments before, was now alive with violence. It wasn't supposed to explode. It wasn't supposed to be anything more than an old building falling apart. But it had been. And that revelation sat heavy in my stomach, a warning I couldn't ignore.

Evan's grip tightened as we moved. His hand, calloused and firm, was the only thing keeping me from falling apart entirely. He led me deeper into the maze of alleys, each step bringing us further from the fire and closer to... what? I wasn't sure. All I knew was that there were answers I wasn't getting, and that gnawing feeling in my gut wasn't going to go away until I had them.

I wasn't about to let him take control of everything, though. I could feel the weight of his gaze on me, the concern in it, but I refused to be a helpless bystander.

"Where are we going?" I managed, my voice barely above a whisper, my throat raw from the smoke.

He didn't look at me as he replied, his pace steady, unflinching. "Somewhere safe. We can talk once we're there."

We kept moving, the night so dark it felt like the sky was swallowing us whole. The only sounds were our footsteps and the distant crackling of the fire. We turned a corner, and suddenly, the chaos of the explosion felt like it belonged to another world, as though it hadn't just happened seconds ago.

I followed Evan into a small, dimly lit bar that looked like it hadn't seen the light of day in decades. It was hidden behind a closed door, tucked away in a corner of the city where no one would think to look for answers. The scent of stale beer and leather hung in the air, mixing with the bitterness of old wood.

Evan gave a nod to the bartender, a grizzled man who didn't seem particularly interested in who we were. He gestured for us to sit at a table in the farthest corner, one that was half-hidden by a peeling curtain.

I sank into the chair, my legs weak, my hands still trembling. I didn't know if it was the adrenaline or something else, but my whole body was on high alert. Evan sat across from me, his expression unreadable, his brow furrowed like he was trying to piece together a puzzle with the wrong pieces.

"So, what's going on?" I asked, my voice sharper than I intended. I was tired of the cryptic silence, tired of him making all the decisions. The building had just blown up in front of us, and I was damn well going to find out why.

Evan's eyes flashed, a mix of frustration and something else I couldn't place. "You should have stayed away. This isn't your fight."

"Oh, and you think you can just waltz in and take over?" I shot back, the words coming out before I could stop them. It wasn't like me to get defensive, but something about his tone, his attempt to control the situation, made my skin crawl.

His lips pressed into a thin line, his jaw clenched. "I'm trying to protect you."

"By putting me in the middle of an explosion?" I wasn't sure why I was so angry, but it wasn't just the explosion. It was the fact that Evan always showed up out of nowhere, always with answers I wasn't allowed to know. He was a ghost in my life, flickering in and out of focus, and every time I thought I had a grip on him, he slipped away again.

Evan ran a hand through his hair, exhaling slowly like he was trying to calm down. "Look, I'm not good at this. I don't know how to make it easier for you. But I need you to understand—there's more to this than you think."

I leaned forward, my elbows on the table. "More to what? You're being vague on purpose. Why can't you just tell me what's going on?"

The tension between us was palpable, a thick wire stretched tight, just waiting for someone to snap. But Evan wasn't about to give in that easily. Instead, he leaned back in his chair, crossing his arms, his eyes fixed on me like I was the only thing in the room that mattered.

"You're not ready for this," he said, the words coming out low, almost to himself.

I froze, the hurt creeping in like a slow burn. It wasn't the first time he'd said something like that. It wasn't the first time he'd underestimated me. But it was the first time it stung so badly.

"I'm not ready?" I whispered, more to myself than to him. "And when will I ever be ready? When you decide I am?"

Evan's gaze softened for just a moment, but it was gone before I could make sense of it. "This isn't about readiness. It's about keeping you alive."

That stung, too. I wasn't sure why, but it did. Maybe because he was right, and maybe because I wasn't sure if I wanted to stay alive if it meant being at his mercy.

"I can handle myself," I said, the words coming out stronger than I felt.

He didn't answer, just stared at me for a long beat, his eyes dark with something I couldn't decipher. Then, without warning, he stood, his chair scraping against the floor. "Stay here. I'll be back in a few minutes."

And just like that, he was gone. Leaving me with nothing but my racing thoughts and the heavy silence that followed.

The seconds stretched into what felt like lifetimes, but in reality, it couldn't have been more than a minute before Evan was gone. Just like that—slipping through the door without a sound, leaving me alone in the quiet hum of the bar. I wasn't sure if I was relieved or frustrated, the emotions fighting for dominance inside me. Relief, because I could finally breathe without him hovering over me like some kind of shadow. Frustration, because I had no idea where this was going. What he was hiding. And worse—why he thought he had the right to keep me in the dark.

The bar felt emptier without him. The neon sign outside buzzed softly, flickering every few seconds like it was about to give out. I picked at the edge of the chipped table, my fingers restless, a knot of tension curling tighter in my chest. The explosion—was it a coincidence? Was he really trying to protect me, or was there something more to it, something he wasn't telling me?

I wanted to scream. I wanted to throw my phone at the wall and demand answers from the universe, but instead, I sat in that grimy corner, feeling the weight of the silence pressing in on me. It was a silence that wrapped itself around me, suffocating, daring me to make a move. I thought about getting up, leaving, but where would I go? And more importantly, where would he be?

Then, the door creaked open again.

I didn't even have to look up to know it was Evan. I could hear the change in the air—his presence filled the space like an electrical charge. And yet, when I did look up, my breath caught in my throat. He wasn't alone.

A man entered with him, tall, lean, his eyes hidden behind dark glasses despite the dim light. He had an aura about him—cold, calculating. The kind of man who could break you with a glance and make you feel grateful for it. I didn't know who he was, but the way Evan stiffened when their eyes met told me everything I needed to know. This was no casual acquaintance.

Evan's gaze flicked to me briefly before he gave a slight nod to the stranger. The man didn't acknowledge me, though his lips twitched upward as he approached the bar. He ordered a drink in a voice so smooth, it felt wrong. Like velvet over steel.

Evan came back to the table, his expression harder than before, like he'd just waged some inner battle he wasn't willing to share.

"Who's he?" I asked before I could stop myself, my voice sharper than I intended.

Evan paused, his fingers gripping the back of the chair before he slid into it. His eyes darted briefly to the man at the bar, then back to me. "Someone I'm trying to avoid."

I raised an eyebrow. "But he's here. So... not avoiding him very well, are you?"

The corner of Evan's mouth twitched, like he might've been amused—though it didn't quite reach his eyes. "Not everything is as simple as it looks."

I didn't know if that was meant to reassure me or just shut me up. Either way, it had the same effect. My frustration grew, coiling inside me like a snake ready to strike. "So you're just going to keep me in the dark about everything? About why this man is here?

About why that building exploded? About why I almost got myself killed—again?"

The words spilled out before I could stop them. Anger, fear, confusion—all of it mixed together in one mess of emotions I had no idea how to untangle. But the worst part was, he didn't even seem fazed by it.

"Sit tight," Evan said, his tone suddenly sharp, hard. "I'll handle it. And you're not going anywhere."

I flinched, but only for a moment. It wasn't the command that bothered me—it was the way he said it. The confidence in his voice, the finality. It wasn't a request. It wasn't even a suggestion. It was a truth I wasn't allowed to challenge.

I wanted to argue. To snap at him and walk out the door, throw caution to the wind and demand that he stop treating me like a child. But I couldn't. I was already too far in, already too tangled in this web to break free. And the part of me that wanted to know the truth—the part of me that had always needed answers—held me back.

The stranger at the bar finished his drink and stood up, his movements measured, almost too controlled. He slipped something into the bartender's hand before he turned toward us. There was no hiding the tension in the room now. The air between Evan and the man crackled with unspoken words, things neither of them were willing to say out loud.

I glanced from one to the other, my chest tightening as I tried to make sense of what was happening. The man walked over to us, and I instinctively braced myself, unsure whether he was a threat or simply an observer in some game I wasn't yet ready to understand.

"Evan," the stranger said, his voice low and even, carrying a weight that settled heavily in my stomach. "We need to talk."

I wanted to look away. I wanted to pretend I didn't hear it, didn't see the way Evan's jaw tightened, his gaze narrowing as he met the stranger's. But I couldn't. I was drawn to it, like a moth to a flame, and I knew—I knew—that whatever this was, it was about to unravel everything. The story, the danger, the mystery that had been tugging at me for so long, all of it was about to come crashing down.

And just when I thought I might get a glimpse of the truth, when I thought I might finally understand what Evan was trying to hide, the man leaned in closer, his voice a whisper meant only for Evan.

"You didn't think she'd be here, did you?"

The words hung in the air, sharp, like a knife poised to strike. My heart skipped a beat, my breath caught in my throat, and I felt every muscle in my body freeze.

Evan's eyes flicked to me. And in that moment, I knew—I knew—nothing would ever be the same.

Chapter 9: A Dangerous Inferno

The fire had burned for hours, yet the air still held that thick, metallic taste, a haunting reminder of destruction. I stood in the parking lot, staring at the charred remains of the warehouse, my fingers clenching around the phone that had been thrust into my hand only moments ago. The screen lit up again—an unknown number flashing across it. I hadn't needed to answer. The message was already there, sitting like an ominous promise.

"You can't stop this. Not now, not ever. I'm going to watch it all burn. Starting with you."

I could almost feel the heat of the words pressing against my skin, searing in a way the flames never could. The arsonist—whoever they were—had made it personal. And worse still, they weren't just targeting me anymore. Evan's name had come through the message, barely visible, buried in a list of threats.

The tightness in my chest wasn't from the smoke in the air or the sting of the fumes. No, this was something else—something far darker, something I wasn't ready to face. Not yet.

"I thought we were getting closer to the end," I muttered, more to myself than to anyone else. But Evan had been hovering nearby, a shadow at the edge of my vision. I could feel his presence like a weight pressing against my back, the steady rhythm of his breathing filling the space between us.

"Nothing ends until it's over," he said quietly, as if the words had a weight of their own, and he'd carried them far too long. I turned to face him, but the look in his eyes stopped me short. There was something—something I couldn't place. I'd seen it before, buried deep in the way his shoulders slumped when he thought no one was looking, the way his jaw tightened when he thought he could outrun the past.

He had seen too much. Lost too much.

"Evan—" I began, but he cut me off with a shake of his head.

"I've lost people before, Iris. People who got too close. People who thought they could outrun what was hunting them." His voice didn't waver, but there was a dark depth there, a warning buried in the way the words hung in the air.

The first spark of fear flared in me—not for myself, but for him. He didn't want me to get any closer, didn't want me tangled in his mess. I could see it in the set of his jaw, the way his hands flexed at his sides as if restraining himself. But there was no way I was backing down. Not now.

"You can't push me away, not now," I told him, my voice firm despite the unease curling in my stomach. "You've seen what happens when we play this game alone. We lose."

He let out a slow, frustrated breath, the kind that carried with it a lifetime of pain. "You don't know what you're getting into. This—" He gestured vaguely, taking in the destruction around us, the charred remains of a building and the fire trucks still flickering their lights in the distance. "This isn't just about us anymore. It's bigger than that."

I resisted the urge to step back. "You're not scaring me away," I said. "You should know that by now."

Evan didn't respond. Instead, he turned to face the wreckage once again, his eyes narrowed, scanning the smoke that curled like ghosts against the gray sky. He was trying to shield me from whatever demons he was carrying. I could see it—the way he fought to keep me at arm's length. But this fight wasn't his alone anymore. We were in this together.

"Whoever is doing this—whoever is trying to destroy everything we've built, they're going to regret it," I said, my voice steady, even if my heart was pounding in my chest.

He shot me a sideways glance, and there was a flicker of something in his eyes, something that looked like reluctant respect.

"You always think you can win, don't you?" he asked, a half-smile curving his lips.

"I don't think. I know."

He gave a soft, bitter laugh. "We're both in too deep, Iris. There's no way out."

"I'm not running," I shot back, my gaze hardening. "And neither are you."

For a moment, there was nothing but the distant crackling of the remnants of the fire, the hiss of water as it was sprayed over what was left of the building. Then Evan sighed, long and drawn-out, like a man who had been carrying a burden far too heavy for far too long.

"You don't get it," he muttered. "When I say they'll hurt you, it's not just a threat. It's a promise. These people don't play fair."

I took a slow step toward him, close enough now that I could feel the heat radiating off his body, smell the familiar mix of smoke and his cologne. It was a reminder of the world we'd walked into, the one we couldn't escape from.

"Then we fight dirty," I said, my voice low but unwavering. "We play by their rules, and we make sure they lose."

For a moment, he didn't move. And then, with a soft exhale, he turned back to face the wreckage. The flickering lights of the fire trucks cast an eerie glow over his features, but it was the way he straightened, the way his shoulders squared, that told me everything I needed to know.

He wasn't going to back down. Neither was I.

We weren't done yet. Not by a long shot.

I found myself standing in front of his door the next evening, the cool autumn air biting at my skin, sharp as the edge of the uncertainty hanging between us. Evan hadn't called after the fire; his silence had been a thick wall, a refusal to let anything break through. I couldn't blame him for wanting distance. He was right about one thing: people got too close, and it was never the right time. But I wasn't going to leave. I couldn't, not with everything unraveling so quickly.

The door creaked open before I could even bring my hand up to knock, and there he was, standing in the dim light of the hallway, wearing that look again—the one that said he was already miles ahead, already deciding how to push me out without having to say a word.

"Thought you'd be somewhere else," he said, his voice low, like it carried a weight he couldn't quite shake off. His eyes were tired, but there was something else there—something darker, like a storm that hadn't fully broken yet.

"Turns out I'm stubborn," I replied, with a wry smile that didn't quite reach my eyes. I wasn't here to argue. Not tonight. "I need you to help me."

Evan stepped aside, gesturing for me to come in. The space was still sparse, just like it had been the first time I'd visited, with only the faintest traces of his personality scattered among the bare walls. His coffee table had a half-finished puzzle, the pieces scattered around like abandoned dreams. It should have been comforting—familiar—but all I could focus on was the tension that had only grown between us.

"Help with what?" he asked, leaning against the back of the couch, arms crossed. I could see the way his jaw clenched, the way his posture grew even more guarded. I had to wonder how many times he'd found himself on the other side of a situation like this, where someone needed him but the price was too high.

"The arsonist," I said, keeping my voice steady, though inside, everything was a mess of urgency and frustration. "We're both targets now, whether we like it or not. We need to figure out who's behind this before they get to anyone else."

Evan's gaze flickered for the briefest moment, like I'd said something unexpected, but just as quickly, he masked it. "I'm not in the business of playing hero anymore."

"Don't give me that." I took a step forward, closing the gap between us. His expression didn't change, but I could feel the faintest pulse of vulnerability that he was trying to hide. "You can't just walk away from this. You're already in it. So am I."

He stayed quiet for a moment, his eyes locked on mine, as if weighing the danger in my words against the truth of them. Then, with a sharp exhale, he dropped his arms and straightened up. "Fine," he muttered, stepping toward the window, his back to me. "We're in it, but that doesn't mean I'm letting you take unnecessary risks."

My brow furrowed. "I'm already taking risks by being here, Evan. You think I don't know that?"

"I don't care what you think you know." He turned to face me now, and I saw it—saw the walls he'd built up, the ones I'd been so eager to tear down. His voice was softer now, but still edged with the same caution. "I've already lost people. If you get hurt because of this—because you chose to chase this thing down—I'm not going to forgive myself."

I opened my mouth to speak, but the words stuck in my throat. I wanted to argue, to tell him that we had no choice but to fight back, to expose whoever was pulling the strings. But the way he looked at me—like he was bracing himself for something he couldn't control—silenced the words before they left my lips.

"You don't have to do this," he said finally, his voice rougher than I was used to. "You don't have to follow me down this road."

I felt a pang in my chest, something soft and unwelcome. "You're not the only one who's lost people, Evan," I said quietly, a weight I hadn't expected settling on my shoulders. "I'm not afraid of losing someone. I'm afraid of not trying to stop it when I know I could."

His gaze softened, just for a moment, but then his shoulders squared again, and he gave a single, almost imperceptible nod. "We do this my way," he said. "No more reckless moves. We stay smart. You follow my lead, no questions."

I nodded, not trusting myself to speak. It wasn't about following his lead, not really—it was about showing him that we could do this together. But I knew better than to push him further. There was a line I couldn't cross, a boundary he'd drawn long before I'd ever stepped into his life. But I was getting closer to finding out what really lay behind that wall.

We spent the next few hours mapping out the threats, piecing together what little we knew. It wasn't much, just a handful of leads that felt more like riddles than answers. But Evan was methodical, his mind sharp as a knife, and it wasn't long before we found a pattern emerging—an eerie consistency to the locations of the fires, the timing of each one. This wasn't random. This was a message.

"What if it's not just about the destruction?" I asked, tracing the locations on the map. "What if they're trying to send a message?"

Evan didn't answer right away. Instead, he stared at the map, as if seeing something I couldn't. Then, with a resigned sigh, he spoke. "You're right. But that's not the part that scares me. It's who they're sending it to."

His words hung in the air between us like smoke, thick and suffocating. And just like that, I knew—we were only scratching the surface. The arsonist was playing a much deeper game than we'd thought. And now, we were both in it.

The following days felt like an extended silence, each hour stretching thin as we tried to piece together the puzzle. But for every lead we followed, every clue we dug up, the picture only grew more tangled. The arsonist didn't just want to destroy property; they wanted to play with our minds, weaving a web of half-truths that only made the truth harder to find. And Evan... Evan was a locked door, one I was desperate to open but not sure I could. His walls were built with secrets that felt as heavy as the burden he carried, and I was starting to wonder if he even realized how much of himself he kept hidden behind them.

It was late, and I was sitting on the floor of my apartment, scattered files and half-finished notes around me. The quiet hum of the city filtered through the cracked window, but even that felt distant, like it belonged to someone else's life. The glow of the desk lamp was warm, but it wasn't enough to chase away the coldness that had settled in my chest. I rubbed my temples, trying to focus, but the fear gnawing at me was relentless. The arsonist had made it clear that they weren't done. Not by a long shot. And now Evan was in their sights too.

The knock on the door was sharp, startling me out of my thoughts. I knew who it was before I even stood up. Evan didn't wait for an invitation, just barged in with that familiar, worn-out expression on his face. The tension between us had thickened over the past week, the unspoken words hanging like smoke in the air.

"Are you sleeping?" he asked, the exhaustion in his voice betraying the hard edge he was trying to maintain.

"I'm fine," I said, pushing aside the papers and standing up. The sudden movement made the blood rush to my head, and I had to steady myself against the desk. "What's going on?"

His gaze softened, but only for a moment. "I think I found something," he said, his voice low. "But you're not going to like it."

I took a cautious step forward, the unease swirling in my stomach. "What do you mean?"

Evan didn't answer immediately. Instead, he reached into his jacket pocket and pulled out a small notebook. He opened it slowly, his fingers tracing the pages as if he could feel the weight of the information inside. "I've been keeping track of the fire locations. There's a pattern," he said, his voice gravelly. "And it's not just about buildings."

I took the notebook from him, studying the scribbled notes and markings. He was right—there was a pattern. But the places the fires were set weren't just random locations. They had been close to certain people—people who weren't just innocent bystanders. They had ties to us, to our past. My heart began to race as the implications hit me like a freight train.

"This is personal," I said, barely above a whisper. The realization settled like a stone in my chest. "They're targeting people connected to us."

Evan didn't look at me, his eyes trained on the floor as he nodded. "Exactly. And the next name on the list..." His voice trailed off, but I didn't need him to finish. I already knew.

"You," I breathed, the air in my lungs suddenly feeling too thick. "You're next."

He didn't flinch, didn't even acknowledge the truth in my words. "They know I'm close to you," he said, his voice dark. "And that makes you a target too."

I swallowed hard, the weight of his words sinking deep into my bones. "Then we need to stop them," I said, my voice firm despite the tremor that ran through my hands. "We can't just wait for the next fire."

Evan finally met my gaze, his eyes searching mine with a intensity that made my stomach flip. "You don't understand," he said quietly, almost pleading. "This isn't something you can just stop. It's bigger than us. They're not playing by the rules anymore."

"And we are?" I snapped before I could stop myself. The frustration bubbled up in me, hot and sharp. "You think I don't know that? You think I don't get how dangerous this is? But we can't let them win. Not like this."

His jaw tightened, and for a moment, I thought he might say something more, but he didn't. He just reached out, taking my hand in his—unexpected, but somehow not. He was always touching me when I least expected it, always in that soft, possessive way, like he was trying to make sure I didn't slip away. But this time, it wasn't the usual quiet reassurance. This time, it was something else—something desperate, something raw.

"You need to stay out of this," he said, his voice low, almost a growl. "For your own sake. If you keep pushing, you're going to get hurt. I can't lose you, Iris. I won't."

I pulled my hand from his, my mind spinning as I tried to make sense of what he was saying. He was scared, but I was scared too. His words were a warning, but they were also a plea. And I wasn't going to be the one to back down.

"We don't have the luxury of backing down," I told him, my voice trembling with determination. "We need to end this now, before it's too late."

His eyes darkened, and for the first time, I saw something in them that unsettled me. A flicker of fear. And then it was gone, replaced by something colder, more calculated.

"We'll do it my way," he said, his voice a hard edge now. "No more risking everything."

I nodded, though a knot had formed in my stomach, the warning signs flashing in my mind. Something wasn't right, and I couldn't tell if it was the game we were playing, or if it was Evan himself. Either way, I knew this wasn't over. It couldn't be.

As I turned to grab my coat, the phone buzzed on the table, the screen lighting up with a message from an unknown number. I didn't need to look at the words to know what it was. I could feel the weight of it—another taunt, another threat, but this time... this time, the message was different.

"Tick-tock, Iris. The clock is running out."

I grabbed the phone, my heart pounding. But before I could process anything further, the door slammed open behind me. Evan's voice, sharp as a whip, froze me in my tracks.

"Get down," he yelled, just as the sound of something sharp and dangerous rang through the air.

The glass in the window shattered with a deafening crash. And I realized, too late, that we had underestimated how far the arsonist was willing to go.

Chapter 10: Kindling Secrets

The air in the room had a thickness to it, like it was holding its breath, waiting for something. It could've been the storm outside, thrashing against the windows with a fury that rattled the frames and made the walls groan in sympathy, or maybe it was just the weight of the truth that hung between us like an iron chain. Evan hadn't told me everything—there were gaps in his stories, stretches of silence that were as loud as any confession. But it wasn't until now that I felt the sting of it, deep in my gut, sharp and cold.

I had stumbled across a photograph, buried under a stack of old letters and postcards in the back of his drawer. She smiled from the corner of the picture, her long, dark hair cascading over her shoulder, the kind of smile that didn't quite reach her eyes. There was a weight to her presence, an undertow of something unspoken. I didn't recognize her, but I knew she wasn't a stranger. Her name was scrawled beneath her image in bold, unfamiliar handwriting: Sarah Manning. That was the name that had haunted me since I'd come across it in the headline of a newspaper article.

"Woman Found Dead in Suspicious Fire." The photo accompanying the article was a blurry black-and-white shot of a charred building, its skeleton still standing amidst the ruin. And there, just at the edge of the frame, was a figure that could've been Sarah—her body half-turned away from the camera, like she was trying to escape the chaos that surrounded her.

I had put the paper down immediately, my stomach tightening. Why hadn't Evan mentioned her before? He'd always been so open with me about his past, about the people he'd lost, about the things that had shaped him. But this? This woman—this fire—had never come up in any of our late-night talks over too many glasses of wine, or the casual chats on lazy Sundays spent sprawled across the couch.

I could feel my pulse quicken as I replayed the moment in my mind. Evan had known her. That much was clear. The photograph was a silent confession, one I wasn't sure I was ready to confront.

The door creaked behind me, and I spun around, instinctively clutching the picture to my chest like a shield. Evan stood there, his hand still resting on the doorknob, eyes dark and unreadable. He looked different somehow, as if the very act of entering the room had unsettled him, made him more distant, more unreachable.

"Is this her?" I asked, my voice barely above a whisper, the weight of the question more suffocating than I had anticipated.

He didn't answer at first. Instead, he let out a slow breath, the kind of exhale you only make when you're bracing yourself for impact. "I didn't want you to find that," he said, his voice tight, the words almost bitter in their delivery. "You're not supposed to know about her."

There it was, the truth I'd been seeking, but it felt more like a slap than a revelation. "Why?" I asked, my chest constricting with a thousand unsaid questions. "Why didn't you tell me?"

Evan's gaze dropped to the floor, his jaw tightening. His hands curled into fists at his sides, and for a moment, I thought he might walk away, leave me standing there with nothing but the puzzle pieces of his past scattered in front of me. But instead, he stepped forward, slowly, deliberately, and I could feel the weight of his silence pressing in on me.

"She was a part of my life a long time ago," he said, his voice lower now, the edges rough with something that almost sounded like regret. "But that part of my life is over, and it needs to stay that way."

My heart skipped a beat at his words. "Over? How? Did she—did she die in that fire?" The words spilled out of me before I could stop them, sharp and accusatory, a jagged edge to them.

His eyes flickered with something I couldn't place, something dark and unsettling. "You don't need to know the details," he said quickly, a little too quickly, as if he were trying to shut the door on the conversation before it could open too wide. "It's in the past."

But I wasn't ready to let him close it. Not this time.

"I deserve to know," I insisted, my voice trembling, but only just. "You've kept so much from me, Evan. How could you—how could you hide something like this?"

He stepped back, and for a moment, I thought he might leave. I was half-expecting him to walk out of the door and disappear into the storm outside. But instead, he ran a hand through his hair, his gaze distant. "I didn't want to drag you into this," he said, his words laced with something like guilt, or maybe fear. "I never wanted you to see me like this, to know what kind of man I was before. You've always known the version of me that's moved forward, that's tried to make up for all the mistakes."

"But Sarah—" I started, but the words died in my throat. "What happened to her? Why didn't you ever mention her to me?"

His jaw clenched so tightly, I could see the muscles in his neck strain against the tension. "I don't want to talk about her," he muttered, his voice colder now, more distant. "I can't."

I felt the sharp sting of his words settle into my chest, like I'd been pierced by something I couldn't see, something that had been there all along but was only now coming to the surface. He was shutting me out, and it was hurting more than I had ever imagined.

I took a step back, my chest tight as the silence thickened around us. His words hung in the air, brittle as glass, and for a moment, I could only hear the storm outside—a constant, relentless roar—as if nature itself was trying to drown out what he'd said. He didn't want to talk about her. He didn't want to talk about her. The words echoed in my head, repeating like a broken record.

But that didn't matter. What mattered was that he was holding something back. And now that I had this sliver of truth, I couldn't unsee it.

"You don't get to make that decision for me, Evan," I said, my voice trembling slightly but growing firmer with each word. "I deserve to know what happened. You don't get to pull away just when I'm trying to understand you, to really know you."

He flinched at my words, and something shifted in his eyes—regret, frustration, maybe even fear. It was enough to make my heart skip a beat, and that terrified me. What was he afraid of?

"I'm not ready to talk about it," he muttered, his back turned now, his hand on the edge of the desk like he was about to push himself away from this conversation, this moment. "Some things aren't meant to be shared, especially not with someone who doesn't need to carry that burden."

It stung. Deeply. His words felt like a rejection, like he was telling me that everything we'd built up until now didn't matter, that I wasn't worthy of his past.

But I couldn't let it go. Not now. Not when I had tasted the bitter edges of it.

"I'm not just someone, Evan," I said, stepping toward him, my pulse hammering in my throat. "I'm the one you've been letting in, the one who's been here, holding your hand while you fumble through whatever this is. You think I don't deserve to know what kind of man you were, what kind of life you've lived before me? Well, guess what? I don't buy it. You don't get to shut me out now."

His shoulders stiffened, and for a moment, I thought he might turn around and walk out—just disappear into that storm outside and leave me with all these fractured pieces of him. But instead, he let out a ragged breath, so sharp and bitter that it made my stomach turn.

"Sarah..." He paused, as though the name itself weighed a thousand pounds on his tongue. He didn't say anything for several long seconds, and I could feel the tension between us stretching, taut like a tightrope. "She was my mistake."

I felt a flicker of confusion, my eyebrows knitting together. "What does that mean?" I asked, the question slipping out before I could stop it. The word "mistake" stuck in my throat, leaving a bad taste there. "You're telling me she was a mistake?"

He turned to face me then, his eyes dark but softening just slightly. His expression was heavy with something I couldn't quite place—grief, shame, regret? Maybe all of them.

"You don't get it," he said, his voice low, almost pleading. "I should've walked away from her when I had the chance. But I didn't. I didn't, and it cost me everything. And when she died... when she died in that fire, it was like the weight of all those mistakes came crashing down on me. I couldn't breathe. I couldn't think straight. And I sure as hell couldn't talk about it."

I stood there, rooted to the spot, unsure of what to say next. He was unraveling in front of me, but in a way that felt like a trap. The more he told me, the less I understood. It was like peeling back layers of a story, only to find there was more darkness underneath than I could stomach.

"Did you start the fire?" I asked, the words slipping out before I could stop them. The thought had been clawing at the edges of my mind since I'd seen the photo, since I'd read the article. It felt cruel to ask, but I needed to know. I needed to hear it from him.

His eyes locked onto mine, and for a moment, I thought I saw something flicker there—a flash of panic, or guilt, or maybe both. But he didn't answer right away. Instead, he looked away, his jaw tightening as if he were forcing himself to stay composed.

"I don't know," he said finally, his voice strained. "I've asked myself that same question a thousand times. But I don't have the answers. I just know that I was there, I was with her when it happened. And I couldn't stop it. I couldn't save her."

The air in the room felt suddenly too thick, too heavy. I could hear my own breath now, shallow and rapid, as if I were drowning in the silence between us.

"I should've told you this sooner," he added, his voice softer now, almost broken. "But I didn't want to scare you off. I didn't want you to see me as that person, the one who made the choices that led to... all of this."

I stepped back, my mind racing as I tried to process everything he had just said. It wasn't just the fire, or Sarah—it was him too. He had been holding onto this pain, this secret, and I had no idea. He'd carried it for years, silently, like it was something too monstrous to share.

But now, it was my turn to feel the weight of it. I had asked for the truth, but I wasn't sure I was ready for it. The world around me felt like it was shifting on its axis, like everything I thought I knew about Evan was being torn down piece by piece.

"I don't know if I can just let this go," I said, my voice low, unsure. "I don't know if I can forget this."

Evan's eyes softened, a hint of vulnerability breaking through the walls he'd built up around himself. He didn't speak, but his gaze told me everything. He was sorry, and that was enough—for now.

But the silence between us was still there, deep and unyielding, and I couldn't shake the feeling that I had only scratched the surface of his secret past. What else was he hiding? What else had he buried beneath layers of guilt and regret? And could I ever truly trust him again if I couldn't get to the heart of it all?

I wanted to shake him, demand more from him. But the way he stood there, his shoulders hunched as if trying to make himself small, made me hesitate. He was unraveling before me, and it was clear that whatever had happened with Sarah—whatever dark chapter of his life he was still carrying—wasn't something he could simply explain away. And yet, the silence between us screamed louder than any explanation could.

I took a step closer, my eyes locked on his, trying to hold onto the last thread of control that had kept me grounded through this whole mess. "You think this doesn't change everything?" I said, my voice more forceful now. "I trusted you, Evan. And you—"

He cut me off, his voice tight, barely audible over the pounding rain outside. "I didn't want to bring you into this mess. I didn't want you to see the parts of me that still... still haunt me. But you're here now. And you deserve to know the truth. Even if it breaks you."

I swallowed hard. The last part of his sentence was like a punch to my chest. The truth—his truth—was something that could easily undo everything between us. I could feel the weight of it settling over me, heavy and suffocating. I had asked for this. I had wanted him to be honest with me, to let me in. But now that he was, I wasn't sure I could carry it.

"Then tell me," I said, forcing the words out through a throat that felt too tight. "Tell me everything. Don't leave me with just the pieces of it. Don't make me guess what happened."

For a moment, there was only the sound of the rain, the steady hum of it as it beat against the window. I watched as Evan's fingers twitched, like he wanted to reach out, to say something, but couldn't find the words. His eyes shifted to the floor, the weight of the moment pressing down on him. His body language was all sharp angles, a stark contrast to the openness I had come to expect from him.

"It wasn't just a fire," he finally said, his voice so low I could barely hear him over the storm. "It was a trap. She wasn't supposed to die. She wasn't supposed to be there. But she was, and now... now it's too late to undo any of it."

I took a step back, blinking as if I had misheard him. "A trap? What are you talking about? Who would—who would want to trap her? Why?"

Evan's gaze flickered to mine, then away, and I could see the struggle in his eyes. He was fighting something—fighting me, fighting himself. "Sarah wasn't just... she wasn't just some woman I once knew. She was part of something bigger. Something dangerous. And I should've walked away from her, but I didn't. I couldn't."

"Dangerous? What do you mean?" My head spun with the sudden shift in tone, my mind trying to wrap itself around the pieces he was giving me. Each one was more confusing than the last.

"She was involved with people I shouldn't have gotten mixed up with," he said, his voice strained. "People who deal in things that don't belong in the light. And I was a fool for thinking I could keep my distance. For thinking that I could walk away without consequences."

I stared at him, my mind struggling to grasp the enormity of what he was saying. "So you're telling me she was involved in—what? Crime? Organized crime?" My voice wavered as I spoke the words, the idea settling on my shoulders like an iron weight.

Evan didn't answer immediately. Instead, he stepped back, running a hand through his hair, his face a mask of frustration. "I shouldn't have brought her into my life. But I did. And now... now she's dead. And I'm still here, and I can't undo any of it. Not for her. Not for me. And certainly not for you."

The more he spoke, the less I understood. His words were like threads pulling me in different directions, each one unraveling a new, darker part of him that I wasn't sure I could follow. But it wasn't just his past that scared me now. It was his present. The way he was talking about Sarah—like he was still tied to her, still haunted by what had happened.

"You're saying she died because of you," I said, my voice trembling despite myself. "Because you couldn't walk away."

His eyes darkened, and he nodded slowly. "In a way, yes. But there's more to it than that. I can't explain it all, not yet. But I promise you—if I'd known how far things would go, I would've stayed away. I would've protected you from this."

"Protected me?" The words caught in my throat. "From what?"

Before he could respond, there was a sharp knock on the door. My heart jumped into my throat. I hadn't been expecting anyone. No one came to the door at this hour—not in the middle of the storm.

Evan's face paled, his eyes flashing with something that bordered on panic. "Don't answer it," he whispered urgently. "Please. Just—"

The knock came again, louder this time, and before I could react, Evan was already crossing the room, reaching for the door handle. My breath caught as I realized something was terribly wrong.

"Evan—" I started to say, but it was too late.

He opened the door, and a figure stood there, silhouetted against the storm, their face hidden beneath a dark hood. The figure stepped inside without waiting for an invitation, and as the door clicked shut behind them, I felt an icy chill snake up my spine.

"I think it's time we had a talk," the figure said, their voice low and dangerous.

Evan's face went ashen, and I saw the brief flicker of something—something I hadn't expected—flash in his eyes. Fear.

Chapter 11: Fanning the Flames

The embers of the past still flickered in the cold, whispering secrets I was never meant to hear. I stood on the edge of the old fire site, where the earth still felt scorched despite the years that had passed. The ground beneath my boots was soft, as though even the land itself couldn't forget the devastation. The trees, once proud, now hunched and twisted, as though their limbs had been permanently singed by the memory of flames.

I watched him, a figure standing tall against the backdrop of a ghostly landscape, his broad shoulders tense and unmoving. His hands, scarred from more than just the fire, clenched at his sides as if fighting against the weight of some unseen burden. I shouldn't have followed him. I knew that. This place was a shadow of his past, a past that neither of us could rewrite. But the pull to understand him, to step closer to the core of whatever it was that haunted him, was too strong.

"Do you ever dream of it?" I asked quietly, my voice barely above a whisper as I closed the distance between us. "The fire?"

He didn't turn to face me, but his breath caught in his throat, a hitch that was all too human, all too raw. I had expected silence, but he spoke, his voice low and ragged, as though each word tore him open a little more.

"All the time." His eyes were distant, as though seeing something I couldn't. "Sometimes it's the smoke that wakes me. Other times, it's the sound of her voice... calling for help."

I felt the air in my lungs tighten, thick with the weight of his words. There was a sorrow in him that I couldn't fully comprehend, but I could feel the suffocating presence of it in every breath he took, every strained muscle in his neck. It was the kind of grief that doesn't ask for pity but demands to be carried. And here, now, in the thick of it, I knew something had broken in him that night, something he hadn't been able to fix.

The silence stretched out, thick and heavy, and I realized just how long I'd been holding my own breath. He didn't seem to notice my hesitation. His eyes, clouded with the weight of memory, finally met mine, and I saw something there, something fragile that he probably didn't even know he was showing. It was vulnerability, stark and unyielding.

"You couldn't have saved her," I said, almost against my will, the words tumbling out before I had time to filter them. "You couldn't have stopped it."

His lips pressed into a thin line, and for a moment, I thought he might retreat further into that fortress of guilt he'd built around himself. But then, as if forcing himself to let the words spill out, he spoke.

"I know." The words were heavy with a conviction that surprised me. "But that doesn't stop the feeling that maybe... maybe if I'd been faster, or smarter, or somehow stronger... I could have."

The guilt hung in the air like a thick fog, and I wondered if there was any way to cut through it, to help him see that he wasn't to blame for the unrelenting flames that had taken someone he loved. But the truth was, I didn't know. I only knew the look in his eyes, the way he carried himself as if his every step was burdened with something he couldn't shake off.

I reached out, my hand brushing his arm lightly, a tentative touch that felt too small for the enormity of the moment. He stiffened at first, but then his body seemed to relax ever so slightly under my hand.

"You're carrying something that isn't yours to carry," I said softly, my voice quiet, but filled with the force of a truth I had known for too long. "And maybe it's time to let it go."

He gave a humorless laugh, the sound harsh and full of edges. "It's not that simple." His gaze dropped to the ground, where the charred remnants of the fire's destruction still marred the landscape. "You think I haven't tried?"

The frustration in his voice made something in me stir, something soft and aching that I hadn't expected. His pain was palpable, so much more real than any of the anger I had ever felt.

"I think you haven't allowed yourself the chance to," I said, my words firming up as I stood my ground. "You can't heal if you don't let go."

For a long moment, he stared at the spot where the fire had raged, and I wondered if he would pull away again, if this quiet moment would turn into one of his usual retreats. But then, to my surprise, he turned toward me, his eyes holding mine with a tenderness that was almost a shock after the storm of emotions I'd witnessed.

"I don't know how," he admitted, his voice barely a murmur, the rawness of his admission both unsettling and endearing.

I smiled softly, the warmth of it somehow reaching out to him, hoping he'd catch it. "Maybe you don't have to know how," I said, my voice a little quieter now. "Maybe you just have to let someone else in long enough to show you."

The world felt like it had slowed around us, like time itself had taken a breath and settled in the stillness between us. His gaze softened, and for the first time, I saw a flicker of something that resembled hope. But it was brief, a mere flash before it was quickly hidden again by the storm clouds of his thoughts.

The quiet stretched on, and I felt the unease in the pit of my stomach rise again, reminding me of the larger shadow that loomed over us. The fire's aftermath wasn't the only thing we were standing in the midst of. The arsonist's reach was closing in, and I couldn't ignore the gnawing feeling in the back of my mind. The danger was growing, and this time, I wasn't sure we could outrun it.

There was something unnerving about the way the sky turned to dust at the edges of his thoughts. It wasn't just the looming absence of the fire's heat that filled the air; it was the quiet certainty with which he bore the weight of it. I had thought, perhaps naively, that standing here in the middle of the wreckage would offer him a sense of release—a kind of closure that he could walk away with. But instead, he stood there as though the fire had never stopped burning in him, a constant, unrelenting ache that seeped into every part of him.

"I don't know how to let it go," he murmured, his voice low, almost as if he feared the words would fall apart before he could finish them. There was no anger in his tone, not like I had expected. Just exhaustion. It was the kind of tiredness that went beyond the physical, something deeper, something that felt like it was carved into his very bones.

I stood beside him, our shoulders just barely brushing, and the electric tension between us felt like it could crack the sky wide open.

"You don't have to figure it out right this minute," I said, trying to keep my voice light, but even I knew how hollow it sounded. Still, I needed him to hear it. The weight of everything didn't have to be carried in one go. I glanced at him, finding his eyes closed, the muscles in his jaw clenched tightly. He was fighting against something I couldn't see, something he might never let anyone see.

He sighed, the sound escaping him like a slow, deliberate surrender. "I thought if I kept busy enough, I wouldn't have to feel it. I thought if I buried myself in work, in the next fire, I could outrun it." His hand tightened at his side, like he was holding something back. "But it doesn't work like that, does it?"

"No," I said, shaking my head. "It never does." There was a kind of ache in me, an old wound I couldn't quite name, that resonated with him. The need to run from grief, to pretend it doesn't exist, was one I understood far too well. "You're here now. That's a start, right?"

His lips quirked, though the smile never reached his eyes. "I suppose. If you consider standing in the middle of the wreckage a 'start.'"

I nudged him gently with my shoulder. "We all start somewhere. Sometimes it's not the prettiest of places, but it's a start."

He looked at me then, really looked at me, and for the first time since I'd met him, I saw something that wasn't weighed down by the past. It was small, a flicker of something that almost felt like relief, and I didn't dare blink in case I missed it.

"I don't know how to do this," he admitted, his voice barely a whisper, like he was afraid I might laugh or walk away.

"Do what?" I asked, my voice softening in spite of myself.

"Let someone in." He paused, his brow furrowing as though the words felt foreign even as they left his mouth. "I've spent so long pretending I don't need anyone, that I don't know how to need anyone."

I swallowed the lump that had formed in my throat. The vulnerability in his words made my heart ache for him in ways I hadn't expected. He'd been alone for too long, convinced that isolation was safer than connection.

"You don't have to do it alone anymore," I said quietly, my gaze never leaving his. "I'm not going anywhere."

For a long moment, neither of us moved. The silence wrapped around us like a heavy blanket, comforting and warm, but still filled with the unspoken things between us. I could feel the faint stirrings of something else, something that danced on the edges of my consciousness, but I couldn't bring myself to acknowledge it just yet. Not while there was still so much of him locked away, hidden behind walls he wasn't ready to tear down.

He let out another slow exhale, his fingers brushing against mine in a fleeting touch that almost felt like an apology. But then he stepped back, his eyes distant again, like he was retreating into his own mind, away from the tenderness I had just offered.

I wanted to follow him, to ask more questions, to press him for answers that he wasn't ready to give. But instead, I held my ground, allowing the space between us to settle in the quiet aftermath of his confession. I understood. I understood the need to pull away, to protect yourself from the things you weren't ready to face.

"We need to go," he said abruptly, the edge to his voice a reminder that we were still bound by something larger than the moment between us. "It's not safe here."

I frowned, confusion knitting my brow. "Safe?"

"The fire," he muttered, as if that was enough of an explanation. "It wasn't just an accident. Someone wanted it to burn."

The words hung in the air like smoke, thick and choking.

"An arsonist?" I asked, barely able to process what he was saying.

He nodded, his jaw tightening once again. "I've been tracking them for months. But they always slip away, always stay one step ahead. The thing is..." He trailed off, his eyes narrowing with suspicion, "I think they've been watching me. Watching us."

The weight of his words settled on me like an icy hand on my chest. I had underestimated the danger. But even as I realized how deep this thing went, something in me refused to back down. There was a fight in me that hadn't been there before, a spark ignited by his confession, by the way he'd allowed me in, even just a little.

"Then we find them first," I said, a fire kindling in my own chest.

His gaze met mine, sharp and uncertain, but there was something else in the depths of his eyes. Something that made me feel like we were in this together. The distance between us seemed to disappear in that single, quiet moment, and for the first time in a long while, I didn't feel alone.

The words hung heavy in the air, and as they sank in, the quiet between us grew unbearable. His eyes—dark with regret, sharp with something deeper—settled on me with an intensity that rattled my bones. I had expected the usual distance from him, the retreat, the cold guard he kept so carefully in place. Instead, he seemed to soften, but not entirely. There was still a tension in his shoulders, a fight within him that refused to settle.

"I'm not going to let them get away with it," he said, voice barely above a growl, like the thought of it twisted him inside out. "Whoever they are, whatever they want... it ends now."

I nodded slowly, the weight of his words anchoring deep in me. The arsonist wasn't just a shadow anymore, not a faceless enemy who could be forgotten or ignored. This person had become something tangible, something we could track, something that connected us in ways neither of us fully understood.

"Then let's find them," I said, my voice firm, though I could feel the chill creeping in. I didn't know what I was walking into, but whatever it was, I wasn't turning back. Not now. Not when the fire, the past, and the danger were tangled up in everything between us.

He turned toward the narrow trail that led back into the forest, his strides long and purposeful. I followed without a word, the crunch of gravel underfoot the only sound between us. The trees loomed tall and dark, their shadows stretching out like fingers waiting to grab at us. The night felt heavier here, the air thicker, as though the earth itself was holding its breath.

"Where are we going?" I asked, breaking the silence, my voice low as I kept pace with him.

"Somewhere safe," he muttered, his eyes scanning the woods around us like he expected an ambush at any moment. "I need to make a call."

His words sent a ripple of unease through me, but I kept it to myself. If he wanted to keep secrets, let him. I had my own, after all.

We reached a clearing, the moonlight spilling down in soft rays, illuminating a small, weathered cabin tucked among the trees. It looked abandoned, but something about it didn't sit right with me. The door, though slightly ajar, seemed to beckon with an eerie calmness, as though it had been waiting for us.

"Stay here," he ordered, his voice flat, a command rather than a suggestion. His gaze swept over me, and there was something about the way he looked at me, something desperate in his eyes. "Don't move."

Before I could ask what he meant, he stepped into the cabin, disappearing into the shadows. I stood still, every nerve on edge, feeling the weight of the night pressing in. My heart hammered in my chest, and I had the sudden urge to run, to follow him into the darkness, but I forced myself to stay put. For once, I obeyed.

Minutes stretched like hours, the cool air biting into my skin as I waited. The cabin loomed before me, quiet except for the occasional rustle of leaves. Something felt wrong, but I couldn't put my finger on it.

Then, a faint sound—footsteps, soft but deliberate—crunched behind me. My body tensed, but I didn't turn, not yet. I didn't need to. I already knew.

"Thought you could use some company," a voice said from behind me, rough and familiar.

I spun around, instinctively reaching for the knife I kept tucked into the waistband of my jeans. But my hand froze halfway when I saw who stood there.

Eli.

His wide grin was almost too easy, too casual, but his eyes... they were different. They weren't filled with the usual humor. There was something darker in them now, something sharp. And it made my blood run cold.

"What the hell are you doing here?" I demanded, taking a step back. My heart lurched, and for a brief moment, I felt like a fool. This whole time, I'd thought he was on my side, that he was the one person I could trust.

"I could ask you the same thing," he replied smoothly, stepping closer. His hands were casually shoved into his pockets, but there was a tension in his posture that hadn't been there before. "But you're not really in a position to ask questions, are you?"

"Eli..." My voice faltered, but I quickly steadied it. "You're with them, aren't you?"

His smile faltered for the briefest second, but it was enough. My stomach dropped. The pieces that had never quite fit together clicked into place, sharp and sudden. Eli wasn't the ally I thought he was.

"You know," he said, his tone almost conversational, "for someone who's supposed to be so smart, you've got a real blind spot when it comes to people." He tilted his head, his expression almost pitying. "You should've seen it coming."

I couldn't move, couldn't breathe. The betrayal was like a weight settling over me, crushing my chest. How had I been so naïve? How had I let myself believe he was on our side?

"Where's... where's Sebastian?" I asked, the name leaving my lips before I could stop it. He had to be okay. He had to be.

Eli's grin widened, but there was no warmth in it. No humor. Just a coldness that sent a chill down my spine.

"You're not as clever as you think," he said, his voice dropping lower, darker. "But that's okay. You'll catch on soon enough. As for Sebastian..." He trailed off, his eyes flickering to the cabin, and

I realized with a sickening certainty that something was wrong—something far worse than I'd imagined.

Before I could react, the unmistakable sound of a door creaking open echoed from behind me. I spun around, my heart hammering in my chest. The cabin door was wide open, and standing there, bathed in the pale light of the moon, was Sebastian.

But something was off. His eyes weren't the same. They were... vacant. And in his hands, he held something that made my blood run cold. A gun.

"Get inside," Eli snapped, his voice suddenly sharper, more commanding. "Now."

I didn't move. I couldn't. My heart was racing, my head spinning as the world around me seemed to collapse in on itself. I had no choice now. No way out.

And then the sharp click of the gun's safety being switched off filled the silence.

"Don't," I whispered, my voice barely audible. But it was already too late.

Chapter 12: Trial by Fire

The heat of the flames presses in, an unrelenting weight. I can almost feel the crackling in my bones, my skin burning with an intensity that isn't just the fire, but something far more sinister, far more personal. The streets stretch out before me, warped by the haze, the thick smoke clinging to the air like an old memory. The fire's glow paints everything in sharp contrast, the shadows long and leaping. But it's not just any fire. It's a fire I've seen before—one I can trace, track, measure.

There's a pattern.

I didn't notice it at first, not in the chaos of it all. The sirens, the shouts, the heat that made the night feel like it had been dipped in molten metal, and everything around us—Evan, me, the city—threatened to melt into one giant puddle of burnt hope. But somewhere in the frantic scramble to pull the pieces together, something clicked. The fires weren't random. Not this time. They weren't merely ravaging the city, they were going after something—someone.

And I had to figure out who. I had to figure out why.

Each one of these fires, in the places they are set, corresponds to a moment in Evan's life. A place. A time. A memory. It's like someone took a map of his past, then threw a match on it and watched it burn. The first was his childhood home. A modest bungalow in a neighborhood that had since been swallowed by a new wave of high-rise apartments and slick townhouses. The fire tore through it like a wild animal clawing for its last breath. Evan had stood there, his eyes wide, too stunned to move, while I tried to pull him away from the wreckage.

"You don't get it, do you?" he had said, a mix of disbelief and horror in his voice. "It's like they knew... knew exactly where to hit me."

He'd spoken like he was still trying to understand it himself. The shock had softened his sharp edges, made him human again, vulnerable in a way I hadn't seen before. But I couldn't let him collapse. I couldn't let myself collapse. Not yet.

It wasn't until the second fire that I saw it. The fire at the old bookstore where he had worked for years after college. The flames had been fierce, but even more fierce had been the sense of nostalgia that clung to the charred remains. I could feel the memories pressing in, and suddenly, it hit me—each fire wasn't just erasing something physical; it was erasing pieces of his past. Pieces of him.

I hadn't said anything at first, unsure if I was just imagining things, if I was reading too much into the smoke and embers. But when the third fire hit, at the café where he and I had shared our first real conversation—one of those moments that felt like it had been stitched into the fabric of time itself—I knew. This wasn't random. This was deliberate. Someone was playing a game, and they were targeting Evan, piece by piece, moment by moment. I could feel the weight of that game pressing on us both, and suddenly, I wasn't just fighting for answers. I was fighting for him.

So I confronted him.

"You're not just a victim of this," I said to him that night, the weight of everything closing in. "This is personal."

Evan had blinked, his hand frozen halfway to his mouth, a cup of coffee trembling between his fingers. His jaw tightened, and I saw the muscles in his neck twitch as if he were battling a wave of understanding he wasn't sure he wanted to accept.

"I don't get it," he muttered. "What are you talking about?"

I had to force the words out. There was so much I wanted to say, but the truth felt like a stone lodged in my throat.

"The fires," I said. "They're following a pattern. Your pattern."

Evan's gaze had narrowed. He set the coffee down with a sharp clink, the sound like a challenge. "You're saying someone is targeting me?"

I nodded, leaning in a little closer, needing him to understand, needing him to see it too. "Each fire marks a part of your past—places you've lived, places you've worked. Even places we've been together."

There was a long silence, the kind that cuts through the air like a knife. I watched him process the information, watched the flicker of realization slowly dance across his face, and then the words came, quiet and sharp, as if he'd been waiting for this moment.

"Do you think they know something about me—about us?"

"I think they know everything."

His eyes widened at that, the shock evident, but so was something else. Something darker. I could see it in the way his posture stiffened, the way his hands clenched into fists at his sides.

"I'm not the only one they're after, am I?" he asked, and there was a sharpness in his voice now, something cutting through the fear. "You're in this too. They've got you in their sights, haven't they?"

It hit me then, with all the force of a sudden storm. This wasn't just about Evan anymore. Whoever was behind this knew more than they should—more than we had ever let on. And now, they were coming after both of us.

"I don't know who they are," I said, my voice barely above a whisper, but the truth of it burned just as fiercely as the fires themselves. "But I think we're both in the crosshairs. And I think they've been watching us for a long time."

Evan let out a low breath, his face clouded with a storm of thoughts. Then, as if coming to a decision, he stepped toward me, close enough that I could feel the heat radiating from his body, his breath coming in short, shallow bursts.

"We'll figure this out," he said, determination threading through his voice. "Together."

And as the fire continued to rage outside, I couldn't help but wonder if the flames had already begun to devour us from the inside, too.

The city, once alive with its usual din of traffic and chatter, had quieted into something that felt more like a funeral march than a normal Tuesday night. The air was heavy with an ash that clung to your skin, making it impossible to ignore the reality of it all. The fires weren't just raging—they were consuming us, our lives, in a way that felt almost personal.

Evan's hands had stopped shaking only once we reached the old diner, the one with chipped booths and a neon sign that flickered like it had seen too much. It was the same diner where we had sat just a few weeks ago, the greasy scent of fries and coffee mixing with the bittersweet memory of what had been a simple conversation turned into something far more complicated. The irony wasn't lost on me. We had tried so hard to keep things light, tried to pretend that nothing existed outside the small bubble we had created for ourselves. But now, here we were, tangled in the aftermath of someone else's destructive game.

As we slid into the booth, the worn leather creaking under the weight of the night, I could see the conflict warring in Evan's eyes. I knew that he didn't want to believe it, didn't want to accept that someone out there knew too much about him—about us. But there was no denying it now. The flames weren't just burning buildings; they were burning bridges, erasing every place and memory that had once been a part of his life.

"They can't know everything," he said, more to himself than to me, though the words still hung heavy in the air between us.

"They do," I replied, my voice steady despite the pounding of my heart. "And they're not stopping until they've erased every single piece of you."

Evan looked down at his hands, the edges of his fingers still raw from the fire he had fought back earlier in the day. He hadn't said much since we left the scene of the third fire, but his silence spoke volumes. His mind was racing, piecing together the puzzle that neither of us had the answers to. The truth was, we didn't know who was behind this—or why. We only knew that the pattern was unmistakable.

His jaw tightened, his eyes flickering to the door as if expecting someone to walk in and confirm the worst. "I've been trying to put the pieces together all day, but it doesn't make sense," he said, his voice low. "The fire at the bookstore—it wasn't just the place where I worked. It was my safe space. It was the one place that always felt like home, even when I didn't have one. And now... now it's gone."

"I know," I said, leaning forward, my hand reaching for his. "But maybe that's the point. Whoever is doing this wants you to feel like you have nothing left. Like you're nothing."

His fingers twitched at the contact, but he didn't pull away. Instead, he locked his gaze onto mine, a flicker of something in his eyes that made my stomach tighten. For a moment, I saw the boy I had first met, the one with the easy smile and the warmth that seemed to light up every room he entered. But that boy had been buried under the weight of the last few days, and now, only the remnants of him remained.

"I don't know if I can keep going like this," Evan said, his voice thick with something I couldn't quite place. "This... this game they're playing, it's like they know me better than I know myself. They're taking everything I've ever cared about and burning it to the ground, and I don't know how to stop it."

"You don't have to do it alone," I said, my voice a little firmer now. "We're in this together, Evan. Whatever it takes, we'll figure it out. I promise."

For a long moment, neither of us spoke. The hum of the diner's fluorescent lights filled the silence, the clinking of silverware in the kitchen the only other sound that broke the stillness. But then, just as the tension threatened to suffocate me, Evan exhaled sharply, running a hand through his hair.

"Maybe you're right," he said, his voice softer now. "Maybe it's just... I don't know. I keep thinking if I can just make sense of it all, then maybe I'll feel like I'm in control again. But I don't think I am anymore. I'm not sure I ever was."

"You never had control," I said, the words slipping out before I could stop them. "None of us ever do. We just like to think we do, because it makes us feel safe."

Evan's eyes flickered up to mine, his lips curving into the smallest of smiles—one that didn't reach his eyes, but still held a trace of the old charm that used to be so easy for him. "You're right about that," he said. "I don't think I've felt safe in a long time."

There was something about the way he said it, like the weight of his own confession had just hit him in the chest. He didn't look at me like I was the girl across the booth anymore. He didn't look at me like the person who had been swept up into this mess. He looked at me like I was the only one who might understand.

And I did. More than he realized.

"I wish I could give you that back," I said quietly, "that sense of safety. I wish I could promise you that everything's going to be okay. But the truth is, I don't know how this is going to end."

"You don't have to promise me anything," Evan replied, his voice steady now, with a firmness I hadn't heard from him before. "But I'm glad you're here. I don't think I could do this alone."

It wasn't much, but it was something. And for the first time in days, it felt like we were standing on the same side of this nightmare, instead of being two people lost in separate storms.

The café was quiet, the kind of quiet that stretched out and settled into every corner, as if the walls themselves were holding their breath. Outside, the night had taken on that oppressive stillness, the kind that follows a storm. The city had gone from chaotic to eerily calm, as if waiting for the next wave to break. I could feel it in my bones, that uneasy sense that the calm before the storm was just a trick, a ruse. And the worst part? Evan felt it too.

The fire had started just a few hours ago. The flames were already licking at the edges of a building that had once been a landmark, a monument to the city's past that now felt like it had been plucked straight from history. The library where Evan had spent countless nights as a child, running his fingers along the rows of books, had been reduced to rubble in a matter of hours. He hadn't said much when we passed by it earlier, but I could see the way his eyes burned—burned with a quiet fury that threatened to spill over.

It wasn't just the fire. It was the feeling of being watched, of being hunted. We were in the crosshairs of someone who knew everything about Evan's life, from the people he had loved to the places he had lived. Each fire was a calculated attack, a step toward something bigger—something far more sinister. But I wasn't going to let it stop us. Not now.

"I'm telling you, it's not over," I said, my voice breaking the silence between us. Evan hadn't taken his eyes off the door since we sat down, as if expecting someone—or something—to walk in at any moment.

"I know," he replied, his voice strained, like he was forcing the words through a wall he didn't want to tear down. "But the longer we wait, the harder it gets. The more they burn, the more pieces of me they take."

I couldn't help but glance at him, my gaze flickering to the way his fingers gripped the edge of the table. There was something dangerous about his stillness, something almost... resigned. The Evan I knew wasn't a man who gave up easily. But tonight, I saw something different—a man on the edge, caught between fighting for survival and the exhaustion of trying to outrun his past.

"You're not alone in this," I said, leaning forward, my voice steady despite the unease that had crept up my spine. "You have me. We'll get through this. Together."

His eyes met mine then, the hesitation in them a clear sign that he wasn't ready to believe that. I couldn't blame him. What we were dealing with wasn't something that could be easily fixed with a promise. There was a deep, gnawing fear that had sunk its teeth into both of us, and no amount of reassurance would shake it. But I was determined to see it through.

Just as I opened my mouth to say something else, the door swung open, the bell above it jangling like a warning shot. I froze, watching the figure that stepped into the room. My heart skipped a beat, the familiar rush of adrenaline flooding my system. But it wasn't who I expected.

The man who entered was tall, dressed in a long coat that brushed the tops of his boots. His face was partially obscured by the shadow of his hood, but I could see enough to know that he was no stranger. His posture was too deliberate, his movements too precise. And when his eyes flickered across the room, landing on Evan and me, it was like he knew exactly who we were—what we were to each other.

The stranger paused just inside the door, his gaze never wavering from us, as if he were deciding whether or not to approach. My breath caught in my throat, my body tensing in preparation for whatever came next. Evan's jaw tightened, but he didn't move. Neither of us did. We simply watched, waiting for the next move, like chess pieces on the same board.

After a moment, the stranger took a step forward, his boots clicking against the floor with each measured stride. I could feel Evan's muscles coil, ready to spring into action at the first sign of danger. But I was faster. Before either of us could say a word, I stood up and met the stranger halfway.

"You've been following us," I said, my voice low but firm. There was no point in pretending. The air between us had thickened with something darker than just the night.

The stranger didn't answer right away. Instead, he studied me, his eyes narrowing as if he were weighing something in his mind. Then, in a voice that sounded too calm for the situation, he spoke.

"Not following," he said, his words clipped and deliberate. "Watching."

There was a chill in his voice that I couldn't ignore. "Who are you?" I asked, my heart pounding in my chest. Every instinct told me that this wasn't someone we should be talking to, but I needed to know who had been pulling the strings from the shadows.

The man smiled, but it was cold, devoid of warmth or humor. "Let's just say... I'm someone who knows what's coming next."

I took a step back, the hairs on the back of my neck standing up. Whatever this was, whatever game he was playing, it wasn't just about the fires anymore. He was toying with us—with me—and I could feel the weight of it settle like a burden in my chest.

"We don't have time for games," I said, my voice barely above a whisper now, though every word felt like it carried the weight of a thousand unspoken questions. "What do you want?"

The stranger's smile widened, but there was no humor in it. His eyes flickered over to Evan, who was now standing beside me, his body tense, his hand brushing against the pocket where I knew he kept his phone, likely ready to call for help at a moment's notice.

"You," the stranger said, his gaze shifting back to me, "have no idea what you're really up against. But you will soon enough."

Before I could respond, he turned and walked out of the café, disappearing into the shadows as quickly as he had appeared. And just like that, the air shifted—tense, charged, electric—and I couldn't shake the feeling that whatever had started with the fires was only just the beginning.

Chapter 13: Into the Flames

The fire crackled fiercely in the distance, the air thick with the sharp bite of smoke. It was impossible to ignore the relentless pulse of heat that seemed to hang in the air, even though we were miles from the inferno. A low hum of tension thrummed in my chest, the kind that always preceded something awful. I didn't need to hear the sirens or see the flashing lights to know that, once again, another fire had torn through the town. Another warning from the arsonist, or whatever he thought he was.

Evan's voice, low and steady, cut through my thoughts as he stood beside me, eyes scanning the horizon. His jaw was clenched so tightly I wondered how it wasn't already broken. He had that look in his eyes, the one that said *I'm keeping you safe—whether you like it or not.*

I had never been one to back down from a challenge, but this felt different. The fires were starting to feel personal, and my resolve to ignore the fear was starting to crack. But Evan? He wasn't going anywhere. And I couldn't deny that his presence, stubborn and unwavering, was comforting in its own way.

"They've gotten braver," I said, my voice barely audible as I crossed my arms tightly across my chest, trying to hold myself together. "This one's worse. It's too close."

Evan didn't reply at first, his gaze locked on the orange glow in the distance, the light dancing in his eyes, casting strange shadows across his face. Then he turned to look at me, his expression soft but unreadable.

"You're not leaving," he said, his voice firm, but with something else, something I couldn't quite place. "We're staying here. Together."

A muscle in my throat tightened, but I swallowed it down. "You don't get it, Evan. This town's burning down around us. And it's getting worse with each fire. You can't keep me safe forever."

He took a step closer, the weight of his presence pressing into me, and I could smell the faintest hint of sweat and gasoline—residue from the fires that had already ravaged parts of the town. It wasn't comforting. It never would be. But when he looked at me, I felt the briefest flicker of something that made the chaos feel less dangerous.

"You're not leaving," he repeated, his voice quieter this time, a silent promise. There was no question in his tone. It wasn't a suggestion. It wasn't even an order. It was simply the way it was. "We'll get through this. Together."

The words made my heart stutter, and for just a second, I let myself believe them. He was so sure of everything—of us, of this town, of his ability to protect me. And maybe, for the first time since this whole nightmare began, I didn't want to fight him.

We stood in silence, the crackle of distant flames a constant reminder of how close we were to something far worse than the threat we were facing. I'd seen too many fires up close to ignore the hollow feeling that churned in my stomach. This wasn't some random act of destruction anymore. This was calculated. Every time the arsonist set another fire, I felt a little more hollow. Like each flame was a thread pulling me further from everything I knew, everything that felt safe.

And yet, Evan was here. He was always here.

But no matter how hard I tried to ignore it, I couldn't shake the gnawing feeling in my gut. Something was about to happen. Something big.

I didn't have to wait long for it.

The next few hours passed in a blur—endless calls, scattered movements, too many people running in too many directions. The fire department was stretched thin, the town's volunteers frantically trying to help. But there was no sign of the arsonist, no pattern I could detect. I couldn't figure out where the next strike would come from. The waiting was the worst part. It made everything feel like a game of Russian roulette.

By the time we reached the edge of the forest, the sky had darkened, the stars barely visible through the haze of smoke. Evan's hand was on my shoulder, guiding me forward, even though the path ahead was as unclear to him as it was to me.

"We're getting close," he murmured, his breath warm against my ear.

"Close to what?" I whispered back, the question escaping before I could stop it. "The next fire? Or the person behind all of this?"

He didn't answer immediately. But when he did, I saw the hesitation in his eyes. The fear he was trying so hard to hide.

"We'll stop them before they can do any more damage. I promise."

I wanted to believe him. I wanted to trust that he had everything under control. But as we moved further into the woods, with only the sound of crackling branches beneath our feet and the distant rumbles of fire trucks, I couldn't help but feel that everything was spiraling. That the flames were just a symptom of something far darker, far more dangerous.

And just like that, the first explosion ripped through the night.

The ground shook beneath me, the heat of the blast sending a rush of adrenaline coursing through my veins. My ears rang with the deafening sound, and for a split second, I couldn't see. Only smoke, only chaos. I barely heard Evan shouting my name, but I felt his grip on my arm, pulling me toward him.

But it wasn't enough. Before I could get my bearings, the world spun wildly, the ground beneath my feet giving way. The last thing

I saw before the explosion engulfed me was Evan's face, contorted in sheer terror as he reached for me.

Then everything went dark.

When I woke up, I was surrounded by smoke. The heat was suffocating. And through the haze, I saw him—Evan—his face pale, streaked with soot and sweat. His hands gripped me tightly, his voice strained with desperation as he pulled me out of the wreckage.

"Don't you dare leave me," he whispered, more to himself than to me.

The fear in his eyes was something I had never seen before.

But in that moment, something in me shifted. And I knew that whatever came next, we would face it together.

I wasn't sure how long I was out for. My head was throbbing, my senses swimming in a fog of fire and dust. I was painfully aware of the heat against my skin, but it wasn't the heat of the flames this time—it was the heat of Evan's hand gripping mine like he was afraid I might slip away. His fingers dug into my wrist, a quiet kind of urgency in the way he pulled me into the safety of his arms.

The world around us seemed distant, muffled, the sounds of distant shouts and crackling flames growing fainter. But Evan's presence, close and solid, was all that grounded me. My throat ached when I tried to speak, but he didn't need words. He already knew what I needed.

"Are you okay?" His voice was strained, but it wasn't anger—it was fear. Fear in a way I hadn't heard before. Fear that made my pulse race in a way I couldn't shake.

I blinked, trying to clear the haze in my mind, and found myself staring up into his eyes, those eyes that always held everything just out of reach. The worry was there, in every crease of his brow, every line of tension along his jaw. He wasn't just afraid for me—he was afraid for us.

"I think I'm fine," I said, wincing as I tried to sit up. The ground beneath me was uneven, the charred earth still warm, the air thick with the smell of smoke. It wasn't the first time I'd been through something like this, but it was the first time I'd seen Evan this... broken.

He helped me to my feet, his grip firm, not letting me go. His eyes searched mine as if trying to pull me into something deeper, something he couldn't say aloud. But I knew. We both knew. There was no going back now.

"I'm not letting you go," he said, and it wasn't a promise—it was a declaration.

For a moment, I wasn't sure what to say. We'd been through hell together—working side by side, chasing down every lead, every fire. But there was something different now, something heavy and suffocating in the way we were standing, the way we couldn't seem to move without each other. It wasn't just the danger. It wasn't even the arsonist. It was us.

"You should," I whispered, a bitterness creeping into my voice. "You should let me go, Evan. This is too much. I'm not who you think I am."

He shook his head, his lips pressed into a tight line, and for the first time, I saw the tiniest crack in his resolve. "I think I know exactly who you are. And that's why I'm not leaving."

His words were simple, but they carried a weight that made my heart thud in my chest. The man I had been working alongside for weeks—making decisions, plotting strategy, fighting side by side—wasn't just a protector anymore. He wasn't just some guy I was forced to trust. He was mine, in a way I hadn't let myself admit until now.

But I couldn't keep up the pretense that everything was fine. The fire, the chaos, the relentless pull of this town—it was burning us both. Every minute we spent chasing shadows, trying to outwit an unseen enemy, was a minute closer to the wreckage we both knew was coming.

"You don't get it," I said, stepping back, trying to put space between us, trying to feel something that wasn't just panic and adrenaline. "You can't just keep me safe by pretending this is all some kind of... love story, Evan. This is real. People are dying. And we're in the middle of it."

He stared at me, and I saw the flash of something in his eyes—something I couldn't quite name. Maybe it was frustration, maybe it was something more, something deeper that we hadn't ever dared to address.

"I'm not pretending anything." His voice was quiet but sure, the words cutting through the night air. "I'm just... not willing to lose you."

I had no response. No clever retort, no sarcastic quip. All I had was the undeniable truth of what he was saying. It settled in my chest like a stone. And I didn't want to admit how much it hurt to hear him say it out loud, to hear him lay bare everything I had spent so long pretending not to notice.

But then the air shifted. The moment of tenderness—the fragile bridge between us—was shattered by the distant sound of tires screeching on gravel. The screech was followed by the unmistakable thud of footsteps, rapid and irregular. Someone was coming.

I froze, eyes darting around as my instincts kicked in, every cell in my body screaming that something was wrong. Evan didn't hesitate. He grabbed my arm and pulled me down, guiding me into a crouch behind the charred remains of a nearby fence. His body shielded mine, and though the tension between us had just been enough to choke the air from my lungs, it didn't matter now. We had bigger problems.

"Stay down," he whispered, his breath hot against my ear.

I nodded, though my heart was pounding, every nerve in my body on high alert. The figure that emerged from the shadows was a silhouette at first, moving too quickly for me to make out any details. But then the outline sharpened, and I saw the glint of metal—just a flash of it. A knife. A threat.

It wasn't the arsonist, but it didn't matter. The danger was still real, and it was still coming straight for us.

Evan didn't hesitate. He pushed me behind him and stood tall, his entire frame braced for whatever came next. There was no bravado in his movements. No fear. Just that steady, unyielding confidence that made me both furious and helpless in equal measure.

And then the first shout rang out, slicing through the silence.

The game had changed.

I felt a cold chill sweep down my spine as the world tilted beneath me. I wasn't sure if I was ready for whatever came next. But there was no backing out now.

The figure in the shadows moved closer, but I wasn't about to wait for Evan's hand to push me further into the dirt. Something told me this wasn't going to be a simple confrontation. It never was when we were involved. The man had a knife, and from the way he was handling it—low and steady, like he'd practiced—it was obvious that he wasn't here for a friendly chat.

I crouched lower, just enough to stay out of sight, but I didn't stop moving. My heart hammered in my chest as I positioned myself, mind racing to calculate the distance, to make sense of what was happening. Evan wasn't an idiot; he knew the risks. But it didn't change the fact that every decision we made right now was a gamble, each second laced with the possibility of disaster.

The footsteps were getting closer. The man was almost upon us. The tension in the air thickened with every breath, as if the night itself was holding its breath, waiting for the explosion.

Evan didn't move. He was still standing, body stiff and resolute, every muscle poised to act. I could almost feel the storm of thoughts behind his steady gaze, that controlled, unwavering expression he always wore when things got intense. He wasn't going to flinch. Not for me, not for anyone. Not when it came to protecting us.

I didn't give him the chance to warn me, didn't let him tell me to stay down again. I was done with that. If we were going to get out of this alive, I needed to act first. I couldn't sit back and wait for someone to decide my fate.

As the man neared, I moved swiftly, stepping out from behind the charred fence and into the open, adrenaline pushing me forward faster than I thought possible. Evan's sharp intake of breath was the only indication that he hadn't expected it, but I wasn't about to let that stop me. I wasn't just trying to survive this. I was going to end it.

I took the first step toward him, the silence between us so thick it practically vibrated. He paused for the briefest of seconds, just long enough for me to get within reach. His gaze shifted, narrowing as he calculated whether I was a threat. A mistake, I thought as I closed the distance, calculating every move like a chess game, knowing that this had to be over in one swift motion.

The moment I reached him, he lunged. But it wasn't me he aimed at—it was Evan. He'd miscalculated, thinking that Evan was my weakness, but I wasn't going to let him get away with that.

Before the blade could come within an inch of Evan's chest, I was there, shoving him sideways, grabbing his arm with the strength of desperation. His knife slid along the edge of Evan's jacket, but it missed. Barely.

For a moment, everything froze. I was holding his wrist, my own hand slick with sweat, every nerve in my body on fire. Evan had moved just in time to avoid being struck, but the attacker's momentum had thrown him off balance. I could feel the heat of his breath as he jerked his arm, trying to break free.

"Get down!" Evan shouted, but there was no time. No time for anything other than what had to happen next.

The man twisted, trying to pull away, but I wasn't letting go. Not now. With everything I had, I forced his arm down, using every ounce of muscle I could gather to shove him backward. He stumbled, tripping over the uneven ground, falling onto his back in a cloud of dust.

I stood over him, breathing heavily, heart pounding, my hand still wrapped tightly around his wrist. The knife had fallen from his grasp, but I wasn't ready to let up. I wasn't sure if he was still a threat or if I could trust the silence that followed. But I didn't want to take any chances.

Evan's voice broke through the tension, his tone sharp. "We need him alive. No more fighting. We need answers."

For a moment, the world around me seemed to shift. There was no more fire. No more chaos. Just me, the man beneath me, and the sharp sting of realization. We were playing a game we hadn't fully understood. Every move we made, every decision, was just pushing us further into danger. We weren't the ones controlling the game. The arsonist was.

I stood there, pulse racing, trying to make sense of it all. The man on the ground was glaring at us, his breath ragged, his eyes burning with hatred. He wasn't just an anonymous face in the crowd. He knew us. He knew this town. He was one of them—the ones behind the flames.

And then, before I could react, he spat. Right into my face.

The shock of it made me stumble back, but I didn't flinch. Not this time. Not with everything hanging in the balance. His hatred, raw and unfiltered, only pushed me forward. I wiped my cheek, my anger flaring, but I didn't take my eyes off him. I wasn't about to let him see me lose control.

"You won't win," he growled, his voice rough with pain but laced with that cold, simmering rage. "You're already too far in."

"Too far in for what?" I snapped back, stepping closer, making sure he knew just how little I was willing to tolerate from him. "What is it that you think you've won? You've set fire to a town. You've killed people. What's next?"

He grinned, a dark, twisted smile that sent a chill up my spine. "You really don't get it, do you?"

Before I could respond, there was a sound behind me—sharp, too quick to be anything but a shot. The world seemed to freeze for the briefest moment. My heart stopped as the man's smile grew wider, darker.

And then I heard it: the unmistakable sound of a click. A new threat. Something worse.

The ground beneath me shifted, and I turned just in time to see a shadow looming, blocking out the distant glow of the flames. But it wasn't the shadow I feared—it was the weapon glinting in the figure's hand. And the look on their face was one I'd never seen before.

It wasn't over. Not by a long shot.

Chapter 14: Ashes and Betrayal

The room smelled of wet earth and damp wood, a lingering scent from the rain that had soaked the ground outside, but it was the cold that wrapped around me like a second skin. I stood in the corner of the room, hands fisted at my sides, my knuckles white against the tension that hummed in the air. We were all on edge, each of us holding our breaths in the quiet aftermath of what had just transpired. The silence was louder than any explosion, louder than the sound of shattered glass and splintered wood.

The others milled about in the background, their movements stiff, eyes darting like startled prey. I could feel their glances, the unspoken questions that hung in the air between us, heavy and uninvited. I wanted to scream at them, ask them what the hell they thought had happened, demand to know why this had to happen to us—but instead, I said nothing. I was too afraid of the answer.

Evan's voice cut through the tension, low and dangerous. "I think it's someone we know."

My heart skipped a beat. My stomach dropped to the floor, and I had to force myself to swallow the lump in my throat. He couldn't be serious, could he?

"You're not serious," I muttered, though I wasn't sure if I was asking him or trying to convince myself.

Evan was staring out the window, his jaw set in that hard line I knew all too well. The one that told me he wasn't backing down. "You heard what they said. This wasn't some random attack. It's personal."

"Who?" My voice cracked. I hated how weak I sounded. But I couldn't help it.

He didn't answer right away, his eyes narrowing as if searching for something that wasn't there. Then, slowly, he turned to face me, his eyes shadowed with something unreadable. "A friend. Someone I used to trust."

A chill ran down my spine, though I couldn't tell if it was the cold or the words he'd just spoken. "Who?"

He didn't respond immediately. The seconds stretched on for far too long, and I felt the walls around me closing in. A part of me wanted to run, to escape this feeling before it consumed me. But there was nowhere to go. Not anymore.

"I don't know yet," Evan finally said, his voice barely above a whisper, like even saying the words out loud might make them too real. "But I'll find out. I always do."

The way he said it made my skin crawl. It wasn't just the words. It was the certainty in his voice, like he had already made up his mind, like he already knew the truth. And that scared me. Because if he was right, if someone we once trusted was behind all of this, then what did that make us? And who was Evan really?

I couldn't shake the thought that something wasn't right. Maybe it was the way Evan's eyes seemed to linger too long on things that weren't there. Or the way he suddenly seemed to know too much. He had always been the strong, silent type, the one who carried his secrets like a badge of honor. But now, every glance he threw my way felt like a warning. Like he was hiding something from me.

"I need to know who it is, Evan," I said, my voice thick with an emotion I couldn't quite name. "I can't—"

But I was cut off as the door creaked open behind me. A figure stepped into the room, blocking the weak light from the hallway. My pulse quickened, and my breath caught in my throat.

"Looks like you've got a problem," a voice drawled, smooth and familiar, but with a cold edge that made my skin prickle.

I turned slowly, my eyes meeting the man who had just entered. His features were sharp, angular—his dark hair slicked back, his suit crisp and immaculate. He looked every bit the part of someone who had it all together, but I knew better. I'd known him too long.

Max.

"Max," I said, the name slipping from my lips like an accusation. "What are you doing here?"

He smirked, a slow, deliberate curl of his lips. "Wouldn't you like to know?"

Evan stiffened beside me, his hand almost imperceptibly moving toward his jacket. I knew that gesture too well. It was the one he made when he was ready to spring into action, to protect, to fight.

"Max," Evan said, his tone colder than I'd ever heard it. "What are you doing here?"

Max tilted his head slightly, studying us both with eyes that never seemed to blink. "I thought I'd drop by. See how you were holding up after the little incident." His gaze flicked to the broken glass scattered across the floor, the remnants of the chaos we had just survived.

"Max," I repeated, the words now sharp with suspicion. "What do you know about all this?"

He stepped further into the room, the air around him suddenly feeling heavier, as if he were carrying some unseen burden with him. "Not much," he said, and there was a flicker of something in his eyes—something I couldn't quite place. "But I know who's behind it. And I know you're all in way deeper than you think."

My heart raced, and the room seemed to shrink around me. He knew something. He was hiding something. And suddenly, everything that Evan had said, everything I had been too afraid to question, started to feel even more dangerous.

The world we had built around ourselves was unraveling, thread by thread, and I couldn't tell if the unraveling was because of Max... or Evan.

Max's smirk never wavered, but his eyes... they weren't the same. They used to be full of confidence, self-assuredness—a kind of quiet power that made him seem untouchable. Now, they flickered with something I couldn't place. Guilt? Fear? Or maybe just the thrill of watching us squirm in our uncertainty.

I crossed my arms tightly against my chest, a nervous habit I'd inherited from my mother whenever she felt the need to shield herself from the world, even if only for a moment. "I don't believe you," I said flatly, doing my best to ignore the nagging suspicion that Max was telling the truth, that he knew exactly what was happening.

"Oh, I think you do," he replied smoothly, eyes flicking between me and Evan. "The question is—how much are you really ready to know?"

Evan shifted next to me, his stance widening, a quiet, dangerous energy radiating from him. He hadn't taken his eyes off Max since he entered the room, and I could feel the tension pulling taut between them, like a snapped wire ready to unravel. There was no doubt in my mind that if Max took one step too far, Evan would strike. And knowing Evan, that step would be minuscule.

"I don't trust you," Evan said, his voice even, but I knew better than to mistake that calm for lack of emotion. His words had the weight of a threat, the unspoken promise of consequences.

Max's smirk grew, though it didn't reach his eyes. "Would you like to hear a little truth, then? I think it's about time someone tells you exactly how deep this rabbit hole goes."

I wanted to snap at him, tell him that we weren't in the mood for cryptic riddles, but the words stuck in my throat. My instincts screamed at me to back away, to shut him out. But the part of me that had always trusted Evan's judgment—no matter how flawed it might have been—told me to listen. Because this... this was too important.

Max leaned in just slightly, as if he were about to divulge a secret too dangerous to whisper aloud. "You think you're just being dragged along for the ride, don't you?" he continued, his voice lowering, more intimate now. "That you're somehow a pawn in this. But I have news for you—you're not. You've always been part of it. Always. From the very beginning."

I stared at him, trying to grasp what he was suggesting. My stomach twisted. A part of me wanted to dismiss it as more of his usual posturing, but the icy certainty in his eyes gave me pause. This wasn't the Max I used to know. This Max was different—more dangerous. And the things he was saying felt too close to the truth for comfort.

"What are you talking about?" I asked, my voice barely above a whisper.

Max straightened, pulling his hands out of his pockets. His eyes glinted with a mixture of amusement and contempt. "You think you've been outsmarting the people who want you gone, right? But they've been watching you the whole time, and they know exactly how to pull your strings. They're just waiting for the right moment to reel you in."

My heart stuttered. The words rang in my ears like a death sentence. I wanted to say something, to push back, but my throat had gone dry, my mind spinning in circles.

"You really are that naïve, aren't you?" Max's tone shifted, hardening. "That's your problem—you trust too easily. And there's only one person who's been behind all this, manipulating you from the start."

I shot Evan a glance. His jaw clenched, his eyes narrowing as if Max's words were poison in the air, something that didn't belong. I couldn't look at him too long. I couldn't let myself believe that Evan was part of whatever Max was implying.

"No," I muttered to myself, more to reassure myself than to convince Max. "You're lying. This is just another one of your games."

But Max didn't flinch. He didn't look surprised by my denial. "You want to believe that," he said, voice like honey dipped in venom. "I understand. I really do. But the truth is that you've been trusting the wrong person. Your precious hero has been playing both sides this entire time, and you've been too blinded by loyalty to see it."

My pulse hammered in my ears. I didn't know what to think, or who to trust, or whether Max was spinning a tale to shake me, to twist something that was already fragile and make it break.

Evan stepped forward, his face hard and unreadable. "I think you've said enough."

Max took a step back, hands held up in mock surrender. "You'll see for yourself soon enough. You always do, don't you? You won't be able to ignore the truth forever."

His words hung in the air like smoke, curling into the corners of the room. I wasn't sure what was worse: the idea that Max might be lying, or the terrifying possibility that he was telling the truth.

Max didn't stay long. He gave us one last look—half pity, half warning—before slipping out of the room with an ease that made my stomach churn.

Evan stood there for a moment, silent, his expression unreadable as he turned back to face me. His eyes softened ever so slightly when he looked at me, but I wasn't fooled. There was something behind that look—something that made me question everything.

"I don't know what he's trying to do," Evan said after a long pause, the words weighing heavily between us. "But you have to trust me. I'm not your enemy."

The warmth in his voice almost made me believe him. Almost. But there was a jagged edge to his words, a hesitation that I couldn't ignore.

And that hesitation... it was enough to shatter the last of my certainty.

The tension in the room felt like a living, breathing thing—every inch of air was thick with unspoken words, accusations hanging like an invisible fog. I shifted uncomfortably, my fingers tracing the edge of the table as I tried to steady my racing thoughts. Max's words kept echoing in my mind, a relentless pulse that made it impossible to think clearly. I wanted to scream at Evan, demand that he tell me the truth, but something in his eyes held me back. That look—a mix of desperation and warning—was something I hadn't seen before, and it was enough to make my throat tighten with unease.

I could feel the distance between us widening, the silence between us more suffocating than any words could be. We hadn't even been together for that long, but already I felt like I was falling for him—completely and utterly—without a safety net. And now, with every passing moment, I was starting to wonder if I was falling for the wrong person.

"Evan," I said softly, barely able to keep the tremor out of my voice. "What did Max mean? About you? About everything?"

He didn't look at me right away. Instead, he seemed to be staring into the distance, his gaze distant and unfocused. It was like he was struggling to find the right words—or maybe the right excuse.

"I don't know, okay?" he said finally, his voice rough. "I don't know what he's playing at, but I'm not the enemy here."

I watched him for a long moment, weighing his words, trying to see if I could find something more in his eyes, some hint of the truth buried beneath the guarded exterior he'd built around himself. But I saw nothing. Nothing except shadows and secrets that were locked away where I couldn't reach them.

"So, what?" I asked, trying to keep the anger out of my voice. "You expect me to just take your word for it? After everything that's happened? After what Max said?"

Evan's eyes flashed, the briefest flicker of something I couldn't quite name. Maybe frustration, maybe guilt. "I don't know what he's trying to do, but it's not going to work," he said, his tone hardening. "You can believe whatever you want, but I'm not going to let anyone drag you into this mess."

My pulse quickened. "I'm already in it, Evan. We're both in it."

I hadn't meant for the words to sound so desperate, but they slipped out before I could stop them. And as soon as they did, I felt the weight of them. Because, deep down, I knew they were true. I was already entangled in this world of lies and danger, and no matter how much I wanted to pull away, I couldn't. Not when Evan was standing there, right in front of me, a contradiction I couldn't ignore.

He took a step toward me, his expression softening just slightly. "I'm doing everything I can to keep you safe."

I shook my head, biting back the words I wanted to say. Because deep down, I wasn't sure anymore if safety was even possible. Not when it felt like every decision I made was dragging me deeper into the chaos, every person I trusted was turning out to be a potential threat.

Just then, there was a sharp knock on the door, followed by the creak of it swinging open. My heart stopped for a moment, the sudden intrusion pulling me out of my thoughts. A tall figure stood in the doorway, his silhouette barely visible in the dim light. He was wearing a long coat, his features obscured by shadows, but I knew immediately who it was.

"Max?" Evan's voice was a mixture of disbelief and something else—something I couldn't quite place.

Max stepped inside without waiting for an invitation, his eyes flicking between us with a look that said he knew exactly how much damage he was causing.

"I didn't come here to stir the pot," he said, his voice casual, as if we weren't in the middle of a crisis. "But I think it's time we talk."

Evan's jaw clenched, and I saw the muscle twitch under his skin. "Talk about what?"

Max smiled, a slow, almost pitying grin. "About the truth. About everything you've been hiding from her."

I turned to Evan, my breath catching in my throat. "What is he talking about?"

Evan didn't answer at first. He just stood there, his fists clenched at his sides. And in that moment, I could see it—whatever Max had just hinted at, whatever secret was buried beneath all of this—it was enough to shatter the fragile trust I'd built with Evan.

"Evan?" I said again, my voice trembling now, unable to keep the fear from seeping in. "What is he talking about?"

Evan's eyes flicked to Max, then back to me, and for a long, painful moment, he said nothing. It was like he was trying to decide how to handle the storm that was about to hit.

Then, slowly, his lips parted, and his voice came out barely above a whisper. "You're not the only one who's been played."

The words hit me like a slap, and I felt my legs tremble beneath me, like the floor was giving way beneath my feet. I could feel the ground shifting, crumbling under the weight of everything that was happening, and I had no idea how to stop it.

Max, leaning casually against the doorframe, seemed to sense my unraveling. "See, that's the thing about secrets," he said, his voice sharp with amusement. "They always have a way of coming to light. And when they do? They change everything."

My heart raced, each beat like a drum in my chest, and I couldn't look away from Evan's face. The man I thought I knew—who had promised me safety, who had made me believe in something more—was slowly unraveling before my eyes.

And just as the tension reached its peak, the door slammed open with a deafening crack, and everything I thought I knew about this mess exploded in a flash of blinding light.

Chapter 15: Embered Memories

The air was thick with the scent of smoke and something else, something sharper, that cut through the cool night like a blade. The fire had long since died down, but the remnants of it still smoldered, clinging to the wreckage of the building, as though the walls were too proud to let go of their heat. I stood at the edge of the lot, watching the distant orange glow from the burning embers, waiting for the moment when the world would finally exhale, when everything would be over. But there was no such moment. The fire never left. Not entirely.

I glanced over at Evan, standing beside me in the shadows, his face drawn and hard in the light from the flames. The way his eyes flickered, his fingers twitching ever so slightly against the sleeve of his jacket—it was almost like he was trying to push something down, something he didn't want me to see. His jaw was clenched, the muscles in his neck taut as if he were carrying the weight of the entire night on his shoulders.

We hadn't spoken much since the fire began to settle into its slow retreat, and the silence stretched between us, thick with unspoken words. But there was a restlessness to him now, an energy that hummed under the surface, something raw and almost reckless, like a spark about to ignite. I could feel it, even at this distance, and I knew this moment would crack open something I wasn't prepared for.

When he finally spoke, his voice was low, almost lost in the sound of the crackling embers. "I've been following these fires for years."

I tilted my head, uncertain whether I'd heard him correctly. "What do you mean, following them?"

Evan ran a hand through his hair, the dark strands sticking to his forehead as though they too were sweating in the heat of the moment. "Not just investigating them," he continued, turning to face me fully. "Tracking them. Keeping an eye on the patterns, the way they spread, the people involved. There's always a connection."

I stepped closer, the hairs on the back of my neck standing up as his words slowly began to sink in. "A connection? Between the fires?"

He nodded, his expression hardening into something I couldn't quite place. "Between the people. People I trusted. People I thought were on my side. Every fire, every ruin—it's always someone I've known, someone I let in. Someone who knew just how to get close."

I could feel the heat radiating from him now, not from the fire behind us, but from the words he was speaking, words he'd clearly been carrying for far too long. He was unraveling in front of me, and I wasn't sure if I was prepared for what that meant. But there was something else in his eyes, a crack of vulnerability hidden beneath the layers of deflection, and I couldn't look away.

"Evan," I whispered, my voice almost lost to the wind. "You've been tracking these fires for so long... Why didn't you ever tell me?"

His gaze flickered to mine, and for a moment, I thought I saw something like regret, something like guilt, pass through his expression. "Because I didn't want to drag you into it," he said, his voice hoarse, like it cost him something to admit that. "You don't deserve that. You deserve better than this. Better than me."

I wanted to argue with him, to tell him he was wrong, but the words lodged themselves in my throat, too tangled with the emotions he'd just exposed. The air between us crackled now—not from the fire, but from the sudden weight of everything unsaid. He was revealing something he'd kept buried for so long, something that shifted everything between us, made it feel like we were standing at the edge of a precipice. And I wasn't sure whether I wanted to leap into it or run the other way.

"So these people..." I hesitated, the questions tumbling out as I struggled to grasp onto something tangible. "They're all... connected to you?"

Evan looked away, his shoulders sagging under the invisible burden he was carrying. "Every last one of them. At some point, they were people I trusted, people who were supposed to have my back. And each one of them—each one of them burned me in some way. And now, these fires, they're just a pattern, a trail of destruction they've left behind. But I can't stop following it. I can't stop trying to figure out why they did it, why they... betrayed me."

The vulnerability in his voice hit me like a freight train, and for a moment, all I could do was stand there, staring at him. The layers of his carefully constructed façade had cracked wide open, leaving only the raw, exposed pieces behind.

"Evan," I said, my voice barely a whisper, "you've been carrying this all alone?"

He didn't answer right away, his eyes dark as he searched the ground, unwilling to meet my gaze. The silence between us stretched out, heavy with the weight of his confession. I didn't know what to say. How could I offer him comfort when I barely understood the depth of his pain?

But then he looked up at me, his eyes locking onto mine with a sudden intensity that sent a shiver down my spine. "I couldn't bring anyone else into this," he said, his voice low but steady. "I couldn't let anyone else get burned. Not again."

I swallowed hard, the knot in my throat tight. I hadn't realized how much I wanted to reach out to him, how much I wanted to pull him into something safe. But instead, all I could do was stand there, caught between the desire to fix everything and the fear that I was already too late.

For a long moment, neither of us spoke. We just stood there, the weight of everything unsaid pressing down on us, until the crackling fire in the distance seemed to grow louder, more insistent, as if it was calling us both back into the heat. Back into the danger of it all.

And in that moment, I understood. The past wasn't done with us yet.

I took a breath, trying to steady the chaos inside me. Evan's words had struck something deep, something jagged and raw, and I wasn't sure what to do with it. My mind raced, grappling with the intensity of the moment, while my heart pounded in my chest, like it had suddenly developed a mind of its own. The fire had died down behind us, but the heat between us—it hadn't gone anywhere.

Evan was staring at me now, and in the dim light, his face seemed almost unreadable. His lips were pressed into a thin line, his eyes burning with some unspoken truth. I should've said something, anything to fill the silence between us. Instead, I found myself standing there, anchored to the spot, as if some invisible thread had tethered me to him. I'd never been one to shy away from confronting things head-on, but right now, all I wanted to do was hold on to this moment, to let it linger just a little longer, before I had to face whatever it was that was crawling out from the dark corners of his past.

"You should've told me," I finally muttered, breaking the heavy silence. My words were softer than I intended, but they felt important in a way I couldn't quite articulate. "I could've helped."

Evan's gaze flickered to me, and there was something in the way his eyes softened—just the slightest trace of regret—that made my pulse quicken. He shifted his weight, turning his body slightly away from me, like he was trying to put some distance between us, but I could see it in the way his hands clenched at his sides, like he was resisting the urge to reach out. Or maybe it was me he was resisting.

"No," he said, the word almost a hiss. "You don't understand. I couldn't—wouldn't—let you get wrapped up in this. It's not something you should have to carry too."

His voice cracked at the end, and for the first time since I'd known him, I saw a flicker of doubt pass through his usually composed demeanor. It was like he wasn't just hiding from his past; he was hiding from me. And I couldn't decide whether I was angry or heartbroken at the realization. Because all this time, I'd believed we'd been in this together. But now it felt like we were worlds apart, and I wasn't sure if I was supposed to cross that distance or turn away from it.

I shook my head, my thoughts tumbling over each other. "You don't get to decide that for me. I've been in the dark for this long. You can't just pull away now."

His eyes snapped to mine, fierce and sharp. "I never wanted you to be in the dark. I've been trying to keep you safe." He paused, exhaling sharply, like the words had somehow become too heavy to carry. "I don't know how to fix it, but I can't bear the thought of dragging you into it."

I wanted to scream, to ask him why he didn't trust me enough to let me help, but the words caught in my throat. Instead, I took a small step forward, closing the distance between us, before I stopped myself. I didn't know if I was making the right move, but something about the way he was standing there, vulnerable and raw, made my heart ache. There was no going back now.

"Evan," I said softly, the words slipping out before I had a chance to second-guess them. "I'm already here."

For a long moment, neither of us spoke, the tension between us building, thick and unyielding. I could hear the distant murmur of the fire trucks as they packed up, their sirens fading into the night. But it felt like the world had paused around us, like everything had come to a standstill. I could almost feel his heartbeat through the silence, each beat a question he was too afraid to ask.

Finally, he exhaled, the sound long and weighted. "I never meant to hurt you."

I nodded, though I wasn't sure what I was agreeing to. I wasn't angry. Not really. I was just... lost. And the more I tried to make sense of what was happening between us, the less clear it all became. The line between us—between what was friendship and what could have been—was no longer clear. It had blurred so much that it was almost unrecognizable.

"You didn't," I said, though the words felt hollow, like I was offering comfort where none was needed. "But I need you to tell me the truth, Evan. All of it."

His jaw tightened again, the flicker of hesitation still there. He ran a hand through his hair, a motion I recognized as his way of thinking, his way of bracing himself. "It's not easy," he murmured, more to himself than to me. "I've spent so long trying to bury it, trying to forget."

"And now?" I pressed gently, stepping closer despite the lump that had formed in my throat.

His eyes locked onto mine then, and for a fleeting second, it felt like I could see everything—the scars, the pain, the weight of years of secrecy. "Now," he whispered, "I don't know what happens next. But I'm done running."

The words hung between us, charged with something I couldn't quite name. Maybe it was hope. Maybe it was fear. But it was there, undeniable, in the way his voice broke on the last syllable, in the way he let himself stand still for once, instead of retreating into the shadows where he'd always felt safest. The air was thick with the unspoken, and for the first time, I realized how much of his battle had been fought alone. I wasn't sure I could fix it, or if I should, but I knew one thing for certain—I couldn't just walk away.

I reached out, my hand brushing his arm in an instinctive motion. The contact was small, but it was enough to make him flinch, like the smallest touch could ignite something he wasn't ready to face. I wanted to apologize for pushing, for pressing him when he'd been so closed off, but the words never came. Instead, I stood there, uncertain and vulnerable, offering him the only thing I could.

"I'm here," I repeated, my voice steady despite the uncertainty in my chest.

For the first time in a long while, Evan didn't pull away. He didn't say anything, either. He just stood there, with me, and the unspoken promise of whatever might come next hung in the air between us.

The words we hadn't spoken seemed to hang in the air, thick and dense, suffocating the small space between us. I wanted to ask him more—so much more—but there was a hesitation in his eyes, a wall he wasn't willing to let me cross just yet. It was in the way he shifted his weight, his hands still clenched into fists at his sides as if he was battling the urge to either let it all go or run away. And I could tell, deep down, he was no longer sure which option was safer.

"I don't know how to tell you all of it," he muttered, his voice tight, low, and far too fragile for my liking. "How do you even explain something like this?"

I wanted to reach out, to touch him, but my body was frozen, unsure of the distance that needed to remain between us or if, perhaps, he was just as terrified of the closeness I craved. The vulnerability he had shown me moments ago—the way his emotions had cracked through the armor he wore so carefully—was something I had never seen before. And I realized that this side of him, the one that had allowed me even a glimpse, was something I wasn't sure I was ready to lose.

Instead of stepping back, I took a step forward. "You don't have to explain all of it at once. Just—just let me in, Evan. You don't have to carry this alone."

His eyes locked onto mine with such intensity that I felt the pull deep in my chest, like gravity had shifted and now, I was being dragged toward him. But instead of answering, he closed his eyes briefly, like he was trying to shut me out, like he didn't want me to see whatever it was he couldn't hide.

"Every fire," he said after a long pause, "was personal. At first, I thought it was just about revenge, about them wanting to destroy me—burning everything to the ground, piece by piece. But the more I watched, the more I realized it wasn't just about me. It was about them too. About the people they lost."

I blinked, confused. "You're saying... you were the one they were after? Or they were all connected to something you've been carrying?"

"Both," he replied, the word sharp as a knife, a bitter laugh escaping him. "I was a part of the fire. Whether I wanted to be or not." He paused, his voice faltering slightly. "I was supposed to stop it, but I didn't. I failed. And now, I have to find out why. Why they chose me, why they wanted to drag me down with them."

I felt my chest tighten, a knot forming deep inside as I pieced together what he was saying. This wasn't just about someone trying to ruin his life. No, it was something darker, something much more complicated—something that had followed him for years. And what terrified me most was the realization that it wasn't over. That whatever he had left unfinished was still coming for him. For us.

"You think it's still happening?" I asked, my voice barely above a whisper. "That they're still after you?"

His eyes hardened, and for the first time in what felt like forever, he stepped closer, close enough that I could feel the heat radiating off of him, close enough that the air between us seemed to grow warmer, charged. "I thought I was done," he said, his voice barely audible now, like he was confessing something he couldn't take back. "But I was wrong. The fires—they're just the beginning. This time, it's different. I can't walk away from it anymore."

The words hit me like a brick to the chest. I could feel the truth of what he was saying—sharp, undeniable—but I wasn't sure I could make sense of it. The weight of his past, his guilt, his responsibility—it was all pressing on him in ways I had never imagined. And here I was, standing right next to him, not sure whether I was supposed to walk away or hold on tighter.

"Evan," I whispered, my voice trembling as I took another step toward him. "Tell me what to do."

His breath hitched at my words, but there was a flicker of something behind his eyes—something almost imperceptible—that made me wonder if he was seeing me differently now too. He opened his mouth to speak, but before he could, the sound of footsteps came from behind us, harsh and quick, interrupting the fragile moment we had been sharing.

We both turned in unison, instincts kicking in, our bodies immediately on high alert. My heart raced, pounding in my ears as I strained to make out the shadowy figure moving toward us through the night. The familiar shape of a person, too large to be anyone I recognized, loomed closer, the clicking of boots against the pavement sharp against the quiet of the night.

Evan stiffened beside me, his posture suddenly tense. He took a step back, moving slightly in front of me as if to shield me, and for the first time since this entire night had started, I could see it—the panic that flickered in his eyes, the realization that whatever this was, it was no longer just his fight.

"Who's there?" I called, my voice surprisingly steady given the adrenaline that had already begun to pump through me.

The figure didn't respond at first, only continued to walk toward us, but there was a dark, menacing energy that seemed to emanate from them, a presence that chilled the air, even before they spoke.

"You should've stayed away, Evan," the voice said, low and almost a growl. "But now you're involved. And that's a mistake you'll both regret."

I didn't have time to process the words, let alone respond, before the figure moved closer, their face hidden in shadow. The scent of something familiar—something smoky—drifted over to us, the same heavy, acrid smell that had clung to the wreckage of the fire.

Before I could react, Evan's grip tightened on my arm, his voice barely a whisper, "Run."

But it was already too late.

Chapter 16: Stoking the Flames

The first time I saw Evan's shadow flit across the hallway, I thought nothing of it. After all, who hasn't caught a glimpse of someone they didn't expect, especially when the house is still too quiet? But when it happened again, and again, each time my gaze flicked up to find his eyes already fixed on me, it wasn't just an observation—it was a silent request, as though he needed something from me that I couldn't quite name. I pretended not to notice, of course. It wasn't my business, not really. I had enough of my own mess to untangle without adding his to the pile.

Still, I couldn't shake the feeling that the more I dug into the mess we were both caught in—the one that seemed to involve fire, shadows, and a history of things better left untouched—the more I needed him closer.

The research wasn't easy. Scanning old case files and government reports on arson was tedious at best, harrowing at worst. The room was stifling, my laptop glowing like an accusing finger as it threw documents at me that I had no business reading. But Evan insisted, his voice quiet behind me, hovering like a constant hum, never quite a whisper, never quite a shout. I could feel his presence more than I could hear his words, like an electric current running just beneath my skin. "This," he would murmur from over my shoulder, pointing at a name, a place, or a date, his fingers brushing mine for a fraction of a second, but it felt like a lifetime.

His insistence on staying close, staying within arm's reach, never gave me space to breathe. It was as though he was tethered to me by something unseen—something that didn't quite make sense, but was far too real to ignore. Every time I shifted in my seat, adjusted the way my hair fell across my face, or sipped my coffee like a nervous tick, I could feel his eyes there, tracking me, dissecting me in ways I wasn't ready for.

But the thing was, I didn't mind. Not at first, anyway. His presence had a way of filling up the room, anchoring me in a way I couldn't explain. His eyes would flicker over my hands when I typed, scanning through the endless records. Every so often, his voice would cut through the murmur of the room. "You're close," he'd say, his tone neither hopeful nor sure, but something else—something almost like fear, though he'd never admit it. And every time, I'd glance up at him, feeling my breath hitch, my pulse quicken for reasons I couldn't sort through.

I told myself it was nothing. That I was simply reacting to the tension of the moment. But then came the night I found the first of what could have been a dozen hidden notes. They were tucked inside a dusty old file, yellowing and fragile, written in a hand that was far too familiar to be a coincidence. The ink was smudged in places, like someone had hurried to pen it, their thoughts jumbled as they worked through the mess. And as I read, a sinking feeling settled in my chest, that sickening twist that grows when you know you've found something dangerous.

The words weren't just about arson. They weren't about destruction or fire or the usual chaos. They were about me. About someone named Grace, my name in sharp, desperate strokes, as though it was a secret no one else should know.

I couldn't breathe. I could barely think. Every part of me wanted to scream, to run out of the room, to tell Evan that it was too much—that I didn't want to be a part of this. But then his voice came, soft but insistent, as he leaned over my shoulder to read the file I had just opened.

"Who's writing this?" His question was a murmur, the quietest hint of urgency leaking through. His breath was warm against the nape of my neck.

I felt his words before I heard them, like they carved a line between my spine and the rest of my body. My heart pounded. The room spun. For a moment, I couldn't look at him. The weight of everything pressing against me made it hard to breathe. "I don't know," I said, trying to keep my voice steady, but failing.

He moved closer, his eyes locked on the file in my hands. His body pressed in behind me, his heat suffusing the space between us like a palpable thing. "Grace," he whispered again, as though tasting the name on his lips. And I couldn't understand why, but I wanted him to say it again. I needed him to say it again.

But his gaze was already moving over the page, studying, analyzing, his jaw set in that stubborn, determined way I had come to know all too well. The silence stretched between us, the kind of silence that should have been comforting, but felt like a battle—like something on the verge of snapping.

Finally, after what seemed like an eternity, Evan stepped back, his presence pulling away just slightly. I didn't know whether to be relieved or disappointed. His voice was low, controlled, though the tension still hummed in the air. "This... this could be a problem."

I nodded, but my mind raced in a dozen directions. What kind of problem? How deep did this go? And, most importantly—why was I involved?

But the question that kept gnawing at me, the one I couldn't shake, was why Evan hadn't let go of me yet. Why he kept lingering in my space, his presence like a thread tied tightly around my chest, pulling me back toward him no matter how hard I tried to escape. It was a weight I didn't want, but couldn't quite shake.

Every time I caught him watching me, his eyes searching, probing, like he was trying to uncover something I wasn't ready to reveal, it only deepened the knot in my stomach. There was more to this than either of us wanted to admit. But for all the questions that flooded my mind, one stood out above the rest: how long could I keep pretending I didn't want him as close as he kept pulling me?

The first time he reached out to steady me, I barely registered the touch. A flash of his hand on my arm as I stumbled backward, a pile of old newspaper clippings scattered across the floor like confetti. My eyes were fixed on the latest document I had uncovered, a file that seemed as if it had been sealed with the weight of decades, and I could barely breathe through the flood of questions that rushed in, drowning out the world around me. I'd been so focused on piecing together the fragments, trying to make sense of the twisted narrative we were both caught in, that I hadn't noticed how dangerously close Evan was. He had that uncanny ability to slip in behind me without making a sound—like a shadow in the dark, always there, always watching.

"Careful," his voice was low, just above a whisper. He didn't try to pull me back or make a fuss. There was something about the way he said it, though, a quiet authority that made me pause for a fraction of a second longer than I would have on my own.

I nodded, the words stalling on my tongue. "I'm fine," I said, but it sounded hollow, even to me. There was no way to explain how everything felt like it was teetering on the edge of something—something bigger than either of us could understand. And even though I was standing still, I couldn't shake the feeling that the ground beneath me was shifting.

Evan didn't move. His presence was like an anchor, pulling me deeper into the chaos, yet giving me no space to breathe. Every glance, every word he spoke, seemed calculated, deliberate. He was always close, yet always out of reach. And it wasn't just his proximity that unsettled me. It was the way his eyes lingered on me, studying me like a puzzle he couldn't quite solve. As if he was trying to figure out a secret I wasn't telling, or maybe something he was afraid to hear.

He wasn't the only one holding secrets. I had my own set of them—ones I hadn't been brave enough to confront. But every time our eyes met, every time his voice slid into the spaces between my thoughts, I wondered how long I could keep them hidden. There was too much at stake now, too much I couldn't afford to ignore. And yet, the longer I spent with him, the more tangled I became in this web we were both caught in, the less I knew where I ended and he began.

"You're good at this," he said, his voice cutting through the silence that had settled between us like a heavy fog. "You're good at finding what people try to bury."

It wasn't a compliment. Not really. Not the way he said it, like it was a warning wrapped in the guise of praise. He didn't look at me when he spoke, his attention fixed on the papers in front of him, but I could feel the weight of his words pressing down on me.

"Not everyone has something to hide," I replied, the words coming out sharper than I intended. I didn't know where that defensiveness had come from. But there it was, sharp and jagged in the air between us.

Evan didn't flinch, didn't back down. Instead, he turned to face me, his eyes steady. "No, but the ones who do... they don't make it easy." He paused, his gaze flickering to the door, like he was expecting someone to walk through it at any moment. "And you don't either."

It was as if he'd cut through every defense I had, exposing the truth I hadn't yet admitted. Not to him, not to myself. I could feel the heat rise to my cheeks, a flush that had nothing to do with embarrassment and everything to do with the fact that he was right. There were things I hadn't said. There were things I hadn't even allowed myself to think. And yet, he saw them—he saw me.

The silence stretched on, thick and heavy, until I couldn't stand it anymore. "You're wrong," I finally said, my voice sounding too loud, too raw in the quiet room. I had to fill the space somehow. "I'm not hiding anything." But the lie tasted bitter on my tongue.

Evan didn't respond right away. Instead, he studied me like I was the last puzzle piece he hadn't yet found. His eyes narrowed slightly, but the hardness in his gaze softened for just a moment. A flash of something—a vulnerability, maybe?—before it was gone again, replaced by that familiar guardedness.

"You're lying," he said, not with accusation, but with the certainty of someone who had learned to read between the lines. "You don't have to tell me, but you can't lie to yourself."

His words settled in my chest, heavy and suffocating. I wanted to argue, to shout, to say something—anything—that would push him away. But the truth was, I didn't want him to go. Not really. There was something about him—something that kept pulling me in, that kept me tethered to him even when I was drowning in my own confusion.

His gaze flickered back to the papers on the table, his fingers grazing the edge of the file before he looked back at me. "But you're close. Whatever this is, you're closer than I thought."

I didn't know what he meant, not really. Was he talking about the investigation? Or was he talking about us? The lines between the two had become so blurred that I couldn't tell anymore. It didn't matter, anyway. Because now, there was no turning back. No way to unsee what we had uncovered. We were both in this together, whether we liked it or not.

I couldn't look at him any longer. The weight of his gaze was too much, too consuming. So, I turned my attention back to the documents, though my mind was no longer focused on the words in front of me. I could feel his eyes on me, though, the intensity of them like a pressure on my skin. He wasn't going to stop watching, not now. And maybe, just maybe, neither of us were going to stop until we found whatever it was we were both searching for.

But as the night stretched on, with the hours slipping by unnoticed, I couldn't shake the feeling that we were both running toward something we weren't prepared to face—together or apart. And somewhere, just beyond the edge of everything, there was a truth that we both knew would change everything.

The days blurred together in a haze of late nights and dimly lit rooms, the silence between us growing heavy with every unanswered question that hung in the air. We sat at the cluttered table, surrounded by stacks of reports, half-empty coffee cups, and the remnants of a research project that had spiraled far beyond what we had anticipated. Evan's presence was constant, a shadow in the corner of my vision, always just behind me, just to the left, just enough to remind me he was there. But even as we worked side by side, there was a wall between us that felt thicker than the papers we were pouring over. A wall that neither of us acknowledged aloud, though it was as impossible to ignore as the shifting tension in the room.

I could feel it more acutely now, the crackling charge in the air that thrummed with an energy I couldn't name. He wasn't just there to help me with the investigation; he was there to protect me, to make sure I didn't dig too deep. But why? Was it because of the connection we shared—whatever that was—or was it something darker, something tied to the danger that seemed to be stalking us both?

Every time I found another clue that suggested my name was somehow tied to the fires, a chill crawled up my spine, like icy fingers pressing against the back of my neck. But it wasn't just the investigation that was unsettling; it was Evan's presence, his constant proximity, his ever-watchful eyes that lingered on me just a second too long. He watched me, as though every glance held more than I was ready to understand. And every time I caught his gaze, there was a flicker of something—something I couldn't quite decipher—before it was gone again.

I tried to push it away, tried to focus on the files in front of me, but the more I dug, the more I uncovered, the more I realized how little I knew. The pieces of the puzzle were all out of order, scattered in a way that made it impossible to see the whole picture. I had no idea what was pulling us together, no idea what thread connected me to this twisted web of fire and deceit. But I knew one thing for sure: Evan was as much a part of this as I was. And the more I worked with him, the more I wanted to understand him—wanted to understand what drove him, what made him tick. There was something in his eyes, something buried deep, that I couldn't help but want to uncover.

When he spoke, his voice was quieter than usual, a murmur that barely reached me, like a breath in the dark. "You're digging too deep," he said, not looking at me but at the pages in front of him. "You need to stop."

I didn't answer right away, didn't acknowledge the unease creeping up my spine. Instead, I kept my focus on the file I was reading, my fingers brushing over the edge of the paper in a nervous rhythm. "I can't stop now," I said, the words coming out in a voice that was both defiant and uncertain, like I wasn't sure if I was talking to him or to myself.

He didn't move, didn't shift in his chair, but I could feel the tension radiating from him. "I'm not asking you to stop," he said, his voice low, "but you need to be careful."

Careful. That word again. It sounded so simple, but I knew it wasn't. He wasn't worried about the investigation; he was worried about me. I could feel it in the way he watched me, in the way he hesitated when he spoke. As if he was holding something back, something that he knew I wouldn't like.

"What is it?" I asked, not bothering to hide the frustration that crept into my voice. "What are you not telling me?"

He met my gaze, and for a moment, I saw something there—something raw, something almost desperate. But then it was gone, replaced by that familiar guarded expression, the mask he wore so well. "You don't need to know."

I didn't back down. "I'm already in this. Whether you like it or not."

The words hung in the air between us, thick with unspoken tension. Evan's jaw tightened, and I could see the struggle in his eyes. He wanted to protect me, I knew that. But in doing so, he was holding me at arm's length, keeping me from the very answers I needed.

A sharp knock at the door broke the moment, and we both turned toward it in unison. The sound was too loud, too jarring, and for a split second, I wondered if it was the kind of interruption we had both been waiting for—something that would force us to face whatever it was we were avoiding.

The door creaked open, and I saw the familiar face of my old colleague, Detective Harris. His expression was tense, his eyes darting nervously between us. "We've got a situation," he said without preamble, his voice clipped.

Evan was already standing, his body tense, his posture rigid. "What's happened?" His voice was sharp, demanding, but underneath the authority was a note of something else—something that wasn't quite fear but was close enough to make the hairs on the back of my neck stand up.

Harris stepped inside, closing the door behind him. "It's... it's not just fires anymore," he said, his voice lowering as though to keep the words between us. "We've found something. Something tied to you."

I froze, my pulse spiking. The blood drained from my face, and I turned to look at Evan, expecting to see some sign that he knew this was coming—that he had known all along. But there was nothing. Just a cold, unreadable expression, as if he hadn't heard a word of what Harris had said.

"Tell me," I demanded, my voice trembling despite myself. "What's tied to me?"

But before Harris could answer, my phone buzzed on the table, the screen lighting up with a number I didn't recognize. And that was when everything started to change.

Chapter 17: Flickers in the Dark

The rain had stopped falling, but the air still smelled like it had been crying. Everything was slick with it, from the worn cobblestones under my boots to the streaked windows of the café where I sat, clutching my coffee like a lifeline. It was early enough that the world felt like it was holding its breath—just before the city woke up in all its chaotic glory. There were no sirens yet, no voices, no honking of horns or hurrying feet. Just the soft, relentless sound of water dripping off rooftops, the hum of the heater under the counter, and the quiet buzzing of my phone.

I should've ignored it. But curiosity had me hooked, like a moth circling a flame it couldn't resist. It was from an unknown number—no name, no clue. Just a message. "You think you're safe, but you're not. The fire's already been lit, and I'm the one holding the match."

My fingers froze mid-swipe as I read the words. The room felt smaller. The low buzz of the heater seemed distant. I glanced around, trying to push the unease down, but it was hard to pretend I wasn't drowning in that awful, familiar feeling of being watched. It wasn't just paranoia this time. It was real. I could feel it in my chest—the tightness of a breath that didn't belong to me, the racing of my pulse, the sense that the world had shifted, and I was standing on the edge of it.

I knew this game. I'd been playing it for weeks now. Whoever this was—this shadow that had been haunting us—they were getting closer. I could feel the heat rising in my cheeks, the flush of something dangerously close to shame creeping up my neck. Evan had warned me. And yet here I was, sitting alone in a café, reading threats from someone who had already proven they weren't afraid to burn everything down.

My phone buzzed again, and I jumped. It was him. Evan.

He wasn't exactly a text-first kind of guy, but his messages always felt like they carried the weight of the world. "Stay where you are. I'm on my way."

He always had that way of speaking, like everything was already settled, like I was safe with him, even when I wasn't sure I believed it myself.

I closed my eyes for a moment, trying to convince myself that the panic in my gut wasn't real. That maybe, just maybe, he was right. But the truth was, I didn't know who to trust anymore. Not even myself.

The door to the café opened, and the bell above it chimed, drawing my attention. Evan walked in, his silhouette outlined in the pale light of the street behind him. His eyes scanned the room before they landed on me, and I felt something stir deep inside, something I couldn't quite name. His gaze was fierce, sharp, like he was already in battle, like he knew this moment was one step too close to the edge for either of us to ignore.

I didn't move as he approached, not because I was afraid of him—never that—but because I wasn't sure I could stand without feeling the weight of his presence pressing against me. He had a way of making me feel like I was both the problem and the solution.

"Don't," he said softly, his voice cutting through the tension like a knife.

I blinked up at him, confused, unsure of what he meant. He nodded toward my phone.

"You were about to text back, weren't you?" he asked, his lips twitching into something like a smile, but it didn't reach his eyes.

I swallowed, trying to steady myself. The truth was, I'd been tempted to send something back—something sharp, something cutting. But in that moment, I couldn't quite find the words.

"I wasn't—" I started, but he interrupted.

"Don't respond to them. Don't play their game. Let me handle this." His voice was firm, unyielding. It should've felt reassuring, but something about it only made the pit in my stomach grow larger.

I wanted to trust him. God, I did. But there was something about the way he said it—like it was too simple, like this was a problem he could solve with brute force, like there was no danger in underestimating whoever was on the other side of the line.

I set my phone down on the table with a little more force than necessary. "You don't get it, Evan. They know things. Things that only the arsonist could know."

His jaw tightened, his eyes narrowing with that look he always got when the world wasn't making sense to him. "I don't care what they know. I care about keeping you safe. That's all that matters right now."

I felt a pang in my chest at the weight of those words. It was hard not to get swept up in his certainty, in the promise he made with every inch of his posture. But promises were fragile things, and I wasn't sure mine were worth keeping anymore.

Before I could answer, the door swung open again, this time with a sharpness that made the hairs on my neck stand at attention. My eyes snapped to the door, expecting trouble, but the person standing there wasn't a threat—not at first glance. A tall man, sharp suit, cold eyes. I didn't know him, but the way he looked at me made my stomach churn.

Evan's reaction was instant, his body stiffening, his hand hovering near the small of my back as if to shield me from whatever was about to happen.

The man didn't speak immediately. Instead, he just stood there, studying us both, his lips curling slightly. "You don't seem to understand the gravity of this situation," he said, his voice smooth, calculated. "The game is just beginning."

I didn't know what game he meant, but in that moment, I was pretty sure none of us would be walking away without being burned.

Evan didn't move when the man entered, not at first. His posture didn't change, and his gaze didn't waver. But I felt the shift in him, a crackle of energy too sharp to ignore. It was as though the air around him thickened, the room holding its breath along with him. I could see it in the set of his jaw, the tension in his shoulders. Every part of him, it seemed, was suddenly at attention, a silent warning that things were about to go wrong, and no one was going to walk away unscathed.

The man, still standing in the doorway, smirked like he knew something I didn't. His eyes flicked between Evan and me, as if gauging how much we knew, how much we could understand. "You're still playing the hero, aren't you?" he said, his voice too calm, too smooth for comfort. It was a game to him—one I wasn't sure I was ready to play, let alone win.

Evan's eyes never left him. "Get out," he said flatly, as if his voice alone could push the man back into whatever hole he'd crawled out of.

But the stranger didn't move. Instead, his gaze shifted to me, the weight of his stare making my skin prickle. "You think you're safe here? You're not. Not while he's around." He nodded toward Evan, and then he looked back at me, his lips curling up at the corners as if he were savoring something dark and dangerous. "You have no idea how deep this goes, do you? But you will."

I could feel the air growing thick between us, the invisible line tightening with every word he spoke. It was a warning, but also a challenge. One that hung there like a shadow I couldn't escape, no matter how hard I tried to ignore it.

I stood, the movement jerky, my chair scraping the floor with an ungraceful screech. "Who are you?" I managed to ask, my voice coming out weaker than I wanted it to. It wasn't that I was afraid—I wasn't sure what I felt, but fear didn't seem to quite fit the emotion gnawing at me.

The man's smile widened, and for the first time, I saw a flicker of something real in his eyes—something cold and calculated, like he was watching me unravel in front of him. "Who I am doesn't matter. What matters is that you're in the way." His voice dropped lower, and for a second, I thought I imagined it, but no, it was there—dark and thick, like oil spilling onto water. "The flames are closer than you think. And when they burn, they'll take everything."

Evan stepped forward, his body a wall between me and the stranger. "You need to leave, now," he said, his voice low, dangerous. It was the kind of threat that didn't need to be repeated. His presence alone was enough to tell the man he wasn't going anywhere without a fight.

But the man only chuckled, a sound that grated against my nerves. "He can protect you all he wants, sweetheart," he said, his words sharp like broken glass. "But it won't matter. You'll be the one to pay. You're always the one who pays."

I took a step back, my legs unsteady beneath me. I couldn't help it; there was something about the way he said it, something cold and final in his tone. I looked at Evan, but he was too focused on the man to notice. His gaze was unwavering, his hands clenched into fists at his sides. I could tell he was holding himself back, fighting the urge to throw the first punch.

The silence stretched between us, a taut, uncomfortable thing that buzzed with unspoken words. Then, the man turned, his movement smooth and deliberate, like he knew how much power he held in that moment. "It doesn't matter," he muttered to himself, as though he were trying to convince himself of something. "It'll happen anyway. One way or another."

He walked out of the café without another glance, leaving behind nothing but a lingering sense of dread in the air, like a storm cloud that hadn't yet decided whether to break.

For a long moment, no one spoke. I was too stunned to say anything, and Evan seemed to be waiting for something—waiting for the right moment to let the tension snap, to break whatever hold the man had on us.

Then, finally, Evan exhaled, long and slow, as if he'd been holding his breath since the man walked in. He turned to me, his face hard, but his eyes softening just a little. "Are you okay?"

I nodded, even though the tremble in my hands betrayed me. "Yeah," I said, my voice barely above a whisper. "I think so."

Evan's eyes narrowed as if he wasn't sure whether to believe me or not. He was the type to see through lies—my lies, anyway. I couldn't hide anything from him, not when it mattered most.

"Don't brush this off," he said, his voice quieter now, but still carrying the weight of his concern. "He knows too much. He's not just playing games anymore."

I wanted to believe that I was fine, that I could handle whatever came next, but the words stuck in my throat. The man's words haunted me, clung to me like a shadow. *The flames are closer than you think.*

"You don't understand," I said, my voice cracking slightly. "I've been getting these messages. They know things, Evan. Things that… no one should know."

He stepped closer, his presence a comfort, a shield I didn't realize I needed. He reached for my hand, his grip firm but gentle, as though he were trying to ground me in the chaos. "Then we'll find out who they are," he said simply. "And when we do, they won't be able to hide."

I didn't know how he planned on making that happen. I didn't know if he had the answers or if he was simply trying to keep me from drowning in my own fear. But I also knew that no matter what, I wasn't in this alone. And for the first time in days, I allowed myself to believe it. I allowed myself to trust that, maybe, just maybe, the flames wouldn't consume us both.

The tension between Evan and me felt like a string pulled too tight, just waiting for something to snap. We didn't speak for a long while after the man left, the quiet stretched thin and taut around us. I was trying to steady my breathing, trying to push the chill from my bones, but it wasn't working. The message still echoed in my mind, the threat hanging over me like a storm cloud that refused to break. The flames were closer than I realized. And it was hard to focus on anything else when my thoughts kept drifting back to that single, horrific idea.

Evan seemed to sense it, though. He always did. He turned to me, his expression unreadable, but there was a flicker of something else there too—something raw, something he didn't want to show. "You're not alone in this," he said softly, like he was reassuring both of us.

I wanted to believe him. I really did. But it was hard to look at him and not feel that knot in my stomach tighten. He doesn't understand. It wasn't that he couldn't protect me; it was that I wasn't sure he could protect either of us from whatever was coming. This wasn't just about me anymore—it was about something far bigger, and as much as Evan was determined to make it go away, the pieces were falling into place in a way I couldn't ignore.

The café was emptying out, the morning rush subsiding, leaving behind only the faintest traces of conversation and the clink of cutlery being cleared. The barista gave us a quick, awkward glance as he wiped down the counter, and I felt suddenly exposed, like the whole world knew the darkness we were standing in.

"Come on." Evan's voice broke through the silence, and I turned to see him holding his jacket, the familiar steely determination in his eyes. "We're getting out of here."

I opened my mouth to protest, but the words stuck. I knew the game was no longer just a game—it was real. Too real. And while Evan's protective nature had always been one of his strongest qualities, it was the first time I'd found myself questioning whether it was enough. *What if he's wrong?*

I stood, gathering my things, but the weight of the message in my pocket felt heavier than it should. "What now?" I asked, my voice barely above a whisper. "Do we just... wait for it to happen?"

Evan's lips pressed into a tight line, his jaw working in that way that meant he was thinking, calculating, deciding. "I don't know," he admitted, but there was no resignation in his tone—just resolve. "But we're not going to let it happen without a fight."

His words hung in the air, and for a moment, they felt like a lifeline. But then the nagging thought surfaced again. *But what if we're already too late?*

We stepped out into the gray morning light, the city sprawled out before us in all its usual chaos. The buildings loomed like silent sentinels, their jagged edges casting long shadows across the streets. I felt small in the midst of it, even with Evan beside me. But he was right—at least in one way. We had to act, and we had to act now.

Evan led the way down the street, his steps brisk and purposeful. I fell into step beside him, trying to shake off the unease that had settled like a second skin. The streets were busier now, the sound of people going about their daily lives blending with the city's constant hum. It all felt so... normal. And that, perhaps, was the most unsettling part of it all. How easily the world could keep moving forward while we were stuck, caught in something dark and relentless that none of us fully understood.

I was lost in my thoughts when a sharp ring cut through the air. I didn't even have to check my phone to know it was him—the arsonist. The chill that crept over me when I saw the number was immediate, a cold prickle along my spine. I wanted to ignore it, but the temptation to pick up was overwhelming. I swiped the screen before I could second-guess myself.

"Hello?" My voice was shaky, but I hoped it sounded stronger than I felt.

"Did you think it would be that easy?" The voice on the other end was smooth, too smooth, like it had been rehearsed a thousand times. "You think Evan can protect you? You think anyone can?" The words dripped with amusement, as if I were a child playing dress-up, pretending to be in control.

"Who are you?" I managed, trying to mask the rising panic in my chest.

The pause that followed felt like an eternity. When he spoke again, it was softer, almost intimate. "You don't need to know my name. But you will know what I'm capable of. Soon enough."

I felt a tug at my heart, a sudden sense of urgency. "What do you want?" The words left my mouth before I could stop them, sharp and desperate.

There was a soft laugh, low and mocking. "You're already too deep, sweetheart. It's too late for you to walk away now. You'll be watching the flames burn, just like everyone else who's been in my way."

The call ended abruptly, the line going silent with a finality that left me reeling. My hands were shaking as I lowered the phone, the words echoing in my head, like a countdown I couldn't escape.

Evan had been watching me closely, his expression unreadable. "What did he say?"

I shook my head, trying to keep the panic from spilling over. "Nothing. Nothing I didn't already know."

But even as I said it, I knew the truth. We weren't safe. Not anymore.

Evan didn't push. He didn't need to. His eyes said everything. We're running out of time.

We continued walking in silence, the city around us moving, oblivious to the storm gathering just a few steps behind us. But I could feel it now, more than ever—the weight of the danger, the flickers of flame threatening to consume everything I held onto. I didn't know what was coming, but I had a sinking feeling we weren't going to get out of this unscathed.

The sudden screech of tires broke the quiet, and I turned just in time to see a black SUV speeding toward us. My breath caught in my throat.

And then, everything went black.

Chapter 18: A Blaze of Longing

The air in Evan's apartment feels thick, charged with the kind of electricity that hovers between two people who have spent too much time circling the edges of something unspoken. His living room is warm, bathed in the dim golden light from a lamp in the corner. The faint hum of the refrigerator in the kitchen is the only thing cutting through the silence. I don't mind it, though. There's something comforting about the quiet between us, even as I try to reconcile the rush of thoughts swirling in my head.

I sit on the couch, my fingers tangled together in my lap, feeling the tension of my body stretching tight. I've been here for hours, yet it's as if time has slowed to a crawl. We've talked about everything and nothing at all—his work, my latest attempts at cooking something that vaguely resembled food, the peculiarities of a city neither of us has quite gotten used to. Yet, beneath all the casual conversation, something else is stirring. I'm starting to feel it in my chest, like a slow burn that keeps getting hotter the more I try to ignore it.

Evan leans back on the opposite side of the couch, his knee just brushing mine. His shirt is slightly unbuttoned at the collar, revealing a smattering of chest hair I've noticed before but never lingered on. There's a familiarity between us now, the kind that comes from hours of shared space and fleeting touches, the ones that speak volumes more than words ever could. He catches my gaze for a split second, his eyes dark with something I can't quite place, before he looks away, almost as if to escape the weight of it.

I can feel the hesitation in the air, thick and palpable. Neither of us is willing to be the first to break. But then he shifts, sitting up straighter and rubbing a hand over his face. It's a small, tired motion, but it feels like the prelude to something deeper. "I don't talk about this," he says, his voice low and rough, like it hasn't been used in a while. His words hang in the air between us, a challenge, an invitation.

I swallow, trying to steady myself, but my curiosity gets the best of me. "What don't you talk about?"

He pauses, glancing up at the ceiling, as if searching for the right words, but they seem to escape him. "Anything real." His gaze flickers toward me again, then drops to the floor. "Anything that's more than just surface-level."

I nod, though it's a slow, unsure motion. Part of me wants to press him, to ask what lies beneath all the layers he's so carefully constructed around himself. But another part, the part that's been aching to get closer to him, knows that whatever it is, it's something he has to offer freely. And I don't want to push him too hard. Not yet.

"So, what do you talk about?" I ask, keeping my voice light. I don't want him to retreat into himself, to shut me out the way he seems to do with everything else. I want to find that sliver of space where I can reach him.

Evan's lips curl into a half-smile, a hint of irony there that makes my chest tighten. "Mostly bullshit. But I'm really good at it." He looks at me again, his eyes a little softer now, more vulnerable than before. "I don't let people get too close. Too much risk of... getting hurt."

There it is. The crack in the armor I've been hoping for. His voice, though quiet, trembles just enough to make my heart skip a beat. It's not an admission I expected, but somehow, it feels like it's been there all along, lurking just under the surface of everything he says and does. He's afraid. And for the first time, I wonder what it would take to make him see that he doesn't have to be.

I shift on the couch, closing the small distance between us until my shoulder brushes his. "I'm not going to hurt you," I say, my voice firm, though I'm not sure where that confidence is coming from.

Maybe it's just the simple truth of the moment. Maybe it's the fact that I've spent the last few weeks getting to know him in ways I never thought I would. Maybe it's just that the more I learn, the more I realize how much I want to be here with him.

He glances at me again, this time holding my gaze for longer, and I see something in his eyes I've only caught glimpses of before—desire, raw and unfiltered, almost desperate in the way it pulls him toward me. His breath hitches, and for a moment, I wonder if he's going to say something else, something that will change everything between us.

But instead, he presses his lips together in a tight line, like he's holding himself back from saying whatever's on the tip of his tongue. I almost wish he would. Almost wish that he'd stop second-guessing himself and just let go. But I won't push. Not this time.

I lean my head back against the couch, letting the tension settle in my body. We sit in silence for a while, the weight of it no longer uncomfortable but rather a shared space where neither of us feels the need to fill the quiet with words. I don't know what's happening between us, or what it will turn into, but I know I'm falling—falling hard—and the more I try to convince myself to slow down, to hold back, the more I realize I'm too far gone to turn back now.

The silence between us stretches, but it doesn't feel oppressive. Instead, it feels like an unspoken understanding, a subtle promise that neither of us is ready to break just yet. The tension builds, slow and steady, like the quiet before a storm. I can feel the weight of it pressing against my chest, a mixture of desire and hesitation, of wanting to reach out and knowing I should wait.

Evan shifts beside me, his leg brushing mine, and the simple touch sends a jolt through me, making my pulse race. He doesn't move away, though. He stays, his presence like a gentle pressure that pulls me closer without a word. I glance at him from the corner of my eye, studying the way his jaw tightens, the slight furrow in his brow. He's trying to hold himself together, and it's almost as if he's afraid of what might slip out if he lets himself go.

"I didn't expect this," he says finally, his voice low, almost a whisper. "I didn't expect to feel this... complicated."

I turn toward him, the words settling deep in my chest, heavy but warm. "Complicated isn't always a bad thing," I reply softly. I'm not sure what I'm saying, or if it even makes sense. But in that moment, it feels right. Like the first honest thing we've said all night.

Evan lets out a quiet breath, something between a laugh and a sigh, before he meets my eyes again. His gaze is intense, like he's trying to see inside me, to understand what's swirling around in my head. "It doesn't feel like it should be this hard."

I smile, a little bit wry, a little bit unsure, but it's real. "Because it's too easy to say something we'll both regret, right?"

His lips twitch, the barest hint of a smile forming at the edges of his mouth. "Maybe. But it's also too easy to pretend it doesn't matter. To act like I don't want something more."

The confession hangs between us, and for the first time all evening, I allow myself to breathe, to let go of the careful restraint I've been holding on to. My heart speeds up, but I can't pull away. There's something magnetic about him, something that pulls me in deeper with every word he says. I want to reach for him, to kiss him until everything else fades away. But I'm waiting, just like he is. Waiting for him to take that first step.

"So what happens now?" I ask, my voice barely above a whisper. I don't know if it's a challenge or an invitation, but I don't really care.

He shifts slightly, leaning closer, the heat of his body pressing against mine. His breath catches, and for a moment, I think he's going to say something profound. Something that will change everything. But instead, his hand brushes against mine, a tentative touch that feels both electrifying and tender. His fingers linger for a beat too long before pulling away, like he's testing the waters, like he's not sure how far he can go without losing himself.

"Maybe we don't know what happens next," he murmurs, his voice rough with an emotion I can't quite place. "Maybe it's just about seeing where it goes. Seeing if this is something worth holding on to."

I nod slowly, feeling the weight of his words settle in my chest. It's a fragile thing, this connection between us. A delicate thread that could snap at any moment, but for now, it feels like the most important thing in the world. I'm not sure how we got here, or what we're even doing, but I can't shake the feeling that I'm on the edge of something big. Something that could change everything.

I look at him, really look at him, and I see the raw vulnerability in his eyes. For all his bravado, all his guarded walls, there's a softness there that catches me off guard. A longing I can almost taste in the air. It's there, in the way his fingers twitch at his sides, in the way he watches me like he's afraid I'll disappear if he blinks.

I want to close the distance, to pull him in and kiss the doubts away, but there's a hesitation in me, too. I don't know what it is—fear, uncertainty, or maybe just the knowledge that this could go wrong in a thousand ways. But it doesn't stop me from reaching out anyway. My fingers find his, tentative at first, but when he doesn't pull away, when his grip tightens just the slightest bit, I let myself believe that maybe this isn't as complicated as we're both making it.

"You know, you're a terrible liar," I say, trying to lighten the moment. My voice is teasing, playful, but there's an underlying current of truth in it.

Evan's eyes flicker with something close to amusement, the smallest smirk tugging at the corners of his mouth. "You have no idea what I'm capable of," he says, but there's a warmth to his words, a softness that belies the challenge.

I laugh, a breathy, almost nervous sound. "Maybe I don't, but I think I'd like to."

For a moment, he doesn't answer. He just looks at me, his eyes searching, like he's trying to figure out if I'm joking or if I mean it. And maybe I'm not even sure myself. But there's a part of me—one I've buried for so long—that wants to know. Wants to dive into whatever this is without holding back.

Evan leans in slightly, his lips brushing against my ear as he murmurs, "I think I'd like that too." His voice is so close, so intimate, that the words feel like a secret shared just between us. And for a fleeting moment, the rest of the world doesn't matter. Only the space between us. Only the quiet yearning that hangs in the air.

The air in the room feels thick, laden with the unspoken words that hover like fireflies just out of reach. Evan's breath hitches slightly as he inches closer, the intensity in his eyes not unlike the heat of a summer storm—electric, inevitable. I can feel the heat of his body, his presence enveloping me, pulling me in deeper with every passing second. The space between us, once just a matter of inches, now feels like an impossible chasm. Yet, at the same time, it feels like the most natural thing in the world to close that distance.

His hand finds mine again, this time with more confidence. The warmth of his skin sends a shiver up my spine, and for a fleeting moment, I'm no longer aware of the room, of the world outside, just the pulse of his touch against mine. His fingers entwine with mine, the pressure gentle but certain. I know, in that instant, that he's not going to pull away, and neither am I.

"Do you always make people wait?" I ask, the words slipping out before I can stop them. My voice is playful, teasing, but it's also a challenge. A dare, really, to see if he's willing to let go, to take that step I know we both want.

Evan's lips curl into a smirk, a mixture of amusement and something more dangerous. "Depends on what you're asking for," he says, his voice dipping low, each word coated in an intimacy that makes my pulse race.

I laugh, but it's not quite enough to cover the flutter in my chest. I want to ask more, to say more, but the words seem to stick in my throat, tangled in the weight of everything unspoken between us. For a moment, I'm not sure where this is going. I don't even know if it matters. All I know is that I can feel the pull of him, magnetic and irresistible, drawing me closer.

"I'm starting to think you like making things complicated," I say, my voice lighter now, the sharp edge of my challenge softened by the grin I can't help but flash.

Evan leans in slightly, the smirk still playing at his lips, but there's a flicker in his eyes—a hesitation that feels almost painfully familiar. "Maybe," he admits, his voice barely above a whisper. "Maybe I like the risk. The not knowing."

I tilt my head, studying him, and for the first time, I see it—the vulnerability beneath the surface, the uncertainty he tries so hard to mask with his easy smile and guarded demeanor. It's there, lurking in the shadows of his gaze, and it makes my chest tighten in a way I can't explain.

"I'm not going anywhere," I say, my voice soft, steady. I don't know if it's a promise or a plea. But the words feel true, even if I'm not entirely sure of what it is we're doing, what we're heading toward.

Evan doesn't respond right away. Instead, he tightens his grip on my hand, his fingers pressing into mine like he's trying to anchor himself, like he's afraid to let go. The air between us shifts, and I wonder if this is it. If this is the moment we stop pretending and start whatever it is that's been simmering beneath the surface.

But then, just as the silence grows unbearable, he leans back, breaking the connection between us, and I feel an unexpected sting of disappointment. His hand falls away from mine, and for a brief second, I wonder if I've done something wrong, said something wrong, to make him pull back.

His eyes flicker to the side, a familiar wariness settling over his features. "I'm not good at this," he admits, his voice rough. "At being... open. Vulnerable."

I swallow, the lump in my throat suddenly heavy. I don't know what to say, don't know how to fix whatever's broken before it even had a chance to start. All I know is that I don't want him to retreat, to shut me out again.

"I'm not asking you to be perfect," I say, my voice steady even though my heart is hammering in my chest. "I just want you to be real. With me."

Evan looks at me then, his eyes searching mine, looking for something I'm not sure I can give him. But in that moment, I realize that maybe I've been searching for the same thing. Maybe we're both just two people standing on the edge of something we're not ready to face.

He leans forward again, but this time, it's different. It's not a question of if, but when. His lips brush against mine, the kiss tentative at first, as if he's unsure how far to go. But when I don't pull away, when I lean into him, the kiss deepens, and the world narrows to just the two of us.

For a moment, I lose myself in him. The kiss is slow, almost lazy in its intensity, but it's enough to make everything else fade away. The doubts, the hesitation, all of it disappears into the sensation of his lips against mine, of his hand finding the small of my back and pulling me closer.

When we finally break apart, we're both breathing hard, our foreheads resting against each other. I can feel the heat of his skin, the thrum of his pulse beneath my fingertips. For a moment, I don't know what to say. I don't know how to explain what just happened, or if I even need to. But I can feel the shift between us, the unspoken promise of something more.

But then, just as I start to breathe a little easier, just as I start to believe that maybe we've finally crossed whatever line was keeping us apart, the door to his apartment creaks open.

And just like that, everything shatters.

Evan freezes, his body going tense as he pulls away, the warmth between us instantly disappearing. I glance toward the door, unsure of who's standing there, but the sharp intake of breath from Evan tells me that whatever's about to happen, it's going to change everything.

Chapter 19: The Arsonist's Game

The air smelled like smoke, heavy and cloying, as though the fire itself had seeped into the very fabric of the world. The sky, once a clear canvas of deepening blue, was now a muted haze, dusted with the ashy remnants of what had burned away. I stepped through the charred remains of what had once been a home—a sanctuary, a place of laughter, warmth, and life—and all that was left now was destruction, a sprawling landscape of scorched earth and twisted metal. The fire had taken it all, every trace of what had made this house a home, leaving only the faint scent of cedarwood and burnt dreams behind.

Evan's jaw was clenched, his eyes fixed on the wreckage, the fury in them so intense it practically crackled in the air. His friend—his oldest friend, the one who had once pulled him from the wreckage of a burning car years ago—had been reduced to little more than a smoldering memory. It wasn't just the house that had been destroyed, but a part of Evan himself, something buried deep inside him that I'd seen flicker in those rare moments of vulnerability. Now, it was all rage. I could feel it in every breath he took, the tension in his broad shoulders, the way his fists were clenched at his sides.

I stood beside him, my own heart beating an erratic rhythm of fear and frustration. The anger inside me was like a wildfire of its own, igniting every nerve, every thought. Whoever had done this, whoever had lit that match and turned this life into nothing but ruin, was still out there, somewhere, hiding in the shadows of their own twisted mind. My hand twitched at my side, a reflex, an instinct. I wanted to track them down, to hunt them, to bring justice the only way I knew how—by making them feel every ounce of the devastation they'd caused.

But Evan wasn't ready to talk about that. Not yet. His voice was low, controlled, as though every word had to be measured, weighed against the violent emotions warring inside him. "I'm going after them. I'm going to make them pay."

"Evan," I whispered, taking a step closer. The gravel crunched beneath my boots as I crossed the space between us. "We can't go in blind. You know that. We need a plan."

He didn't look at me, but I could feel his anger swirling around me, wrapping itself around my chest like a noose. It was a dangerous thing, this fire inside him. A thing I couldn't let consume him. Not when we were this close, not when I could still see the man I loved buried beneath the fury.

"I don't care about a plan," he muttered, his voice rough, like it was being dragged across shards of glass. "I care about stopping them. And I won't wait."

I saw the flicker in his eyes then—the same look he'd given me that first night we met, when the world had been black and the city had felt so heavy on our shoulders. It was the same mixture of determination and something darker, something wild. The kind of look that made you believe there was nothing he wouldn't do to protect the people he loved.

But it was also the kind of look that scared me. And it wasn't the kind of thing I wanted to see right now, not when everything we'd fought for could unravel with one rash decision.

"Evan," I said again, this time more firmly, placing my hand on his arm, feeling the tremor beneath his skin. "Listen to me. I know how you feel. But we need to do this right. We need to understand who we're dealing with, how they think. You can't just rush in. You'll get yourself killed."

His eyes finally met mine, and in them, I saw the internal war playing out—a battle between the rage that had driven him for so long and the quieter part of him that still listened to reason. His lips pressed into a thin line, and for a long moment, neither of us said anything. The sounds of distant sirens and the crackling of embers were the only things filling the space between us.

"Do you think they're still here?" I asked quietly, trying to change the subject, if only for a moment, to distract him from the darkness I could feel creeping over him.

He didn't respond right away, but I saw the shift in his posture. He was thinking, his mind whirring through possibilities. The arsonist had gotten bolder, more reckless, leaving behind nothing but destruction in their wake. Whoever they were, they had a message to send, and they were playing a dangerous game. And we were right in the middle of it.

Finally, Evan shook his head. "No. I think they've moved on. But we need to be ready. They'll be back. This isn't over."

I nodded, though the weight of those words settled heavily between us. There was something deeply unsettling about the idea of this person watching from afar, knowing they had the power to destroy everything Evan held dear. Knowing they'd already done it once, and they'd do it again.

The smoke still lingered in the air, a constant reminder of the devastation that had unfolded here. But as the last of the fire trucks began to pull away, and the flicker of the flames gave way to the quiet hum of a town in mourning, I knew one thing for certain: we weren't done yet. Not by a long shot.

We didn't speak much after that. The hours bled into one another, a slow crawl through the haze of that devastated neighborhood, while my mind churned with possibilities. I couldn't shake the image of the flames licking the sky, the crackle of wood and the soft pop of embers as they broke free. Something about the way the fire had spread, the particular patterns it had left behind, made it feel like this wasn't just an act of destruction—it was something more, something personal.

I wasn't sure when we got back to the house. Or when the tension between us became so thick it was suffocating. But by the time the front door closed behind us, I realized how badly my hands were shaking. I didn't think about how to hide it. Evan didn't either.

He moved across the room with purpose, grabbing the whiskey bottle from the cabinet. The way his hand gripped it, almost possessive, told me everything I needed to know about the storm brewing inside him. I sat at the kitchen table, trying to keep my mind on the simple act of breathing, trying to push away the image of that burning house. I could hear the sound of the bottle being unscrewed, followed by the sharp clink of the glass. His footsteps were heavy, but they didn't sound like someone who was walking toward me—they were more like footsteps of someone trying to escape from whatever it was that was chasing them.

"You want a drink?" he asked, his voice rough, more gruff than usual.

I shook my head, not trusting myself to speak. The air between us was thick, charged with everything unsaid, everything dangerous that neither of us was ready to acknowledge.

He took a long swig from his glass and stared at the wall, but not really at it. His eyes were distant, focusing on something far beyond the familiar surroundings of the kitchen. The silence stretched out for what felt like an eternity. I hated that silence, because in it, I could hear the weight of his thoughts pressing down on him. The weight of a thousand questions, the anger, the loss, and worst of all, the helplessness that was eating away at him.

"Do you think I'm crazy?" His question came out of nowhere, and for a moment, I wasn't sure if I was supposed to answer.

"What?" I blinked, thrown off guard.

He took another drink, his eyes never leaving the spot on the wall where a picture of us once hung, now missing. "I mean, look at us. We're chasing ghosts. I'm chasing fire. All because some sick bastard wants to play games. I don't know if I'm ready for this anymore." His voice was softer now, less controlled. Vulnerability bled through the cracks of his carefully built walls, and it sent a shiver up my spine.

I stood up, pushing the chair back with a scrape that filled the silence like an accusation. "I don't think you're crazy. I think you're angry, and I think you're scared."

The truth hung in the air between us, delicate yet sharp, like glass poised to shatter at the slightest touch.

He exhaled through his nose, a short, frustrated breath, but this time when he looked at me, there was something else behind the fury. Something darker. Something raw. "What if we don't catch him? What if this keeps happening, and it gets worse? What happens to us then?"

I knew the answer, but I wasn't ready to give it voice. The arsonist had already proven he was capable of pushing limits we hadn't even considered. If he wasn't done, if there was no reason behind what he was doing, it could get worse. Much worse. And we were both too close to the fire, too entangled in it, to walk away now.

"I don't know," I said, my voice barely above a whisper. "But we'll fight. We won't just stand by and watch."

Evan's gaze softened, just slightly, but the tension in his jaw remained. His hand rested on the edge of the counter as if holding on to something that wasn't really there. I wanted to reach for him, to pull him out of the abyss of his thoughts, but I didn't know how to. The silence grew heavy once more, stretching long between us like a taut wire, until I finally broke it with the question that had been eating away at me for hours.

"Why are you so afraid of what happens if we don't catch him?"

Evan didn't look up at first. When he did, his eyes were stormy, filled with a thousand unspoken words. "Because, what if it never ends? What if this is the thing I can't fix? I've been able to fight everything else, but this... I don't know if I can stop this."

I didn't say anything at first. What was there to say? I understood that fear all too well, the kind that settled in your bones and refused to leave. The kind that didn't let you sleep at night.

"You're not alone in this," I finally said, my voice quiet but firm. I took a step toward him, but stopped when he held up a hand.

"I don't want you to get hurt."

"You don't get to decide that for me," I said, my own voice sharp, sharper than I intended. "I'm here because I want to be. I'm not going anywhere."

The words hit the air between us like a challenge, and for a moment, there was nothing but the raw energy between us, crackling like an unspoken promise. Evan didn't respond right away, but I could see the muscles in his shoulders relax, just the slightest bit. As if he'd been holding on for so long, and now, he wasn't alone anymore.

"Then let's do this," he said, his voice low and steady again, like the storm inside him had passed, just for a moment.

It wasn't the calm before the storm. It was the storm, finally contained.

The morning light didn't feel like light at all. It felt heavy, a weight pressing down on my chest as I stood at the foot of Evan's driveway, watching him pace like a caged animal. His fists were clenched, his jaw working against some invisible restraint, but there was something in his movement—something jerky and tight—that made it clear he wasn't sure where to go next. And neither was I.

We'd spent the last few hours gathering our thoughts, piecing together the ruins of what was left after the fire, trying to make sense of the pattern the arsonist had left behind. But it wasn't just the fire we were chasing now—it was the idea of it. The weight of what had happened. The ghosts of his friend's home, the place where laughter had once echoed off the walls, where memories had been built brick by brick, now reduced to ash. That's what we were up against. Not just a person with a match and a death wish, but a phantom haunting the edges of our lives.

"You're quiet," Evan said, not looking at me. His voice was strained, low, like he was trying to keep it from snapping in two.

"I'm thinking," I said. I wasn't. I was just watching him, watching the way his frustration coiled in his movements, the way he seemed on the verge of exploding into a thousand pieces. It was clear that the plan to track down the arsonist, to bring him to justice, had become more of a personal vendetta for Evan than I was ready for.

"About what?" he asked, glancing over at me, the first real acknowledgement of my presence since we left the scene of the fire. His eyes were dark, still that storm swirling beneath the surface, but the question was genuine. He was looking for a way out of this mess we'd found ourselves in, and I wasn't sure I had the answer he wanted.

I chewed on my lip for a second, glancing at the gravel beneath my boots. I wanted to say something to calm him down, something that would make him feel like he wasn't alone in all this, but I wasn't sure how. What was the point of speaking if the words couldn't fix anything?

"Do you ever wonder," I began slowly, "why someone would do this?"

Evan stopped pacing. The question hit him like a slap in the face. He didn't respond immediately, just stood there, staring at the ground as though searching for some meaning beneath the dirt. His silence was a weight. The kind that settled deep in your bones.

"What do you mean?" His voice came out rough, like he hadn't quite processed what I was asking.

"I mean, this isn't just about the destruction. This person... they want something from us. Something more than just fire and ruin."

He snorted, the sound bitter, almost sarcastic. "What's that supposed to mean?"

I glanced at him, meeting his eyes, but there was no anger there, not this time. Just exhaustion. "It's a game to them. They know we're watching, Evan. They're trying to make us jump through hoops, to chase something that doesn't make sense. They're making us burn."

The realization hung in the air for a moment, the silence pressing down like a weight I couldn't ignore. And then, finally, Evan spoke again, his voice quieter this time, as if the idea had settled into his bones.

"I hate feeling like I'm not in control." His words were slow, deliberate, as if he was testing them in the air before committing.

"I know," I replied, my voice soft. "But that's what they want. To make us feel powerless. To turn the tables on us."

There was a long pause, and then Evan moved, faster than I expected. He crossed the distance between us in two steps, his face close to mine, and for a split second, I thought he was going to push me away. Instead, he stopped just short, his breath heavy on my face, and for the first time in hours, his eyes seemed to clear, as though he was seeing me for the first time.

"I don't want you to get hurt," he said, and there was a desperation in his voice that I wasn't prepared for.

"I'm not some delicate thing you need to protect," I shot back, a little too quickly, the words out before I could stop them.

He paused, studying my face for a long moment, as though he could see the way the fire had already taken root inside me, the way I was already too far gone to turn back now. I wasn't sure if he was trying to decide whether to push me away or pull me closer, but I wasn't ready to let him make that decision for me.

"I know you're not," he finally said, his voice calmer now, almost apologetic. "But this—this thing we're doing, it's dangerous."

"I'm aware," I replied, a small smile tugging at my lips. "I'm not exactly known for making safe choices."

He chuckled, though it was dark and short-lived, like the sound had been squeezed out of him. He ran a hand through his hair, and I could see the frustration building again, like the storm inside him was gathering speed. "I don't know how much longer I can keep pretending like I'm not the one who caused all of this."

His words hit me like a physical blow. I blinked, taken aback by the rawness of it. "What?"

Evan turned away, his back stiff, his shoulders tight with the weight of something I wasn't sure I understood. "I should've known something was coming. I should've stopped it before it reached this point. If I hadn't—"

"Don't." The word slipped out before I could stop it, the sharpness in my tone making him freeze. I wasn't sure what had made me snap, but the idea that Evan would blame himself for something he couldn't have predicted—it wasn't right. "None of this is your fault."

His eyes flicked to mine, and in them, I saw the self-recrimination, the guilt that had been eating him alive for days. But before he could say anything else, the sound of a phone vibrating broke through the tension.

I fished mine out of my pocket, my heart leaping into my throat when I saw the text.

"Check the perimeter. He's been here."

I didn't need to ask who the "he" was. The arsonist had just taken his game to a new level. And now, it was our turn to move.

Evan grabbed my arm before I could take a step. "No," he said, his voice low, but firm. "We're not going in blind."

I met his eyes, the intensity between us crackling like a live wire. "We don't have a choice."

And that's when I heard it—the soft sound of footsteps coming toward us from behind.

Chapter 20: Whispers of Betrayal

The scent of stale coffee clung to the air in the dimly lit office, mixing with the sharp tang of burnt paper that lingered from the fire weeks ago. Evan sat across from me, his fingers drumming on the edge of the desk in a rhythm that echoed the restless energy building between us. His jaw was tight, the muscle in his cheek twitching with every breath he took, but it wasn't his usual, controlled manner. This was different. This was tension. A crack in the mask.

"You're quiet," I said, the words falling out without thought. The silence had stretched between us long enough to feel like a weight. His eyes flickered up to mine, the dark circles under them deepening, making him appear older than his years.

"I'm thinking," he replied, his voice too even, too calm for the storm brewing underneath. He looked away, eyes flicking to the window where the pale light of the setting sun filtered through the blinds, casting long shadows across the room.

I leaned back in my chair, the creak of the leather sending a shiver through the air. We had been chasing this lead for weeks, pulling at threads that seemed to vanish as soon as we grasped them. Every time we thought we had something solid, it slipped through our fingers like sand. I hated this. I hated the uncertainty gnawing at the edges of my mind, the questions that kept popping up like weeds in a garden I couldn't keep under control.

"You're telling me the department is divided," I said slowly, choosing my words carefully. "But you haven't told me why." It was more accusation than question, though I didn't mean it to be.

Evan looked at me then, really looked at me, and for a moment, I saw something I hadn't expected—fear. The tiniest flicker of it, but enough to send a chill down my spine. He exhaled, rubbing the back of his neck, and I could see the weight of the situation pressing down on him.

"People are... unsure," he said, his voice tight. "They don't know where to draw the line anymore. Some think it's all a case of arson gone wrong. Others think it's personal. Someone's feeding the firebug information, but no one knows who. And there's..." He trailed off, his lips pressing into a thin line. "There's the possibility that one of us is the mole."

I froze, the words settling over me like a heavy cloak. A mole. I swallowed hard, trying to push past the sudden tightness in my chest. The thought of someone in the department, someone I had trusted, turning on us was unfathomable. But then again, I had learned the hard way that betrayal could wear the face of anyone, even the people closest to you.

"Is that what you think?" I asked, my voice almost a whisper, betraying the unease gnawing at me.

Evan didn't answer immediately. Instead, he sat back in his chair, running a hand over his face. His shoulders sagged, as if the weight of the situation was finally taking its toll on him. The cracks in his facade were becoming more apparent, and I couldn't help but wonder just how deep this thing went.

"I don't know," he admitted, his gaze drifting back to me, filled with something I couldn't quite read. "I'm not sure who to trust anymore." His words hung in the air, thick with the implications of what he was saying. And then, just when I thought he might say more, he stood up abruptly, his chair scraping against the floor. "I have to go. There's more to this than we're seeing, and I can't figure it out from here. We need to find out who's been playing both sides."

I watched him leave, the door clicking shut behind him, and for the first time since this whole mess began, I felt completely alone.

The office was suddenly too quiet, the hum of the fluorescent lights overhead too loud, as if the room itself was holding its breath. I ran a hand through my hair, a nervous habit I had picked up in the last few weeks, and glanced at the pile of notes on my desk. The investigation had started as a simple arson case, but now, it felt like we were uncovering something much darker, something that twisted its way into the very core of the department.

I grabbed my jacket and headed for the door, the cool air of the hallway a sharp contrast to the stuffiness of the office. Outside, the city was alive with the sounds of traffic and the distant hum of life moving at its usual pace, indifferent to the chaos unfolding within the walls of that office. But to me, the world felt different now. I was no longer certain who I could trust. The cracks in Evan's story had already started to show, and I had no idea whether he was hiding something from me or if he, too, was being played.

The question of loyalty, of truth, weighed heavily on my mind as I made my way to the car. My fingers clenched around the steering wheel, the leather cold under my fingertips. This wasn't just about an arsonist anymore. This was about a betrayal, one that was creeping closer with every passing moment. And as much as I wanted to believe Evan, there was a nagging feeling in the pit of my stomach, telling me that the truth was far more complicated than I could have ever imagined.

I pulled out of the parking lot, the city lights blurring as I drove, trying to piece together the puzzle. But the harder I tried, the more the pieces refused to fit. The investigation had taken on a life of its own, and I was left struggling to keep up, all while wondering just how much of the story Evan was keeping from me.

The night air hit me like a slap as I stepped out of the car, the kind of crisp chill that sneaks past your jacket, settles in your bones, and lingers for hours. I hugged my coat tighter around me, wishing I could somehow push the doubts that had begun to knot inside my chest. I had never been one to question Evan, but now, the silence between us felt different. He wasn't just a partner anymore, not in the way I had once thought. He was a puzzle, and with every piece I thought I had figured out, another one seemed to vanish.

I made my way down the street, the click of my heels echoing against the sidewalk, the city alive in all its restless energy. The lights were a blur of yellow and white, and the low hum of conversation from nearby cafes seemed out of place, given the chaos I was feeling inside. I wasn't just looking for answers about the case anymore—I was looking for answers about him, about everything he had yet to say. His half-truths. The way he looked at me when I asked him the hard questions.

There was a bar just around the corner, a quiet little place where we had met a few months ago, back when the world was simpler, when we were still just two people figuring things out. The bartender knew me by name, a smile that was familiar but not overbearing. I didn't need to explain myself; he just slid a glass of whiskey across the counter before I could even sit down. I hadn't ordered it, but then again, I hadn't come here for a drink. I'd come here for clarity.

The burn of alcohol was sharp on my tongue, but the heat didn't quite match the cold running through my veins. I had never imagined myself tangled up in something like this—some personal vendetta that seemed to stretch back further than the fire itself. I wasn't naive enough to think people's loyalties were always pure, but I'd never expected betrayal to come so close to home.

I took another sip, the whiskey doing little to ease the anxiety crawling beneath my skin. If it was true, if there really was someone in the department feeding information to the arsonist, it was only a matter of time before everything came crashing down. But who? The list of suspects felt like a sea of faces, all blurring into one—a series of people I had trusted, who had all seemed so... so solid. But the truth was, no one was invincible. No one could wear that mask forever.

A voice behind me pulled me from my thoughts, low and grating, and I didn't need to turn around to know who it was.

"You don't look like you're here for a drink," Carl said, his tone a mix of curiosity and concern, as he took the seat beside me. He was a detective from the same unit, a friend of Evan's before all of this had started, and while I couldn't claim we were exactly close, he had a way of reading people, of reading me, that left me feeling exposed. His eyes flicked to the glass in front of me, the unspoken question hanging between us.

"Just thinking," I muttered, swirling the drink in my hand, watching the amber liquid catch the light.

Carl wasn't the kind to push, but he could sense when something wasn't right. He leaned back in his chair, studying me for a moment before speaking again. "Evan's in a bad place. You know that, right?"

I didn't respond right away, unsure of where the conversation was heading. Was this about the investigation, or was it something more? I couldn't tell anymore. Carl wasn't an idiot, and Evan's moods had become harder to ignore. But then, Carl had always had an odd way of speaking without saying much.

"He's a stubborn guy, but he means well," Carl continued, his voice lowering to match the intimacy of the moment. "I think he's just... worried. He doesn't like seeing things slip out of his control. Especially not something like this." He paused, his eyes darting around as if ensuring no one was listening in. "I don't know if I can say this, but..." Another pause. "He thinks someone's got it out for him."

I sat up straighter, the words hitting me harder than I expected. "What do you mean? Someone in the department?"

Carl hesitated, then nodded slowly. "Could be. It's hard to say. There are whispers, you know? About who's been leaking info to the firebug. A lot of fingers pointing, but no one willing to take the heat. And Evan..." He trailed off, his gaze moving toward the door as though he was suddenly aware of the distance between us. "You should talk to him. He's... been keeping things from you, I think. Not because he wants to, but because he doesn't want you in the line of fire."

The implication settled between us like a brick, and for a moment, I couldn't quite breathe. I had trusted Evan more than I had trusted anyone in a long time. To hear that Carl thought he was hiding something—it wasn't just unsettling; it was like a gut punch. And the worst part? Part of me didn't want to hear it. I didn't want to believe that he could be keeping secrets from me, that his stonewalling was more than just a protective instinct.

"I'll talk to him," I said, the words coming out more curt than I intended. Carl's eyes narrowed, but he didn't push me further. Instead, he gave me a knowing look—one that said, I told you so, but in the gentlest way possible.

I finished my drink in silence, the world outside the window seeming to pulse with a rhythm I couldn't match. The truth was, I was on the edge of something, teetering between trust and doubt, and I wasn't sure how to stop myself from falling. The pieces were slipping away, faster now, and I didn't know if I had the strength to put them back together. But I would try. For Evan. For whatever had brought us here.

Because deep down, I didn't want to believe that everything I had built with him could be a lie.

The apartment was quiet when I arrived, the kind of quiet that presses in on you, fills the spaces between your thoughts and makes everything feel a little too heavy. I kicked off my shoes by the door and made my way to the kitchen, the dim light casting long shadows across the room. The day had been a blur of questions and half-answers, each one more convoluted than the last. I should have felt relieved to be away from the noise of the investigation, but instead, it was like everything was closing in on me. I couldn't escape it, no matter how hard I tried.

I opened the fridge without thinking, grabbing a bottle of wine that had been sitting there for too long. The label promised something complex, something bold, but I wasn't in the mood for complexity. I poured myself a glass, the deep red liquid catching the light like liquid fire, and took a long sip.

I hadn't heard from Evan since our conversation in the office, and I found that strange, but not surprising. He wasn't one to offer explanations without a reason, and when he did, they were never the whole truth. There had been something in his eyes earlier—something guarded, something distant—that told me he wasn't ready to let me in on everything. And I hated it.

I leaned back against the counter, swirling the wine, my thoughts spinning in the dark spaces between the sips. It wasn't just the investigation that had me on edge. It was Evan, his sudden detachment, his refusal to open up, even now, when everything was falling apart. Carl's words kept echoing in my mind: He's hiding something from you.

I set the glass down a little too forcefully, the sharp clink of it on the counter snapping me out of my thoughts. I didn't know if Carl was right. I didn't want to believe him. But part of me knew that I couldn't keep ignoring the signs—the way Evan had pulled away, the secrecy, the way he'd thrown out half-truths as though they were shields.

I needed answers, and I couldn't keep waiting for him to provide them.

The phone rang just then, cutting through the silence like a knife. I glanced at the screen, my heart skipping a beat when I saw Evan's name flashing.

I picked it up, trying to sound casual. "Hey, you."

There was a pause on the other end, a long stretch of silence that made me wonder if he was going to hang up. But then his voice came through, low and strained, as though he was fighting against something just out of reach.

"I need to see you," he said, the words rushed, almost desperate.

The urgency in his voice sent a spike of unease through me, but it also made my pulse quicken, like a signal that something was finally moving, something was about to shift.

"Where?" I asked, the question almost slipping out before I could stop myself.

"Just... meet me at the old warehouse. The one by the docks. I'll explain everything. I swear."

I hesitated, the wine still sitting in front of me, the taste of it now sour on my tongue. There was something about the location he'd chosen—quiet, isolated, out of the way—that made my instincts scream. But then, another part of me, the one that always wanted to believe in him, pushed those doubts aside.

"I'll be there in twenty," I said, my voice steady despite the nerves tightening my stomach.

The call ended abruptly, and I stared at the screen for a moment, trying to read between the lines of his words. What did he need to tell me that couldn't wait? Why this place, of all places? The warehouse by the docks had always been a place for people who didn't want to be found, a place where deals were made in the shadows. I hadn't been there in months, and I had no real reason to go back now, except for him.

The wine wasn't helping anymore, so I grabbed my jacket and hurried out the door, the cool night air biting at my skin as I made my way to the car. The engine purred to life, and I drove, the streets blurring past me, my mind a whirlwind of questions. Was this a trap? Had Evan finally reached the point where he couldn't keep lying to me? Or was he being led into something deeper, something darker, than either of us could have anticipated?

The drive felt endless, the city's skyline looming in the distance as the familiar landmarks passed by in a haze. When I finally reached the docks, the air was thick with salt and the distant sound of waves crashing against the shore. The warehouse stood ahead of me, looming like a sentinel in the dark, its windows dark and empty, as if it had been abandoned for years.

I parked a little ways off, the tires crunching on the gravel as I stepped out of the car. My breath misted in front of me, and I could feel my heart pounding in my chest, the adrenaline coursing through my veins. This was it. Whatever was about to happen here, it would change everything.

I walked toward the entrance of the warehouse, my footsteps echoing in the stillness of the night. The door creaked as I pushed it open, the smell of rust and old wood filling my nose. Inside, the place was almost pitch black, save for the slivers of moonlight that filtered through the cracks in the walls.

I took another step, the sound of my breathing the only thing breaking the silence. And then I heard it—footsteps. Slow, deliberate, and just close enough to make my skin crawl.

I turned, my pulse racing, but no one was there.

A voice, low and cold, came from the darkness. "You shouldn't have come."

It was Evan's voice, but it wasn't right. There was something wrong in the way he said it, something too flat, too distant.

I felt a chill settle in my bones, and before I could react, I heard another sound—this one closer, sharper. The sound of a gun being cocked.

And then everything went black.

Chapter 21: The Heat Between Us

The evening air was thick with a tension that could almost be tasted, heavy and sticky, like honey left too long in the sun. I pushed the strands of hair that had escaped my ponytail back into place, but it didn't matter. The heat of the day was still hanging on, pressing against my skin, crawling under my clothes, making the smallest movements feel like a betrayal of every cell in my body. The office was empty now, save for the click of the keyboard and the occasional shuffle of paper as I sifted through the mountain of files in front of me.

Evan was sitting at the desk across from mine, the light from his laptop casting a pale glow on his face, softening the sharp edges I'd become so familiar with. He had always been this person to me—intense, focused, driven to a fault. But there was something different tonight, something raw in the way his jaw clenched whenever he glanced at me. It wasn't the usual unapproachable determination. No, it was more like... hunger. The kind you feel when you've been starved for too long, and finally, there's something to feast on.

I thought I could ignore it. I thought I could keep my distance, keep my focus on the work that had brought us together in the first place. But the way his gaze lingered, tracing the curve of my neck as I adjusted my shirt, made it impossible. And then, in the quiet of the office, with only the hum of fluorescent lights above us and the distant chatter of the city outside, Evan's patience snapped.

He was across the room in an instant, too fast for me to process, too quick for my body to react. Before I knew it, I was caught—his hands on my arms, pulling me to him, his breath hot against my ear as he whispered something I didn't quite catch.

The words didn't matter. They were nothing compared to the pressure of his lips on mine, urgent and demanding. It was like a dam had broken, releasing a flood of emotions I hadn't even known I was capable of feeling. The heat between us was unmistakable, like a spark igniting a fire that had been smoldering beneath the surface for far too long.

I didn't know when I had surrendered to it—when I had stopped fighting and started pulling him closer, needing more. But somewhere, in that chaotic moment, I found myself wrapped around him, my hands tangled in the fabric of his shirt as if he might slip away if I let go.

He tasted like coffee and something richer, darker, like the kind of warmth that burns you alive and leaves you wanting more. His lips moved over mine with a desperation that matched the pounding of my heart, and for a few moments, it was just the two of us—no work, no deadlines, no reason to stop.

But as quickly as it had started, it came to an end. His hands released me, and I was left standing there, breathless and disoriented, like I had been caught in a storm. Evan stepped back, his eyes suddenly avoiding mine, as if the very act of looking at me might shatter something inside him.

I could feel the distance creeping between us, the room shrinking, as if he had put up invisible walls around himself. The warmth that had pulsed between us now felt like a ghost—fading, slipping through my fingers. I opened my mouth to say something, but the words died before they could leave my throat.

For a moment, all I could do was stand there, the aftermath of everything that had just happened pressing on me like an unspoken question. I wasn't sure what was worse—the kiss, the sudden shift in his demeanor, or the gnawing sense that I had just been pulled into something far deeper and more complicated than I could handle.

"Evan?" I finally managed to whisper, but the way his eyes flicked to mine, then away again, told me everything I needed to know. The spark that had flared between us had ignited something neither of us were ready to confront.

"I didn't mean—" he started, then paused, his words as jagged as the silence that followed. He ran a hand through his hair, and I could see the frustration bubbling just beneath the surface. "I didn't mean to make things... complicated."

Complicated? The word hung in the air like a challenge. My heart was still racing, but my mind was reeling. What had just happened? Was it a mistake? Was it something he regretted already?

"You don't get to decide that for me," I said, the sharpness in my voice surprising even me.

He froze, his face hardening. "You think I want this? Want this..." He motioned between us, his fingers twitching, unsure of what to do. "We don't exactly fit, do we?"

I wanted to argue—wanted to throw back every excuse I could think of. But deep down, I understood. The tension between us had always been something that hovered in the background, something neither of us had dared acknowledge. And now that it had been pulled into the light, there was no ignoring it. The truth, no matter how inconvenient, was staring us in the face.

We couldn't be what we wanted to be—not now, not with the world we had built around us. There were too many things left unsaid, too many walls built up between us that couldn't just be torn down in a single kiss.

I turned away before I could say anything else. My chest ached, but I couldn't let him see it. Not now. I wasn't sure if I wanted to be angry at him, angry at myself, or just angry at the entire situation.

But when I heard his footsteps behind me, I knew—this wasn't over. Not by a long shot. The fire between us had only just begun to burn.

The silence between us was like a heavy fog, the kind that presses down on your chest, thick and suffocating. My skin still hummed with the memory of his touch, but that was fading, disappearing into the space that had suddenly opened up between us. I couldn't look at him—not yet. If I did, I was afraid the vulnerability would spill out, like water rushing over a dam, and I wasn't sure I was ready to drown in it.

I focused on the sound of my own breath, the rush of air that wasn't quite as steady as I wanted it to be. The tension had settled around us like a second skin, the kind you can't peel off without tearing something in the process. And I wasn't sure either of us was ready to do that, not yet.

I turned my head slightly, catching a glimpse of him in the corner of my eye. Evan was standing by the window now, his back to me, his posture rigid, as though he was holding himself together by sheer force of will. He had a way of pulling away like that, retreating into himself when things got too close. When emotions got too messy.

"Why do you do that?" I found myself asking, my voice quieter than I'd intended. There was no anger in it, just a thread of confusion that I couldn't seem to shake. "Why pull away like you're afraid of something? You can't keep doing this, Evan."

He didn't answer right away, and I hated how that silence seemed to stretch out longer than it should have. It made my chest tighten, the words hanging in the air like an unspoken question. Finally, he turned, but his eyes never quite met mine. They were focused on the floor, his jaw tight, as though he were chewing over every word.

"I'm not afraid," he said, but there was an edge to his voice, a sharpness that didn't quite match his words. "I just don't... I don't want to mess things up."

I blinked, the words hitting me like a punch in the gut. "What things, Evan? What do you think you're going to mess up?"

He shook his head, a tight smile tugging at the corner of his lips, but it didn't reach his eyes. "Everything," he said, his voice softening just a fraction, enough that I could almost believe him. "I don't want to screw this up."

This... what? The kiss? The fire we'd just ignited between us? Or was he talking about something else entirely? Something deeper, something that had been festering beneath the surface long before we'd ever crossed paths.

I stood there, frozen for a moment, watching him struggle with whatever battle he was waging inside. I wanted to reach out, to pull him back into the warmth we'd just shared, but something told me he wasn't ready for that. Not yet.

"I don't need you to have all the answers," I said finally, my voice steady, despite the uncertainty swirling inside me. "I just need you to stop running from this. From me."

He looked at me then, really looked at me, and for the first time since everything had shifted, I saw the cracks in his armor. The vulnerability that he tried so hard to keep hidden. "I don't know how not to," he admitted, his voice almost a whisper. "I've been doing it for so long, I don't even remember what it feels like to let someone in without worrying they'll just leave."

The words stung, though I knew they weren't meant to hurt. He wasn't talking about me. He was talking about something that had happened before I'd entered his life—something that had shaped him into this man who could pull me close one minute and shut me out the next.

I didn't know the specifics, didn't need to. But I could feel the weight of it, the layers of grief and regret that clouded the air around him. I stepped closer, my hand instinctively reaching out, but I stopped myself just before I touched him. The last thing I wanted was to force him into something he wasn't ready for.

"I'm not going anywhere," I said, trying to make my voice as steady as his had been. "You're not alone in this."

He didn't respond right away. Instead, he closed his eyes for a brief moment, his hand resting against the edge of the desk like it might anchor him to the present, to something real. When he opened them again, there was a rawness in his gaze that sent a shiver down my spine.

"You think I don't know that?" he asked softly. "I do. But that doesn't make it any easier. You're too good for me, and I'm not sure I know how to handle that."

I laughed, a short, sharp sound that felt almost foreign coming from me. "Good? You think I'm good?" I shook my head, disbelief coloring my words. "I'm a mess, Evan. A complete and total mess. But if I can figure out how to let someone in, so can you."

He sighed, a deep, weary sound that made my heart ache for him. "I'm not asking for a perfect solution. I don't need you to fix me." His gaze softened then, almost tender. "I just need you to stop pushing me away. Just... be here. With me. If that's possible."

The simplicity of the request, the way he framed it as though it was the hardest thing in the world, made everything inside me settle. Maybe we didn't need to have it all figured out. Maybe all we needed was to stay in the same place, to not let go, even when it seemed easier to do so.

"Alright," I said quietly, my voice a little shaky. "I'll be here. I'm not going anywhere."

His lips curved up into a small, genuine smile, the kind that didn't try to hide the cracks. "Good," he murmured. "Then let's just... take it one step at a time."

I watched him move, the stillness of the room stretching between us, filled with unsaid things that felt like they might explode at any moment. He was at the desk now, his fingers drumming on the edge of his laptop, his gaze fixed on the screen in front of him as if the numbers and letters on it could offer him some kind of escape.

I wanted to scream at him, shake him out of whatever thought prison he had locked himself in, but I swallowed the urge. He was as far away from me as if we were miles apart. Every inch of him seemed closed off, sealed tight like the vault of a bank, keeping everything that mattered hidden. I could feel the walls he'd built up, thick and unyielding, and it frustrated me.

"Tell me what's going on in that head of yours," I said, forcing the words out before the silence suffocated me. My voice was low, almost tentative, but I wasn't sure why. I wasn't afraid of him, but I was afraid of what I'd see if he ever truly opened up.

He stiffened at the sound of my voice, and I immediately regretted it. The air between us thickened, and I could almost hear the click of his internal lock turning. "It's nothing," he said, his tone flat and practiced, like he'd said it a hundred times before.

But I wasn't buying it. Not this time. Not after everything that had passed between us.

"Evan." I stepped closer, daring to close the space between us, hoping my presence would pull him back from the edge. "I'm not asking for your life story. But I need to understand why you keep pushing me away."

He didn't look at me, not immediately. He dragged his hand through his hair, exhaling sharply, as if the very act of answering would hurt. "It's not you," he began, his voice tight with something I couldn't name. "It's just... I don't do this. I don't do... us." He finally met my eyes, his gaze dark and stormy, full of a thousand unsaid things. "I don't know how."

"You've got a funny way of showing that," I muttered, trying to keep the bitterness out of my tone, but it slipped through anyway.

"You kiss me like there's no tomorrow, and then act like I'm the one who's complicated."

He winced, the words hitting harder than I intended, but they were out there now, hanging in the air like an accusation. He opened his mouth to respond, but I didn't let him.

"No," I said, holding up my hand. "Don't. Just... stop acting like I'm some kind of liability. Either you want this, or you don't. I'm done with the back-and-forth."

He sighed heavily, as if carrying a weight too heavy to bear. "It's not that simple," he said, his voice strained. "I don't... I don't want to hurt you. And I'm pretty damn good at doing just that."

I scoffed, fighting to keep the sting from my voice. "Hurt me? You've got to be kidding me. I'm not made of glass, Evan." I took a step back, suddenly feeling the full weight of the distance between us, not just physically, but emotionally. The distance that had always been there, no matter how close we got.

His gaze softened, and I hated the pity in it. "You don't even know what it's like," he said, his words barely above a whisper. "The things I've done... the things I've had to do."

I froze, the hairs on the back of my neck standing on end. "What do you mean? What things?"

He didn't answer at first, his mouth pressing into a thin line, like he was waging a silent war with himself. "I can't get into it," he said finally, his voice colder than before. "Some things are better left unsaid."

Something inside me snapped—an instinct that had been building ever since I met him, an urge to push through his walls, to uncover whatever it was that haunted him. I crossed the room in two long strides, my heart racing, a mixture of anger and something else burning in my chest. "No," I said, the word firm and final. "I won't let you do this. If you're not going to let me in, then there's no point in this—in us."

The look he gave me then could have frozen lava. His eyes were dark, unreadable. "You're right. There's no point. Because I'll destroy everything around me if I let you in."

The air in the room seemed to crackle with the intensity of his words, and for a brief moment, the only sound was the frantic beating of my heart, loud and deafening in my ears.

I took a step back, my breath shallow. "Is that what you think? That you're some kind of... monster? That I can't handle whatever it is that makes you act this way?"

His gaze darkened further, and for the first time, I saw the true depth of the battle raging inside him. "I'm not who you think I am," he said quietly. "I'm not the guy you want me to be."

I shook my head, my chest aching. "You don't get to decide who I want. I get to choose that."

A silence stretched between us, thick and suffocating. He looked like he wanted to say something, but the words never came. Instead, he turned away again, his back to me, a final wall between us.

"I don't want you to be disappointed when you figure it out," he said, his voice barely a murmur. "When you find out who I really am."

I opened my mouth to respond, but something stopped me—something in his tone, something in the way his shoulders slumped. It was the kind of finality that made my stomach twist with dread.

And then, just as I was about to say something—anything—his phone rang, cutting through the silence like a knife. He glanced at the screen, his face hardening, and without a word, he picked it up.

"Yeah?" he answered, his voice suddenly businesslike, the walls coming back up.

I stood there, frozen, unable to move or speak as I listened to him, my heart pounding. Something wasn't right. I could feel it, deep in my gut. And when he hung up the phone and turned to me, his expression unreadable, I knew. Whatever he'd been hiding—whatever secret he'd been so afraid of revealing—it was about to surface.

Chapter 22: Ashen Truths

I clicked through the old files on Evan's laptop, the screen's soft glow casting a faint, sickly light across the dark room. It wasn't like me to snoop—really, it wasn't—but I'd started feeling uneasy in a way that wasn't exactly rational. The edges of everything he said had started to fray, unraveling like the cheap seam of a sweater caught on a loose thread. It was supposed to be a quick check, a simple search for a name, but the more I went through his documents, the deeper I sank into the silence between us.

The fire reports weren't labeled with the kind of urgency you'd expect—no bold red warning signs, just a quiet line of text buried in the middle of a folder for 'Non-critical Casework.' I clicked open the first document, letting the air around me still, the scent of old coffee and the faintest trace of cologne lingering in the air. There it was: a case from ten years ago. A fire. A name I didn't recognize.

My fingers stilled as I read through the details, the haze of the past seeping into the present with each word. The arson had been gruesome, the details chilling—a building reduced to ash in minutes, lives lost. But it wasn't just any fire. This one had a story, one that didn't belong to the police or the insurance companies, but to someone I'd never known. His former fiancée.

It hit me like a slow wave, creeping up until I was submerged. This was it. The truth I'd been looking for. Evan's eyes never once strayed toward the past when we spoke about work. Always careful, always guarded. And suddenly, the protective layer of his silence clicked into place. I knew then, without a shadow of a doubt, that I wasn't just dealing with secrets. I was dealing with guilt.

I could hear his voice in the other room, a low murmur as he spoke to someone on the phone. He sounded distant, but there was an edge to his words, something sharp enough to make my stomach churn. The house felt too quiet around me, like it was holding its breath, waiting for me to make the first move. And when I stood up, the floor creaked beneath me, the sound of a thousand small warnings.

I didn't know what I was looking for, only that I needed to know everything. I needed to find that missing piece of the puzzle, the one that had always been just out of reach. The one that would finally explain why he had been so damn protective of me.

The door opened before I could even gather my thoughts, and there he was—tall, broad-shouldered, with a look of someone who'd just had the wind knocked out of them. His eyes immediately went to the screen, to the papers spread out like a confession. He didn't need to ask what I'd found. I could see it in the way his jaw clenched, in the way his hand fisted at his side.

I didn't say anything at first. What was there to say? He wasn't surprised. Not really. He'd known this day would come. I could tell by the quiet regret that wrapped itself around him like a shadow.

"Evan," I said, my voice softer than I wanted it to be. "Why didn't you tell me?"

He walked slowly into the room, a hand running through his hair as he exhaled, like he was trying to find the right words but couldn't. "I didn't think you needed to know."

"Why? Because I'm supposed to be some kind of fragile flower? I'm a journalist, Evan. This is what we do. We find the truth."

He flinched, the words cutting deeper than I intended. But he didn't pull away. He just stood there, staring at me as if he was weighing every word he might say next.

"She was a journalist too," he said, almost to himself. "That's why. She was chasing a story when it all happened. She—she disappeared, just like that. And the only thing left was the fire. No trace. Just ash."

The weight of his words settled in the room like a fog, dense and heavy. I stared at him, searching for something, anything in his face that might offer an explanation for all the secrecy. For all the fear he had of me doing the same thing she had.

"So she was investigating this arsonist?" I asked, my voice barely above a whisper.

He nodded, his eyes losing their focus. "She was relentless. Too damn good at what she did. And she didn't stop, even when things started getting dangerous. I—" He stopped, swallowing hard. "I couldn't protect her. I couldn't save her. And that's the part I hate the most."

A silence fell between us, but this time, it wasn't uncomfortable. It was something else—something far heavier. My heart squeezed in my chest as I tried to make sense of what he was telling me. The pieces were all there, but they didn't fit. Not yet.

I closed the laptop with a soft click and looked at him, really looked at him for the first time. The fear in his eyes wasn't just about losing me—it was about history repeating itself. About me being that same reckless journalist chasing the same dangerous story, just like she had. I knew it, and he knew it too.

"I'm not her," I said, taking a step toward him, my voice low but firm. "I won't end up like her."

But even as I said it, a part of me wondered if I was lying. Because wasn't I already chasing a story that could end in flames?

Evan didn't answer right away. Instead, he pulled me into his arms, and for a long moment, neither of us spoke. There was nothing to say. The truth was already out, and now, there was nothing left but the fear that came with it.

The air between us hung thick, a blend of the kind of intimacy that could either heal or destroy, depending on how it was handled. I could feel the weight of his confession pressing down on both of us, and for a moment, I just wanted to escape it. To flee, to go back to the carefree mornings we used to share, where the hardest decision was choosing what we'd have for breakfast.

But no, I wasn't that naïve. Life didn't work like that, and neither did Evan. His past wasn't something he could simply close away in a drawer. It was the kind of history that refused to stay quiet, no matter how many times he tried to bury it.

I stepped away from him, not because I wanted to put distance between us, but because I needed to breathe. Needed to gather my thoughts before they completely overwhelmed me. He watched me, standing perfectly still, as though waiting for the ground beneath us to swallow him whole.

"I don't understand," I said after a long silence, my voice quieter than I wanted it to be. "You never mentioned her before. You never talked about any of this."

"I didn't know how," he admitted, his voice low, almost apologetic. "And I wasn't sure you'd understand. I didn't want to drag you into the past I couldn't save her from."

I laughed, though it felt hollow, like I was trying to break through the thickness of the moment with something far too thin. "You're kidding, right? I'm a journalist, Evan. I live in the past. It's what we do. It's what we dig for."

He shook his head, his lips pressed tightly together. "It's different when it's someone you—" He faltered, looking away like even saying the words would burn him. "It's different when it's someone you loved."

The weight of those words landed between us with a finality that took my breath away. Someone you loved. I looked at him, seeing him as if for the first time in days, maybe weeks. He wasn't the strong, invincible man who seemed to have all the answers. He was a man carrying the kind of grief that dug deep and stayed with you, a grief you couldn't outrun, no matter how fast you ran. It wasn't about protecting me anymore. It was about protecting himself from the ghosts that had been haunting him long before I came into the picture.

"Evan, I need you to understand something," I said, stepping closer to him, keeping my voice steady despite the storm I felt rising inside. "I'm not afraid of you telling me the truth. I need the truth. You think I'm scared of the past? You've got it backwards. I'm scared of living in the dark. Of never knowing what really happened."

He swallowed, his eyes shifting back to me, raw and vulnerable, like he was fighting a battle he wasn't sure he could win.

"I thought if I kept it buried," he whispered, almost to himself, "maybe the fire wouldn't spread."

I shook my head. "It doesn't work like that. We can't bury things, Evan. Not forever. Not when they're this big."

He looked at me then, a flicker of hope passing through his eyes. Maybe he had thought, all this time, that I wouldn't push him. That I'd be content to live in whatever half-truths he was willing to offer, just so long as we could keep pretending that things were fine. That we could keep living in the safety of the story we had created together.

But I wasn't content. Not anymore.

He exhaled sharply, running a hand through his hair again. "Her name was Isabelle. Isabelle Darnell. She was brilliant. Determined. I... I loved her. And I couldn't stop what happened to her. The night she disappeared, she was on the trail of someone—the same person who caused the fire. I should have stopped her. I should have made her stop. But she wouldn't listen. And then she—" He choked on the rest of the words.

"I'm sorry," he said, his voice breaking. "God, I'm sorry."

I didn't know what to say. What could I say to that? My heart ached for him, for the man who had been carrying this weight around for so long. The guilt, the pain—it wasn't something I could fix. Not in one conversation, not ever. But I could try to understand. I could try to be there for him, even if I didn't know how to help him carry it.

"You don't have to apologize to me," I said, my voice gentle, though my chest felt tight with emotions I didn't know how to sort through. "I'm not Isabelle. I don't need you to protect me from the world. From the truth. I just... I just need to know I'm not walking into the same trap."

"Don't say that," he said, his voice fierce. "Don't even think it. You're not her. You're not chasing a story for the sake of it. I know you, and I know you won't let it consume you like that."

But there it was, lingering like an unwelcome guest—his fear. His fear that I would go too far. That I'd get too close to something dangerous.

I exhaled, a shaky breath, feeling the weight of the world pressing down on me. "I'm not her, but I'm still chasing something, Evan. I have to. I can't walk away from this. Not when we both know how much is at stake."

I could see the storm in his eyes, the moment of conflict. He wanted to argue, to tell me to stop. But I wasn't the type to back down. Not when the truth was so damn close.

Finally, after a long pause, he nodded slowly, his eyes searching mine. "Then promise me one thing."

"What's that?"

"That you won't push too hard. Not yet. Not until we know everything. Until we're ready."

I didn't make any promises. Not yet. There was still too much left unsaid. But I nodded, and in that moment, I think we both understood that we were already tangled up in this, together.

The words hung in the air like smoke, swirling in a slow, suffocating dance that I couldn't escape. Evan's confession still felt too raw, too close to the edge of something dangerous. We'd crossed a line, and now there was no going back. I wasn't sure if that terrified me more or if it was the way the past was echoing through every moment we shared. The fire. Isabelle. The fact that she had once been as obsessed with the truth as I was now.

I could feel the tension growing, thick as the walls between us. I wanted to reach for him, to reassure him, but I couldn't seem to move. Everything in me was pulling in opposite directions. Part of me wanted to hold him, to remind him that I was different, that I wouldn't make the same mistakes. But another part of me, the one that had always thrived on the chase—the investigation, the pieces that fit together like a perfect puzzle—felt a gnawing urgency. I had to know more.

"You said Isabelle was chasing a story," I said slowly, my voice trembling just a bit as I tried to steady my breathing. "What was it? Why would she risk everything for a story?"

Evan ran a hand over his face, his brow furrowed in thought, like he was trying to piece together something he'd buried long ago. "She was brilliant, you know. Obsessed with finding the truth. I thought... I thought it was just her nature, but I never realized how deep it went. She got fixated on this arsonist. A man who'd burned down dozens of buildings across the state, and no one could catch him. She thought there was something more to it. She thought he was connected to something bigger."

I shook my head, the disbelief creeping in despite myself. "Bigger? What do you mean, bigger?"

He hesitated, his gaze turning inward, as if he was staring through the walls, seeing something that wasn't there. "She thought the fires were a cover for something else. Something darker. A criminal syndicate that used the chaos as a cover for laundering money, for doing all sorts of things that wouldn't get traced back to them. I didn't think she was wrong. I just didn't think she'd... push so hard."

I leaned back against the table, feeling the weight of his words pressing down on me. I had known Evan was cautious, protective in ways I hadn't understood. But this? This was more than that. This was guilt wrapped in years of suppressed terror.

"And then what happened?" I asked, though I already knew. There was only one way a story like this would end.

He swallowed hard, his voice barely above a whisper. "She followed the trail to a warehouse, somewhere on the outskirts of the city. She told me she was close. She was getting closer to the man behind the fires. But then... then she went silent. She never came back. No phone call. No texts. Just... nothing."

I let out a breath I didn't realize I was holding. "And no one ever found her? No trace?"

"Nothing," he said quietly. "No body, no evidence. It was like she just vanished into thin air."

The silence between us felt suffocating, too thick for words. I wanted to tell him that I understood—truly, I did. That the fear, the guilt, the sense of helplessness—it all made sense now. But as the minutes ticked by, the fear inside me grew too. I wasn't sure what it was I was afraid of anymore. Was it the thought of losing myself in this story, like Isabelle had? Or was it the idea that, somehow, I might become the next casualty in this game of secrets and lies?

"What if I do end up like her?" I asked, the words slipping out before I could stop them. "What if I push too hard? What if I—"

"Don't," he interrupted sharply, his voice low and insistent. "Don't even think about it."

I looked up, meeting his gaze. His face was hard now, his eyes flashing with something fierce, something desperate. "You don't get it, do you?" I said, my voice rising despite myself. "You don't get that this is my life. This is what I do. I don't just sit by and watch. I chase after things. I dig for truths. I need to know what happened to Isabelle. I need to understand why she disappeared. Because if I don't, it'll haunt me the way it haunts you."

"You don't need to do this," he said, stepping closer, his voice trembling with something I couldn't quite name. "You don't have to follow in her footsteps. You don't have to put yourself in danger just because it's your job. You can walk away from this, right now."

I stared at him, his words hitting me like a slap, but I didn't back down. "And if I do? If I just walk away, what happens? We go back to pretending nothing happened? You think I'll forget about this? About her?"

"No!" He snapped, his hands coming to rest on my arms, pulling me closer. "I just—I just want to protect you. I can't lose you. Not like I lost her. Not like that. Not again."

I felt my heart skip a beat, a pang of understanding running deep through me. This wasn't just about Isabelle. This was about Evan—about his fear, his guilt, and the ghosts that haunted him. I saw it now. I wasn't just investigating an arsonist. I wasn't just chasing a story. I was wading into a past he couldn't outrun, no matter how hard he tried.

But even knowing that, I couldn't stop. Not yet. There was too much at stake, too many unanswered questions.

"I can't walk away, Evan," I said, my voice softer this time. "I won't. You've already shown me too much. I can't unsee any of it."

He closed his eyes, his forehead resting against mine for a moment, his breath shaky. "Promise me you won't go too far. Promise me you'll be careful."

I opened my mouth to say something—anything—but before I could, the sound of the door slamming shut downstairs sent a jolt of alarm through me. I pulled away from him, my heart pounding, instinct kicking in.

I didn't need to say anything more. We both knew. Something was about to happen. Something we weren't prepared for.

And just like that, the ground shifted beneath us again.

Chapter 23: Fractured Flames

The rain had come in sheets, slamming against the windows of the apartment like a thousand angry hands. I could hear it, a constant rhythm, like a drumbeat echoing through my bones. But it wasn't the rain that was making my pulse race—it was Evan. His words had cut through me like a blade, and no amount of storm outside could drown the sound of his voice inside my head.

"You're not doing this," he said, his voice hard with finality, his face pale with something I couldn't quite place—fear, maybe, or anger. Or both.

"Watch me," I shot back, my words too sharp, too eager, desperate to hold onto something. Anything. The cool air from the rain seeping through the open windows couldn't touch the heat building between us. The kind of heat that could burn you alive if you didn't let it go. But I didn't want to. I wanted to press forward. I had to.

His hands were gripping the edge of the kitchen counter, his knuckles turning white, but his eyes—those dark, familiar eyes—flicked to me with something different. Something colder. He wasn't looking at me the way he used to, like I was someone to protect, someone to hold close. No, now it felt like I was a nuisance—one more complication in a life that had become increasingly difficult for him to navigate. His lips thinned, his jaw tightening, and for a moment, I saw it—the unspoken words that danced between us, sharp and dangerous.

"You can't. Not after everything that happened to Marissa. It's too dangerous," he continued, his voice low, like the threat of it might dissolve the room into something darker. He was still watching me, like he was waiting for me to cave, to back down, to stop being so stubborn. But there was something inside me, deep down, that refused to let him win this.

"Stop," I said, my voice trembling, though I hated that it was. "I'm not her, Evan. I'm not going to stand on the sidelines while the story is unfolding. I'm the one who's been chasing it, who's been following every twisted little thread you and your team left hanging. You think I'm just going to let it go? Let you make that decision for me?"

He opened his mouth to protest, but I didn't give him the chance. "No. I'm doing this. It's my choice, not yours."

There it was—my moment of defiance. My voice rang in the room, as if daring the universe to challenge me. But Evan wasn't going to back down, either. I knew that, even before he spoke again.

"You don't understand what you're getting yourself into. This isn't some—" he cut himself off, swallowing hard. He was walking a fine line, I could see that, but I didn't care. The taste of his concern wasn't sweet—it was suffocating.

"I'm not afraid of the truth," I said, my voice hoarse. But I didn't believe it. Not entirely. Truth, when it came to this case, felt like a dangerous, elusive thing, wrapped in secrets I wasn't sure I wanted to uncover. But I needed to know. I needed it more than anything else.

He stepped closer to me then, his face inches from mine, his breath warm against my cheek. There was no more space between us now, no distance, nothing that could soften the words that were coming. "I can't lose you, too. I've already lost too much," he said, his voice cracking on the last syllable.

I sucked in a breath, my chest aching, but the heat in my heart was there, burning bright and fierce, unrelenting. "Evan—"

But he was already shaking his head, his eyes pleading with me. "You don't get it. If you keep pushing, if you keep chasing this, you'll end up exactly like she did. Exactly like Marissa." His eyes were wild now, and for a split second, I saw something flicker—something raw and desperate and terribly, heartbreakingly familiar. It was as though he was seeing something inside me he couldn't bear to look at, something I hadn't even fully realized was there.

I wanted to scream. I wanted to tear at the walls between us, to fight for everything we'd ever shared, to make him see that I wasn't about to let him make my choices for me, but I didn't. Instead, the silence between us stretched, too long, too thick. My thoughts spun, a whirlwind of anger, fear, and something I couldn't name. It was suffocating.

We stood there, breathing in the same air, but it felt like a hundred miles separated us now.

"You'll regret it," he said, his voice barely above a whisper, like he didn't want to say it out loud in case it made it true.

I opened my mouth, but no words came. What was there to say to that? How could I promise him I wouldn't?

"I have to do this," I said instead, softer now. And there it was. The truth. I didn't know if I could live with the consequences, but I knew I had to try. The need for answers gnawed at me like a relentless hunger, something deep inside that I couldn't ignore anymore.

His eyes softened, just for a moment, but it was enough to see the battle waging in him—between the man who loved me and the man who couldn't protect me any longer. "I won't stand by and watch you walk into this," he said quietly, stepping back, his eyes closing as if to shut me out.

I didn't move. I couldn't. Instead, I watched him walk away, the space between us widening, and with each step, something inside me began to crack. The rift was real now, and I wasn't sure if either of us could bridge it.

As the door slammed behind him, the storm outside seemed to quiet. But inside, I felt like I was drowning.

I spent the night staring at the ceiling, the sound of Evan's words echoing through my mind, a drumbeat of regret I couldn't quite silence. It was too quiet in my apartment, too still. The city outside pulsed with life, but in here, it felt like something had died, and I wasn't sure what was worse—the silence or the echo of everything we'd just lost.

I couldn't tell if I was angry at him for pushing me away, or angry at myself for letting him. My fingers itched to grab my notebook, to scribble down something—anything—to get the chaos in my head to stop. But no words came. It was like everything had turned into a dull ache, and every time I tried to move forward, I hit a wall of frustration.

By morning, the rain had stopped, but the clouds still clung to the sky, low and heavy, as though holding their breath. I dragged myself to the kitchen, blinking in the harsh light of day. The coffee machine greeted me with its usual hum, a small comfort in the midst of the mess that was my life right now. I poured a cup, taking it black, no sugar, the way Evan liked it when we first started seeing each other. I could still see his face, the way his eyes would light up at the first sip, as if he'd just tasted something he couldn't quite believe. But now, I wasn't sure who he was anymore—or who I was in relation to him.

I took a slow sip, the warmth of the coffee running through me, trying to hold onto something familiar, something that didn't hurt. It didn't help.

I grabbed my phone off the counter and checked the time. Late, as usual. Another day I was going to be late to the office. My boss wasn't going to like that, but that was the least of my problems. I wasn't sure what had hurt more—Evan's insistence that I step away from the investigation or the look on his face when I didn't. That wounded expression, as if I was too much of a risk, too much of a liability. I knew he'd meant it with love, but somehow, that made it worse.

I grabbed my jacket, tugging it on as I walked to the door. The decision was made. I couldn't sit here and wallow any longer. I had to move. I had to get back to the story, even if it meant walking into fire. Even if it meant losing everything.

The elevator ride down was the longest three minutes of my life. I watched the numbers on the screen count down, each one a reminder of the tension that still buzzed in the air around me. My fingers were gripping the handle of my purse so tightly that my knuckles were white, but I couldn't let go. Not now. Not when the story was just beginning to take shape, when the answer was out there, somewhere. I had to find it.

The street outside was alive with the usual bustle of city life, but today, the usual hum of cars and people felt like a distant noise, far away from the thoughts swirling in my head. I wasn't sure where I was going—only that I couldn't go back to my apartment, couldn't go back to the place where Evan's voice still haunted the air.

I walked for what felt like hours, but in reality, it was just a few blocks. The city was sprawling around me, every corner a new distraction, and I wasn't looking for distractions. I was looking for something to make sense of everything that had happened.

My phone buzzed in my pocket. I pulled it out, half-expecting it to be a message from Evan. But it wasn't.

It was from the one person I knew I should have contacted days ago. The one person who would never judge me for chasing down the truth. The one person who understood what it was like to be driven by something you couldn't quite explain.

Tessa.

I hesitated for a moment, then opened the message.

"You okay? I've been hearing things. Thought you might need some company. Call me when you're free. And remember, you're stronger than you think."

I smiled a little, but it didn't reach my eyes. Tessa had a way of making me feel like everything was going to be alright, even when I knew it wasn't. She had that innate gift—one I envied and adored all at once.

I quickly typed a response, trying to sound more upbeat than I felt. "I'm fine. Just... busy. Let's catch up soon, okay?"

I hit send before I could second-guess myself. The truth was, I wasn't fine, but I didn't want to drag her into the mess that was unfolding. Not yet.

I shoved the phone back in my pocket and continued walking, letting the city swallow me up. The streets stretched out before me, a maze of possibilities, but none of them felt like they led to the answers I needed.

A few blocks later, I ended up in front of a small, unassuming café. The scent of freshly baked pastries drifted out to greet me, a rich, buttery warmth that almost made me forget the ache in my chest.

I pushed open the door and walked inside, the bell overhead jingling as I entered. The place was quiet, cozy, the kind of place that made you want to linger with a book and a cup of coffee for hours. I settled into a booth in the back, as far from the front window as possible, wanting to remain unnoticed, just for a little while.

I ordered my coffee, black, just like Evan liked it, and waited. The clink of the espresso machine and the soft murmur of conversation around me became a backdrop to the thoughts swirling in my mind. But no matter how hard I tried to focus on anything else, the only thing I could hear was Evan's voice—faint but insistent, warning me to step back.

But it was too late. I couldn't stop now. Not when everything was so close.

The café was a quiet refuge, the kind of place where you could disappear into the shadows, bury yourself in a cup of coffee, and pretend the world didn't exist. Or at least, that's what I had hoped. But there was no such luck. Every time I tried to lose myself in the steam rising from my cup, Evan's face haunted me like a phantom, a specter of everything that had gone wrong.

I stared at the black liquid, feeling its warmth seep into my fingers. Maybe I was doing the wrong thing. Maybe stepping into the chaos of this investigation was just another way to avoid dealing with what was happening between Evan and me.

I'd never been good at navigating relationships, never been able to figure out where the line was between love and self-preservation. But this—this wasn't just about me anymore. It was about the story, the truth that was buried under layers of lies, and I couldn't walk away from it. Not when I was so close to finding the answers.

The door to the café swung open with a jingle, and the soft murmur of the conversation around me shifted. I didn't look up, knowing full well it wasn't Evan. He wouldn't have come after me. Not this time. He was too proud. Too stubborn. And honestly, I wasn't sure if I wanted him to come after me.

But then I heard the voice, low and unmistakable, cutting through the ambient noise.

"Mind if I join you?"

I didn't need to look up to know who it was. His voice still had that edge, that smooth undertone that always made me feel like I was both home and in danger at the same time.

I looked up slowly, and there he was—Lucas.

He'd changed since the last time I'd seen him, though I couldn't quite pinpoint how. His jaw was tighter, his eyes sharper, as if something deep inside him had shifted, and not for the better.

He still carried that same confidence, that undeniable aura of control, but it felt different now. Heavy.

"You always show up like this?" I asked, trying to mask the knot of anxiety that formed in my stomach.

He slid into the seat across from me without waiting for an invitation, his eyes flicking to the empty coffee cup in front of me, then to my face. He didn't smile. Not a real one.

"I like to think of myself as a surprise guest. Keeps life interesting." His words were coated with something I couldn't quite identify, but it made my skin prickle.

I narrowed my eyes at him, more wary than welcoming. "What do you want, Lucas?"

He leaned forward slightly, his gaze intense as he studied me, like I was the most fascinating thing in the room. "You're chasing something, and I want in."

I blinked, trying to decipher his words. Was he serious? "I'm not sure what you mean."

"You know exactly what I mean," he said with a wry smile, leaning back in his chair. "You're investigating things. You're digging into stuff you have no business uncovering. I can help you with that. We can make this easier, make it all go faster." His voice lowered to a near whisper. "And safer."

I felt a flicker of unease, the words settling into my chest like an ice cube. "Safer for who?"

Lucas paused, his eyes gleaming with a mix of something almost sympathetic and something much darker. "Safer for you. Because you've been playing with fire, and one of these days, it's going to burn you."

I could feel my heartbeat picking up speed, but I didn't let it show. "I don't need your help. I'm perfectly capable of handling this on my own."

He chuckled, a sound that was half amusement, half something else—something calculating. "Are you? Really? Because last time I checked, you were caught between two worlds—one where you're pretending this is just a story, and another where you're stepping into something a little more dangerous than you realize."

I stared at him, trying to gauge whether he was bluffing or if there was something deeper at play. But Lucas had always been good at playing games. He had a way of making you feel like you were the one who was out of control, even when you knew you weren't.

"Is that why you're here?" I asked, my voice hard. "To remind me that I don't know what I'm doing?"

"No." His voice dropped, becoming a little softer, a little more dangerous. "I'm here because I can see what's coming. And I don't want to see you get caught in the crossfire. Not this time."

There was an undeniable sincerity in his eyes, but underneath it, I could feel the pull of manipulation. He wasn't just offering help. He was trying to position himself as the person I'd need. The person I'd turn to when things got messy.

I leaned back in my chair, folding my arms across my chest. "I don't need anyone, Lucas. Not you. Not anyone."

His gaze darkened, the smile fading as he sat back in his chair, eyeing me with quiet intensity. "You're wrong about that. You might not need me now, but when things start falling apart, you'll remember I offered. And when that time comes, I'll be here."

I said nothing, but his words lingered in the air like smoke, both suffocating and impossible to ignore. He was right about one thing—I wasn't in control anymore. But the idea of accepting his help felt like surrendering to something far worse than I was willing to admit.

"Is that a threat?" I asked, my voice steady despite the storm raging in my chest.

Lucas stood up, his eyes never leaving mine. "Take it however you want. Just remember—you'll find yourself wishing you'd listened sooner."

He left before I could respond, the door swinging shut behind him with a quiet thud. I sat there for a long moment, the weight of his words pressing down on me, and yet, despite the unease, a part of me wondered—what if he was right?

Chapter 24: Kindled Shadows

The fire was already licking the sky by the time I arrived. A terrible thing, that fire. You'd think you'd get used to the acrid scent of burning wood, the crackling roar that echoed through the streets, but you don't. Every time, it felt like my lungs were on fire too, the air choked with thick smoke that stung the eyes and made your throat burn from the inside out. I pulled the collar of my jacket higher, squinting through the haze, trying to pick out familiar faces in the chaos. But no one here was looking for me. They were looking for flames, for the thick, black smoke swirling like a living creature, devouring everything in its path.

The street was lined with people, most of them standing in small groups, their faces painted with panic and disbelief. Some were covering their mouths, others were frozen in place, unable to look away from the inferno. The fire trucks were already in full swing, but I could tell from the way they moved—sluggish, uncertain—that they were fighting a losing battle. The blaze was too fierce, the wind too unpredictable. It had spread quickly, almost too quickly. A few minutes late, and I'd be hearing about another building lost to the flames.

I scanned the crowd, hoping—praying, really—that Evan wasn't here. I couldn't explain it, not then, but I felt a sudden, gut-wrenching certainty that somehow, this fire had something to do with him. It wasn't just another one of those random incidents, something that happened to someone else. No. I wasn't that naïve. And as soon as that thought settled in, something snapped in me.

I made my way through the crowd, avoiding the first responders who were trying to control the chaos. I ducked under a yellow caution tape, moving toward the rear of the building where the fire was most intense. I had to get closer, had to see it for myself. I needed to know what was really going on. There was no mistaking it anymore—the arsonist had struck again. I could feel it in the air, the way everything smelled like gasoline, sharp and bitter, mingling with the fire's natural bite. This wasn't an accident. This was personal.

I was almost there, almost through the side alley where the fire's edge barely reached, when I heard the voice. A low, cold chuckle that sent a wave of dread down my spine.

"You're always in the thick of it, aren't you?"

I spun, my heart leaping into my throat, but I couldn't see anyone. Just the shadows, long and stretching in the firelight, obscuring any trace of a body. A man's voice, rough but familiar. So familiar.

The voice drifted closer. "You really think you can stop me? That you can run from me? You can't, you know."

I froze. The world around me seemed to stop moving, as if everything had fallen into slow motion.

And then, as if pulled from the very darkness itself, a figure stepped forward. Tall, cloaked in shadow, his features hidden beneath the brim of his hat, but I knew—I knew—who it was. My breath caught in my throat as the last of the flames illuminated his face.

He was smiling. A smile full of teeth, sharp and knowing, like he'd been waiting for this moment longer than I had.

"You think you've figured it out, don't you?" The voice was smooth now, laced with a quiet mockery. "But you haven't. Not by a long shot."

I took a step back, my heart thumping so hard I thought it might break through my ribs. I should have run. I knew I should have. But something kept me rooted in place. A feeling I couldn't shake, like this was all meant to happen, like I was meant to be standing here, facing whatever came next.

"How long have you been watching us?" I asked, my voice trembling but steady. I was trying to hold on to something, anything, that made sense. But the truth of it was unraveling too quickly.

The arsonist—no, he—chuckled again. "Long enough to know what makes you tick. Long enough to know you, Evan, your little secret." He leaned closer, his breath warm against my ear. "It's all tied together. Every little thing you've done. Every mistake you've made. It all leads back to this."

I shoved back a wave of nausea, refusing to show fear. I couldn't. Not now. I had to stay strong.

"What do you want?" My voice was hoarse, my palms clammy as I gripped my phone tightly. "Why this? Why now?"

He stepped back, and for a moment, the shadows swallowed him whole. I wanted to scream. I wanted to run. But before I could make any move, I felt it—a cold hand pressing against my shoulder, just enough to make me shiver.

"You'll find out soon enough," he whispered, and just like that, he was gone.

I didn't wait a second longer. I turned and ran, my pulse pounding in my ears, adrenaline coursing through my veins. I had to find Evan. I had to find him before it was too late.

Somehow, I knew the truth now. It wasn't just the fire that was personal—it was everything. The arsonist, Evan, me. All of it was connected, like strings pulling tighter, leading us toward something neither of us could escape. We had been caught in a web of lies, and the threads were slowly, inevitably, pulling us back into the heart of the storm.

It wasn't just about the fire anymore. It was about survival.

I stumbled into the dimly lit alley, trying to regain my breath, the echo of the arsonist's voice still ringing in my ears. It felt like the walls were closing in, the world shrinking into this small, suffocating space between me and a shadow I couldn't outrun. I forced myself to slow down, each step heavy, deliberate. The last thing I needed right now was to collapse in a panic attack, though everything inside of me was screaming to do just that.

I had to find Evan. He would be the first to understand. He would—he had to—know what this meant, what the fire meant. But the thought of dragging him into this mess, of pulling him deeper into whatever twisted game the arsonist was playing, made my stomach churn.

I stopped outside the door to his apartment building, my fingers hovering just over the buzzer. For a long second, I wondered if I'd even get an answer. If I had anything left to offer him that wouldn't drag him down further. But I pressed it anyway, that instinct that told me I had to see him, had to make sure he was okay. The door buzzed open, the dull hum filling the silence before the heavy weight of it gave way to the sound of footsteps. My heart skipped, knowing the only person it could be.

Evan. Of course.

His face appeared in the doorway, his eyes narrowing in concern when he saw me, wild-eyed and breathless. "What the hell happened?" His voice was soft, but there was an edge to it. That sharpness I didn't always hear unless something was wrong. His gaze flicked over me, then to the night, as though he too was already bracing for some impending storm.

I didn't wait for him to invite me in. I pushed past him into the apartment, barely registering the familiar scent of his place—the mix of coffee and something else, something uniquely him.

"I didn't just run into a burning building, if that's what you're asking," I said, a little too harshly, though my voice cracked in the middle of it. I pressed my palms against my forehead, trying to get rid of the buzzing inside my head. "We're in it now, Evan. All of it. The fire. The thing that's been stalking us both."

He didn't argue with me. Didn't ask me for the full story or waste time pretending we were still safe. Instead, he came over to where I stood, his hands gentle but firm as he pulled me toward the couch, settling me beside him. He didn't let go, didn't release the tension from his grip, as if worried I'd disappear if he did.

"I told you, I—" he started, but I shook my head.

"I know. I know you told me." My breath came out shaky, words a jumble, but I couldn't stop the flood now. "But I didn't listen. I thought it was all just... coincidence. The fire at the office, the one by the diner, everything. But it's not." I swallowed hard. "It's all connected, Evan. We're connected. And I think he knows—"

Evan's eyes darkened. "Who? Who knows?"

I swallowed again, my throat raw. "The arsonist." I couldn't say it any other way. The name had been on the tip of my tongue for too long now, and there it was. Truth. Pure and ugly. I knew there would be no escaping this now. Not from him, not from the fire, not from whatever this was that clung to the air between us.

"You think it's..." He trailed off, his voice tight. "You think he's watching us? Watching me?"

I nodded. "Yes. Not just watching. He's... playing us. Using everything he knows. Using you. Using me. He said it." I paused. "He knows about us."

I watched Evan's face shift, a mixture of disbelief and fear flickering in his eyes before he masked it, slipping back into that calm exterior he always wore when things were falling apart. His hand tightened around mine. "You're sure? This isn't just some—"

"It's real," I interrupted, my voice louder now, insistent. "I saw him. I heard him."

We sat in silence for a long while. I wasn't sure how long. Long enough for the weight of the truth to settle between us, thick and suffocating, curling around our throats like smoke.

Evan ran a hand through his hair, then stood abruptly, his movements jerky as if something was unraveling beneath his skin. "I don't get it. Why now? Why this? Why us?"

"I don't know." I shook my head, pulling my knees to my chest, trying to hold everything in. "But he's after something, Evan. This isn't just about fires. This is personal. And the more I think about it, the more I realize we've both been part of it for a long time."

"You mean..." He was pacing now, back and forth, voice tight with frustration. "This whole time? This has been about us?"

I didn't answer. I couldn't. It wasn't a question I had an answer to, not yet. But I saw it in his eyes—the same realization that had hit me. We were connected to this mess, deeper than I ever wanted to admit. We'd both been pawns in a game, and the game wasn't over.

I glanced up at him, my hands trembling. "You have to stay close to me. We both do. This isn't something we can outrun. It's too late for that."

He stopped pacing, his gaze intense, searching mine. "And if he comes for you again?"

"I won't be alone," I said, the words a promise, even though the fear coiled in my gut. Even though it felt like every inch of me wanted to run.

Evan's mouth tightened into a thin line, but there was something else in his eyes now—something that wasn't just fear. It was resolve. "I'm not going anywhere."

And just like that, we were bound together. Not just by fire, but by something darker, something that would chase us down no matter how far we ran. Something that would keep us in its grip, and neither of us was ever going to let go.

The evening dragged on in slow-motion, as though time itself was caught in the haze of the fire's aftermath. The apartment felt too quiet now that the adrenaline had started to ebb, leaving only the pulse of fear humming beneath my skin. The weight of everything—Evan's closeness, the arsonist's taunting words, the looming sense of dread—pressed in on me like a storm gathering strength. I couldn't shake the feeling that we were at the eye of it, suspended for a moment before the chaos would crash down again.

Evan's face was unreadable as he moved around the kitchen, his hands working with a precision that was foreign to him. The stove clicked on, a soft hiss filling the silence as he set a pot of water to boil. I watched him for a beat, unsure of how to fill the space between us. It was as though the fire outside wasn't the only thing that had burned through the day, but everything we thought we knew.

"Are we just supposed to wait?" I finally asked, my voice cutting through the thick quiet. I knew the answer. I didn't need him to spell it out. But I had to ask. The uncertainty gnawed at me. "I mean, how do we even know where he is? What he's planning next?"

Evan turned slowly, his expression a mask of carefully controlled tension. "We don't. But we're not sitting here twiddling our thumbs, either." His voice was tight, too tight. The kind of controlled anger I recognized all too well from the few times I'd seen him on the edge of losing it. His jaw worked, the muscles there tightening. "But I'm not about to let him drag us through this any longer. We need to figure out what he wants, why us."

I knew that tone. I'd heard it before, when he was determined to move mountains with nothing more than stubbornness and will. It was a dangerous thing, because Evan didn't stop once he made up his mind. Not even when he should.

I ran my hand through my hair, a knot tightening in my chest. "He said—he said we were connected. That we've been part of this mess for a long time."

The words hung between us, heavier than I expected, because as soon as they left my mouth, something shifted in his eyes. The guarded part of him cracked, just a fraction. Just enough for me to see the flicker of realization. And it wasn't the kind of realization I wanted to see. Not the kind that felt like a death sentence.

"You think it's because of me?" Evan asked, voice low and careful. But I could hear the tremor in it, the edge of something else, too. Something sharper. His eyes narrowed, searching mine. "You think this is all about my past?"

I shook my head quickly. "No. It's not like that. I don't know what it is, Evan. But I think it's personal. I think…" I paused, swallowing the lump in my throat, because saying it out loud was like giving life to the nightmare. "I think we're being used to draw him out."

Evan's expression darkened further, his jaw tightening like he was trying to keep control of the fury swirling beneath the surface. "Great. So we're pawns in his little game. How does that make us any different from the others he's torched?"

I wanted to tell him we weren't the same. That somehow, we were better than this, that we had more control. But the truth was, we were all just waiting for the next fire, the next disaster to strike. And as much as I wanted to escape this, as much as I wanted to take Evan's hand and run, I knew that was no longer an option.

"I need to know everything," I said, my voice firmer now, not willing to let this feeling of helplessness take root. "Everything about your past, Evan. All of it. I need to understand why he's targeting us. We can't hide from this. Not anymore."

He was silent for a long moment, eyes cast down, lips pressed into a thin line as if weighing every word carefully. Finally, he exhaled, a soft puff of air, before his gaze met mine again.

"Fine," he said, the word leaving his mouth like he was tasting it for the first time. "But you have to promise me something, okay?

You can't run from this. You can't—" He stopped, swallowing the rest of it. "We're in this together now, whether we like it or not. You need to trust me, because I'm not letting you get caught up in this any more than you already are."

I wanted to argue, to tell him that I'd been caught up in it long before I even knew his name. That none of this had ever been a choice. But I couldn't. Instead, I nodded, swallowing back the storm of emotion I couldn't quite name.

"I trust you," I said quietly. The words felt like an anchor, though they didn't quite hold me steady. Not yet.

He reached over, placing his hand over mine in a rare, unspoken gesture of solidarity. For the first time since this madness had begun, I felt the weight of what we were up against. The depth of the fire that threatened to consume us both. This was no longer a game of chance, no longer about escaping with our skin intact. It was something much darker.

Evan stood suddenly, a sharp movement that made me jump, but before I could react, he was at the window, staring out into the night, his hands clasped behind his back.

"Tomorrow," he muttered. "Tomorrow, we find out exactly who's been pulling the strings. I'm done with running."

I stood as well, heart racing. "What do you mean? What's tomorrow?"

He turned to me, a dark glint in his eyes that made my blood freeze. "Tomorrow, we go to him. And we end this."

The doorbell rang before I could process his words. A sharp, insistent sound that sliced through the air like a blade.

I didn't have to ask who it was. The look on Evan's face said everything.

And then, in the middle of the night, everything shifted again.

Chapter 25: Smoldering Wounds

The smell of smoke lingered in the air even hours after the fire had been put out. I could still taste the ash on my tongue as I stood in front of the charred remnants of what used to be my life. The house was gone. Every room, every photograph, every memory reduced to blackened skeletons and the scent of destruction. But it wasn't the house I was grieving, not exactly. It was the pieces of myself that had been lost along the way.

Evan was beside me, hands buried deep in the pockets of his coat, his eyes darting around like he was trying to outrun the memories, the guilt that clung to him like the smoke. He hadn't said much since we got here, and I could tell he was torn between wanting to fix things and wanting to retreat back into whatever shadows haunted him. I wasn't going to let him.

"Evan," I said softly, my voice cutting through the quiet. "You're not alone in this."

He didn't answer immediately, and I didn't expect him to. I knew what it felt like to want to push everyone away, to believe that if you just kept enough distance, the weight of it all wouldn't crush you. But I wasn't about to let him fall into that trap. Not this time.

"I dragged you into this mess," he said finally, his voice low, thick with guilt. "You didn't ask for any of this. I never should have—"

"Stop," I cut him off, stepping closer. I didn't want to hear him blame himself. Not when we both knew it wasn't his fault. "You didn't drag me anywhere, Evan. I chose this. I chose you."

He turned to face me then, and there was something in his eyes—something raw, desperate. It almost felt like he was looking for a reason to believe me, something to pull him out of the hole he was digging for himself. "You're too kind," he muttered, shaking his head. "I don't deserve—"

"Don't." The word snapped out of me, sharp and final. "You do deserve it. You've been through hell, just like I have. And if you think for one second I'm going to walk away now, then you don't know me at all."

There was a flicker of surprise in his eyes, quickly masked by a grimace. He wasn't used to people fighting for him, I could tell. Not when his guilt weighed so heavily on him, when he had so much blood on his hands—at least in his mind. But I wasn't going to let that be the end of his story, not when we'd just begun.

The silence stretched between us, thick and suffocating, before I finally spoke again. "We're not done, Evan. We're going to get through this. Together."

He swallowed hard, his eyes flicking away from mine, and for a moment I thought I might lose him. But then, slowly, like he was testing the waters, his hand reached out, tentative, unsure, but there. And when I took it, the rawness of that simple touch settled into my bones like a promise.

The world around us was falling apart, but in that moment, it didn't matter. For once, there was something I could hold on to—something real. Evan was still here, and I would be too, no matter how dark it got. We'd rebuild this, piece by piece, like we were stitching our lives back together, one fragile thread at a time.

The night air felt different now, heavier somehow, but there was a certain calm to it. The sirens, the chaos, the lingering smoke—it all felt distant, like a bad dream I was slowly waking up from. But I knew better than to think it would stay that way. There was more to face. More to uncover. And we weren't out of the woods yet.

Still, for now, we had this—this quiet moment between us, a fragile truce in a war we didn't start but would see through to the end.

I squeezed his hand, gently this time, feeling the weight of everything he hadn't said, all the things he'd buried deep. "I'm not asking for you to fix anything," I said softly, my voice just above a whisper. "I just want you here. With me."

His grip tightened, and I felt something shift between us. A crack in the wall he'd built around himself, just wide enough for me to slip through. "I'm here," he said, the words raw but real. "I'm not going anywhere."

And just like that, the night seemed a little less suffocating. The ruins of my home, of our lives, didn't feel quite as overwhelming. There was still work to do, still so much left undone. But for the first time in weeks, I felt like maybe, just maybe, we'd be able to face it together.

It wasn't just the house that had been reduced to ashes. Somewhere in the thick of everything that had happened, I'd realized that Evan had, too, become a shadow of the man he once was. I couldn't fix it—whatever was broken inside him—but I could try to stand beside him while he stumbled through it. We both needed a crutch. And at that moment, I would be his.

We hadn't spoken much since the fire. Conversations had turned into one-sentence exchanges, as though we were both afraid to open the floodgates and drown in the other's grief. I'd made coffee this morning, the warm steam curling from the mug, and he'd stared at it as if it were a foreign object. The silence between us felt heavier than ever, but the weight of it was familiar. Too familiar, perhaps.

"Do you want to talk about it?" I asked, as I settled into the worn armchair across from him, the same one we'd shared more than a few arguments and quiet mornings in. But today, it didn't feel the same. Nothing felt the same.

He didn't answer, his gaze fixed on the mug in his hands as if he could somehow dissolve the mess of his thoughts into the coffee's surface. His lips were pressed tight, the set of his jaw more rigid than it had been in days.

"Evan," I said again, my voice a little softer, less insistent. "I can't fix this if you won't let me in."

He exhaled a sigh, deep and heavy, and finally lifted his eyes to meet mine. "You shouldn't have to fix anything," he murmured, the words nearly breaking as they left his lips. "I'm the one who dragged you into this. You were safe before. You didn't ask for any of this."

I couldn't keep my frustration in check any longer. "I don't care about your guilt. I care about you. And it's my choice to be here, Evan." My voice wavered, but I stood my ground.

He looked away, as though the weight of my words were too much to carry, too much to bear. "I've never been good at this, you know. At letting people in. It's easier when you don't let anyone get close enough to... to break." The confession hung in the air like smoke, heavy, suffocating.

"I'm not going anywhere," I said firmly, my heart pounding harder than I wanted to admit. "You don't get to push me away. Not like this."

His eyes softened, but the ghosts that lived behind them remained—too many years of pushing people away, too many layers of armor that I wasn't sure I could ever pierce. He shook his head, a ghost of a smile pulling at the corner of his lips. "You're stubborn," he said, his voice low but affectionate, the closest thing to warmth I'd felt from him in days. "I didn't know that when we first met."

"Well," I said, a little smile tugging at the corners of my mouth, "I'm glad you know now. Stubborn is sort of my thing."

There was a beat of silence before he finally spoke again, quieter this time. "I don't want to hurt you."

I reached out, my fingers brushing against the back of his hand. The touch was tentative at first, unsure, but then he allowed me to hold it, his fingers curling around mine like it was something he wasn't sure he should trust but was willing to give in to. For a moment, it felt like we had time. Like the rest of the world could wait while we figured this out, while we allowed ourselves to breathe in the mess of everything we'd gone through.

"I know," I whispered, looking at him with all the sincerity I had left. "But sometimes, Evan, the only way out is through. We don't have to fix everything right now. But we can start, little by little."

The tension in his body loosened just slightly, but the battle was far from over. There was so much he was carrying, things I couldn't even begin to understand. And yet, in that moment, I knew he wasn't pushing me away. He was just scared of what it would mean if I really saw him, if I understood the depths of the damage he'd endured.

"I don't know how to let someone in like this," he said, his voice quiet but genuine, raw with emotion. "How to be the person you need me to be."

I squeezed his hand, grounding myself in the warmth of his touch, the only thing right now that felt real. "You don't have to be anyone other than yourself, Evan. I'm not asking for perfection. I'm asking for you. Just... for you."

His eyes flickered with something unreadable, but for the first time in a long while, I thought I saw a glimpse of hope. Maybe we didn't need to rebuild everything all at once. Maybe the weight of his past didn't have to be carried alone. Maybe, just maybe, there was room for both of us in the rubble.

"I don't know how to love without expecting something to fall apart," he said, his voice rough. "It's always been that way."

"Then maybe," I said slowly, "we take it slow. No expectations. No grand gestures. Just... us, figuring it out."

There was a pause, a long, lingering silence. The kind that spoke volumes without needing words.

And then, almost imperceptibly, he nodded. Just a slight movement of his head, but it felt like the world had shifted. In that single motion, I knew that whatever it took, whatever walls we had to tear down, we would face it together. Slowly, carefully, but together.

"Okay," he said softly, his voice still rough but lighter than it had been. "We'll do it your way."

I smiled, the relief of hearing those words washing over me like a gentle wave. It wouldn't be easy. I knew that. But as long as we were willing to fight for each other, there was a chance. And for the first time in a long while, I felt the weight on my chest lighten, if only a little.

"We'll figure it out," I murmured, my thumb brushing against the back of his hand. "One step at a time."

The sun was low in the sky, casting a hazy orange glow through the dust-covered windows. Evan had gone out, just as he did every evening, taking walks to clear his mind. I suspected he was looking for answers in the shadows, hoping the quiet solitude would give him the peace he hadn't found in the noise of his thoughts. I couldn't fault him for it. I, too, had been learning to find comfort in the silence.

But tonight was different. The house was too still, the kind of stillness that felt like it was holding its breath, waiting for something to break. I paced the living room, fingers drumming against the back of the chair, the weight of my own thoughts pressing in. I was tired—tired of watching him retreat, tired of waiting for him to let me in. But I wasn't sure how much more of this distance I could stand.

I heard the front door creak open, and I didn't need to look up to know it was him. There was a rhythm to the sound of his footsteps now, one I'd come to recognize in the late hours of the night, when sleep was too elusive and everything felt like it was teetering on the edge.

"I thought you'd gone to bed," he said, his voice rough with the kind of fatigue that had nothing to do with sleep.

"I couldn't sleep," I replied, my back still to him. I wasn't sure why I was so hesitant to face him, why the words didn't seem to come as easily as they used to. Maybe it was the way he stood there now, always half-guarded, like a man waiting for a blow to land.

There was a long pause. I felt his presence behind me, heavy but not oppressive. I wanted to turn around, to see the expression on his face, but something kept me rooted to the spot. I wasn't sure what I'd see. Or maybe I was afraid of what I wouldn't see.

"Do you ever wonder if it would have been easier if we never met?" His voice was quieter now, almost a whisper, the kind of question that hung between us like a smothering fog. "If we had just stayed out of each other's orbit?"

I wasn't sure how to answer that. I didn't want to lie to him, but I wasn't ready to tell him the truth, either. Not yet.

"I think about it sometimes," I said, my voice tight. "What if we'd stayed strangers? What would life be like?"

"And what do you think?" His voice was even softer now, as though he wasn't asking for the answer, but merely for me to hear him. To listen.

"I think..." I paused, feeling the words settle in my chest like stones. "I think it would have been a lot less complicated."

He exhaled, the sound long and weary. "Yeah. It's always easier when it's just simple. When the complications don't have a way of eating you alive."

"Evan." My voice cracked, the truth slipping out before I could stop it. "You're not alone in this. Whatever it is. Whatever's happened. You don't have to carry it by yourself."

He didn't answer, but I could feel the tension in the air, stretching thin. It was the kind of silence that felt loaded, like a gun just waiting to go off.

I turned around then, finally, finding him standing there, his face shadowed in the dim light, but his eyes burning with something I couldn't quite place. There was so much in those eyes—regret, fear, and something else, something darker, like he was holding back an ocean and I was standing on the shore, waiting to be swept away.

"You think you're the only one who's scared?" I asked, taking a step forward. My heart was pounding, and the words tumbled out before I could stop them. "You think I don't feel all of this? That I don't see the way you pull away every time I try to get close?"

He flinched, the movement barely perceptible, but it was enough to make me pause. I had said it. I had finally said the thing that had been clawing at my throat for days, weeks, months.

"I'm scared too," I continued, my voice trembling. "I'm scared that I've invested everything into this—into us—and that you'll just shut me out, like you've always done. I'm scared that the more I care, the more it will hurt when you push me away. And maybe that's why I've been holding back, too."

The words hung between us like smoke, thick and acrid, but as they settled, something shifted. The air felt different now, charged with a tension that was somehow lighter, like we were standing at the edge of something new. Something we hadn't been able to face until now.

He opened his mouth as if to speak, but then froze, his eyes narrowing as he looked past me, toward the window.

"What is it?" I asked, instinctively glancing over my shoulder. But there was nothing outside, just the empty yard bathed in moonlight.

Evan's expression had changed—his jaw clenched, his eyes narrowing in a way that made my stomach twist with sudden dread. "Someone's here."

Before I could respond, the sound of a car door slamming echoed through the stillness of the night, followed by the unmistakable crunch of gravel underfoot. The hairs on the back of my neck stood up, my pulse quickening.

It wasn't the sound of a familiar visitor. It was something else—something I hadn't heard in weeks, not since the fire had burned everything to the ground.

"Get down," Evan hissed, pulling me with him toward the floor, his grip strong and urgent.

I barely had time to process his words before the unmistakable creak of a door opening echoed from the front porch.

Chapter 26: In the Line of Fire

The air in the old fire station smells like dust, mildew, and the unmistakable scent of burned wood—lingering ghosts of a fire that had ravaged this place years ago. The heavy silence presses down on me as I step carefully over the charred remnants of what used to be a sleek red fire truck, its wheels long gone, leaving only rusted skeletons behind. Sunlight filters through the broken windows, casting long, jagged shadows across the room. The floor is a maze of debris, every step a gamble, my boots crunching against shattered glass and scorched timbers.

Evan's voice breaks the stillness, his low murmur carrying an edge of urgency. "This place... It's all wrong, isn't it?"

I glance at him, feeling the tension in his posture as he surveys the room, his hand resting lightly on his gun. I don't blame him. There's a palpable sense of unease in the air, like this place isn't abandoned—it's just lying in wait. Waiting for something. Or someone. And I'm starting to think that someone is us.

"Wrong? In what way?" I ask, my voice steady, but my eyes scanning every corner of the room.

"The way it feels," he replies, his tone darker now. "There's a pattern here. A sort of methodical chaos." His gaze shifts to the walls where, under layers of soot and smoke, I can make out faint markings—symbols, numbers, something that's been deliberately scratched into the stone.

I step closer, brushing my fingers over the markings, tracing the deep grooves in the wall. They're deliberate, purposeful, as though someone had spent hours, days even, creating them. The hairs on the back of my neck stand up. I don't know why, but I feel like we're being watched. "This isn't just some abandoned building. It's been turned into something else."

"Yeah," Evan agrees, his voice a bit tighter now. "A message. But for who?"

Before I can answer, the distant sound of something shifting in the dark recesses of the building catches our attention. It's faint but unmistakable—a low creak, like the groaning of an old house settling under the weight of something more sinister.

"Stay close," Evan murmurs, stepping closer to me. His hand finds mine, his fingers warm against my skin despite the chill in the air. There's something unspoken between us now, a bond forged through too many close calls. His presence is both comforting and dangerous—like standing next to a lit fuse. And I don't know whether I want to lean into that danger or run as far from it as possible.

We move deeper into the building, the darkness closing in on us, wrapping around us like a suffocating blanket. The walls seem to pulse with a hidden energy, every step feeling like it could be the one that triggers whatever trap is waiting for us. I half expect the floor beneath us to collapse or the ceiling to cave in, but we press on. We have no choice.

A door at the far end of the room creaks open with a slow, painful groan. My heart skips a beat, but I don't stop. I can feel Evan's breath on my neck as he follows me, his hand never once leaving mine. We reach the doorway, and I peek through, my breath catching in my throat.

It's a small room, barely bigger than a closet, filled with shelves of old files, half-burnt papers, and blackened, forgotten equipment. But it's not the mess that catches my attention. It's the photographs. Hundreds of them, pinned to the walls in a chaotic pattern. Some are faded, others so recent they practically shimmer with clarity.

"I don't like this," I whisper, my voice barely audible over the pounding of my own heart.

Evan stands beside me, scanning the walls. His hand tightens around mine as he stares at one photo in particular. It's of a man in a fire department uniform—dark hair, steely eyes, a face I don't recognize but somehow feel like I should. I don't know why, but looking at him sends a chill down my spine. The man is smiling, but there's something off about it. Something wrong in his eyes.

"I've seen him before," Evan mutters. His gaze flicks to me, the tension in his face deepening. "It was a few months ago, at a fire on Miller Street. He was there. In the background."

I'm about to ask more when a distant rumble shakes the walls, followed by the unmistakable sound of an explosion. The air shifts violently around us, the force of it knocking us both off our feet. I scream as the floor beneath us tilts, sending us tumbling into the room, debris raining down, smoke filling the air. My ears ring, and my vision blurs as the world tilts and spins like a cyclone.

Through the haze of dust and smoke, I hear Evan's voice, strained but clear. "Stay with me, Sophie!" His grip tightens on my hand, and suddenly, he's pulling me towards him, wrapping his arms around me, shielding me with his body as more debris rains down. I can feel his heart hammering against mine, his breath ragged in my ear.

"Evan..." I gasp, trying to push myself up, but my legs are unsteady, my body trembling from the shock. "What just happened?"

"An explosion," he growls. "And we're not alone."

The words are barely out of his mouth before I hear it—footsteps, rapid and heavy, echoing through the smoke-filled room. A silhouette emerges from the haze, a figure too tall, too broad to be anyone we know.

"Get down!" Evan shouts, pushing me to the ground as he draws his weapon.

In the split second before I hit the floor, I catch a glimpse of the man's face. It's him—the man from the photograph.

And my world tilts again, only this time, I'm not sure which way is up.

The air in the room tastes bitter, thick with the sting of smoke and the sharp, metallic tang of charred wood. My breath comes in shallow gasps, the walls seeming to close in around me, pressing down on my chest. I can't tell if it's the smoke or the weight of everything that's just happened, but my heart is hammering in my ears.

I feel Evan beside me, his body pressed close, his hand still wrapped around mine like a lifeline in this chaos. His breath is ragged, but there's an urgency in his touch, a sharpness that I'm starting to recognize as his quiet brand of resolve. He won't let me fall. Not now. Not ever.

I try to focus, to clear the fog in my mind, but all I can hear is the ringing in my ears, all I can see is the creeping darkness that blurs the edges of my vision. And then, just like that, a sharp whisper of movement cuts through the haze.

The man from the photograph.

I feel it before I see it—his presence, heavy and cold, a shadow against the flickering light of the explosion's aftermath. I manage to turn my head, and there he is, framed in the doorway, his eyes cold and calculating, like a predator finally cornering its prey. My heart lurches, a sickening twist of dread coiling in my stomach.

"You didn't think it would be that easy, did you?" His voice is low, smooth, and far too calm for the situation we're in. It's the kind of voice that promises pain without hesitation.

I hear Evan growl under his breath, a sound so raw, so primal, it sends a shiver up my spine. But there's something else in his eyes now—something sharper than the steely resolve I'm used to seeing. Something dangerous.

"I'm going to need you to step away," Evan says, his voice cold but steady as he pulls me behind him, his body a shield between me and the man. "Now."

I catch a glimpse of the man's hand, casually resting at his side. It's almost too casual, like he's not even remotely concerned with the gun Evan's holding, or the fact that we're both trapped in this room with no clear way out.

"You're not in a position to make demands," the man says, his smile curling up at the corners like a cat that knows it's about to pounce. "Not yet."

The words hang in the air, thick with an unspoken threat, but there's something else there, too. A flicker of recognition in his eyes when he looks at me. My pulse spikes as I try to recall where I've seen him before—his face, his voice—but it's like trying to grab a handful of smoke. Slippery. Elusive.

Then it hits me. A whisper of a memory, buried deep in the recesses of my mind. I've seen this man once before, years ago. A fire. A case I'd long forgotten. And the realization comes crashing into me like a freight train. This is no random arsonist. This is someone who knows us, who knows the ins and outs of every fire we've ever investigated.

Evan must see the shift in my expression because his grip tightens on my hand, pulling me even closer to him. "Sophie," he murmurs, his voice tight. "What's going on? You know this guy?"

I shake my head, the memories too scattered, too jumbled to make sense of. But I know enough to understand one thing—this man isn't here for us. He's here for something far bigger, something that's been brewing for a lot longer than we realized.

"You've been playing a dangerous game," the man continues, his voice dripping with sarcasm. "But the thing about games is, eventually, someone gets to flip the board."

The words hang in the air, full of meaning I can't quite grasp, but I know they're not good. Nothing about this is good.

Evan steps forward, his jaw clenched, his eyes narrowing. "You're going to regret this."

The man's eyes flicker briefly to the gun in Evan's hand, and for a split second, I think he might actually hesitate. But then his lips curl into that same predatory smile, and he pulls something from his jacket. It's a flare gun, and he's aiming it straight at the ceiling.

I don't even have time to scream before he pulls the trigger, a bright, blinding flash of light filling the room, followed by the screeching hiss of fire erupting above us. My skin prickles, the heat from the flare burning through the air like an oppressive weight. I instinctively pull back, but Evan doesn't budge, his hand never leaving mine as he keeps his body between me and the fire.

"Get down," he orders, his voice low but commanding.

I don't question him. I drop to the ground, instinctively curling into a ball as the flare continues to hiss above us, casting everything in an eerie, flickering glow. The man doesn't make a move, standing there like he's waiting for something—waiting for us to react.

I hear Evan muttering under his breath, his fingers tapping against his leg like he's thinking, calculating. I can practically feel the tension in the air, a tangible thing, vibrating with the potential for chaos.

"You're out of your depth," the man says, his tone almost pitying as he watches us from above. "You don't understand what's happening here. But you will. Soon enough."

And then, without another word, he turns and walks away, his footsteps echoing in the smoke-filled room, leaving us alone with the flare, the heat, and the growing sense that we're standing on the edge of something far more dangerous than we ever imagined.

I push myself up, my legs shaky, my mind reeling. I look at Evan, searching his face for any sign that he knows what to do next.

He meets my gaze, his eyes hard, but there's something else there too—something softer, more vulnerable, like he's letting me see the cracks in his armor.

"Sophie," he says quietly, "we're not done here. Not by a long shot."

And in that moment, I realize he's right. This isn't just about surviving anymore. It's about making sure we uncover the truth, no matter the cost. And whatever happens, we'll do it together.

The flare's light is a cruel, hot glow, the kind that makes your skin prickle and your chest tighten. It flickers against the walls like a dying heartbeat, casting jagged shadows in every corner. I blink through the haze, the air sharp with the tang of smoke and the burnt metal that clings to the wreckage. Every breath is a struggle, my lungs aching with each shallow gasp. It feels as though we're suffocating in this room, trapped not just by the walls but by the dark weight of uncertainty hanging over us.

I glance up at Evan. He hasn't moved, not an inch. His eyes are locked on the door where the man disappeared, a storm brewing in his gaze. There's a heaviness to him now, an urgency I've never seen before. I want to ask him what comes next, but the words get caught in my throat. What can come next? The man who's playing this twisted game is already steps ahead, and here we are, fumbling in the dark.

"We need to get out of here," I say, my voice sounding thin and distant, even to my own ears.

Evan's lips press together in a hard line, his jaw clenched with the kind of tension that always precedes action. But there's something else in his eyes, a flicker of something that's unsettling. Doubt, maybe? Fear? Or is it just the weight of everything pressing down on him, on us both? I wish I could read him the way he reads me, but tonight, nothing makes sense. Not anymore.

"We're not leaving until we get answers," he says finally, his voice lower than before, almost too calm for the situation we're in.

"Evan, we don't know where we are in this building—how do you even know we're going to find anything useful?"

His gaze meets mine, and there's a brief, unexpected softness there, like a crack in the ice. "Because we're running out of time. This is bigger than just you and me."

His words hang heavy in the air, as though they're not meant just for me but for himself too. A reminder, perhaps, that the stakes have never been higher. We've both known this is more than a simple case of arson from the beginning, but I didn't expect it to hit this close to home. I didn't expect to be caught in a game where the rules are still being written, where every decision could be the last.

I swallow hard, pushing the thought aside as I force myself to my feet, my legs wobbling with the sudden movement. The room is spinning, the smoke crawling up into my lungs, but I push through it. We've come this far; I can't let us fall short now.

Evan's hand wraps around my arm, steadying me before I can stumble again. "We stick together, Sophie. No matter what. Got it?"

I nod, my throat tight. There's a promise in his words, but the shadow of doubt is too strong to ignore. How much can we really trust each other when we're both being played? The man we're chasing doesn't seem to care about the lines we've drawn between us, between right and wrong. He's blurring them, and we're running out of time to figure out what he wants, and why.

We move through the smoke-filled room, my eyes burning as the flare flickers out, the faint light swallowed by the darkness. The building groans around us, the walls shifting as though the entire structure is unstable. There's no sign of the man, no hint of his presence. He's gone. And I'm left wondering if that was his plan all along—lead us into this trap and disappear before we can even lay a finger on him.

"Which way?" I ask, trying to ignore the creeping panic that's starting to claw at my mind.

Evan doesn't answer right away, his eyes scanning the shadows as he takes a slow step forward, testing the ground beneath him like he's waiting for it to give way. The silence is oppressive, making the slightest sound feel like a gunshot in my ears.

"Over there," he finally says, nodding toward a narrow hallway that disappears into the darkness. "Stay close."

I don't hesitate. I follow him, my steps quick, my pulse thudding in my neck. The hallway is cramped, claustrophobic, the air thick with the scent of rot and decay. The walls are lined with shelves that haven't been touched in years, filled with fire-fighting gear, old helmets, and scorched uniforms, all of them relics from a life long past. It's like walking through the remnants of a forgotten world, one that's been consumed by its own ashes.

"Do you ever get the feeling that we're just... playing catch-up?" I ask, my voice barely above a whisper.

Evan shoots me a glance, the corners of his lips twitching slightly, like he's trying to suppress a smile. "All the time," he says dryly. "But we're still breathing, so there's that."

I can't help the small laugh that escapes me. It's sharp, desperate, but it feels good to break the tension, even just for a second. We're in this together. I remind myself of that, but the truth is, I don't know how much longer we can keep up with this game.

We round a corner, and the hallway opens into a large room, one that looks like it was once the heart of the fire station. The walls are lined with old equipment, now covered in a thick layer of dust, the tools of a forgotten trade. There's a dark, greasy stain on the floor that smells like something more than just smoke—something darker, more dangerous.

And then I see it—a large black box, sitting in the center of the room, barely visible under a pile of charred debris. My heart skips a beat. That's it. That's what we've been searching for.

"This is it," I say, the words almost a breath of relief. "This is the thing that connects it all."

Evan steps forward, his hand brushing against the box, sending a shockwave through me. "Careful," I warn, but it's too late. He's already lifting it, his fingers brushing against something cold and metallic inside.

The box opens with a sharp snap, and I freeze. Inside, neatly tucked beneath a layer of old rags, is a set of files. But not just any files. These are marked with official fire department insignia, and the names on the tabs are ones I know—ones I shouldn't know. Firefighters who've gone missing over the years. Investigators who vanished without a trace.

And then, at the very bottom, a single note.

It's simple, written in stark black ink.

"You're too late."

And that's when the lights go out.

Chapter 27: Burned Bridges

The air is thick with the scent of scorched earth, a sharp, metallic tang that clings to my skin, no matter how many times I scrub at it. The stench of smoke curls around me, a constant reminder of how close I came to death tonight. My hands shake, not from fear, but from the rush of adrenaline still coursing through my veins, mingling with the stinging reality that we're not dead. We should have been, but here we are, alive, and that should mean something, right?

Evan stands beside me, a shadow of the man I know. His clothes are singed, his hair a mess, and his face—well, it looks like he's aged five years in the span of five minutes. But it's his eyes that are the most striking. They're distant, the usual spark of humor and mischief replaced by a bleakness I've never seen before. He's staring ahead, hands in his pockets, his jaw tight, like every inch of him is trying to hold something back—something I know is coming.

"You okay?" I ask, my voice hoarse from the smoke, though the question feels absurd even as I say it. Neither of us is really okay.

Evan's eyes flicker to me for the briefest of seconds, like he's just realized I'm still standing next to him. "I'm fine," he mutters, but there's a flatness to his tone that immediately sends a jolt of unease through me. "Just—just get some rest. You've been through enough."

I want to argue, to say that we've both been through enough, but the words get stuck in my throat. Instead, I just nod, pulling the thin hospital blanket around my shoulders tighter as if that might somehow shield me from the cold growing between us.

We're in one of those sterile, white hospital rooms where the smell of antiseptic and old linoleum floor tiles clings to everything. The beeping of machines, the murmur of nurses in the hall, it all feels so ordinary, so achingly normal compared to what we've just survived. It's almost too much. It doesn't fit. And neither does the silence between us.

I try again. "Evan—"

"I don't want you involved in this anymore," he interrupts, his voice low, but firm. The words land like stones, heavy and final. "This whole thing... it's dangerous. You're not safe. I'm not gonna let you keep getting caught up in it."

My heart stutters, not from the physical injury but from the weight of his words. "You don't get to make that decision for me," I say, my voice barely above a whisper. There's a twinge of anger there, something sharp and raw, but it doesn't fully cut through the overwhelming sense of dread that's settling in my chest. "I'm not just some damsel in distress. I can handle this. We can handle this."

Evan runs a hand through his hair, exhaling sharply. He looks tired—more tired than I've ever seen him. There's something defeated in the way he holds himself, like he's already given up, not just on the situation but on me, too. His eyes meet mine again, and for a moment, I see the flicker of something—something I can't quite name—before it's gone, smothered by the same coldness that's taking over his face.

"You think I don't know that?" he says, his voice tight. "But I'm not willing to risk you, not like this. Not for anything."

My breath catches, and for a moment, the world tilts on its axis. "Evan—what are you saying?" My chest tightens, and it's hard to breathe around the lump in my throat.

"I'm saying," he pauses, as if the words are too heavy to say aloud, "that maybe it's time we... stop. For your sake."

I blink at him, feeling as if I've been slapped. "You're leaving?" The words tumble out before I can stop them, and they feel as foreign as they do raw, like they don't belong in the same sentence as his name.

His eyes soften just a touch, and for a second, I think he might take it back. But then he looks away, and it's like I've been struck by something colder than the sterile air around us. "I'm not leaving. I'm just... stepping away. From you. From everything. For your own good."

The silence that follows feels suffocating. My heart beats too loudly, the sound drowning out everything else. I don't know what to say. I don't know how to fight back against something so final, so absolute. It's as if the universe has pulled the rug out from under me, and I've fallen so far that I don't even know where the ground is anymore.

"You can't do this," I manage to whisper, my voice shaky now. I want to scream, to demand that he stay, but the words feel like they'll crumble to dust before they even leave my lips.

Evan takes a step back, his hand moving to the door, but not before he looks at me one last time. There's no warmth in his gaze now, no trace of the man I thought I knew. Only a kind of quiet devastation. "I already have," he says, before turning and walking out of the room.

And just like that, he's gone. The door clicks shut behind him, and the finality of it hits me harder than the explosion ever could. My hands are trembling again, but now it's not from the remnants of fear. It's because I know that something is broken between us—something that may never be fixed. And no matter how much I want to, I can't chase after him, can't try to put it back together.

So, I sit there, alone in the sterile silence of the hospital room, with nothing but the scent of smoke clinging to my skin and the aching emptiness where he used to be.

The hospital room is too quiet, too still, like the world has held its breath and hasn't yet let go. I sit on the edge of the bed, my legs swinging like a child's, though I'm far too old to still be behaving this way. The faint hum of the fluorescent lights overhead does nothing to fill the space, nor does the soft rustle of the nurses' shoes as they pass by the door. I reach up, almost absentmindedly, to wipe at my cheek, but there's no tear. It's just ash, like everything else around me. Everything I thought was solid, secure, real, is covered in this gray, brittle dust.

I should be angry. I should be throwing something, stomping my foot in defiance, telling the universe just how unfair this all is. I should be demanding answers, forcing him to stay. But all I feel is the exhaustion that comes with realizing how powerless I am in this. How small. He's made his decision, and I know—deep down, somewhere that still refuses to admit it—that there's no changing his mind.

The door creaks open, and I barely register it at first, too wrapped up in my own thoughts to notice. When I look up, I see Dr. Rojas standing in the doorway, her clipboard in hand, her brow furrowed as if she's been about to call out my name for a while now.

"Still awake, huh?" she says, her voice an easy mix of concern and amusement. "I figured after everything you've been through today, you'd be passed out cold."

I shrug, offering her a smile that doesn't quite reach my eyes. "I'm fine. Just... thinking."

She steps fully into the room, her sneakers squeaking softly on the tile. Her white coat swishes with her movement, and her stethoscope dangles around her neck like a reminder that she's the one in charge here, the one who can fix everything that needs fixing. Too bad she can't fix this.

"Well, don't think too hard. You've got a few bruises and some scrapes, but I don't need you worrying yourself into something worse." She pauses, studying me closely. "What happened out there, anyway? I know you're not the type to just end up in a place like this for no reason. You didn't accidentally walk into an explosion, did you?"

The question is lighthearted, but I feel the weight of it like a rock sinking into my stomach. I laugh, though it sounds thin and brittle. "Not by choice," I reply. "Let's just say it was... unavoidable."

Dr. Rojas raises an eyebrow. "Uh-huh. Well, I hope for your sake that's not the case every time. We don't have a lot of rooms left here for people who can't avoid explosions."

I let the joke hang between us for a second, then offer a nod. I know she's trying to lighten the mood, but right now, the tension in my chest makes it hard to find humor in anything. Her expression softens when she sees my face.

"Okay, okay. You're not in the mood for jokes. Just... make sure you take it easy for a while. Get some rest." She takes a step back toward the door, then pauses, looking back over her shoulder. "If you need anything—anything at all—don't hesitate to ask."

I nod, but I don't speak. She exits with one last glance at me, and I'm left with the feeling of being untethered again, adrift in a sea of confusion and uncertainty.

I should sleep. My body's crying out for it, begging for the relief of losing consciousness, but I can't. Every time I close my eyes, I see Evan's face, his final look before he walked out of this room and out of my life. I can't forget it. His words replay in my mind, on a loop I can't seem to stop, each one cutting deeper, each one like a new wound that hasn't had time to scab over before it's reopened.

You're not safe. It's not worth it.

I try to focus on my breath, the slow rise and fall of my chest, but it's hard. Everything is hard.

It doesn't take long for me to give up on the idea of sleep. I slip out of bed, the cold tile biting at the soles of my feet as I make my way toward the window. The city stretches out before me, a sprawl of lights and motion that feels so far removed from the chaos I just survived. The world keeps spinning, indifferent to what's happening inside these walls, inside my mind.

I need a distraction. I need to feel something—anything that isn't the weight of the hole Evan's left behind. But there's nothing. Nothing to fill the space he used to occupy.

I'm still standing there when I hear the footsteps again. This time, I don't have to turn to know who they belong to. There's only one person who could make the entire hospital feel as though it's holding its breath again.

He's back.

I keep my gaze trained on the skyline, unwilling to acknowledge him, unwilling to face whatever he's come to say—or not say. The silence stretches on, thicker than the last one, and I almost convince myself he's left again. Maybe it's for the best.

Then, the soft sound of his voice, so close I can feel it in my chest, breaks through the stillness.

"I don't know what I was thinking." Evan's voice is raw, like he's saying something he's been holding back for far too long. "Leaving like that. I... I don't know what I'm doing anymore."

I bite my lip, my fingers curling into fists at my sides. The anger I'd been trying to suppress stirs again, simmering beneath the surface. But it's not the anger I thought it would be. It's confusion, wrapped up in a kind of brokenness I can't quite place.

I don't look at him. I don't give him that satisfaction. "I'm fine, Evan. You don't have to explain yourself." The words come out sharper than I intend, but I can't pull them back. Not now.

His sigh is heavy. "I'm not here to explain myself," he says, his voice lowering, as though he's walking a tightrope. "I'm here because I'm not sure I can let you go."

And just like that, everything shifts. The air grows heavier, charged with a kind of electricity I can't quite understand.

I stand there, frozen in the moment, as Evan's words reverberate in the quiet of the room. His footsteps, hesitant at first, then resolute, retreat down the hall, each step a reminder that I've been abandoned, left to confront whatever comes next alone. My fingers curl into my palm, the sting of a bruise under the skin as if my body has been trying to keep pace with my emotions. I want to scream, to tear something apart—anything—to drown out the sound of him walking away. But instead, I stand in the silence, the weight of his absence pressing down on me like a thick, suffocating fog.

The world outside my window continues its ceaseless motion, the distant hum of traffic a harsh contrast to the stillness in my chest. There's something tragically absurd about it all. The world spins on, and here I am, caught in the ruins of something I'm not sure I ever understood. How did we get here? How did we go from that instant of pure, unfiltered connection to this, to a fractured silence where every word feels like it might push us further apart?

I sink back onto the edge of the bed, my hands trembling as I clutch the blanket to my chest. I can still smell the smoke, faint but persistent, woven into my clothes, my skin. It's the only reminder left of the explosion, the only trace of the chaos that's left a gaping hole in my heart. I need to get up. I need to find him. But my body feels heavy, weighed down by everything I can't change, everything I can't undo.

The door clicks open again, and my heart lurches, every muscle tensing in anticipation of something—anything—that could pull me out of this haze. But it's not him. Not Evan. It's a nurse, a young woman with tired eyes who's probably seen more than her fair share of patients who don't belong here, who don't deserve to be here. She glances at me with an unreadable expression, clipboard in hand, the routine of her job a sharp contrast to the emotional wreckage I'm trying to navigate.

"Everything okay?" she asks, her voice soft but not soft enough to mask the professionalism in it.

I nod, though the lie feels like it's crawling up my throat. "Just... tired."

She gives me a look, one that says she's seen it before—the way grief and exhaustion can mimic something much more dangerous. "Rest is good. But I'll have the doctor come check on you in a bit. Make sure those cuts don't get worse."

"Yeah, sure," I mutter, not really listening. She doesn't know what's worse than the cuts—she doesn't know that my heart's in pieces that no doctor can stitch back together.

She hesitates before leaving, a flicker of concern in her eyes. "You're sure you don't need anything?"

I force a smile, but it's thin and brittle, like old paper. "No, I'm fine. Just need some time."

The door shuts behind her with a soft click, and the silence envelops me again. I want to believe the lie I just told, but I don't. The room feels too small, too suffocating. Everything about it—everything about tonight—feels like it's closing in on me.

I grab my phone from the bedside table, my fingers hovering over the screen. The temptation to call Evan, to reach out to him, is almost unbearable. But I know it won't change anything. It never does. He made his choice, and whatever happens now—whatever we could have been—it's all in the past, buried under the rubble of what was. And yet, I find myself scrolling through my contacts anyway, my thumb brushing over his name as if it might bring him back into the room.

Just as I'm about to press the call button, a soft knock interrupts my thoughts. The sound is polite, hesitant, but it sends a ripple of panic through me. I place the phone back down, smoothing my hands over my knees like I can hide the mess of emotions swirling inside me.

The door opens a crack, and a familiar voice calls out, low and cautious. "Are you decent?"

It's Sarah. My breath catches in my throat as I look up, my heart hammering in my chest. Of course, it's her. Who else would dare step into this mess of a room? I nod wordlessly, though I don't know if I'm nodding for her benefit or my own.

She steps in, shutting the door quietly behind her. Her eyes scan the room, landing on me, then flicking to the bed, as though taking in the disarray of my mind. Her expression softens as she sits down next to me, the familiar warmth of her presence grounding me, even if just for a moment.

"You look like hell," she says, her tone light but there's a knowingness in it that catches me off guard. "And I'm guessing that's not just from the explosion."

I don't laugh. I don't even smile. I just shake my head, the weight of it all pulling me deeper into the bed, deeper into the dark space I'm trying to avoid.

"I don't know what to do anymore," I say, my voice barely above a whisper. "He's gone, Sarah. And I don't even know what I'm supposed to be feeling. Part of me wants to scream, to tell him he's wrong, that I don't need saving. But the other part... it just feels so final."

Her hand rests on my arm, warm and steady, her fingers curling gently around my skin. "It's okay to feel lost," she says softly. "But you know what? That doesn't mean it's the end. Maybe it's just the beginning of something else."

I meet her gaze, and for the first time tonight, I feel a flicker of something like hope, though it's fleeting, like a candle about to be snuffed out by a gust of wind. She squeezes my arm and stands up, her voice calm, resolute. "You'll find your way. I know you will."

She turns to leave, but just as her hand touches the door handle, the sound of something—someone—moving outside the door catches my attention. My breath catches in my throat as I see the shadow of a figure standing just beyond the threshold, hesitating as if uncertain whether to enter or not.

And then, in a voice that makes everything inside me freeze, I hear Evan.

"I can't walk away from you, not when you need me the most."

My heart skips a beat, the air thick with the unspoken words that hang between us.

Chapter 28: Kindling My Own Fire

The dust in the archive is thick, hanging in the air like a secret waiting to be discovered. I swipe at the old ledger, my fingers leaving a trail of smudges on the yellowed pages. The smell of ink and age lingers, a musty scent that wraps itself around me as I search for any clue that might lead me to the truth. My eyes burn from the strain, each page feeling heavier than the last. The noise of my breath, shallow and quick, is the only thing that grounds me. There's no one here but me, and that's how I like it. No distractions. No one to tell me to stop, to move on, to give up.

I flip through the brittle paper until I reach the photograph. It's a group shot, the sort of thing any firehouse might have hanging on the wall—four men standing side by side, their gear worn and faces weathered from years of hard work. But it's the man in the center, arms crossed, jaw set in a way that suggests he's been asked the same question too many times, that stops my breath. Evan. His dark eyes stare back at me, sharp and alert, as though he knew the camera was a threat. There's a tension in his posture, in the way he holds himself next to the others. But the most unsettling part of this photograph? The man standing beside him. Or, rather, the man who isn't there.

The photograph is old, cracked in places, but there's a clear tear mark across the face of the man beside Evan. Someone had gone to great lengths to deface it. The others in the picture are all present, their faces slightly faded with time, but the scratched-out man—his face is obliterated. It's deliberate. The violence of the marking stands out, as though the act of erasure was an attempt to erase the person entirely. But no one can disappear like that. There are always traces. Always threads to pull on.

I squint at the photograph, trying to make sense of the anger seeping from it, from this very moment frozen in time. What had happened here? Why had this face been marked so aggressively?

The air around me thickens as the realization hits. This photograph holds the key to something. Something dark. I feel it in my bones, the way the tension in Evan's face mirrors the tightness in my chest. But before I can think too much about it, the door to the archive creaks open.

I freeze, hoping the sound was nothing more than the building's groaning frame settling, but it's not.

A voice echoes down the narrow hallway. "I thought you were supposed to be resting."

It's Karen. Her voice is laced with concern, but there's something else there too. Something I can't quite place. She steps into the room, her presence filling the space like a slow-moving storm. She's in her usual attire—dark, practical—but there's an edge to her today. Maybe it's the way her eyes narrow when they land on the photograph, or how she stands just a little too still. She knows. She knows I'm not here to simply research fire safety.

"I'm fine," I reply, trying to keep the irritation from my voice. "I need to keep going. There's something here. I just need to figure it out."

She doesn't respond at first, her gaze lingering on the photograph. "Do you know what this is?" she asks, stepping closer, her boots making soft sounds on the wooden floor.

I nod, not taking my eyes off the image. "It's a group photo from the department. But one of them is gone, wiped out. I think he has something to do with this whole thing. The fires. Evan's disappearance. Maybe everything."

Karen's gaze flicks back to me, and I feel her watching me carefully, weighing my words. She's not convinced. "I don't know if you should be diving into all of this, you know. You've already got a lot on your plate. People in this department... they've got a history. You don't want to stir up old ghosts."

I shake my head, pushing past her words, my hands gripping the edges of the photograph tighter than I mean to. "Ghosts are already stirring. I'm just trying to make sense of it. What happened to this man?" I say, holding up the photo, the question hanging in the air between us.

She steps back, her gaze softening. She seems torn, almost as if she's wrestling with something—some unspoken truth. "I don't know. But I've been around here long enough to see that some things are better left buried."

There's a pause, a silence that stretches far too long. The kind that makes your skin crawl, your instincts scream that you're on the verge of discovering something that was never meant to be found. Finally, she speaks again, her voice quieter now. "You need to be careful. People don't like their pasts getting dragged into the light."

I turn to face her, frustration bubbling beneath the surface. "I'm not afraid of what I might find."

For a moment, she just stares at me, and I can almost see the gears turning in her head. Then, without a word, she turns and walks away, her footsteps fading down the hall, leaving me alone with the photograph and the weight of her warning.

I stare at the defaced image once more, my fingers trembling slightly as I trace the edges of the tear. There's more here. So much more. I can feel it in my bones, in the way the photograph seems to pulse in my hands, as if it's alive with the secrets it's been hiding for years. And I'm not about to let it slip away without uncovering every last one of them.

I'm going to find out who this man is. And why he's been erased from history.

I barely register the passage of time as I sit there, staring at the photograph, my heart pounding in my chest. The faint hum of the fluorescent lights overhead is the only sound, a quiet counterpoint to the rising chaos in my mind. It's as if the photograph is pulling me deeper, its secrets beckoning like an open door I've been too afraid to walk through. I flip it over, hoping for a clue, a name, anything. But the back is blank—silent as the grave.

The old man behind the front desk must have gone home by now, his chair empty, the archives left to their own devices. The air in the room feels cooler, as though the walls themselves are exhaling a sigh of relief that I'm here alone. No one to tell me what's sensible, what's appropriate. I reach for the photo again, tracing my fingers over the scratched-out face. I can feel the fury in that mark, the rawness of it, and I wonder if the anger was meant for someone else entirely, if it was never meant to be erased at all but left as a warning.

I set the photo down carefully on the table, trying to quell the shaking in my hands. The weight of it all is starting to settle in my bones, heavy and unyielding. The fire department's walls are more tangled than I realized. This isn't just about a series of arson cases. This is about betrayal. Long-held grudges. People who had been burned—figuratively and literally—by the very ones they trusted. The connections between Evan and the others in the photo are sharper than I'd first thought, and if this man was erased from the story, then he's the one I need to find. If he's alive.

I push away from the table, pacing the narrow aisle between the rows of filing cabinets. There has to be something more—something that ties this man to the fires. I run my hand over the cold metal handles of the cabinets, pulling at my frustration, willing it to break free. There's a gnawing suspicion crawling under my skin, one that refuses to be ignored. But I don't know how to follow it yet. Not without more evidence.

The sound of footsteps echo down the hallway again, a slow, deliberate cadence that stops my breath. I glance toward the door, the hairs on the back of my neck standing on end. I'm not in the mood for interruptions tonight, especially from someone who might try to talk me out of what I'm about to do.

The door creaks open. I don't turn around. I don't have to.

"Thought I might find you here."

I recognize the voice immediately. It's Karen, again, her tone thick with something I can't place, but it's not the usual concern. This time, it feels... weighed down. Like she's been holding something back for too long.

I don't respond at first. The tension in the air is palpable. Instead, I let my fingers hover over the edges of the photograph, unwilling to turn and face her. If I do, I might lose the thread of thought I'm desperately clinging to. If I let myself feel her judgment, I might stop.

She sighs, a soft sound that betrays her impatience. "You know, when you dig too deep into these things, you're asking for trouble. People—"

"I'm not asking for trouble," I snap, whirling around to face her. "I'm trying to make sense of everything. I can't just sit here and pretend I don't know something's wrong. Evan's gone, and no one's talking about it. This—" I gesture toward the photograph on the table, "—is the one thing that could lead me to answers."

Her gaze flickers from me to the photograph and then back again, her mouth pressing into a thin line. "And what happens when you find those answers? What then? You think it's going to fix everything? Evan's gone for a reason."

I frown, my patience snapping. "I'm not looking to fix anything. I'm just trying to understand why it happened in the first place. Why people close to Evan—people in his own department—are being erased from history."

She takes a cautious step closer, her movements slow, deliberate, as if trying to gauge just how far she can push me before

I snap. "Not everything is meant to be understood. Some things are buried for a reason. You've got to let it go."

I stare at her, the walls closing in around me. She's right, of course. I should let it go. I should stop poking at things that don't want to be disturbed, and I should go back to being the quiet, obedient investigator, nodding when I'm told, asking the right questions at the right time. But something in me refuses. Something deep inside me, something I didn't even realize I'd been holding onto for so long, bursts free.

"I can't," I whisper, my voice raw. "I can't let this go."

For a long moment, neither of us moves. The silence is thick, heavy with unspoken truths. She opens her mouth as if to say something, but stops herself. Maybe she's realizing there's no more room for half-measures, for pretty words that soften the truth.

"I know what you're feeling," she says at last, her voice barely audible. "But you're playing with fire."

I glance down at the photograph once more, the scratch still mocking me. "Maybe I'm the fire, Karen. Maybe I'm the one who needs to burn this all down."

I can see the hesitation in her eyes, the flicker of something she wants to say but can't quite bring herself to. Her gaze shifts toward the door, and then she's gone again, leaving me alone with the burning question that's haunted me from the start.

What really happened here? And why does it feel like it's all just waiting for me to light the match?

The next few hours blur into an endless stretch of paper and ink, my fingers numb from rifling through dusty files, my mind tethered only to the photograph. The room feels colder now, the weight of it pressing against me with every breath I take. The quiet is oppressive, a far cry from the noise I've been living with lately—Evan's absence ringing in my ears like an unanswered call. The investigation isn't just about finding the truth anymore. It's personal. It's about confronting the ghosts that have been lingering in my life long before this fire ever started.

But I can't shake the feeling that I'm not alone anymore. I can feel it, like a presence, lingering just behind me, lurking in the shadows of my thoughts. Every time I flip through a new page or scan a new file, I sense something else. Someone else.

And then, just as the pressure in the room becomes unbearable, the door creaks open again.

This time, I don't even flinch. I've been expecting it. The question is, who is it this time? Karen? Someone else entirely? My back is to the door, but I know I don't need to look. I'll feel it in the air before I see their face.

"Still here?" The voice is deep, familiar, but not Karen's. It's low and edged with something I can't quite place.

I finally turn to face him, and there he is—Marcus, standing in the doorway with his arms folded across his chest. His presence fills the room with a heavy stillness, his eyes unreadable as they meet mine. I've always known he had a knack for showing up at the wrong moments. Or maybe they're the right moments. I haven't quite decided yet.

"Do you ever knock?" I ask, trying to sound nonchalant, though there's a sharp edge to my voice I can't hide. I'm tired. My head aches from too much time spent chasing shadows, and I'm not in the mood for his games.

He shrugs, the movement fluid and effortless. "You seemed busy. Figured I'd spare you the trouble of pretending you weren't in here." He steps further into the room, his boots clicking on the old floorboards like a slow, deliberate countdown.

I bite my lip, not wanting to give him the satisfaction of knowing how much his presence unnerves me. "What do you want, Marcus?"

He doesn't immediately answer, instead looking around at the files scattered across the room. "I could ask you the same thing. What's all this? Looks like you're trying to dig yourself out of a hole."

I stand up abruptly, too quickly, and the chair behind me creaks loudly in protest. I hate the way he's always able to disarm me with that half-smirk, that knowing look he's mastered.

"I'm not digging myself out of anything. I'm just looking for answers," I snap.

His gaze hardens at the edges, but there's something almost sympathetic in his eyes. "I get it. You want closure. You want to understand why everything went sideways. But you've got to stop doing this to yourself. You're chasing ghosts, and they won't give you the answers you're looking for."

I hold up the photograph between us, a gesture meant to silence him, to make him understand that I'm not letting go. "You think this is just some ghost story? You think I'm just going to let it go because someone tells me to? This is real, Marcus. This—" I gesture toward the image of the erased man, "—this is why I can't stop. This is the man no one wants me to find, and that's exactly why I have to."

For the first time, Marcus looks genuinely taken aback. He steps closer, his voice dropping lower as if sharing a secret. "You don't know what you're dealing with here. Not really. You think you can handle it, but you don't. People get hurt when they start poking around in this department's past."

I take a step back, away from him, shaking my head. "And what? You're going to tell me to stop? To give up?"

He doesn't answer right away, instead studying me with a mixture of concern and something else—something deeper. "You don't know what it's like, do you? To really know someone, to trust them, and then watch everything burn because of one decision. One mistake."

I freeze at his words, and for a split second, I'm certain he's talking about something more than just this investigation. There's a crack in his mask, a brief moment where the façade slips, revealing something I didn't expect. Regret? Fear? Something darker?

"What are you talking about?" I ask, my voice barely above a whisper.

He doesn't answer immediately. Instead, he turns away, his jaw tightening. "Just... be careful, okay? This isn't some game. It's not just about finding answers—it's about surviving what you uncover."

I stand there, speechless, watching him. He's a man who's been haunted by something, something I can't quite place. And I have a feeling it has everything to do with the history I'm trying to uncover.

Before I can respond, the air in the room shifts again, this time with a sense of urgency that cuts through the tension between us. Marcus, sensing it too, stiffens.

We both hear it—footsteps approaching, slow and deliberate, the kind of rhythm that suggests someone's on a mission. I turn toward the door, but before I can react, the sound stops. Silence hangs in the air like a held breath, thick and unnerving.

Then the door slams open, and I feel my heart skip a beat.

"Get down!" a voice shouts.

The warning comes too late.

Before I can even think to move, the explosion rocks the building, sending the entire room into chaos.

Chapter 29: The Blaze of Betrayal

The room felt colder than it had moments before, the air thick with an unspoken tension that seemed to cling to the walls like the heavy scent of burning wood. I hadn't expected the phone call with Evan to go like this. His voice, low and hesitant when I first rang, had unraveled the last of my own hesitations. He agreed to meet. I'd gathered my evidence, pieced together the tangled threads of the truth with the careful precision of someone holding a fragile bird in their hands. Now all I had to do was deliver it—and pray I didn't crush it.

The café was bustling, as always. The murmur of voices, the clink of spoons against mugs, the occasional hiss of the espresso machine, all blended into the background noise of my thoughts as I waited. The table between us felt miles long, a gulf of space I could neither fill nor ignore. I ran a finger absentmindedly around the rim of my coffee cup, the warmth of the porcelain a small comfort against the cold truth I was about to unfold.

When Evan walked in, the door creaked behind him, and I could almost feel the world shift. He was dressed in his usual well-tailored, almost-too-pristine way, the sleeves of his shirt rolled back with a precision that seemed both comforting and unsettling at once. But his eyes—they were the same. Dark, thoughtful, but now edged with a layer of wariness I hadn't seen before. I thought about how his gaze had once been a safe place, a refuge from the noise of everything else. Today, it was a battlefield.

He settled across from me, the chair scraping against the floor like a whispered question. There was an awkward pause, then he leaned forward, folding his hands together in that familiar gesture that had always meant he was ready to listen, but today, it felt like he was bracing himself for impact.

"You said you had something for me," Evan said, his voice carrying a hint of wariness. He didn't look angry, not yet. But I could see it in the tightness of his jaw, the way his fingers twitched just a little. He was already calculating, already distancing himself from whatever he thought was coming.

I placed the photograph on the table between us, the edges slightly curled from where I'd carried it around with me for days. The paper felt like a heavy weight, pressing down on everything around us. His eyes flickered over the photo at first, just a casual glance. But then, like a ripple on the surface of calm water, his gaze froze.

I had seen that reaction before, but this was different. This wasn't just recognition; it was shock. His fingers twitched again, a little less controlled this time. Without a word, he picked it up, the photo trembling between his hands, as if the image was suddenly too real, too dangerous to hold.

"I don't understand," he whispered, almost to himself. "This can't be—"

His voice trailed off as his eyes locked onto the scratched-out face in the photo. The man was familiar to both of us, though we hadn't seen him in years. A former colleague, a man Evan had once trusted implicitly. Until the day he disappeared without a trace, leaving behind nothing but a trail of accusations—negligence, misconduct. The kind of thing that made you doubt everything you thought you knew about people.

It had been the kind of scandal that rocked their small, insular world, the kind that Evan had never fully confronted. Maybe he'd hoped that time would sweep it under the rug, that the man would stay gone, his actions buried in the murky past. But that photo, the one I had found tucked away in an old file, it had pulled all of that back to the surface. It wasn't a mistake. It was a message.

"What does this mean?" Evan finally asked, his voice tight, almost too controlled.

I watched him carefully, my own heart beating out a rhythm I didn't want to acknowledge. "It means," I said slowly, deliberately, "that the man who disappeared... didn't disappear. He was hiding."

There was a long pause, the kind that stretched long enough to make the space between us feel as suffocating as a cloud. Evan's fingers tightened around the photo, the muscles in his arm straining as though he were holding onto something that might slip away at any moment. He didn't look at me, didn't speak. Just stared at the image, lost in whatever storm was brewing inside his head.

"This... this is real?" he asked, his voice barely audible now. The doubt, the disbelief was palpable. I could see it, feel it, as if the air had thickened around us, filling every inch of the room with the weight of everything unspoken.

I nodded. "It's real. And it's just the beginning."

Evan's eyes finally met mine, the rawness in them enough to make my breath catch. He looked different now, as if something deep inside him had cracked open, revealing all the broken bits of trust and memory he'd buried for so long. His shoulders sagged, just a little, the weight of the truth finally pressing down on him.

"This doesn't make sense," he murmured, half to himself. "Why now? Why bring this up?"

I leaned back in my chair, the motion almost instinctive. I had my answer, but I wasn't sure he was ready to hear it. Still, I couldn't hold it back any longer. "Because there's more. Much more. I've been digging into everything—into his disappearance, his records, everything I could find. And there's a thread that runs straight back to you, Evan. To us."

He didn't react at first, just blinked, as if the words were too much to absorb all at once. But I could see the shift in him, the way his muscles tightened, the slow realization starting to sink in. Whatever calm facade he had been holding onto was starting to crack.

"Are you saying...?" His voice trailed off as he looked down at the photo again, his expression unreadable.

"Yes," I said, my voice steady. "I'm saying that the person who betrayed you wasn't just the man who disappeared. It was someone else, someone you never suspected. Someone close."

The silence between us stretched on, thick and suffocating. Evan's fingers, still wrapped around the photo, were white with the effort of holding it steady. I could almost hear the cogs in his mind grinding against each other, wrestling with the chaos of the revelations I'd just dropped on his lap. The man in the picture was nothing but a shadow of a past neither of us wanted to confront, yet here we were, pulling that shadow back into the light.

His gaze didn't leave the image, and for a moment, I thought maybe he was hoping it would dissolve under his scrutiny, that he could blink and make it disappear. But it stayed stubbornly in place, mocking him with its clarity. His lips pressed together in a thin line, his eyes narrowing with a sharpness that spoke of a brewing storm.

"This is..." he started, his voice a low rasp. "This is impossible."

I could hear the strain in his words, the way they cracked as if they were too heavy for him to carry. I didn't want to be the one to bear the weight of it all, but there was no turning back now. "Impossible, maybe. But real, yes."

The words were out before I could stop them, and I saw the flicker of hurt pass across his face. It wasn't just shock now; it was a deeper, more complex kind of pain. I knew it because it mirrored something inside me, the knot of disappointment that tightened every time I had to remind myself that nothing in this situation was what I wanted it to be.

Evan's gaze met mine, his brow furrowing as he set the photo down, the edges curling slightly. His voice dropped lower, as if trying to speak around the anger that was building, not quite there yet but on the verge of breaking through. "You think someone I worked with—someone I trusted—did this? You think they're the one pulling the strings behind all of this?"

I shifted in my seat, suddenly uncomfortable under the weight of his stare. "I don't know who's pulling the strings, Evan. But I know you're not the only one who's been played."

The words hung in the air between us like a challenge, an invitation to dive deeper into a pool neither of us wanted to wade through. He didn't move, his eyes still fixed on me, but there was a new tension in his shoulders. He was holding himself together, but just barely.

For a long moment, I thought he might dismiss me entirely, that he'd turn on his heel and leave without a word, too overwhelmed by everything to process it. But he didn't. Instead, he took a deep breath, leaned back, and let his hand fall to the table, the motion sharp but controlled. When he spoke again, his voice had shifted, a dangerous calm settling over it.

"You're telling me you've been investigating this for how long?"

I winced. The question felt like a slap, the truth of it sinking in like a lead weight. "A few weeks," I admitted. "It's not like I planned it. I just... couldn't stop digging."

"And you didn't think to tell me?"

His eyes were cold now, the flicker of trust I had once seen in them long gone, replaced by something much harder to stomach. The worst part? I didn't blame him for it. I'd kept him in the dark because I was scared. Scared of what the truth might do to us, to everything we'd built. But that fear was nothing compared to the terror of letting the lies continue. The past was catching up with us, and we had no choice but to face it.

"I didn't think you were ready for it," I said, my voice steady despite the way my hands trembled under the table. "You were never going to take me seriously if I'd just come to you with a suspicion. But now... now it's clear. We have to deal with it."

Evan's jaw clenched, the muscles in his face twitching as he processed what I had just admitted. His breath came out in a sharp exhale, his gaze flicking back down to the photo. The air between us crackled with a thousand unsaid things, all of them hanging over us, waiting for one of us to make the first move.

But instead of the confrontation I had braced myself for, Evan did something unexpected. He let out a short laugh, almost bitter in its humor. "I should've known," he muttered, more to himself than to me. "Should've known it wasn't just about negligence. Should've known there was more."

I stared at him, confused. "What do you mean?"

His laugh faded, but the wry smile remained, curling at the corner of his mouth like a secret he wasn't sure he wanted to share. "The guy who vanished? I always wondered if it was more than just the stuff they accused him of. But I never looked too closely. I never wanted to know how deep it went. And now..." He stopped, as if realizing what he'd just said.

"And now?" I pressed, leaning forward slightly.

He hesitated before looking at me again, this time with a rawness I hadn't seen before. "And now I'm starting to think I've been the one in the dark all along."

The words stung, not because they weren't true, but because they were so achingly honest. Evan had never been someone to admit to being out of his depth, and the fact that he was now told me more than anything he'd said in the last few months. We were both lost in this mess, and neither of us had the answers, no matter how hard we tried to convince ourselves otherwise.

"I never thought it would be this," Evan murmured, almost to himself. He rubbed his temples, his fingers leaving behind a trail of exhaustion that only added to the weight pressing down on him. "I never thought it would be this messy."

"Life rarely turns out the way we plan," I said, my voice softer now, the tension between us easing, if only just.

He met my gaze, the storm in his eyes subsiding, replaced by something I couldn't quite name. Maybe it was understanding. Or maybe it was just the grim reality settling in. Whatever it was, it wasn't enough to keep him from looking away, the weight of it all too much to bear for even a moment longer.

"Just promise me one thing," he said, his voice thick with an emotion I couldn't decipher.

"What's that?"

"That we keep this between us. For now. I don't know if I can trust anyone else yet."

I nodded, and for a moment, I almost believed it. That we could keep the world at bay, just for a little while longer. But I knew deep down that the storm was coming, and it was bigger than either of us could control.

The hours between our meeting and the moment I stepped back into my apartment felt like they stretched on for days. The weight of Evan's words still hung in the air around me, his voice laced with disbelief, regret, and something darker—an almost imperceptible layer of guilt. I couldn't shake the feeling that I'd opened a door we might not be able to close, even if we tried.

The apartment was quieter than I remembered, a stark contrast to the buzzing energy of the café, where everything had felt urgent, pressing, like we were two people racing against an unseen enemy. I set the photo down on the counter, still staring at the man whose face had been scratched out, a ghost that seemed to haunt not just the picture but every decision we had made up until now. I rubbed my temples, trying to clear the fog that was settling in. The questions were piling up faster than I could answer them, and every answer felt like it led to more uncertainty.

I didn't want to be the person who carried all the weight of this. Evan had his demons, but I had mine too, and they were starting to rise to the surface. The only thing I could do was wait for him to make the next move, to tell me how we were going to handle the mess we had stumbled into. But as the minutes ticked by, I realized he might not come to me first. Not this time. Not when his trust had been shattered, when everything he'd believed about his past—his life—was now up for question.

And that realization hit harder than anything else.

I moved around the apartment, making little noise, letting my fingers brush over the things that once gave me comfort. The worn leather chair by the window. The old, chipped mug I kept for coffee, even though it had long ago lost its handle. Nothing here felt safe anymore. I didn't even know if I could trust my own instincts.

The soft hum of my phone broke the silence, and my heart skipped a beat. I didn't need to check the caller ID to know who it was. The brief hesitation I felt before answering was less about doubt and more about how much of myself I was willing to reveal.

"I need to see you," Evan's voice came through, rough around the edges, but steady. "Now."

"Evan," I said, trying to keep my voice neutral, my grip tightening around the phone, "I don't know if we should—"

"I don't care," he interrupted, his tone leaving no room for argument. "I'm outside."

I didn't know how to respond. My gut told me this wasn't going to be one of those quiet, reflective meetings where we tried to sort things out. No, the urgency in his voice suggested something more—something larger, something that was about to explode.

I was already heading for the door before I could process it. The air outside was sharp, colder than I had expected for the late evening, but it didn't matter. I was moving on autopilot now, drawn to Evan like a magnet. He was standing by his car, hands jammed into his pockets, the lines of his suit still sharp and pristine despite the tension that radiated from him. There was no time for pleasantries. No exchange of greetings.

"You're here," he said, his gaze darting toward me but quickly turning away, as if he couldn't bear to meet my eyes for too long. "I need you to come with me."

"Where?" I asked, my voice steady but uncertain. I hadn't expected him to ask me to follow him—he wasn't the type to push when he wasn't ready. But something had shifted.

"The last place I ever thought I'd go," he said, the words laced with bitter irony. He turned, moving with purpose, as though he knew exactly where he was headed.

I didn't argue, not this time. I followed him to his car, my heart pounding with each step. Whatever had happened during the time I'd spent waiting in my apartment, it had pushed him over some kind of edge. There was no turning back from this. We were both past that point.

The drive was quick, too quick, with the city lights flickering by in flashes of neon and shadows. I sat in the passenger seat, my mind whirling with questions, but I didn't ask. There was no point. Evan wasn't in the mood to talk. Instead, I watched his profile, the tension coiling in his jaw, the way his hands gripped the steering wheel like he was trying to keep control of something that was already slipping through his fingers.

When he finally pulled into a parking lot, the sight of the building made my stomach drop. The abandoned warehouse, dark and looming in the night, stood there like a relic of forgotten decisions. This place hadn't seen life in years, but here we were, drawn to it like moths to a flame.

"Why here?" I asked, stepping out of the car. My voice was barely above a whisper, like the building itself was watching us.

Evan didn't answer immediately. Instead, he walked toward the entrance, his footsteps muffled against the cracked pavement. His expression was unreadable, his face a mask of determination. Whatever we were about to uncover in that place, it wasn't going to be good.

Inside, the air was stale, thick with the smell of mold and dust. The low hum of forgotten machinery echoed in the distance, as if the building itself was holding its breath. My boots echoed on the concrete floor as we moved deeper into the cavernous space. The shadows seemed to move around us, swallowing up the light from the small flashlight Evan carried.

"Keep up," he muttered, his voice low and tense, as if the place itself was something he feared. We moved swiftly, the silence between us growing more oppressive with each step. I couldn't help but feel the weight of it—the weight of the secrets we were about to uncover. Whatever lay ahead was not something I could change, not something we could undo.

And then, suddenly, we stopped. Evan stood still, his body rigid as he pointed to something on the floor. My breath caught in my throat as I stepped closer, the beam of the flashlight illuminating a small pile of papers, carefully arranged, almost as though they had been waiting for us.

But the last thing I expected to see—sitting on top of the papers, staring back at me with cold, accusatory eyes—was a photograph.

The same photograph. The one with the man whose face had been scratched out.

And beside it? A note.

It read: You should have stayed away.

Chapter 30: Rekindled Passions

The kitchen smelled of coffee, dark and rich, as I stood at the counter, watching the steam swirl up from the mug in my hand. It was a quiet moment, too quiet, as though the world was holding its breath, waiting for something to shift. The sunlight had just begun to filter through the slats of the blinds, casting golden streaks across the worn countertop. I hadn't slept much the night before, and the exhaustion clung to me like a second skin, but there was something else now, a tightness in my chest, a knot that hadn't been there before. I knew what it was—Evan.

The memory of him was fresh, too vivid, lingering on my skin like the taste of wine long after the last sip. Our bodies had collided with a force that left no room for doubt. The tension that had been building between us for weeks had finally exploded, and for a moment, it felt as though nothing else mattered. The chaos of our lives, the mystery of the arsonist who had been stalking us, even the weight of our pasts—all of it had faded into the background as we stood there, tangled in each other's arms.

But now, with the soft light of morning spilling into the room, the reality of it all crashed back. It had been a fleeting escape, a temporary reprieve from the mess we'd both created. I felt the bitter sting of it—the knowledge that I couldn't just walk away from the past, from everything that had happened. The world hadn't stopped turning just because we had surrendered to our desires.

I didn't hear him approach until his voice broke the silence, low and rough, like gravel scraping against metal. "Coffee?" he asked, his eyes never leaving me, as if trying to gauge how much damage had been done by the night before.

I nodded, unable to find the words to answer him, still not sure if I wanted to. The air between us crackled with something electric, something dangerous. He moved behind me, the heat of his presence undeniable as he reached past me for the coffee pot, his fingers brushing against mine in a brief, charged contact. It sent a jolt through my body, but I didn't pull away. Neither did he.

The minutes stretched, thick and heavy with the weight of unspoken words. I wasn't sure how to act around him now, wasn't sure what had changed. I hadn't expected to feel this way. I had thought I was stronger than this, that I could handle whatever came after. But as he stood there, his gaze never wavering, I realized I didn't know what came next. I didn't know if I could go back to the way things were.

"You're thinking too much again," Evan said, his voice just above a whisper, breaking through my thoughts like a soft wind brushing against a window. "We're still here. We're still us."

Still us. The words hung in the air, both a comfort and a challenge. Because if we were still us, then everything that had happened before, all the reasons we'd kept our distance, still mattered. And that thought made the ache in my chest twist harder.

"Are we?" I finally asked, my voice quieter than I intended. I hadn't meant for it to come out like that, but the doubt slipped out before I could stop it. "After everything?"

He set the coffee down and turned to face me fully, his eyes searching mine with an intensity that made me feel exposed, like he could see right through me. "We've been through worse. We're still here, and that's what matters."

I wanted to believe him. God, I wanted to. But the reality of the situation felt so much more complicated than that. The fire. The mystery. The fact that neither of us could trust anyone, not even each other at times. It was all too much to carry, too much to just let go of. I couldn't ignore the fear that had begun to creep into my bones.

"Evan," I began, my voice trembling with the weight of everything I wasn't saying, "what if we're just...running away? From the danger, from the people who want to hurt us?"

He stepped closer, his hand finding mine, the touch warm and grounding. "Running away won't fix anything," he said softly, his thumb brushing over my knuckles in a soothing, almost rhythmic motion. "But we don't have to do this alone. You don't have to carry it all by yourself."

I felt the sting of tears, a sharp ache in my throat that threatened to spill over. I didn't want to cry—not in front of him, not now. But everything was too much. The uncertainty, the fear, the longing. The passion we'd shared only hours ago felt like a distant memory, a fragile thing that could slip through my fingers if I wasn't careful.

"I don't know what to do anymore," I admitted, my voice small, barely a whisper. "I don't know if I can keep doing this."

He didn't answer right away. Instead, he cupped my face in his hands, his touch tender, his eyes soft with understanding. For a moment, everything else faded away. There was just him. Just us. I closed my eyes, allowing myself to lean into him, feeling the steady rhythm of his heartbeat. But even as I allowed myself this fleeting moment of peace, I knew that the storm was far from over.

The silence stretched between us, heavy and thick with the weight of words unsaid. I could feel the pulse of the morning air against my skin, cool and fresh, but it only made the ache inside me grow. Evan's hands were still on my face, his fingers warm against the chill, but I was no longer certain if the touch was meant to soothe or to tether me.

I pulled back slightly, just enough to catch my breath, to gather the pieces of myself that had scattered during those frantic hours the night before. The mess we'd made, or maybe the mess we'd uncovered, had the potential to tear us apart just as quickly as it had pulled us together. The realization hit me harder than I expected: this wasn't just about us anymore. It was about everything else—the fire, the secrets, the lies. Evan had already been a part of that world long before he'd found his way back to me, and I wasn't sure how I fit into it all anymore.

His expression didn't change, but I could feel the heat of his gaze as it traced the curve of my jaw, down the length of my neck, as though committing every inch of me to memory. I wondered if he could see how unsure I felt, how much I was struggling to find the balance between what my heart wanted and what my head screamed.

"You're still thinking too much," he said, his voice low and teasing, but with an edge of sincerity that made it impossible to ignore. "What happened last night... wasn't a mistake. We both know that."

His words, simple and direct, hung in the air. I wanted to argue. I wanted to remind him that we couldn't just pretend that everything was fine—that the danger, the tension, all of it was still real. But his eyes were soft, and there was something about the way he looked at me that made it hard to remember why I shouldn't trust him.

I shook my head, taking a step back. The space between us felt wider now, though I hadn't moved far. "I don't know what to do with this," I admitted, my voice barely above a whisper. "With us. With what we're doing."

Evan's expression shifted, just a touch, like he was trying to decipher the puzzle that had always been me. "I'm not asking you to know everything right now. Hell, I don't even know how we got here, but I don't regret it." He stepped closer, closing the gap between us, and for a fleeting moment, I let myself lean into the comfort of his presence.

But then, just as quickly as it had come, the moment passed. My mind raced, and the reality of everything that had happened before, the fires, the shadow of the arsonist still lurking just beyond the edges of our lives, slammed into me like a cold wave.

"I can't just forget about everything," I said, my voice edged with frustration. "I can't ignore the fact that someone is still out there, playing games with us, with our lives."

Evan paused, the intensity of the situation not lost on him. "I don't expect you to forget. But we don't have to carry this alone." He reached for my hand, this time more tentative, as if giving me the space to pull away if I needed to. I didn't pull away. Instead, I squeezed his hand, grounding myself in the warmth of it.

"You think we can stop him?" I asked, the words tasting bitter on my tongue. I hadn't realized how much hope I'd placed in the idea of us, in the idea that we could be more than just two people in a tangled mess of circumstances.

He gave a slow nod, his gaze unwavering. "I'm not saying it's easy. Hell, I don't know what the next step is. But we're still here, right? We're still fighting. And I'm not going anywhere."

That was the thing with Evan—I knew he wasn't a man who would run from a fight. And maybe that was part of what had drawn me to him all those years ago. He had this way of standing firm, of digging in when everything else was falling apart, and for all my cynicism, I admired it. I just wasn't sure it would be enough this time.

"Yeah, well," I said, forcing a smile that didn't quite reach my eyes, "sometimes fighting isn't enough."

He seemed to hear the edge in my voice, and his expression softened. "We'll figure it out. One way or another." His hand dropped from mine, and I suddenly felt the loss of it, as though the thread that had briefly connected us was unraveling.

I looked away, unable to meet his eyes for the moment. The truth was, I wasn't sure if I could keep doing this. The weight of the mystery, of what we were up against, felt like a burden that was already too heavy to carry. And the idea of relying on anyone—especially him—terrified me.

"You're thinking too much again," he said, the words familiar, a gentle reminder that I wasn't fooling anyone with my walls.

"Yeah, well," I said, forcing my tone to be light, though it trembled under the weight of my thoughts, "maybe that's what I do best."

He didn't laugh like I expected. Instead, he studied me quietly, his gaze searching. "You don't have to do this alone," he repeated, his voice quieter now, as though the words held more weight than I realized.

For a moment, I wanted to believe him. I wanted to say yes, to let myself trust again, to allow myself to lean into the unknown with him at my side. But there was still something holding me back. Something in the pit of my stomach that twisted at the thought of surrendering, of letting go of control.

I took a deep breath and stepped back, putting a little more space between us. "Maybe you're right," I said, my voice uncertain but steady. "Maybe we'll figure it out. But not today."

His eyes softened, and for a second, I saw something there—something that looked like understanding. But just as quickly, it was replaced with the familiar spark of determination that had always been a part of him. He nodded, stepping back as well.

"Tomorrow then," he said, his voice low, but the promise in it clear. "We'll figure it out tomorrow."

The world outside was quiet, a stillness that almost felt unnatural given the chaos that had swirled around us in the past few days. But inside, the air was charged, thick with the unspoken words and unfinished thoughts that hovered between us like the edge of a storm. I couldn't shake the feeling that, just as the calm of dawn had briefly given way to the fire, everything else—everything we had been trying to outrun—was about to resurface with the same intensity.

Evan stood near the window, his broad back to me, his silhouette framed by the soft light that poured through the half-open blinds. I couldn't see his face, but I knew what he was thinking. We both had the same thoughts, I realized. The same burden, the same fear that lingered like smoke in the air, invisible but suffocating all the same. He'd said we'd figure it out. And while his words were full of that quiet confidence that I used to find so reassuring, today they felt more like a fragile promise, one I wasn't sure either of us could keep.

I finally broke the silence, my voice sounding too loud in the quiet of the room. "You're right, though. We don't have to do this alone. But I don't know how we even begin to fix this."

He turned then, his gaze meeting mine, and the sharpness in his eyes was almost enough to make me flinch. "You start by trusting me. Let me help you."

The way he said it, like it was a simple thing—like trust could be given as easily as a coin in a wishing well—made me feel foolish for hesitating. He was right, of course. We couldn't go back to how things had been. The fact that we were here, facing down a mystery we hadn't fully unraveled, had already changed everything. I wasn't sure what I wanted anymore, but I knew I couldn't keep walking this tightrope without a net beneath me.

"I trust you," I said, but the words tasted empty, as though I were trying to convince myself as much as him. "I just... I don't know how to stop feeling like we're running in circles."

Evan crossed the room in a few strides, and before I knew it, he was standing in front of me, his hand gently cupping my cheek, the warmth of his touch grounding me. I wanted to resist it, to pull away, but I didn't. Instead, I let myself sink into his touch, feeling the comfort of it, even as my mind raced with everything we still didn't know.

"You're not alone," he repeated softly, this time with a certainty that cut through the fog in my head. "We'll figure it out. But you have to let me in."

I swallowed hard, fighting back the wave of emotion that threatened to overtake me. He was right. I had to let him in. But letting him in meant exposing everything—the doubts, the fears, the pieces of myself I'd kept hidden for so long. And maybe that was what I was afraid of the most. Not the mystery. Not the danger. But the possibility of vulnerability.

Evan leaned in closer, his forehead brushing mine, his breath warm against my skin. I could feel the tension in his body, the same tension that had fueled our reckless moments together, and it pulled at something deep inside me. But this time, it was different. This time, there were no easy answers. No quick fixes. Just the raw, undeniable truth that neither of us knew where this path would lead.

"We'll find him," Evan said again, as if he were speaking a promise, not just to me, but to himself. "And when we do, we'll end this."

It was that last part that stuck with me, that lingered in the air like the smoke from a fire that refused to die. We'd end this. But what did that mean? What did it really mean to end it? And at what cost?

Before I could voice the thousand questions swirling in my mind, the sound of a knock at the door broke through the moment, sharp and unexpected. My heart skipped a beat, the tension in the room shifting instantly as we both turned toward the sound. Evan's face hardened, the momentary softness replaced by a hard edge.

Without a word, he moved toward the door, his movements quiet but purposeful.

I didn't need to ask who it was. I already knew. My pulse quickened, and I instinctively reached for the gun at my side, the cold metal a sharp reminder of the danger we were still facing. Evan paused with his hand on the doorknob, glancing back at me. His eyes were narrowed, but there was something else there now. Something unreadable.

"Stay here," he said in a voice that brooked no argument, but I could see the flicker of uncertainty in his eyes. "I'll handle this."

But I wasn't about to sit on the sidelines while things played out. Not this time. I shook my head, my gaze locking with his. "No. I'm not staying behind again."

He didn't argue further, but the tension between us flared again, thicker than before. We both knew what was at stake, what we were about to face. I reached for my jacket, pulling it on with a quickness that belied my unease.

Evan opened the door, and standing on the threshold was a figure I hadn't expected. A figure I thought we were done with. A ghost from our past. His face was as familiar as the line of his jaw, the same arrogance in his stance, the same coldness in his eyes.

"You didn't think it would be that easy, did you?" he asked, his voice smooth and mocking.

I froze, a chill crawling up my spine. The game had just changed.

Chapter 31: Into the Inferno

The smoke was thick, choking the air as we pulled up to the address, its outline already obscured by a rising cloud of black. It swirled and danced above the building like a bad omen, the fire crackling in a slow, deliberate rhythm that sent shivers down my spine. I knew we were too late. The flames had already begun their work, but that didn't stop us. We had no choice.

I turned to Evan, whose jaw was set, face grim, eyes narrowed like he'd seen this before—maybe too many times. His hands gripped the wheel, knuckles white, as the engine idled in front of the structure. There was a faint tremble in his breath, almost imperceptible, but it was there. It was always there before he threw himself into the chaos, before he became something else entirely—the firefighter, the savior, the man who would risk everything for a stranger.

"Stay here," he ordered. The command was sharp, no room for discussion. But we both knew there was no real question.

I nodded, even as my hands curled around the seatbelt, refusing to let go. There was no part of me that wanted to stay behind, but I had learned enough to know when Evan was in that zone, there was no talking him out of it.

"Be careful," I managed, my voice too thin in the roar of the fire that seemed to be growing by the second.

His eyes flicked over to me briefly, a half-smile tugging at his lips before he pushed open the door and disappeared into the chaos. I barely had time to process the motion before the sirens wailed again in the distance, signaling the arrival of backup. But that felt like a lifetime away.

The heat was unbearable, even from here. I leaned forward, watching the flames curl around the edges of the windows like hungry snakes, eager to consume whatever it could. There were people inside. I could feel them, even though I couldn't see them. Evan would find them. He always did. But the question still lingered—what had they been hiding in this building? And where was Leon?

The seconds felt like hours as I sat there, staring at the growing inferno, my heart in my throat, every instinct screaming at me to do something. Anything. I drummed my fingers on the dashboard, the waiting unbearable, until I could no longer stand it.

I pushed the door open, my feet hitting the gravel with a crunch, the heat from the fire slapping my face like a reprimand.

"Stay back!" someone shouted from across the yard, a firefighter waving me away.

I ignored him. I was going to find Evan, make sure he was okay. But as I took a few more steps forward, I saw him, emerging from the smoke like a force of nature. His figure was framed by the orange glow, his face smudged with soot, eyes wild but determined.

"Get back!" he barked, his voice hoarse, but there was something else—something urgent. "There's someone inside. I need backup!"

The words hit me like a slap. Someone was still inside? Panic gripped me, but I fought it back, knowing he needed me calm. "I'll stay here," I said, keeping my voice steady, even though my legs were shaking.

Evan didn't even acknowledge me. Instead, he ran toward the building again, charging back into the heat without a second thought. I watched helplessly, the air thick with smoke and ash, the ground beneath my feet unsteady as if the earth itself were buckling under the weight of the fire.

It seemed like an eternity before he emerged again, dragging a man with him, his clothes singed and his eyes wide with terror. Evan didn't stop, didn't pause to check his own injuries. He shoved the man toward the waiting medics, then turned back, eyes scanning the inferno as if willing something—or someone—out of the flames.

"Leon?" I asked, my voice barely audible over the crackling fire. I didn't expect an answer. But I needed to hear it anyway.

He shook his head, face a mask of frustration. "No sign of him." He wiped a hand over his face, smearing soot and sweat across his forehead. "Nothing. He's not here."

I watched him, the frustration in his eyes now mirroring my own. "Then what now? What do we do?"

He didn't answer right away. Instead, he stood there for a long moment, looking at the burning wreckage as if the answer was buried in the flames themselves. Finally, he spoke, his voice low, almost to himself.

"If Leon was here… then he's either too smart or too lucky to get caught in the fire." He turned toward me, his gaze hardening. "Or he's already gone."

Gone. Just like that. The man who had been pulling strings behind the scenes, always one step ahead, always just out of reach. He could be anywhere now. And there was nothing we could do but wait for the next lead, the next clue, the next piece of the puzzle to fall into place.

The fire continued to burn, but it felt like it had burned everything, even the hope I'd been clinging to.

I didn't know which hurt more—the weight of the smoke still heavy in the air, or the bitter taste of defeat that lingered on my tongue. Leon, that ghost of a man, had once been part of Evan's life in a way that neither of us fully understood. He had always been more shadow than substance, and now, it seemed, he was nothing more than a mirage, slipping away just as we thought we were close to catching him. The fire still raged behind us, but it felt distant, as though the heat and noise belonged to someone else's nightmare.

The paramedics had taken the terrified man away, leaving only the scent of burnt wood and regret. I couldn't help but wonder if Leon had been the one who set the fire—or if it had just been a cruel twist of fate. I watched as the flames licked at the sky, an angry, unforgiving beast that cared nothing for the lives in its path. Was it all a distraction? A diversion?

Evan paced beside me, his boots crunching in the gravel with each step, his eyes scanning the wreckage as if he might find some hidden truth buried in the ruins. I knew what he was thinking—the same thing I was. Leon was here, he had to be. And yet, no sign of him, not even a footprint. It was like trying to catch smoke in your hands, futile and maddening.

"I don't get it," Evan muttered, running a hand through his already messy hair. "If he was here, he was never planning to stay."

I didn't answer right away. There was no point in arguing the obvious. Leon was a ghost, a man who thrived in the shadows, who never stayed in one place long enough to be caught. "Maybe he got scared," I said, though even as the words left my mouth, I knew how ridiculous they sounded. Leon wasn't the type to be easily frightened.

"Yeah, or maybe he's been one step ahead of us this entire time." Evan's voice hardened, his frustration simmering just beneath the surface. I didn't have to look at him to know his mind was racing, spinning webs of possibilities that would lead nowhere.

The sirens finally began to quiet in the distance, their wail fading as the last of the fire trucks rolled away. The wreckage of the building loomed over us, silent now, but still hot to the touch. The sense of urgency had started to seep out of the air, replaced by a deep, suffocating quiet. The only sounds were the occasional crackle of embers and the soft crunch of footsteps on the broken ground.

"I need a drink," I said suddenly, the words tumbling out of me before I could stop them.

Evan turned to look at me, raising an eyebrow. "At this hour?"

"Yes," I said firmly, brushing the loose strands of hair from my face. "After all this, I deserve one. You deserve one."

He seemed to consider it for a moment, and then his lips curved into a small, reluctant smile. "I guess I'm not one to argue after a day like today."

"Good. Meet me at the diner down the street. You can drink your troubles away, and I'll drink my frustration. Deal?"

"Deal," he agreed, though there was a flicker of something else in his eyes—something deeper, darker, like the storm clouds that had gathered in the distance earlier. It was the same storm I had seen in him every time we faced a dead-end. The one that always simmered just beneath the surface.

The diner was quieter than I expected, the hum of the neon lights overhead the only company. The booths were old, the cushions cracked with age, but the coffee—oh, the coffee—was rich and steaming, just the way I liked it. I slid into a booth by the window, the glass streaked with rain that had begun to fall like a quiet sheet of sorrow, as if the world itself was mourning the loss of whatever we had hoped for today.

Evan followed, sitting across from me, his eyes now back to that unreadable distance they so often adopted. He took a long pull from his coffee, the heat of it not quite enough to melt away the cold of whatever had happened to him out there in the fire.

"I thought I was going to find him," he said, his voice rough, the words slow like he was trying to piece them together, like they didn't belong in the same sentence. "I thought maybe..."

He trailed off, and I knew the rest. Maybe this was the one time he couldn't save the day. Maybe he had finally met a man who was smarter than him, faster, more slippery than anything he'd ever chased before.

"You did everything you could," I said, though I knew the words were hollow. There was no real comfort in them, no magic spell to fix the situation. But Evan, stubborn as always, seemed to need the reassurance. So I gave it, even if it was just a thin thread of hope in a sea of disappointment.

He looked at me, his dark eyes narrowing, but not in anger. It was more like he was trying to figure me out, trying to see if I believed the lie I was telling. "I'm not sure I did. Maybe I missed something. Maybe if I'd—"

"You didn't miss anything," I interrupted, leaning forward just enough to make sure he understood. "Sometimes things fall through the cracks. Sometimes people are just too good at disappearing."

Evan didn't argue, didn't fight me on it. Instead, he stared out the window, his gaze distant, and for a long moment, we both just let the silence settle between us, the weight of what we didn't know hanging in the air like smoke.

I should have expected it, really. The fire, the chaos, the endless chase for a man who knew how to vanish like smoke in the night. But standing in that diner, with Evan across from me, I couldn't shake the feeling that this wasn't just another lead gone cold. It felt different this time, heavier, like we'd stumbled into something far darker than we realized. And still, there was no trace of Leon. No sign of the ghost who had haunted Evan's past, the one who always seemed to be a step ahead, hiding just beyond our reach.

Evan's hand trembled slightly as he took another sip of coffee. It wasn't the kind of thing anyone would notice unless they were paying close attention—like I was. But I had spent enough time with him to understand the subtle shifts, the moments when his guard slipped, when he was human instead of just the man who put out fires and saved lives for a living. I knew this was eating at him, gnawing at his confidence. And I hated that.

"I should have gone further in," he muttered, his voice barely more than a whisper. His gaze flickered to the door, to the street beyond, as if Leon might walk in at any moment, laughing at our fruitless efforts. "If I'd just taken one more look... maybe—"

"Stop," I said, cutting him off with the force of a command, even though I didn't mean for it to sound so sharp. "You did everything right. You don't need to go back into that building and risk your life just to prove a point. Leon's not that kind of man. He knows how to hide."

The silence stretched between us, and for a second, it felt like we were in two completely different worlds. I could feel his frustration hanging in the air, a tangible thing that was thick with regret. But that wasn't going to help us now. Regret didn't find people. And Leon was still out there. I had no doubt about that. But what if he wasn't running from us? What if he was playing a much more dangerous game?

"Maybe he's not hiding," I said quietly, my voice steady, even though the words made my stomach flip. "Maybe he's waiting for us to make the next move."

Evan's head snapped up, his dark eyes meeting mine, intense and sharp. "What are you saying?"

I leaned back in the booth, folding my arms across my chest. "Think about it. We're not the only ones looking for him. He knows we're on his trail. What if he's setting us up? What if the fire was just the beginning?"

He stared at me for a moment, as though I'd said something too outrageous to process, but then his expression shifted. A flicker of realization passed across his face. "You think he wants us to come after him."

"Exactly. He's not scared of us. He's baiting us. And I don't know about you, but I'm not about to walk straight into whatever trap he's setting up."

Evan's lips pressed into a thin line, and I could see the gears turning behind his eyes. He wasn't buying into the fear just yet, but I could tell that what I was saying was starting to make sense to him. Leon wasn't running. He was orchestrating. And the longer we stayed in the dark, the easier it would be for him to win.

"We need to figure out what he's really after," I said, my voice firm. "We've been chasing ghosts, but there's something bigger at play here, something we haven't seen yet."

Evan set down his coffee, his eyes narrowing. "You think this is bigger than Leon?"

"I think Leon is the tip of the iceberg. We need to know who's pulling his strings, because this game, it's not just about him. We're part of it now. And if we don't figure it out soon, we're going to be the ones who get burned."

Evan's gaze locked with mine, the weight of what I said sinking in. "So what now?"

"We go back to the beginning," I said, leaning forward. "We start digging into Leon's connections. Who has he been talking to? Who has he been working for? Someone's behind this. And if we find that person, we find Leon."

Evan nodded, his jaw tightening. "Alright. Let's do it."

We didn't say anything more. We both knew that from this moment on, nothing was going to be the same. We were no longer just chasing Leon. We were chasing something much darker, something much more dangerous. And we didn't have the luxury of time on our side.

I paid the bill with quick, efficient movements, and we left the diner in silence, the weight of our next steps hanging heavily between us. The streets were slick with rain, the world outside the diner washed in a gray haze. It wasn't just the rain that made the world feel heavy; it was the nagging sense that we were being watched. The air itself felt thick with tension, as if the universe were holding its breath, waiting for the next move.

We split up at the corner, heading in opposite directions. Evan had his contacts in the fire department; he would track down anything related to the fire, any scrap of evidence that might have been overlooked. And I had my own network of people, each with a piece of the puzzle, if I could only put them together in time.

The night had fallen fully now, and as I walked down the street, the rhythmic slap of my boots on the wet pavement was the only sound. That's when I saw it—just a flash, a shadow darting across the alley up ahead. I froze, my heart leaping into my throat. It was too quick to be a trick of the light. Someone was there, and they knew I was watching.

I took a step forward, then another, careful, deliberate. The alley was dark, but I could make out the shape now, a figure standing just at the edge of the streetlight's reach. As I stepped closer, my pulse quickened. I wasn't alone anymore.

Then the figure turned. And for a split second, I thought I recognized the face.

But the words never left my mouth.

Chapter 32: Scorched Trust

The air in the office was heavy, as though the weight of unsaid things lingered like an oppressive storm cloud, threatening to burst at any moment. I could feel the tension in the pit of my stomach, knotting tighter with each passing hour. Evan was distant, more than usual. It wasn't just the case, though that was enough to set anyone's nerves on edge. The fires, the mysterious arsonist, the backstabbing—everything had begun to wear on him. I could see it in the way he narrowed his eyes when he thought no one was watching, his jaw clenched tight like a vice. It wasn't just the case anymore; it was everything. The question that burned in my mind was whether it was the case that was pulling us apart, or something deeper, something that I couldn't see, and I feared I might never be able to.

"Lena," Evan's voice broke through my thoughts, but it wasn't the warm tone I had once known. This was clipped, like he was holding back something volatile, as though I might shatter if I got too close.

I looked up from my desk, meeting his eyes across the room. There was a flicker of something there, but it was hard to place—distrust? Or was it guilt? Either way, it unsettled me.

"You've been quiet," I said, trying to keep my voice steady, but I knew he could hear the edge that had crept into it. How could he not? We used to finish each other's sentences, laugh about our day, share everything. Now, it felt like we were strangers in the same room.

Evan didn't answer immediately. Instead, he looked away, running a hand through his hair in that way that always made me think he was trying to push something away—something he didn't want to confront. His posture stiffened as he took a step closer, but the space between us felt vast, as if he were miles away instead of a few feet.

"I've been thinking," he said, his voice low, "there's a leak somewhere. Someone's feeding the arsonist information."

I nodded slowly, but the words were like ice in my veins. "You don't mean—"

He cut me off. "I mean, someone here. In the team. Someone is giving them exactly what they need to stay ahead of us."

My heart pounded in my chest. The air felt even thicker now, and I could barely breathe. "Evan, you don't think…?"

His eyes turned hard, cutting through me. "I don't know who I can trust anymore, Lena. Not even you."

The words struck like a slap, and for a second, I couldn't speak. The room felt too small, too suffocating, as though the walls were closing in. I wasn't sure what hurt more—the accusation or the look in his eyes. I thought I knew him, had known him for years, but this—this wasn't the man I had given my heart to.

"I—" My voice caught in my throat, and I had to swallow to steady it. "You think I'd betray you?"

"I don't know who you are anymore," he said, his gaze not quite meeting mine, his voice tinged with frustration. "Everyone's hiding something, Lena. Even you."

The sting of his words cut deep. I opened my mouth, but the words got stuck somewhere between my chest and my lips, too tangled up in the hurt to come out. There was no way to explain, not when the walls between us had gotten so high, so thick.

Instead of answering, I stood up from my chair and moved toward him, my legs shaking beneath me. "I've been with you through every fire, Evan. You know that. I've never lied to you, never hidden anything from you."

He took a step back, his eyes not leaving mine. "It's not just about what you've done or haven't done. It's about trust, Lena. Trust that's been burned, one piece at a time."

I could see the cracks forming, the slow, inevitable collapse of something once solid. Each word he spoke tore at the fabric of our relationship. Every accusation, every look, every unspoken thing between us pushed me further away. My heart ached for what we were losing, but I couldn't break through. The distance was growing too wide.

I wanted to yell at him, to tell him he was wrong, that I hadn't done anything to hurt him. But the truth was, I couldn't even tell myself that anymore. What was I supposed to say to a man who no longer saw me as someone he could trust? My chest tightened with the realization that the cracks we'd been ignoring were now yawning wide, and I couldn't even begin to fill them.

"I'll find out who it is," he said, turning on his heel and heading toward the door. "And when I do..."

I watched him leave, my breath shallow. I wanted to call out to him, to beg him to stop, but the words were gone. What did I even have left to say?

The silence that followed was deafening. I stood there in the middle of the room, my hands trembling at my sides. What had happened to us? Where had we gone wrong? I didn't have the answers, and I didn't know if I ever would.

It wasn't just the arson anymore. It wasn't even the case. It was the slow, seeping poison of doubt that was tearing through everything we'd built, everything we'd shared. And I didn't know if it was something we could survive.

The silence that had settled in the room was oppressive, like the aftermath of a thunderstorm. A lingering tension crackled in the air, one that seemed to grow heavier with each minute that passed. I found myself staring at the door Evan had left through, wishing I could do something—anything—to bridge the chasm that had opened between us. But I knew better. There was nothing I could do right now but wait, and I wasn't sure how much longer I could bear the quiet. The weight of his words—the accusation, the suspicion, the coldness—pressed against my chest, suffocating me with every breath I took.

I paced the floor, my shoes clicking against the polished tiles like the ticking of a clock counting down to some inevitable end. What was I supposed to do now? How could I fix this, when the thing that had held us together, that thread of trust, had been snapped in two? I could feel it unraveling between us, piece by fragile piece. Each moment without him, without the warmth of his touch or the comfort of his voice, felt like a slow erosion of everything we'd built.

I tried to focus, to distract myself with work, but the files in front of me blurred into meaningless shapes. My mind kept returning to Evan, to the shadow of his doubt that seemed to loom over us both. How had we gotten here? Where had the love, the passion, the certainty gone? And, more terrifying than any of that, was the fear that it might never come back.

I was still lost in these thoughts when the door to the office opened again. For a moment, I thought it might be him, returning with some apology or explanation, but the figure that stepped inside was unfamiliar—a man in his late thirties, with sharp eyes and a grin that didn't quite reach them. He was one of Evan's colleagues, I remembered, though I couldn't quite recall his name.

"Lena, right?" he said, his voice smooth, too smooth. There was something about him that immediately set me on edge, though I couldn't put my finger on why.

I nodded, half-heartedly glancing at him. "Yeah, that's me."

He closed the door behind him with a soft click and then leaned casually against the desk, his eyes scanning the room before settling back on me. "Evan's not in today, huh?"

I looked up, irritation sparking in my chest. "No. He's... otherwise occupied."

There was an unsettling pause before he continued, his gaze shifting just a little too quickly, too deliberately. "You know, it's a real shame. A lot of people around here are starting to talk. It's not just the arson case anymore. It's... well, it's Evan, isn't it?"

My heart skipped a beat. His tone was too casual, too familiar, but there was an underlying edge to it that made my skin crawl. "What are you talking about?" I asked, trying to keep my voice steady, but it came out sharper than I intended.

He straightened up, pushing himself off the desk with a slight grin. "Oh, nothing. Just that he's been a little... distracted lately. Some people are saying he's too focused on the case, you know? Not seeing the bigger picture."

I didn't like the insinuation. My stomach twisted, a feeling of dread creeping over me. Who was he to say anything about Evan? And what did he mean by "the bigger picture"? I wasn't in the mood for games or vague threats.

"Listen," I said, standing up abruptly, "I'm not sure what you think you're implying, but if this is some kind of... power play, or whatever it is you're doing, it's not going to work."

He chuckled, the sound dark and hollow, like someone who had been laughing too long without finding anything funny. "Oh, don't worry, Lena. I'm not here to cause any trouble. Just... curious, that's all."

His eyes lingered a moment longer, reading me like an open book, then he shrugged and turned toward the door. "Just remember, people are always watching. Especially in situations like this."

And then, just as quickly as he'd come, he was gone, leaving behind a lingering unease that gnawed at me. I stood there for a long time, my mind racing. What was that all about? Why had he come here? What did he want? His words echoed in my mind, like a siren call I couldn't quite shake. People are always watching. I couldn't ignore the possibility that someone was trying to sow discord—trying to drive a wedge between Evan and me. But who? And why?

The knock at the door startled me, and I swung around, half expecting it to be the same man from before. But this time, when I opened it, I found Evan standing there, his face drawn tight with something between frustration and guilt.

"I've been looking everywhere for you," he said, his voice a mix of anger and exhaustion.

I stepped aside to let him in, my heart racing. I wanted to ask him where he'd gone, what had happened between us, but the words stuck in my throat. Instead, I just stood there, waiting for him to speak.

He didn't waste time with pleasantries. "We need to talk," he said, his gaze flicking to the door behind me. "Not here, though."

I nodded, leading him to a small conference room at the back of the office, away from prying eyes. The room was empty, but the tension between us was palpable. I could feel the weight of what was unsaid, hanging between us like a thick fog, obscuring everything.

When we sat down, he didn't immediately meet my eyes. Instead, he looked at his hands, flexing them nervously. His usual confidence was gone, replaced by something much more vulnerable.

"I... I don't know what's happening with me," he said, his voice low, almost a whisper. "I'm sorry. I've been pushing you away, I know. But I don't know how to stop. I've got this... weight on my shoulders. I can't even think straight sometimes."

I didn't know how to respond. Part of me wanted to reach out to him, to tell him it was okay, that we could work through this. But another part of me was too scared. Too scared to believe him. Too scared to trust that this wasn't just another manipulation.

But then, just as quickly as the coldness had come, it softened. He looked at me, his eyes searching, as though trying to find a way back to something we'd lost.

"I need you to trust me, Lena," he said quietly. "I know I've been terrible to you. But I can't do this without you. I need you with me. Please."

And for the first time in days, I let myself believe him, even just a little. Because maybe, just maybe, we could still find our way back.

The weight of Evan's words hung in the air like a dense fog, and I couldn't escape it. He needed me. And for the first time in what felt like forever, I wasn't sure if I could give him what he was asking for. My chest felt tight as I sat across from him, watching him fidget with the cuff of his sleeve. I knew he was trying, but part of me wondered if it was too late. The cracks in our relationship were too large, too jagged to ignore, and no amount of apologies or promises could fill them.

"I don't know how to fix this, Lena," he said, his voice barely above a whisper. "I don't know who to trust. The team—hell, even you—I feel like everyone's hiding something."

I wanted to reach across the table and take his hand, to remind him that I was still here, that I hadn't gone anywhere, but I stayed frozen in my seat. What was the point? What was the point in trying to patch up a bond that was quickly unraveling?

"I'm not hiding anything from you," I replied, my voice coming out too sharp, but I couldn't stop it. "If you're not going to believe me, then what's the point? You're pushing me away. You're pushing everyone away."

He didn't answer right away. Instead, his eyes flickered toward the door, as though he was expecting someone to burst in at any moment. The paranoia was suffocating, and I could see it in his eyes. He was consumed by it, and no matter how much I wanted to help, no matter how much I tried to soothe him, it felt like there was an invisible wall between us, one that I couldn't climb over.

"I never wanted this to happen," he said finally, his voice rough, like he was fighting back emotion. "I never wanted to push you away. But I can't think straight anymore, Lena. All I see are the flames, the destruction. I don't know who I can trust."

His gaze met mine then, and for the briefest moment, I saw something there—something raw, something vulnerable. It was enough to make my heart ache for him, but it wasn't enough to make me forget what had happened. What had been happening for weeks, for months. The way he'd distanced himself from me, the way his suspicions had eaten away at us, turning everything we had into a series of tense silences and bitter glances.

"You think I'm part of this?" I asked, my voice trembling despite myself. I wasn't sure what I wanted the answer to be, but I needed to hear him say it. I needed to know if he really believed I was the one betraying him.

He hesitated for a long moment before shaking his head. "No. But I don't know who is, Lena. And I can't stand not knowing."

The words hit me like a punch to the stomach. He didn't trust anyone, not even the people who had been with him through everything. And that included me.

"I'm not your enemy, Evan," I said, my voice breaking just a little. "You need to start believing that. Or we're both going to lose everything."

I pushed away from the table, standing abruptly, the chair scraping across the floor. I didn't want to cry. I didn't want to break down in front of him, but I could feel the tears starting to sting the corners of my eyes. I turned away quickly, pretending I wasn't affected, pretending the cracks hadn't begun to deepen, spreading into every part of my soul.

But Evan stood, following me across the room. "Lena—"

"Just stop," I interrupted, whirling around to face him. "Stop acting like I'm part of the problem. You're the one pushing everyone away. You're the one who's so deep in this mess that you can't even see what's right in front of you."

My heart was pounding now, the tension between us thick and suffocating. But something inside me snapped. I was done. Done trying to reach him when all he wanted to do was pull away. Done being the one who always had to hold everything together.

"I'm sorry," he said, his voice quieter now, softer. "I don't know how we got here. I don't know how to make it right."

"You can't just apologize and expect everything to go back to normal," I shot back, my voice trembling with frustration. "This isn't just about us anymore, Evan. This is about trust. And right now, I'm not sure we have any left."

I took a step back, as if putting some distance between us could help clear the fog in my head. But I couldn't shake the feeling that I was standing on the edge of something I couldn't stop, something that was slipping further and further away from me no matter how hard I tried to hold on.

"I'm trying, Lena," he said, his voice desperate now, his hand reaching out for me. But I couldn't let him. Not yet.

"You're not trying hard enough," I whispered, my voice barely audible. "You don't get to shut me out and expect me to keep fighting for something that doesn't exist anymore."

I turned to leave, to walk out of the room and let the silence fill the space between us. But just as I reached the door, I heard a soft knock. My pulse quickened, and I spun around, half-expecting someone else to walk in. But no. The look on Evan's face told me something was wrong, something worse than I had imagined.

"You should check the phone," he said, his voice strained. "I think someone just sent a message."

The sudden cold dread that washed over me was instant. My hand hovered over the door handle, but I froze. Something told me that whatever was waiting for me on that phone was the one thing that could break everything open. The last piece of this twisted puzzle.

I pulled the phone from my bag, my fingers trembling as I unlocked it. The message was simple, but the words felt like ice in my veins.

I know what you're hiding. And I'll make sure everyone else does too.

I stared at the screen, my breath catching in my throat. And before I could even process what was happening, the phone buzzed again. This time, there was a photo. One that made my blood run cold.

Evan and me. Together.

From a time I couldn't remember. But someone else clearly did.

Chapter 33: Sparks of Hope

The morning light slanted through the blinds, casting long shadows across the cluttered desk. I sat in front of the computer, my fingers hovering over the keys like I was about to summon something both dangerous and necessary. The clicking of the mouse seemed louder than it should have been, and my breath caught each time I flicked through another file, another trail, another clue.

Evan sat across from me, his elbows on the edge of the desk, eyes narrowed as he examined the screen. His usual confident air was gone, replaced by something I couldn't quite place—a tension, a weariness. Maybe both. I wanted to ask if he was okay, but I had a feeling the answer wouldn't be the one I was looking for. He was in it now, just like I was.

"Look at this," I murmured, pointing at a series of names on the screen. "They're connected. They're all part of the city's old guard—the people who have held influence here for decades."

Evan leaned forward, eyes narrowing as he scrolled through the pages. "I see it. These aren't just firefighters. Some of them... they have ties to city council, private investors, local businesses."

I could almost feel the weight of the truth pressing in on me. It was one thing to investigate an arsonist—it was another to uncover a tangled mess of corruption, betrayal, and unspoken alliances. The fire we'd been chasing was just the spark, the outward manifestation of something far more sinister. I had thought the fires were personal, driven by anger or revenge. But now, they felt like a statement—a loud, explosive declaration that the city's foundation was cracked, and the arsonist was intent on tearing it apart.

"The target's always the same," I muttered, more to myself than to Evan. "Something old. Something important. The first building, the second one... and now, the third."

Evan's gaze flickered to the paper I had tacked to the wall—three fire-damaged buildings, all part of the city's historical landmarks. The one we were about to face was different, though. It wasn't just a relic of the past. It was a symbol, a place that represented everything the city had built, everything it had fought to protect.

"They're going after the city's heart," Evan said, his voice rough. "And we're supposed to stop it?"

I let out a breath, the sharpness of the situation sinking deeper. "We don't have a choice. The next fire—if we don't stop it—it'll be the one that destroys everything."

Evan's lips pressed into a thin line. I knew what he was thinking. If it were anyone else, he might've said it out loud: What are we even doing here? But he didn't. He was a man of action, and that was why we were both sitting in this hellhole of a fire station, staring at evidence that would have crippled most people.

I flicked through the files one last time. Names, dates, locations, all jumbled together like pieces of a puzzle I couldn't quite fit together. But then, just as I was about to close the folder, something caught my eye. A discrepancy. A time stamp. A missing piece.

"Wait," I said, louder this time. "This is it. This is where they're going next."

Evan's eyes snapped to mine, and I could see the shift in his expression—surprise, then understanding. "That's... that's right in the middle of the city. The oldest part of it."

I nodded, already pulling up the map on the screen. My mind was racing, piecing together the plan in an instant. The building—an old, ornate theater—was surrounded by a maze of narrow streets, cobblestone alleys, and dense crowds. It wasn't just a building. It was a place of memory, of pride. People came from all over the city to see performances there. The fire would be more than an act of destruction. It would be a death blow to the soul of the city.

"They're not just trying to burn it down," I murmured, more to myself than to Evan. "They're trying to erase it from existence. To make the city forget."

Evan's silence stretched between us, thick and charged. I could feel the weight of his gaze on me, and I didn't need to look up to know he was thinking the same thing I was: How are we supposed to stop this?

But we didn't have time to question it. Not anymore.

"We need to warn the people at the theater," I said, pushing my chair back. "And we need to get there before the fire starts."

Evan stood, his chair scraping against the floor. "I'm going with you."

I turned to him, meeting his eyes for the first time since we'd started this mad hunt. He was all business now, no trace of doubt or hesitation. It was a stark contrast to the man who had walked in here hours ago, a man still grappling with his own demons.

He was with me, and that meant everything. We might've been fighting fire with fire, but at least we weren't doing it alone.

The city's heartbeat pulsed in my ears as we left the station. The streets felt different now, charged with an energy I couldn't explain. The world was holding its breath, waiting for something to happen. And I couldn't help but wonder: When the smoke cleared, would we still be standing?

The theater stood like a sentinel from another time, its ornate façade gleaming in the fading light. It was beautiful, a relic of the past, but I couldn't shake the sense that it was more than just a building. It felt… fragile, as if the city's heartbeat was held together by its crumbling brick and peeling paint. And somewhere, in the shadows of those once-gleaming walls, a fire was waiting to be lit, a match poised to erase not just the theater but the very memory of it.

I turned to Evan as we approached the theater, our footsteps echoing in the narrow alleyway. The tension between us was palpable, but it wasn't just the weight of the task ahead—it was something more, something unspoken. It had been building all afternoon, in the way his eyes lingered just a second too long on mine, in the way we worked side by side without any of the usual banter. The quiet had its own language, one we were both fluent in.

"This is it," I said, my voice barely a whisper. I glanced at the building again, my stomach knotting as I saw the shadows stretching out like fingers, crawling across the stone. "We can't afford to make any mistakes."

Evan gave a curt nod, his expression hard as granite. He didn't speak, but the way he clenched his jaw told me everything I needed to know. He wasn't just committed to stopping the fire. He was invested in preventing something even worse. Something we hadn't yet fully understood.

The theater's doors stood wide open, as if inviting us in, but I had no illusion that what waited behind them would be anything but trouble. Inside, the air was thick with dust, the kind that settled over forgotten things, over things that no one cared to look at anymore. But I wasn't here for nostalgia. I was here for answers.

"We need to find the fire traps, the points of entry, anything that'll give us an edge," I muttered, more to myself than to Evan.

His eyes scanned the darkened interior, his voice low. "If they're here, we won't see them until it's too late."

That truth hung in the air between us, a chilling reminder that everything we had been chasing might slip through our fingers at the last possible second. I wanted to argue, to say we could still stop it, but the words felt hollow in my throat. The reality was harsh and unforgiving. Time was running out.

As we moved deeper into the theater, the faint creak of the floorboards beneath our feet made the silence even more oppressive. The place had a history, but it was being buried under layers of neglect. Once, it had been a hub of culture, a place where people gathered to watch performances that brought the city together. Now, it was just an empty shell. But it wasn't the building that had been chosen as the target—it was the heart of the city's soul.

"I don't like this," I said, half to Evan, half to myself. "It feels like a trap."

Evan stopped in his tracks, his eyes scanning the room. He didn't seem surprised, though. Maybe, deep down, he knew it, too. He just hadn't said it aloud yet. "You think they're waiting for us?"

"Maybe." I shrugged, pulling my jacket tighter around my shoulders. "But they might be waiting for more than just us."

I was talking about the city. About the people who didn't know what was coming. I didn't even know how we would explain it to them. How could I tell them that this wasn't just an arsonist with a vendetta, but a person willing to burn the entire city down to send a message?

We moved toward the back of the theater, where the backstage area loomed like a labyrinth of forgotten props and half-dismantled sets. The smell of old wood and dust was overwhelming, but it was the coldness that unsettled me most. The deeper we went, the more the temperature seemed to drop. It was as if the place itself was holding its breath, waiting for something terrible to happen.

And then I saw it.

A faint line of light flickered through a crack in the wall, barely noticeable, but there nonetheless. I was on it before Evan could even say anything, pushing against the wall with a strength I didn't know I had. The wall groaned as I pried open a small door that had been hidden behind layers of crumbling plaster. Inside, the smell hit me immediately—gasoline, thick and suffocating.

I stepped back, my heart racing. "It's here," I said, my voice tight with a mixture of relief and horror. "This is where it starts."

Evan didn't hesitate. He stepped into the narrow space, his flashlight slicing through the dark like a knife. "We need to make sure they don't get to it first."

He was right. This wasn't just about finding the fire. It was about keeping the arsonist from lighting the match. But what if we couldn't stop them? What if, despite all our preparation, despite all the time we'd spent chasing this, it was already too late?

I pushed those thoughts out of my mind, focusing instead on the task at hand. The trap had been set. Now we just had to make sure we were the ones who caught it.

We moved quickly, checking every corner, every shadowed alcove. But it wasn't just the arsonist we had to worry about anymore. The more I thought about it, the more I realized that there were bigger forces at play. Someone had orchestrated this. Someone with a vested interest in making sure this fire wasn't just another act of destruction—it was a statement.

I could feel the weight of it all settling over me like a storm cloud, thick and suffocating. This wasn't just about stopping a fire. This was about saving everything I cared about.

And somehow, in the midst of it all, I couldn't help but wonder: What if the fire wasn't the end? What if it was just the beginning of something far worse?

The darkness behind the theater felt alive, like it was pulsing with a heartbeat all its own, a slow and steady rhythm that matched my own erratic pulse. My fingers tightened around the flashlight as I scanned the backstage area, the damp, musty air making each breath feel heavier than the last. I could hear Evan's boots scuffing along the floor behind me, his presence a solid reassurance even as the danger tightened its grip around us.

"How sure are we that this is it?" Evan asked, his voice breaking the silence like a shot in the dark.

I glanced over my shoulder at him, keeping my voice low. "As sure as we can be. It's too quiet here—there's no sign of anyone, and this is where the gasoline's been stored. Whoever's behind this wants us to find it, to think we've got a lead. It's a distraction."

His eyes narrowed. "A distraction? So, what? We're walking right into a trap?"

I didn't answer right away, letting the weight of his question sink in. Because the answer was both simple and terrifying. "Maybe." The word hung between us like smoke.

Evan's hand slid under his jacket, his fingers brushing the cool metal of his weapon. "Then we'll just have to make sure they don't spring it on us."

We moved through the maze of darkened corridors, every creak and whisper of the old building making my skin crawl. I had to admit that Evan was right—this wasn't just about stopping the fire anymore. It was bigger, much bigger, and whoever was behind this wasn't concerned with the flames alone. No, they wanted something more. They wanted to burn the city's memory to the ground, to erase the past.

And maybe—just maybe—they wanted to erase the people who still cared about it.

We came to a small door tucked in a far corner of the theater's backstage. The kind that was never meant to be seen, much less opened. But it stood ajar now, and I knew that whatever lay beyond it would be the final piece of the puzzle. The question was whether we were ready for the truth it held.

"Stay close," I whispered, already feeling the familiar weight of the uncertainty that had become my constant companion.

Evan's response was a terse nod, his hand brushing against the handle of the door, testing its weight. When it didn't budge, he gave it a firm push. The door opened with a sharp creak, revealing a narrow staircase leading down into the unknown.

"We're going down there," I said, though it wasn't a question.

"Apparently," Evan answered with a dry chuckle. But there was no humor in it, just the tight edge of someone who knew what kind of trouble we were walking into.

We descended together, every step echoing through the hollow space, until the air turned colder, like the breath of something ancient and forgotten. There was no light down here, only the dim flicker of our flashlights cutting through the gloom.

And then, we saw it.

A room at the end of the stairs—larger than I'd expected, with the smell of gasoline thick in the air. The faint, almost imperceptible hum of machinery buzzed in the distance. But it wasn't the machinery that caught my attention. It was the sheer number of gasoline canisters stacked in neat rows across the floor, their labels worn and faded, some of them half-empty, others full to the brim.

This wasn't just a fire waiting to happen—it was the setup for a catastrophe.

I stepped closer, my heart pounding in my chest as I tried to make sense of the room. The walls were lined with old furniture and remnants of theater props, stacked in haphazard piles as if someone had been preparing for a massive event, one they hadn't quite finished. A sense of wrongness gnawed at my gut.

"This doesn't feel right," I muttered, eyeing the stacks of cans. "This place—this room—it's been set up for a controlled burn. But why here? Why now?"

Evan crouched next to one of the cans, inspecting the nozzle. "It's not just about starting a fire," he said slowly. "It's about ensuring it's uncontrollable. Whoever's behind this wants to spread it far and wide."

I swallowed hard, the weight of his words sinking in. The arsonist wasn't just trying to burn down a building. They were trying to set the entire city ablaze. Every landmark, every old stone, every piece of history reduced to ash in one night.

I shook my head, trying to clear the thought that threatened to overwhelm me. "We have to stop them," I said firmly, more to myself than to him. But I already knew that stopping them wasn't going to be enough.

Evan stood, his gaze flicking across the room as if searching for something hidden in the shadows. "We need to make sure we're not too late," he said. "There's no telling how many places like this there are."

That was the truth of it. The fire was the least of our worries. This wasn't about one arsonist anymore—it was about a network, a web of people who had enough power to make things like this happen without anyone noticing.

But I couldn't think about the people behind it, not yet. Not while the room we were standing in felt like a ticking bomb.

I reached for my phone, dialing the fire station before I could second-guess myself. The line rang three times, then four. Finally, someone picked up.

"Fire station, how can I help you?"

"Send everyone. Now," I barked. "The theater's about to go up in flames. It's worse than we thought. We need backup, we need reinforcements, and we need it fast."

The operator's voice faltered for a second, then steadied. "Understood. Help is on the way."

I hung up, the weight of the moment crashing over me. We had to act fast, but the longer I stood there, the more the pieces seemed to be slipping out of reach. The building was rigged to explode—there was no doubt in my mind about that anymore. And somewhere in the dark, someone was waiting for it to all go up in smoke.

Evan met my gaze, his face grim. "It's too quiet. They're already here, aren't they?"

I couldn't answer him. My breath caught in my throat, my body stiffening as the unmistakable sound of footsteps reached my ears. We weren't alone anymore.

And this time, the enemy had the advantage.

Chapter 34: The Heart of the Flame

The weight of the night pressed down on me, each step through the cold, dimly lit hallway a reminder that we were running out of time. The old building groaned beneath its own age, the air thick with dust and the faint scent of mildew that clung to the corners like an unwanted memory. I tried not to look at the floor as we walked, knowing the wood beneath our feet was fragile—too fragile. The building had survived decades, but tonight, it felt like it might not survive us.

Evan's presence beside me was a steadying force, though I didn't dare turn my head to look at him. His silence was more reassuring than words ever could be. The slight brush of his hand against mine as we reached the corner was almost imperceptible, but it grounded me in the chaos of the moment. In a world where the unseen threat was just one corner away, it was the smallest touch that kept me tethered to the reality I was trying desperately to hold onto.

"Stay close," Evan muttered under his breath, his voice low but intense, a touch of something that might have been concern buried beneath the calm exterior. It was odd—his usual bravado was gone. The arsonist had done that to us. The fear. The uncertainty.

I nodded, even though I knew he couldn't see me in the dark. My heart thudded heavily in my chest, and every breath seemed like an effort, each inhale and exhale coated in a fine layer of smoke that wasn't quite there yet but felt like it was. I had the nagging sensation that it was only a matter of time before the fire would start—the fire I wasn't sure we'd be able to stop this time.

There were no signs of the sabotage, no telltale wires or ticking devices in the places we checked. It felt wrong—too wrong—and yet, there was something satisfying about the quiet that lay thick between us. Too quiet. And in a place like this, silence was never a good thing. It wasn't natural. Old buildings never stayed silent, not even when they were standing still.

Then, out of nowhere, a sound. A shift, like the air itself bending to a new shape. A soft click. A door creaking open behind us. I froze, and Evan's grip on my hand tightened, a signal that he'd heard it too.

"We're not alone," I whispered, though I already knew that much. The tension in the air thickened, curdled into something sharp, something predatory. We weren't alone. The arsonist had finally decided to show his face.

I felt the cold prickle of anticipation rise along my spine. I had spent the better part of the last hour steeling myself for this moment, expecting him to appear in a cloud of smoke, but the reality was far more disorienting. There was no grand reveal. No dramatic lighting. Just a voice, steady and calm, cutting through the silence like a blade.

"Well, well," the voice said, as if we were nothing more than an inconvenience to his plans. "You really thought you could stop me?"

I didn't need to turn around to know who it was. The familiarity of the voice—the unremarkable arrogance in it—was enough. I couldn't place him exactly, but I'd heard it somewhere before. It wasn't just the sound of someone who had learned to be unbothered; it was the voice of someone who knew they were already two steps ahead. And that made him more dangerous.

Evan's hand shifted on mine, and the briefest, most electric shiver ran down my arm. I had no words, no response, no witty retort. I just had the feeling, deep in my gut, that this would be the moment we'd finally lose the battle.

There was a faint hiss—just enough to register before the world exploded around us.

A flash of light. A deafening roar. My ears rang, the ground seemed to shift beneath my feet, and then I was thrown backward, my body slamming into something solid. The air was suddenly thick with smoke, acrid and biting. Coughing, I struggled to sit up, my hand grasping blindly for something to steady me. The taste of ash was in my mouth, burning my throat as I tried to breathe.

"Evan!" My voice came out in a hoarse rasp, swallowed by the chaos, but there was no answer. I tried again, panic rising. "Evan, where are you?"

A low groan answered me, and I quickly pushed myself to my feet, my legs unsteady. The entire hallway was bathed in orange light, flickering as if the building itself were alive, pulsing with the promise of destruction. The floor beneath me felt too soft, like it might give way at any moment.

There he was, his form slowly emerging from the smoke, his face streaked with soot, but his eyes still locked onto mine. He wasn't dead. Thank God, he wasn't dead.

"We need to move," he said, his voice rough but commanding, like a man used to giving orders even when the world was falling apart around him.

I didn't need to be told twice. I moved toward him, my hand instinctively reaching out for his, and together, we stumbled down the hallway, toward the exit that seemed too far away. The building seemed to groan again, like it was remembering its own fragile history, and with each step we took, I could feel it crumbling beneath us.

The arsonist had set the trap. And now, it was up to us to escape it.

The smoke was relentless, choking, like the very air had turned on us. It twisted into every corner, snaked into my lungs with a fury that made my chest tighten in protest. I could hardly see my own hand in front of my face, let alone the collapsing hallway. The fire had already spread faster than we had imagined—its ferocity somehow matching the quiet confidence of the man who had set it all in motion. The heat was unbearable now, clinging to the walls, crawling up the floors like a living thing.

Evan was beside me again, though it felt as if he had somehow become a part of the smoke itself—just a shadow, a breath away from disappearing. I could hear the rasp of his breath, quick and labored, and his footsteps as they fell into a rhythm with mine. But still, he wasn't looking at me. We both knew that we couldn't afford the luxury of checking on each other, not now. Not with everything crumbling around us.

"This isn't just sabotage," Evan muttered, his voice strained but urgent. "This is... personal."

I glanced at him quickly, his face just visible through the haze. His jaw was set in that stubborn way of his, but his eyes—his eyes were burning with something deeper than fire.

"I know," I whispered, my words barely carrying through the smoke. "But we don't have time to figure out his motivations. We just need to get out."

His grip on my arm tightened, pulling me forward as if his mere touch could shield me from the flames at our backs. "I don't know if we can. It's too fast. We're too slow."

I didn't respond. We both knew he was right. Each footstep we took seemed to take us further into the heart of the chaos. It felt like the building itself was folding in on us, pressing down on our shoulders with a silent cruelty. The fire had already claimed its first victims—structure, stability, sanity. There was nothing left but ash and the promise of more destruction. The walls had begun to warp, the once-solid beams groaning under the weight of their own demise.

Then came the sound—a low, almost reverberating thud that made my bones rattle in my chest. It came from behind us. A door slamming shut, the unmistakable sound of something being locked. And the unmistakable sound of the arsonist's voice—smooth, too calm, as if this were some twisted version of an art show.

"Did you really think I'd just let you walk away?"

The words hung in the air like a fog of their own, and for a heartbeat, I couldn't breathe. I turned, ready to fight, but it was too late. The flash of movement was barely visible through the smoke, but I could hear the distinct scrape of metal on stone, the unmistakable click of a fuse being set into motion.

"Run!" Evan's voice cracked through the tension just in time.

We didn't need any further prompting. The trap had been sprung, and we were already too close to the flames to waste time trying to outthink it. We sprinted down the hallway, feet pounding against the splintering wood beneath us, the floor buckling slightly with each step. The fire was everywhere now, consuming anything it could find, and I could feel the heat licking at my skin, the pressure of it pressing me forward even as it threatened to burn us both alive.

Ahead, the hallway split into two directions, one path leading to the stairwell and the other to a long corridor that I knew would eventually take us to a side exit. The problem was that I had no idea which way would get us out faster. The fire was spreading too quickly for logic, too wildly for reason. But Evan didn't hesitate. Without a word, he pulled me toward the stairs.

I didn't argue, because I knew. In moments like this, you follow. You trust, even when you're not sure of the destination. His confidence, even in the face of impending doom, was something I envied. His steady hand, his unwavering resolve—it was like a light in the suffocating darkness. I tried to ignore the sting in my lungs, the dizziness creeping up on me as I fought for breath. I could taste the ash, thick and acrid, coating my tongue.

As we reached the stairwell, I realized something else. We weren't alone.

A sound—footsteps, soft but deliberate—echoed behind us. Someone was trailing us, staying just out of sight, like a predator playing with its prey. I risked a glance over my shoulder, trying to make out anything in the haze of smoke, but there was nothing. Not at first. Then the shadow flickered again, more defined this time, a silhouette against the firelight.

It was him. The arsonist. He wasn't just hiding in the smoke. He was making his way toward us, as calm as ever, his pace leisurely, like he had all the time in the world.

I could feel my heart rate spike. "He's coming," I whispered, my voice thick with fear and disbelief. "He's right behind us."

Evan's grip on my arm tightened, and I could feel the muscles in his arm coil with the same tension that gripped my chest. "We're not losing him now."

The stairs groaned under our feet as we rushed upward, the heat growing hotter with every step. We needed to move faster, but every part of me felt like it was being pulled in different directions—my body begging for air, my mind screaming for a plan that I didn't have.

And still, the arsonist followed, like a shadow that refused to let us escape.

The air felt too thick, almost suffocating, as if the fire wasn't just behind us but all around, inching closer with every breath. We were trapped in a pocket of chaos, a twisted dance of smoke and flame, and somehow, we were supposed to outrun it. My legs burned with the effort to move faster, but the heat clung to us like a living thing, growing heavier with each passing second.

I didn't dare look back. I knew he was there—closer now, his footsteps steady and deliberate, echoing in the suffocating silence that followed each explosion. Each crackle of fire felt like it was a heartbeat away from consuming us both. Evan's grip on my arm was the only thing keeping me from losing my mind, but even that didn't seem like enough. We were running blind, and there was no way out that didn't lead directly into the inferno.

I could hear Evan's labored breathing beside me, but his pace never faltered. He was focused, determined, as if he was certain this would end in victory, even though the odds were stacked against us. His jaw was clenched, and every inch of him was bracing for impact. There was no fear in his eyes—not yet. But I could see the shadow of it there, waiting, simmering just beneath the surface.

"We can't outrun it," I gasped, the words dragging themselves out of my lungs like they were caught in the smoke. "We need to think of something else."

His grip tightened, pulling me closer, urging me to move faster. "Thinking won't help us if we're dead."

I bit my lip to stop from snapping at him. The air was too thick for argument, too full of the noise of destruction. The fire was creeping faster than we could run, the entire structure groaning and buckling beneath its heat. The walls seemed to have taken on a life of their own, twisting in unnatural directions, bending toward the flame as if they welcomed it.

Then there was a scream. A sharp, hollow cry that split through the thickening fog of smoke, cutting through the panic that had already taken hold. My heart dropped into my stomach. That scream wasn't from Evan, and it wasn't from me. It was the sound of someone who had no hope, who had realized just too late that they were already lost.

I stumbled, nearly crashing into Evan as he halted abruptly. I didn't even need to look at him to know what had happened. I could hear it in the sudden change of his breathing, the tense way he stood still, like a lion catching the scent of prey. He had stopped. And he was listening.

The scream echoed again, closer this time. Too close.

"Evan," I whispered, my voice catching on the edges of the fear I could no longer hide. "What's going on?"

He didn't answer right away, his eyes darting around us, trying to make sense of the chaos unfolding in front of us. The air around us was growing hotter, but the fire was coming from deeper in the building, pulling us back toward the one thing we couldn't escape: the source of the destruction.

"We need to find another way," he muttered, his voice low and rough. But his eyes were locked on the direction of the scream, and I knew he was weighing the choice. There was nothing else to do. Someone was still here—someone who hadn't gotten out, who was trapped, just like us.

"Evan, no—" My protest died in my throat as he started to move again, pulling me forward with him.

I wasn't sure whether to be furious or grateful for his unwavering determination. There was no time for either, though. The longer we lingered, the less likely we were to make it out in one piece. The fire, it seemed, had a mind of its own now, carving paths through the old building like it was searching for something—or someone.

As we approached the corner, a flicker of movement caught my eye. A silhouette, just beyond the reach of the flames, struggling in the heat. I couldn't see who it was, but I could see the desperation in their movements, the way they were clawing at the smoke that surrounded them like a physical barrier.

Without thinking, I broke into a sprint. The distance between us seemed to stretch impossibly long, but I was too far gone to care. Evan's shout followed me, sharp and cutting through the chaos, but I was already committed, already too close to stop. The figure was stumbling now, slipping on the slick, burning floor as the flames closed in.

And then I saw him—the arsonist—standing behind the figure, watching as if he were merely an observer to his own destruction. His calmness was maddening, like he was enjoying every second of our suffering, feeding off the fear that pulsed through the air like electricity. He didn't flinch as the fire grew closer, didn't seem to care that the building was on the verge of collapse. He had no more interest in us than in the flames themselves.

"Don't!" I screamed, but it was too late. The figure collapsed to the ground, and the arsonist made no move to help them. His face, twisted into a mask of cold indifference, didn't even flinch.

I reached for my sidearm, fingers slick with sweat as I fumbled to draw it out. But the moment I did, the arsonist's eyes locked onto mine. His lips curled into a smile—thin, cruel—and he took one deliberate step toward the flames, as if to challenge the fire itself to do its worst.

Evan was already on the move, pulling me back toward the stairs. "Not like this," he grunted, dragging me away. "Not now."

But the arsonist was smiling as he watched us retreat. And that smile—it didn't promise escape.

Chapter 35: Trials of the Firefighter's Heart

The heat hit first, like an unexpected slap across my skin. Not the sudden, searing burst I had expected, but the kind that lingered—hot, insistent, and all-consuming. Smoke curled in on itself, twisting around the beams above us like an angry beast, hungry and unforgiving. The air was thick, cloying, every breath a battle, every step a small war.

Evan's hand gripped mine, fingers tight as the heat, his pulse rapid against my palm. He didn't have to say anything; his eyes—wide, alert, yet shadowed by something I couldn't name—said it all. We were in deep. Deep in the kind of trouble that didn't just eat at your body, but gnawed at your soul. And I was right beside him, not because I wanted to be, but because somehow, the universe had conspired to place me here.

"You good?" Evan's voice was low, thick with smoke, but still sharp, still his.

I nodded, though every part of me screamed no. The air tasted like charred wood and something else—something metallic that I couldn't quite place. But I wasn't going to give him the satisfaction of seeing me flinch. "As good as anyone can be when their lungs are full of fire."

A flicker of something passed through his eyes, something that made my heart stutter in my chest. Regret? Guilt? The fear of whatever haunted him? But before I could decipher it, he yanked me forward, pulling me closer to his side as we navigated the thickening smoke, the crackling fire eating away at the building we had just stepped into. The walls groaned under the pressure, as though they, too, were fighting to stay upright, unwilling to give in to the inevitable collapse.

"Stay close," he barked, his voice tight. And there was that edge again, the one that had never quite left him. The one that felt like a thread pulled taut between us, every word, every glance, every move we made together, threatening to snap at the slightest wrong turn.

I followed, each step taking me deeper into the belly of the beast, and with every breath, the smoke thickened. But Evan—Evan was a different kind of creature in these moments. His movements were instinctual, graceful in a way that made it seem like he had done this a hundred times before. Like he'd walked through hell in a pair of boots a hundred times over. But I knew better. I knew that whatever he was fighting, whatever darkness simmered beneath the surface of his confidence, it wasn't just the fire. Not anymore.

"You ever been this far in before?" I asked, trying to sound casual, but the tremor in my voice betrayed me.

"No," he answered simply, but his eyes flickered. A twitch at the corner of his mouth that might have been a grin if the circumstances were different. "But I've been to places worse than this. And I'm not losing anyone else today."

The words hit harder than the heat, slicing through the smoke and fear that clung to my chest like a second skin. They weren't just words—those were the ghosts he'd been fighting, the shadows of past choices, of things that couldn't be undone.

We rounded a corner, and I barely avoided slamming into him when he stopped abruptly. His arm shot out, blocking my path, and I barely had time to register the movement before he was already scanning the space ahead of us, eyes flicking back and forth with a precision I'd come to expect from him. This was his world. He belonged here. I was just a passenger in the chaos.

"Down," he ordered, and before I could process, he dropped to the floor, pulling me with him. The air tasted like burning paper, thick and suffocating. I could feel the heat from the flames licking at my back, but Evan didn't seem to care. He was too busy, too focused on the path ahead.

I followed his lead without question, because when he looked at me like that, his face set in determination, it made me believe that maybe, just maybe, we could get through this. That there was a way out.

But the smoke was thickening faster now, smothering us, the world around us fading into a haze of heat and destruction. The crackling of the flames grew louder, a distant roar that was all too close.

"We have to move, now," Evan said, rising quickly, and pulling me with him once more. His grip was ironclad, a lifeline in the sea of chaos. I didn't question him. Not here. Not now. Not when every second felt like it might be our last.

"Where are we going?" I gasped, the smoke crawling into my lungs, burning like acid.

"There's an exit." His voice was tight, each word clipped as he pulled me through the narrowing corridors, past fallen beams and shattered glass. The heat was unbearable, stinging my skin, making it feel like I was suffocating, and yet, I couldn't pull away. Couldn't escape the pull of his presence, the quiet intensity that seemed to fill every inch of space between us.

The world outside the fire seemed so far away. And yet, the only thing that mattered in that moment was the rhythm of Evan's movements, the pulse of his heartbeat in sync with mine as we navigated the maze of flame and destruction.

But then, just as quickly as he'd pulled me through, he stopped, his head whipping around, eyes scanning, wide with something I couldn't place. Something worse than the fire, something that froze the blood in my veins.

There was no way out.

I saw the realization in his eyes before he spoke. "There's no way through."

And then I understood. Whatever he was running from, whatever he feared, it wasn't the fire. It was the price we'd have to pay to escape it.

The room was closing in, the heat like a living thing, breathing down my neck and wrapping itself around my chest, squeezing the air out of my lungs. I could feel the sweat, thick and bitter, trickling down my spine, but it wasn't just the heat anymore. It was him—the weight of the moment pressing down between us, heavier than the flames licking at the walls.

Evan's eyes, still locked on the burning path ahead, flickered briefly to mine, and for just a heartbeat, I saw it. That hesitation. That fleeting moment when everything, even the fire, took a backseat to something else. Fear. Fear that I was the next one he couldn't save.

"Stay close," he repeated, his voice lower now, not because he was afraid, but because his command carried the weight of a thousand unspoken apologies. I didn't question it. Didn't dare to. Not with the fire closing in on us.

I wanted to say something—anything to lighten the air between us. To tell him that I wasn't afraid. That whatever happened, I wasn't going anywhere. But the words caught in my throat, swallowed by the smoke that clouded the world around us. Instead, I just nodded, clutching his hand tighter. We both knew that in this chaos, it wasn't words that mattered. It was the unspoken trust we had in each other.

We moved forward, the floor beneath us crackling with the sounds of fire eating through the building like a ravenous beast. The beams above groaned, and for a moment, I wondered how much longer this fragile structure could hold. How long before the whole damn thing came down on us.

Evan didn't seem to hear it. His focus was absolute, his movements instinctual, a dance of survival that I was fortunate enough to be a part of. I'd seen him work before, seen him save people in ways that felt almost like magic—quick, precise, and without hesitation. But this time was different. This time, it wasn't just a matter of saving someone else. This time, it was personal. The flames weren't the only thing threatening to consume him.

We turned another corner, and the heat intensified, wrapping around us like an iron fist. I stumbled, but Evan's grip was there, always steady, always guiding. His arm swept out to steady me, but I could feel the strain in his shoulders, the tension in his jaw, the way he gripped the doorframe as if it was the only thing keeping him from losing control.

"Evan," I whispered, my voice barely reaching his ears over the roar of the flames. "Are you alright?"

He didn't answer immediately, and when he did, his words were laced with something that might have been anger, but I couldn't quite tell. "We don't have time for that."

I wanted to argue, to tell him that we could make time. But there was no arguing with him when he was like this. No pleading for him to let down the walls that separated him from everyone else. He was locked in this battle with himself, and no amount of talking would change that.

His hand tightened on mine again, and this time, I didn't feel the burn of the flames on my skin, but the heat from his touch. The way his fingers gripped mine—tight, desperate, like I was his lifeline. And maybe I was. Maybe, in some small, ridiculous way, I was the one thing he was still fighting for.

"I'm not going anywhere," I said quietly, my voice hoarse, but unwavering.

He didn't look at me. Didn't let his eyes linger on mine for even a second. But I saw it. The slight flicker of something in his gaze—the barest sign of relief, or maybe it was just the faintest hint of hope.

For a split second, I thought we might make it. Thought that maybe, just maybe, the universe had finally decided to give us a break. But then, the building seemed to sigh, and the entire floor beneath us buckled, sending a shockwave through the air. The ground shifted, sending us both to our knees.

"Move!" Evan's voice was sharp, cutting through the disorienting crash of debris falling around us. His arm shot out to catch me before I could fall too far, pulling me back to my feet with a force that felt almost painful.

The sound of the building collapsing around us was deafening. I could hear the creak of the beams snapping, the shattering of glass, the desperate, angry crackling of the fire as it consumed everything in its path. We ran again, faster now, the air thick with smoke and ash, the heat like a wall pressing against us, urging us to keep moving, to keep fighting.

My lungs burned, my muscles screamed in protest, but Evan's grip never loosened, his hand never faltered in its hold on mine. We didn't speak. There was nothing to say. Just the sound of our feet pounding the floor, the rush of adrenaline pulsing through my veins, and the smell of smoke clogging my senses.

I didn't know where we were going. I didn't know if there was even an exit left. But I knew one thing: if we made it out of here, it wouldn't be because of luck. It would be because Evan had decided that I was worth saving.

And maybe, just maybe, I was beginning to believe that I wasn't the only one fighting to survive.

The air was thick with the acrid sting of burning wood, but even that couldn't mask the deeper scent that lingered between us—something far more personal. It clung to the back of my throat, bitter and desperate, and I could almost taste the fear that had settled between Evan and me, unspoken but undeniable. The fire wasn't the only thing consuming us. There was something else, something we hadn't acknowledged, and for the first time, I understood what it meant to be truly trapped. Trapped between the blaze and the man who was as much a part of it as the flames themselves.

"Keep moving," Evan ordered again, his voice steady despite the wild, frantic pulse of energy that radiated from him. Every fiber of his being was honed on survival, but in the way he gripped my hand, his fingertips pressing into my skin as if afraid to let go, I knew that somewhere beneath that hardened exterior, something was breaking.

I didn't dare stop to think about it, though. Not now. There would be time to unravel whatever was happening between us later. After we survived. I glanced up at him, studying his profile as we ran, sweat glistening on his forehead, his jaw set with that familiar resolve. He was the same man who had pulled me out of more trouble than I cared to admit. And yet, for all his training, for all his strength, there was something raw about him now, something vulnerable.

We rounded the next corner, the heat of the fire following us like a shadow. The walls were crumbling, but Evan didn't hesitate. He guided us through the ruins with a steady, almost unnerving calm, as though he knew exactly where we were going. Or maybe he didn't. Maybe he was just making it up as he went, hoping that the next turn would be the one that led us out.

The sound of crackling wood grew louder, a deafening roar that threatened to swallow us whole. My heart pounded in my chest, and I could feel the rhythmic thud of Evan's steps syncing with mine, the pulse between us almost like a silent communication, as if we could read each other's thoughts without saying a word.

"Over here," he said abruptly, pulling me to the side as a large beam came crashing down just inches from where we had been standing.

I stumbled but caught myself just in time. "You know, I thought I'd be dead by now. But I guess this is better than the alternative."

Evan shot me a quick, grim smile. "Stick with me, and I'll make sure you make it out in one piece."

I wasn't so sure about that, but I wasn't about to argue with him. We kept moving, ducking under low-hanging beams, sidestepping the occasional burst of flames that seemed to appear out of nowhere, like vengeful spirits clawing at our heels.

And then, just as the corridor ahead of us seemed to open up into something resembling an escape route, the ground beneath us shifted again. It wasn't a tremor this time, but a distinct, sharp cracking sound that echoed in the silence before the entire floor buckled beneath us.

Without thinking, I grabbed onto Evan, my body instinctively seeking his for stability. But the floor was already giving way, and I felt the earth drop out from under me. I screamed as we both fell, the air rushing up around us as we plummeted, falling, falling—

The world came to a violent halt.

For a moment, I couldn't breathe, couldn't think. My body ached from the impact, my mind scrambled to make sense of what had just happened. I groaned, rolling over onto my back, trying to push past the dizziness that clouded my vision.

And then I heard it.

A voice—soft, strained, but unmistakably Evan's. "You okay?"

I turned my head slowly, blinking against the sudden sharpness of the world around me. The rubble from the collapse was scattered everywhere, pieces of debris and charred wood blocking our path in every direction. The only light now came from the flickering orange glow of the flames above us, casting long shadows across the uneven ground.

"I've been better," I replied, my voice thick with dust. I tried to sit up but winced as a sharp pain shot through my side.

Evan was already on his feet, his eyes scanning the wreckage around us, calculating, weighing options in that quiet, methodical way he always did. "We're not out of this yet," he said, his voice quiet but full of the kind of grim certainty that made me wish I could just pull him out of this—pull him out of whatever mess he was in, whatever torment had driven him to be so damn good at this.

The fire above us raged louder, the smoke swirling around us, thick and suffocating. I glanced up, wondering how much longer the roof would hold before it caved in completely. The air felt heavier, thicker, as if the building itself was collapsing on top of us, one layer at a time.

"We need to move," I said, my voice more urgent now.

Evan gave me a look—a silent exchange of sorts—and then nodded. Without another word, he moved forward, his steps sure and steady despite the obstacles in our way.

But as we began to pick our way through the rubble, something caught my attention. A faint light, flickering in the distance. It wasn't the fire—it was too controlled, too steady. A flashlight. Someone else was here.

Evan must have noticed it too, because he stopped dead in his tracks, his posture immediately shifting, tense. "Stay behind me," he ordered. His voice was low, but there was a command in it that I didn't dare question.

I nodded, my heart racing. But as we took another step forward, the sound of footsteps ahead of us made the hairs on the back of my neck stand up.

Who else was in here with us?

Chapter 36: After the Ashes

The fire flickered out, and the last of the smoke curled lazily toward the evening sky. My eyes stayed fixed on the horizon, watching the once-persistent orange glow fade to nothing. The forest around us, now eerily still, felt like an old friend I hadn't seen in years, familiar and unsettling all at once. The scent of burnt wood lingered in my nostrils, sharp and acrid, as though it had been embedded into my skin. I turned to face him, knowing this moment was coming, knowing it was inevitable.

"Tell me," I said, my voice quieter than I'd intended, but there was no room for pretense now. The dust from the fire still clung to his clothes, making him look more like a phantom than the man I'd spent countless hours fighting beside. His eyes were haunted, the weight of everything we'd been through evident in the way his shoulders sagged beneath the exhaustion.

He didn't meet my gaze, his eyes fixed instead on the ground between us, where the remnants of a crumbled building had once stood proud.

"You know," he muttered, his voice low and rough. "I never wanted any of this. You, me, this—whatever it is. It was never supposed to happen. I never thought I'd survive long enough to let myself want something, someone. Not after everything."

His words hung in the air like smoke, lingering and choking out the space between us. He rubbed his hand over his face, his movements jerky, as if trying to shake off some ghost that refused to leave.

"You've always pushed me away," I said, stepping forward. "And I need to know why. Not in the way I think I know, but in the way you know. Why do you keep doing this? Why keep me at arm's length?"

There was something almost tragic about him in that moment. His usual air of control, of indifference, had crumbled like the ashes beneath our feet. His lips tightened, a hint of regret flashing across his face before he shoved it away. He wouldn't look at me, but his voice, when it came, was raw and exposed.

"Because I'm terrified, okay?" His words cracked, jagged like glass. "I'm terrified that you'll leave. That I'll lose you. Just like I've lost everyone else."

I was taken aback. His confession hit me harder than I expected, catching me off guard like a wave that rose higher than the storm had promised. There it was, the truth he'd kept buried under layers of deflection and anger. I took a step closer, trying to bridge the distance that had always been between us, even when it felt like we were standing in the same room.

"You think I'll leave you?" I asked, my voice barely a whisper now. "You think that, after everything we've been through, I'd walk away?"

His laugh was bitter. "I'd never blame you if you did. I'd walk away myself if I thought I was capable of it. But I'm not. I've tried. I've told myself over and over to just let go. That I didn't deserve you, didn't deserve to feel what I feel when I'm with you. But that doesn't change the fact that it scares me. It terrifies me."

I wanted to reach out, to close the gap between us, but something—pride, perhaps, or the remnants of my own insecurities—kept me frozen in place. My hands fisted at my sides, nails digging into my palms as I processed what he was telling me. The man who had spent so much time keeping me at arm's length was afraid of the very thing that had drawn us together in the first place.

"Do you think I'm going to leave you?" I asked again, and this time, my voice held an edge of something sharper. Something that wasn't just wounded, but demanding.

Finally, he met my gaze, and I saw it then—the vulnerability, the raw fear. The fear of losing me was a ghost that had haunted him long before I ever came into the picture, and it was a ghost he hadn't been able to exorcise. His lips parted as though to say something, but the words caught in his throat.

"I'm not going anywhere," I said, stepping forward until I was just close enough for him to reach out. "Not unless you push me away. And I won't let you do that."

For a moment, we stood in silence, the wind gently stirring the charred remnants of the forest around us. It was like the world was holding its breath, waiting for him to make a decision. And then, almost imperceptibly, his hand reached out. Tentative at first, like he was afraid I'd pull away, but I didn't.

When his fingers brushed mine, it felt like a quiet acknowledgment, a truce between two forces that had clashed for far too long. I looked at him then, really looked at him, and in that moment, I saw everything—the layers of grief, the anger, the heartache that he'd carried for so long. I saw the man who had been running from the very thing he wanted most.

"I'm not going to let you carry this alone," I said softly, my voice steady despite the wild, uncontrollable beating of my heart. "I'm here. I'm not going anywhere. Not now, not ever."

He didn't respond immediately, but when he finally did, his voice was a whisper, barely audible against the backdrop of the evening's stillness.

"I'm scared of losing you," he admitted. "But I'm more scared of pushing you away. More scared that I won't ever get to fix the mess I've made of everything."

The weight of his words hung between us, heavier than any fire or smoke we'd survived. It wasn't just fear now; it was something deeper, more real. It was love. And for the first time, I could see it clearly, see him clearly. And it was terrifying in its own way. But it was also beautiful.

I took a step closer, and this time, he didn't pull away. "Then let's fix it together," I said, my voice sure. "We'll face it. All of it. Together."

The air was still, hanging heavy with the weight of unspoken words. There was something almost absurd in the quiet between us—like we were the last two people left on earth, both survivors of something far larger than we could comprehend. But the silence was no longer uncomfortable; it wasn't awkward, not the kind that lingered uninvited. It was, for the first time, something we could settle into.

I watched him, noting how the light from the fading sun caught on his features, the small cracks in his stoic expression. For a man who'd mastered the art of appearing unreadable, there was something too honest in his eyes now. And it wasn't just the confession he'd made that shattered the walls; it was the simple fact that he'd made the decision to speak it aloud, to let me in.

"You really are ridiculous, you know that?" I said, the teasing edge in my voice a soft counterpoint to the heaviness of the moment. He raised an eyebrow, and a half-smile tugged at his lips, the first sign of the man I'd grown familiar with—the man who didn't do anything unless it was on his terms.

"You're the one making this sound easy," he countered, leaning back against the charred remains of the building. "I'm the one with all the emotional baggage here, remember?"

I grinned, despite myself. "Well, it's hard to keep up with someone who insists on carrying around a suitcase full of existential dread wherever they go."

He snorted. "Existential dread. That's rich. You've been telling me for weeks that I need to get out more, and now you're calling it 'existential dread.'"

I crossed my arms, shrugging in mock innocence. "I'm just trying to find a way to enjoy the show. Watching you wrestle with yourself is more thrilling than anything on Netflix."

He let out a short laugh, the tension between us momentarily defusing, but the reality of what had just passed between us wasn't lost on either of us. We were standing on the edge of something new, something neither of us had anticipated when we first crossed paths, and that thought made the corners of my heart tighten with something I couldn't quite place—hope, maybe? Or fear. Or both.

"What do we do now?" he asked after a long pause, his voice steady, but I could hear the flicker of uncertainty buried beneath it.

I tilted my head, considering. "Well, we're already standing here, pretending that the world isn't on fire around us, so I'd say we've taken the first step."

"Good start," he murmured, the sarcastic edge back in his tone, but I could hear the relief there too. Like a crack had appeared in the dam he'd built so carefully around his heart, and though he tried to plug it, I could see the water still seeping through.

"Tell me," I began, stepping closer, "did you really think I'd let you do this alone?" I didn't wait for an answer, because I already knew. I could see the remnants of that doubt in the way he held himself, in the way he'd always kept a safe distance from me, even when everything inside me screamed that we were already there—together, in a way that meant more than just proximity.

He opened his mouth to respond, but nothing came out. For a brief second, I thought I might have pushed too hard, but then I saw it in the way his shoulders sagged, in the soft exhale of breath that escaped him, like a man finally allowing himself to let go of the weight he'd been carrying for years.

"I never thought I deserved you," he admitted, the words coming out in a rush, as though he couldn't stop them if he tried.

"It wasn't just about the risk of losing you—it was about the risk of you realizing that maybe I wasn't worth sticking around for."

That stung, but it wasn't just the pain of his words that hit me; it was the quiet truth in them. For all the bravado he projected, for all the times he'd pushed me away, he had never really believed he deserved any of this—deserved the kindness, the warmth, the way I fought for him when he wouldn't fight for himself.

"You know," I said, my voice softer now, quieter, "that's not something you get to decide. Not anymore. I'm not leaving, and I'm not going anywhere."

He turned to look at me, his eyes meeting mine in a way that made everything feel sharper, more vivid. The weight of the world had lifted, just slightly, but it was enough to see him for what he really was: a man who had been running, even when there was nowhere left to go.

"I don't want to push you away," he said, almost too quietly for me to hear, but the sincerity in his voice made me stop in my tracks. "But I don't know how to let someone in. Not like this. Not with everything I've been carrying around."

I reached for him then, not with hesitation, but with the kind of certainty that comes from knowing, deep down, that there was no other option. He didn't flinch when I took his hand, didn't pull back like he had done so many times before. Instead, he let me close, let me be the anchor that kept him grounded.

"You don't have to know how," I said, squeezing his hand. "I'm not asking you to have all the answers. I'm just asking you to take a step with me, one step at a time. That's all I need from you."

He didn't respond immediately, but the warmth in his gaze said everything that needed to be said. It wasn't a perfect resolution, but it was enough. We were here, together, and for the first time, I believed in it. I believed in us.

"So, now what?" he asked, his lips quirking upward in that familiar, teasing way, the one that had always been just a little too self-assured for his own good.

"Now we figure it out," I said, the weight of the world still there, but somehow lighter, as though we might finally be strong enough to carry it together.

The night was unnaturally quiet, save for the distant rustling of leaves. The fire had long since given up its rage, leaving only the faint scent of burnt timber to cling to the air. We had walked out of the wreckage, side by side, as if the very act of survival had bound us together in some unspoken contract. The lingering adrenaline from our escape buzzed in my veins, but there was something else too—a new kind of tension, as though we were both holding our breath, waiting for something else to happen.

His hand brushed mine as we walked, a touch too casual to be an accident, but not yet a promise. My heart thumped erratically in response, as though it couldn't quite decide if it should race ahead or linger in the safety of the moment.

"Tell me this isn't one of those times when I should be saying 'I told you so,'" he said, his voice teasing, but there was an undercurrent of something more vulnerable there, something that made his words falter at the end.

I couldn't help but smile, the kind of smile that felt half-forced, half-relieved. "If you were anyone else, I'd be convinced you were just trying to distract me."

"And if I were anyone else, you'd probably listen," he shot back, his grin widening at the soft shove I gave him in response.

"You're lucky I like you," I said, the teasing lightness in my voice concealing the thudding in my chest.

"I think it's the other way around," he muttered, but there was something more in his eyes than the usual playful deflection. I wasn't sure if it was the aftermath of everything we'd been through, or if it was the slow realization that we hadn't been as far apart as we thought. That maybe, just maybe, we had been standing at the same crossroads the entire time—both too afraid to cross, to meet in the middle.

His words from earlier echoed in my mind. The ones where he'd said he didn't know how to let someone in. I knew the struggle too well; I'd been there, barricading myself with walls no one had been allowed to breach. But something had shifted between us in the last few minutes, something that no longer felt like a battle. Instead, it felt like an invitation—an unspoken promise to be there for each other, no matter what happened next.

"Let's just walk," I said, my voice low, but steady. There was something about the simplicity of it that made sense.

"Walk," he repeated, almost to himself. "Right. I can do that."

And so we did, side by side, in comfortable silence, letting the night swallow us whole. It was the kind of silence that, despite its stillness, didn't feel empty. It felt full—full of everything we hadn't said, everything we still needed to say.

"Do you ever wonder," he began, his voice cutting through the quiet, "if we're both just too stubborn for our own good?"

I laughed, a soft, amused sound that felt strange coming from me, considering everything that had happened. "You? Stubborn?" I raised an eyebrow. "I think we both know who the real stubborn one is here."

He grinned, and for the briefest moment, I could see him—truly see him—without the weight of the past pulling at his shoulders, without the burden of uncertainty clouding his eyes. There was something endearing about that, the way his defenses crumbled in the most unexpected moments.

But then, just as quickly, that familiar guardedness returned. The glimmer of vulnerability faded, and in its place was the same man I'd met days ago—the one who was careful with his words, his actions, his very self. It was the man who had pushed me away, even as I'd tried to close the distance. The man who had kept me at arm's length, convinced that I wouldn't—or couldn't—understand.

"I wasn't kidding, you know," he said, his voice suddenly quieter. "I don't know how to do this. This...whatever this is."

I stopped walking, turning to face him. "What do you mean, 'this'?"

He hesitated, as though the answer might be too much to give, but when his eyes met mine, there was no hiding it. No more walls between us, no more defenses to hide behind.

"I don't know how to trust it. Trust you." His words hung in the air, suspended between us like fragile glass. "I'm scared, okay? Scared that if I let myself...really let myself, I'll lose it. I'll lose you. Just like I lost everything else."

My chest tightened, the words sinking deep into me. I could feel the weight of his fear, the way it pressed against my ribcage, making it hard to breathe. The vulnerability that had been buried beneath his bravado was raw now, too real to ignore.

"You won't lose me," I said, my voice softer than I'd intended, but full of certainty. "I'm not going anywhere. I won't leave you like that."

But as the words left my mouth, something shifted. It was subtle, like a shadow creeping into the corners of the room, but it was enough to make my stomach tighten with unease. His gaze flickered to the distance, and I followed his eyes just in time to catch the faint outline of something—someone—moving through the trees at the edge of the clearing.

I felt the shift in the air, the sudden change from calm to tension, as though the very earth beneath our feet had recognized the threat before either of us had. My breath caught in my throat. This wasn't the kind of peace I'd been hoping for, the one where we could finally settle into something real.

It was a warning.

"Did you see that?" I whispered, my heart hammering in my chest.

He didn't answer right away. Instead, he turned slowly, his body going rigid. The shift in his demeanor was instantaneous. And as he met my eyes, I saw it—the recognition. The realization that our fragile moment was about to break.

"Stay behind me," he ordered, his voice low and tense.

Before I could ask any more questions, a figure stepped out from the shadows, and my blood ran cold.

Chapter 37: A Flicker of Truth

The coffee shop smelled like burnt caramel and something I couldn't quite place. Maybe it was the heavy scent of impending rain, or the soft, chemical edge of too many air fresheners masking the stale air. It didn't matter. What mattered was the man sitting across from me, his shoulders hunched like he was trying to disappear into the booth. Frankly, he didn't have a prayer. The old firefighter with too many lines on his face and a chip on his shoulder was about as good at blending in as a bull in a china shop. Still, I let him talk.

"You don't get it, do you?" he rasped, his voice like gravel grinding against the pavement. "Leon's got a way of working people. Knows how to twist 'em into thinking he's the victim. But he ain't." He coughed, hacking up what sounded like regret, but I didn't buy it. Regret and guilt don't usually show up at the same time.

I let my fingers tap on the edge of my coffee cup. "You seem pretty sure of that. How'd you know Leon's name in the first place?"

He scowled, glancing nervously toward the window like someone might burst in at any moment. He wasn't wrong. The world had a way of making you paranoid when you'd spent too many years dodging trouble.

"I know him," he muttered. "Used to work with him. A lifetime ago. He and Evan, they both... they were there. That night. The fire. That's when everything changed. You think you can escape something like that, but you can't. Not when it follows you around, waiting."

I leaned forward, trying to catch the flicker in his eyes. That's where the truth always hid—the eyes. And this man's were hiding something. Something bigger than fire.

"Tell me about the fire," I prompted, not expecting the floodgates to open, but hoping for a crack, just a crack that would let the truth seep through.

He took a deep breath and winced. "You don't want to know. Hell, I didn't want to know what happened either. But you can't unsee that kind of thing. You can't forget it once it's burned its way into your soul."

His words made the room feel a little smaller, a little tighter, like someone had turned down the air conditioning just enough to make the sweat bead on the back of my neck. I could almost hear the flames crackling, smell the smoke curling in the corners of the room.

"Tell me anyway," I said, quieter this time, coaxing him like you would a scared animal. "You want to help, don't you?"

His eyes darted away, and I watched him wrestle with the decision. Finally, he met my gaze. "Evan didn't set the fire. But Leon? He… he wanted something to burn. Wanted to watch it all go up. To watch everyone else burn too. It's like he thought if he could just make everyone feel the heat, he'd be free. But he never was. Not really. It just made him darker. Made him dangerous."

A chill ran down my spine. "What do you mean, dangerous?"

"Leon had a score to settle. A list. And he was going through it, one by one. People from the fire, from the old crew, they were getting hit. Different ways, different fires, but the same end result. And Evan? Evan didn't know, not at first. But after, after he figured it out, after the first few names started dropping off the list, Evan started to get scared. That's when it clicked for him. Leon wasn't playing games anymore. This was personal."

I leaned back in the booth, my mind spinning, the pieces of the puzzle swirling and shifting into something far worse than I'd imagined. Leon wasn't just angry. He wasn't just bitter. He was methodical, and every fire, every victim, was part of some twisted plan. A plan that, according to this man, had started with the fire that had nearly destroyed them all.

I ran my fingers over the rim of the coffee cup, thinking about Evan—about how his face had changed when he'd talked about Leon. How he'd looked over his shoulder, like the past was breathing down his neck. That fear, that nagging unease? Maybe he had more to hide than he was letting on.

"What happened that night?" I asked, my voice softer now, pulling at the thread of his memory like I was coaxing a wound open.

The old firefighter closed his eyes, and for a moment, I thought he wouldn't answer. But then he spoke, his voice low and rough.

"I thought I could save them all," he whispered. "Thought I could save the kids trapped in that building. But... it was too late. Too many of us got caught in the flames, including Leon. He got burned. Bad. Real bad. But he wasn't the worst off. Evan, though..." He trailed off, rubbing his face, like he was trying to wipe the memory away.

I waited, my heart beating faster. "What about Evan?"

"He made it out. Barely. But not the way you think. He didn't get burned. He got away clean. Too clean. Like he wasn't really there. Like he didn't care what happened to the rest of us. That was the first crack. And when Leon... when he woke up in the hospital, he blamed Evan. Blamed him for everything. Said he wasn't even trying to save anyone. He said Evan turned his back, and it cost lives. And that, that was the start of all of this."

My stomach tightened, a knot of understanding forming. Evan hadn't just been a survivor. He'd been a target. And Leon had been planning his revenge for years, using the very thing that had destroyed them both as a tool to carve through their lives.

"So what does he want?" I asked, the words almost too heavy to say. "What's the endgame here?"

The firefighter looked at me, his eyes hardening with the weight of something old, something he could never forget. "Evan's the last one on the list." He paused, watching me closely. "And he's next."

The words hung in the air like smoke, thick and suffocating, as the room seemed to close in on me.

I wasn't sure how much more of the truth I could swallow in one sitting. The old firefighter was right, I hadn't wanted to know any of this, but now that it was out there, all jagged and messy, I couldn't unhear it. Leon wasn't just angry—he was on a mission, a relentless, unforgiving pursuit that had started long ago. The idea that Evan could have been a target all along? That twist felt like it might choke me, like I'd been sucker-punched by a memory I hadn't even known was mine.

I glanced at the man across from me, still hunched like a man caught in the crossfire of his own mistakes. The coffee shop felt quieter now, as though the whole world had suddenly shifted on its axis. I could feel the weight of every second ticking by, the minutes stretching thin as if the universe was testing my patience, daring me to ask the next question.

"You're sure about all this?" I asked, the words tasting different on my tongue now. Like a secret, and a heavy one at that. "About Leon wanting to finish what he started?"

He didn't even blink. "Yeah, I'm sure. Leon... he's been setting fires for years, picking off people one by one. But it's all been leading to this. He's been waiting, planning. And now it's Evan's turn. He thinks he's owed something, something that was taken from him that night. And he's not gonna stop until he gets it back."

I nodded slowly, the storm brewing in my chest as the pieces clicked into place. Leon wasn't just an arsonist; he was an avenger, and the only thing that could satisfy him was seeing Evan fall. It didn't matter how many people got burned along the way—it was all part of his sick equation. Evan had been the catalyst, the moment Leon's world had splintered, and everything since then had been a slow burn toward this.

I stood up from the booth, my fingers wrapped tight around the handle of my coffee cup. The sound of ceramic clinking against the table felt too loud in the quiet, but I didn't care. "So what's the next move?" I asked, already knowing what the answer would be. There was no going back now. "Do I warn Evan, or do I go find Leon and deal with this myself?"

He finally looked at me, and for the first time, I saw a flicker of something like regret in his eyes. "You don't get it, do you?" he said, his voice quieter now, more measured. "Leon's not a man you can just confront. He's got people, connections. You think you're gonna walk up to him and shake some sense into him? He's too far gone for that. He's not just angry. He's... he's a force now. And if you go after him, you'll be pulling Evan right into the middle of it."

I felt a pang of frustration, but I held it in check. It wasn't the time for pushing, not now. I had bigger fish to fry—mainly Evan, who was probably out there somewhere, blissfully unaware that he was about to walk into a trap set years ago. A trap that could snap shut at any moment.

"Fine," I said, my jaw tight. "So I warn Evan. But if Leon's been planning this for years, we don't have a lot of time, do we?"

"No," the firefighter said, standing up with a groan. "You've got about as much time as it takes for Leon to finish whatever sick little plan he's cooked up. And believe me, he's cooking."

I left the coffee shop feeling like I was carrying the weight of an entire city on my shoulders. I could hear the buzz of traffic, the distant hum of streetlights flickering on as the day turned to night, but none of it felt real anymore. It was all just noise in the background. The only thing that mattered was finding Evan before it was too late.

I made the drive back to Evan's place, my thoughts a tangled mess of guilt and dread. I could feel it in the pit of my stomach—something was off. Even though the house was quiet when I pulled up, I couldn't shake the feeling that I was too late. Maybe I was being paranoid. Maybe not. I parked a little too quickly, my tires screeching against the pavement as I threw the car into park, but I didn't care.

I ran up the steps, two at a time, my heart pounding in my chest. I rang the doorbell, a little harder than necessary, but I needed Evan to answer. I needed him to know that he was in danger. The kind of danger that wasn't just a matter of a few bad decisions. This was life or death.

When the door finally opened, Evan's face was the picture of confusion, his eyebrows furrowing like he couldn't quite place me in this moment. But when he saw the look on my face, that confusion melted into something closer to fear.

"What is it?" he asked, his voice steady but low, like he already knew something was wrong.

"You need to listen to me," I said, pushing past him into the entryway, not waiting for an invitation. "Leon is coming for you."

His expression hardened, like I'd slapped him, but then something else shifted, something darker, like the shadows in his eyes deepened. "Leon's already been here," he said, his voice barely above a whisper.

My blood ran cold. "What do you mean, 'already been here'?"

Evan ran a hand through his hair, his usual calm demeanor cracking like fragile glass. "I should've seen it coming, but I didn't. It's not just the fires. He's been... manipulating everything. The other victims. The stories. Even you. I'm not the first person he's gone after, and I won't be the last."

I froze, the words hanging between us, heavy and suffocating. This wasn't just a vendetta anymore. It was a campaign, a systematic effort to break everything Evan had built, to tear apart the remnants of his life until there was nothing left but ashes. And now, for the first time, I understood the true scope of Leon's obsession.

Evan's confession hit me harder than I expected. Not because I didn't understand the weight of his words, but because they confirmed something I'd been trying to deny for far too long. The fires weren't random. They were deliberate. Each one had been meticulously planned, part of a twisted tapestry that had been unfolding in the shadows while I was busy chasing the wrong leads. I could feel the air in the room shift, thickening with a tension I couldn't quite place.

"You're telling me Leon's been pulling strings behind the scenes all this time?" I asked, barely recognizing the tightness in my own voice.

Evan nodded slowly, the weight of his gaze sinking deep into me. "It's not just about revenge anymore. It's about proving something—about making everyone who's ever wronged him pay. He's methodical. He's patient. And now he's coming for me. And there's nothing I can do to stop it."

I could see it—the shadow that had been following him for years, finally catching up. It had all started with that fire, with the moment everything had shattered. Now, it felt like that shattered glass was scattered across every corner of his life, and each piece was sharp enough to cut through to the truth. The air between us hummed with something darker than the usual tension. It was the feeling you get when you realize that your whole life has been a step away from collapse and you didn't know until the moment the floor fell out beneath you.

"You think he's already made his move?" I asked, my pulse quickening.

"No," Evan replied, shaking his head, his voice betraying an edge of something close to panic. "Not yet. But he's close. I can feel it. I've been waiting for him to make the first move, but instead, he's been playing everyone around me. You've seen the fires, right? Those weren't accidents. Those were deliberate, carefully orchestrated."

"I know," I said, my hands moving to my hips, the weight of what was happening settling into my bones. "But I think it's more than just revenge for him. Leon's not just trying to hurt you, Evan. He wants to destroy everything. Every piece of what you've built. What you are. And once he has that... he'll be satisfied."

Evan ran a hand over his face, like he could scrub the tension from his features, but it didn't work. It never did. "I've been running from him for years. I didn't know it, but I've been on the defensive since that night. Now it's coming to a head. And I don't know how much longer I can keep it together."

I stepped closer to him, my voice softer now, coaxing, but the gravity of the situation was still present, weighing us both down. "You don't have to do this alone. We're going to stop him. Together."

For a split second, there was something in Evan's eyes—a flicker of hope, of a possibility that maybe, just maybe, there was an out. But it disappeared almost as quickly as it appeared, buried under layers of fear and exhaustion. "I'm not sure that's possible," he muttered, more to himself than to me. "He's not just a man anymore. He's... a force."

The word hung in the air, settling between us like a heavy, insurmountable weight. A force. And Evan was right. Leon had become something beyond a person. He'd turned himself into a storm—no longer someone with a face or a name, but a presence that loomed over everything Evan had ever known. A presence that was now coming for him.

"We don't have time to waste," I said, the urgency in my voice spurring me into action. "We need to figure out where he's going to strike next."

Evan nodded, his face drawn and pale. He didn't have the luxury of time. Neither of us did. "I've been trying to think—track where his movements are. But he's too careful. He's good at making sure no one's looking in the right direction." He paused, his hand brushing through his hair as he exhaled deeply. "It's like he knows every move before I make it."

"Then we think like him," I said, leaning forward, the spark of determination flaring in my chest. "We need to predict where he's going, what his next step is. What's his pattern?"

Evan's eyes flickered with a recognition that I could see he hadn't fully understood before. "The fires... they've always been personal, right? Each one targeted someone close to me. People who were involved, people who witnessed what happened. The thing is, these fires aren't just about making a statement. They're about destroying the people who've got the power to stop him."

I narrowed my eyes. "So, who else does he want?"

Evan's face hardened as he said the name, barely a whisper in the room. "My family."

My stomach twisted. I didn't need to ask what that meant. If Leon had already set his sights on Evan, there was no telling who would be next. "How do you know?"

"Because he always knows where to strike. My brother. My parents. They're all part of it. If Leon can't get to me, he'll go after them. And that's the part I'm afraid of—the part I can't protect them from. The ones I love. That's the ultimate punishment for him."

The door behind us creaked. It wasn't the wind, it wasn't the house settling—it was something else, something far too deliberate to be an accident. I froze, my heart skipping a beat.

"You hear that?" I whispered, holding my breath.

Evan's eyes went wide, his hand going to the back of his neck, like he could somehow erase the sudden tension crawling up his spine. "It's him. I know it's him."

Before I could respond, the sound came again—a heavy thud from upstairs. Then the unmistakable scrape of a door creaking open, followed by a low, guttural laugh.

My pulse raced, and I was already halfway toward the stairs before Evan could stop me. I knew the danger, I knew how foolish this was, but I couldn't help myself. Leon was here. And I wasn't going to let him walk away again.

Chapter 38: The Flames Within

The night was thick with the kind of silence that presses against your skin like a heavy, wet blanket. It was the kind of silence that makes you question whether the world was holding its breath or whether it had already exhaled everything worth saying. We walked through the empty streets, the pavement slick underfoot with the dampness of a rain that had long since passed. There was a chill in the air, but it wasn't the kind of cold that nips at your nose and cheeks. No, this cold settled in the marrow of your bones, the kind that makes you feel like something is coming—something bad.

Evan's stride was long, purposeful, the weight of whatever was about to happen pulling him forward. I stayed close, too close perhaps, but I couldn't bring myself to let him go alone. Not this time. He had that look in his eyes, the kind that says he's ready to face whatever nightmare Leon had planned, but I knew better. Leon was a different kind of monster. The kind that doesn't just tear things apart with brute force. No, Leon had a mind that could twist and contort, make you see things that weren't there, convince you that fire wasn't just an escape—it was a cleansing.

We reached the building—Leon's fortress, or what remained of it. The cracked windows and peeling paint were the least unsettling things about it. Inside, it was nothing but shadows and the kind of emptiness that makes you wonder if the walls had ever truly been whole to begin with. The dim light spilling from the doorway barely cut through the dark, casting long, crooked lines across the floor, like something out of a nightmare. Leon was waiting for us. Of course, he was. The man never had a problem with timing.

Evan pushed the door open with a deliberate slowness, like he was preparing himself for the worst. And maybe he was. Maybe we both were. I could feel the knot in my stomach tightening, like it was trying to warn me of something. But then Evan stepped inside, and all the caution in the world couldn't hold me back. I followed him, my footsteps a soft echo of his, my heart racing in time with his.

Leon was standing in the middle of the room, his figure cast in shadow, just enough to make him look larger than life, but not enough to give him any real presence. It was an illusion, like everything he did. The smell of smoke was in the air, faint but persistent, clinging to the space as if it had never truly left.

"Well," Leon's voice slid through the air, smooth like oil, "I didn't think you'd come, Evan. You never were one for theatrics." He stepped forward, and the dim light caught the sharp angles of his face, the cold gleam in his eyes.

Evan didn't flinch. He didn't even blink. "You know why I'm here."

"I know why you think you're here," Leon replied, his smile stretching wider. "But that's the funny thing about thinking. It never really gets you where you need to go, does it?"

I wasn't sure if it was the flicker of his grin or the way he said those words, but something in the air shifted. It was subtle, like a spark before the full blaze of a fire. "What's your endgame, Leon?" I asked, stepping forward, my voice steady despite the chaos swirling inside me. "You've burned enough bridges. You've ruined enough lives. What's next? What's the big finish?"

Leon's eyes flickered to me, a brief flash of something—annoyance? Respect? Hard to tell with him. He tilted his head, considering me. "You really think you can stop me? You're all just pawns, in a game much larger than you can comprehend."

I didn't hesitate. "You're wrong." My voice was firm, more confident than I felt. "This isn't about some game. This is about you trying to destroy everything we've worked for, everything Evan's built. And I'm not standing by and letting you do it."

Leon's laughter echoed in the room, unsettling in its hollow ring. "Everything he's built?" He repeated the words, like they were foreign to him. "You still don't get it. It was always about control, about resetting things to how they should've been. One final fire, one last act to bring it all crashing down."

The words hit me like a physical blow. I glanced at Evan, his jaw clenched, his eyes burning with something that could've been fury or something much darker. Leon was playing with us, I realized, his words carefully crafted to lure us in, to make us doubt our every move.

"So, this is it?" I said, fighting to keep my voice steady. "You think you can just burn everything to the ground and walk away from the ashes?"

Leon's eyes glittered, the corners of his mouth twitching like he knew something we didn't. "I don't need to walk away," he said, taking a slow step toward us. "I'm already gone. You just don't know it yet."

There was a moment—a long, drawn-out stretch of time where nothing moved. And then, just like that, the truth fell into place. Leon wasn't just planning a fire; he was planning the end of everything. Not just for Evan, but for all of us. Everything we held dear would be reduced to ash if we didn't act fast.

I turned to Evan, meeting his gaze. For the first time since we stepped into this hellhole, I saw a flicker of doubt in his eyes, a hint of uncertainty. But there was also something else. Determination. He wasn't going to let Leon win. Not this time. And neither was I.

The air was thick with the smell of burnt wood, a lingering memory of the destruction Leon had left in his wake. Each word he spoke seemed to hang in the air, thick and heavy, waiting to settle into the corners of the room like dust. I could feel the weight of it all pressing in on me—the years of suffering, the lives lost, the pieces of a world that had once felt whole, now scattered and crumbling. Leon's obsession with control was as consuming as the fires he set, each one a symbol of his twisted vision, a vision that had no place in the world we were fighting to protect.

I glanced at Evan again, his eyes narrowing with a quiet fury. He had always been the one to stand firm, to carry the weight of the world on his shoulders without complaint. But now, there was something different in him. Something... dangerous. He wasn't just angry anymore. He was determined. And that made him unpredictable. I saw it in the way he held himself, the tension in his muscles as if he were on the edge of a precipice, ready to leap into whatever chaos Leon had set in motion.

"You think you can stop me?" Leon's voice was smooth, but there was an edge to it, a flicker of something that suggested he wasn't quite as confident as he wanted us to believe. "You really think you can change everything I've set in motion?"

Evan didn't answer immediately. Instead, he took a step forward, his eyes never leaving Leon's. I knew that look—he wasn't just confronting Leon. He was confronting the man who had turned their shared past into a battlefield, a place where no one could win without losing something vital in the process.

"You're wrong," Evan said finally, his voice low but steady. "You think all these fires were about cleansing. About resetting. But you're not fixing anything. You're destroying everything."

Leon's lips curled into a smile, but it wasn't a smile that reached his eyes. "Destroying? Oh, Evan. You don't understand, do you? I'm not destroying. I'm purging. Cleansing the world of its rot." His voice was almost soothing, like he was trying to explain a simple fact to a child. "You, of all people, should appreciate that."

"I'm nothing like you," Evan bit out, his fists clenched at his sides. "I never was."

For a moment, Leon's expression faltered, just enough for me to see the mask crack. His eyes flickered with something I couldn't place, a brief flash of vulnerability, of something almost human, before it was buried beneath his carefully constructed facade. He took a step toward us, his every movement slow, deliberate. "You still don't get it, do you?" he murmured, his voice almost pained. "This isn't personal, Evan. This is about survival. About creating a new world—one without the failures of the past."

I watched Evan carefully, waiting for him to react. But his gaze didn't waver. He was holding on to something I couldn't quite understand, some thread of belief that still connected him to the man who had once been his ally. It was the same thread that had kept him from walking away from this nightmare, the thread that had tied him to Leon even when it should've been severed long ago.

"You're not saving anyone," I said, my voice cutting through the tension between them. "You're only tearing down what's left."

Leon's eyes shifted to me, his gaze calculating, as if deciding how best to handle me. "And you," he said with a sneer. "You're nothing more than a bystander in this. You always have been, haven't you? You're just a spectator, watching the world burn."

I felt my blood boil, but I didn't back down. "You're wrong, Leon. I'm not standing by while you burn everything to the ground. I'm here to stop you."

Leon's laugh was low, almost affectionate. "You think you can stop me? After all this time? After everything I've done?"

"I don't think," I replied, my voice colder now. "I know."

There was a brief, heart-stopping moment of silence, a space where time seemed to stretch and snap, like a wire pulled taut between us. I could see the frustration in Leon's eyes, the way he was trying to regain control of the situation, trying to make it all fit into the narrative he had created for himself. But he was slipping, and he knew it.

"Do you really think you can just walk away from this, Evan?" Leon asked, his voice softer now, as if trying to coax something out of him. "You've always had a choice. But it's too late for you now. There's no going back."

"I never needed your permission," Evan said, his voice hardening with each word. "And neither does she."

Leon's gaze flickered to me, something like recognition passing over his face. "Ah. So that's how it is." His smile was thin, almost sad. "You really believe you can change anything?"

Evan took another step forward, and I followed suit, standing firm at his side. "I believe in the fight. And I believe in us."

Leon's expression twisted, his eyes narrowing as the reality of what we were saying sank in. He had always thought he was untouchable, that he could bend the world to his will with fire and manipulation. But he hadn't accounted for one thing: he had underestimated us.

"Then you'll die with that belief," Leon said, his voice barely a whisper, but it was enough to make the hairs on the back of my neck stand on end. He was playing his final card, ready to burn everything in one last act of desperation.

But I wasn't going to let him. Not now. Not after everything.

"Not today," I said firmly. The words came out with a clarity I hadn't expected, but they were true. Leon might have thought he was the one in control, but he hadn't counted on the one thing he couldn't predict: our resolve.

Leon's gaze darkened, the light in his eyes shifting from calculated indifference to something far colder. A deeper, sharper kind of anger that felt like the breath before a storm. It was as if the very air around us had thickened, the tension clinging to my skin like the soot from his flames, every word he spoke landing with the weight of a promise he meant to keep.

"You think you can stand against me?" His laugh was hollow, nothing like the earlier amusement. "You'll never win this fight, not the way you think. The fire is already here, whether you see it or not. It's been coming for a long time."

The words hung in the air, heavy with the anticipation of something terrible yet to come. My pulse quickened, not just from fear, but from the sharp clarity that came with the realization. Leon wasn't bluffing. Whatever plan he had, it wasn't just about burning buildings. He had something much larger in mind.

Evan's hand twitched at his side. I knew him well enough to know that the silence between us was no longer one of uncertainty. It was a moment of preparation. Every muscle in his body was coiled tight, like a storm about to break.

"I told you," Leon continued, his voice taking on a strange gentleness. "It's all about cleansing. You're too blind to see it. But maybe she can finally understand." He turned his attention to me, his gaze a cold, calculating sweep from head to toe. "Maybe she'll be the one who gets it."

I met his eyes with a defiance that surprised even me. "You're delusional. You've been tearing people apart because you think it'll make everything better. You've destroyed everything you touch."

The muscles in his jaw tightened, the frustration visible now, but he still smiled. "I'm not destroying. I'm creating. You'll see soon enough."

There it was. That sick, twisted vision of his. That belief that destruction wasn't an end—it was a beginning. A new world, shaped by fire and ash. And somehow, he had convinced himself that this was the only way forward. But I wouldn't let him finish the job.

Before I could speak again, there was a sharp, sudden sound—like a snap in the air—and the floor beneath us seemed to tremble, faintly at first, then more insistent. Evan's eyes darted toward the door behind Leon, his expression turning to one of disbelief.

"No," he whispered, the word more of a growl. "You didn't."

But Leon's smile only widened. "I told you, Evan. It's already started."

I turned, and for the first time, I saw what Leon had been hiding behind that cryptic calm. The distant rumble that I'd mistaken for a storm wasn't just the wind. It was the low, ominous hum of machinery, a steady, relentless sound that seemed to grow louder with each passing second.

Evan reached out, grabbing my arm, pulling me back toward the exit. But it was too late.

The sound shifted—louder, sharper—and then a blast of heat rushed toward us from the far side of the room, followed by the unmistakable scent of smoke. The floor seemed to tremble harder now, as if the building itself was awakening to the destruction Leon had set in motion.

"No," I said, my voice rising with panic. "He's setting it off. The fire—he's—"

Evan didn't let me finish. He was already pulling me toward the door, urgency in his every step. But as we neared the threshold, Leon's voice rang out, louder than the chaos around us.

"Run, then. Try to save yourselves. But remember—this is the end of everything."

We didn't need any more words. We didn't need the final confrontation to prove how far gone Leon was. The fire was real now. The destruction wasn't just an idea in his head. It was tangible. It was happening.

"Move!" Evan shouted, dragging me forward, but even as we reached the door, I could hear it. The crackling of flames, the sound of something large and dangerous igniting. A fire that had been waiting to unleash itself.

The door swung open, and we stumbled into the night, the heat already at our backs, but there was no escaping it. No matter how far we ran, no matter how quickly we moved, the fire would follow us. Leon had seen to that.

But as we reached the street, I could feel the desperation rising. We hadn't just been running from Leon. We were running from the consequences of his actions. From the destruction he had set into motion long before we'd ever arrived.

"Evan," I gasped, looking around. The world seemed to be closing in on us. The sky was stained orange from the flames licking at the edges of the building. It was like the entire city was starting to burn.

"I'm not leaving this behind," Evan said, his voice cold with determination. "We can still stop it. We can still take control."

I grabbed his arm, my hand shaking. "How? How do we stop it? There's nothing left to fight."

He didn't answer. Instead, his eyes darted toward something in the distance. A glow on the horizon, growing brighter with every second. The fire had spread, yes, but there was something else now. A larger, more deliberate force at work.

And then I saw it.

A figure in the distance, moving through the smoke, walking calmly toward us. Leon. His silhouette was unmistakable against the blazing backdrop, his arms spread wide like he was embracing the inferno.

The realization hit me like a blow to the chest. He wasn't just setting fires. He was becoming them.

Chapter 39: Consumed by Fire

The heat hit me like a slap across the face, its intensity searing the air around us. The building groaned, its bones rattling under the weight of Leon's plan—our plan now, whether we liked it or not. I could taste the smoke, thick and acrid, swirling around my mouth as if it were trying to choke me before the fire could. I had no idea how long we had before the whole place collapsed, but I didn't plan on finding out.

Evan was close, his shadow cast long on the crumbling walls as we navigated the narrow corridor. He moved with purpose, each step sure, each breath controlled. I had always admired that about him, his unwavering calm in the face of disaster. But even now, with flames licking at the edges of the hallway, I saw something else in his eyes—something darker. His determination was as sharp as a knife, but there was a flicker there, a deep fear, the kind that comes when you know that survival isn't a guarantee, no matter how good you are.

"Stay low," Evan murmured, his voice barely rising above the crackling heat. His hand shot out, guiding me through a jagged doorframe that had barely held on through the blast.

I obeyed, crouching down as the air thickened with smoke. The fire had spread quickly—too quickly, for my liking. It was an impossible situation, and every step forward felt like it might be my last. But there was no turning back.

Through the haze, I caught sight of the fire eating away at the walls, embers flying like angry sparks. The building moaned again, this time louder, as if it, too, was struggling against the inevitable. My mind flashed to Leon, the man who had set this chaos into motion. His face, twisted in rage when we last saw him, flashed in my mind like an angry ghost. He wasn't just trying to destroy the building. He wanted to destroy everything I cared about, and right now, that included my life.

I couldn't let him win.

"Evan, do you think we can—"

A sudden crash echoed through the hallway, followed by a thunderous roar. A piece of the ceiling collapsed with an ear-splitting crack, just inches from where I stood. Evan's grip on my arm tightened, pulling me backward with a strength that surprised me. I was about to protest, to scream that I could handle it, when I looked up and saw the flames in his eyes, bright and unwavering.

"Not yet," he said, voice low, his teeth clenched against the suffocating heat. "We need to get to him. We have no time."

I nodded, even as the world seemed to tilt around us. The fire surged, its roar like a wild beast being unleashed.

We moved forward, ever closer to the heart of the blaze, where Leon waited. I could almost feel him there, lurking just beyond the corner, his presence like a heavy shadow that filled the space between the flames.

When we finally rounded the corner, the sight of him nearly stopped my heart. He stood in the middle of a massive firestorm, the flames curling and leaping around him like hungry snakes. His eyes were wild, manic, a grin stretching across his face. He looked less like a man and more like a force of nature, his whole body consumed by the inferno he had created.

"You really think you can stop me?" His voice, twisted and distorted by the heat, reverberated in the air. "You're just as trapped as I am."

My stomach twisted into a knot. He was right. The building was coming down around us, and there was no easy way out. No safety net.

Evan stepped forward, pushing me behind him. "You're insane, Leon," he said, his voice cutting through the chaos with a calm that was almost unsettling. "This doesn't have to end like this."

Leon's laughter filled the air, harsh and cruel. "It already has," he sneered. "It ends with you dead and me standing over your ashes."

I couldn't breathe. I couldn't think. The air was thick with smoke, my body screaming for oxygen, but all I could focus on was the look in Evan's eyes. There was a fire there, one that matched the one around us. It wasn't fear. It wasn't doubt. It was the kind of determination that made me believe, for the first time in what felt like forever, that we might actually make it out of here.

"We're not going anywhere," Evan said, his voice steady, unwavering. And then he moved.

The fight was brief but brutal. Leon was a force, his rage a thing that burned as hot as the flames around us. But Evan didn't back down. Not even when the smoke thickened to a point where we could barely see each other, not even when I could feel the heat of the fire in my chest, threatening to consume me.

In the end, it wasn't the fire that took Leon down—it was the fight in Evan's eyes. I watched as he struck, his movements swift, precise, his hands steady as they fought back the madness that had taken hold of our adversary.

And then, just as the building seemed ready to collapse in on us, we heard the first of the cracks—the sound of the foundation breaking. I knew it was time to go.

"Now!" Evan yelled, pulling me toward the exit. The fire surged behind us, but his grip never faltered. Together, we ran, the world around us a blur of smoke, flames, and chaos. And just as the floor beneath us gave way, we leapt into the unknown, escaping the inferno by mere inches.

The flames roared behind us as the building collapsed. But I wasn't thinking about the destruction. I was thinking about the fire in Evan's eyes—the fire that had carried us through to the other side.

The ground shuddered beneath my feet as the last of the structure's foundation gave way. It wasn't an explosion that ripped through the building, but something much more ominous—the slow, inevitable collapse of something too far gone to be saved. Each tremor sent a fresh wave of panic through me, but somehow, it also felt oddly familiar, like the last moments of a terrible dream where nothing is real, yet you know it's about to swallow you whole.

Evan's hand was still clamped around mine, his grip as fierce as ever. I could feel the pulse in his fingers, each thud against my skin a reminder that we weren't out of danger yet. We weren't even close.

"You okay?" His voice was low, barely audible over the chaos, but there was that same quiet strength in it, the one that always anchored me when the world threatened to go off the rails.

I nodded, though the truth was far messier than my simple answer. My lungs ached from the smoke, my throat raw, and I could taste the bitter metal tang of fear, but there was no time to indulge it. Not now. Not when the world was falling apart around us and the only thing keeping us standing was the fragile thread of each other's presence.

"Can you see it?" Evan's voice had shifted, a hint of urgency threading through it. I strained my eyes, squinting against the haze, trying to make sense of the chaos ahead.

A figure loomed in the distance, a silhouette draped in shadow and fire, the flames dancing around him like they were a part of him, feeding his madness. Leon. The reason we were in this mess to begin with. His insane plan hadn't just been about destruction. It had been a statement. A reminder that he could destroy everything, even us, if he wanted.

But there was something more in his eyes now. It wasn't just the hunger for power or the wildness that had driven him to this point. No, what I saw now was something almost tragic. The flickering madness was still there, but so was something else—something raw and desperate, like a man who knew he had no way out, but couldn't bear to admit it.

"We need to finish this," Evan said, more to himself than to me. But I heard the steel in his voice, the unwavering commitment that I had always relied on.

We stepped forward, the heat growing unbearable with each step, the sound of crackling timber reverberating in my chest. There was no escape. There was only the confrontation. The final face-off that had been inevitable from the moment Leon set his plan into motion.

When we reached him, Leon didn't move, didn't even acknowledge us at first. He just stood there, a dark, eerie figure in the heart of the flames, his gaze fixed on the destruction around us.

"You really think you've won?" His voice was eerily calm, a stark contrast to the madness in his eyes.

I wanted to snap back, to tell him he was insane, to scream that none of this had to happen. But instead, I found myself holding Evan's gaze, grounding myself in his silent strength. The weight of the moment hung heavy between us, and all I could think was that it wasn't about winning anymore. It was about survival.

Evan stepped closer, his movements slow and deliberate, the tension crackling in the air. "We haven't won," he said, his voice carrying that quiet intensity that had always seemed to cut through the noise. "But you've lost, Leon. We're not doing this anymore."

For a moment, I thought Leon might laugh, might relish the chaos he had caused just to see the world burn. But instead, something shifted in him. The corners of his mouth twitched, a strange, almost painful smile playing at the edges. "You don't get it, do you?" he whispered, his voice thick with a bitterness that was almost too much to bear. "I never wanted this. Not really. But you forced my hand."

I glanced at Evan, confusion creeping in. This wasn't the same man who had once looked at us with nothing but contempt. This wasn't the man who had plotted this destruction with cold calculation. This... this was someone else.

But before I could process it, Leon moved, his body shifting as if the weight of his own words had finally pushed him over the edge. He lunged, wild and desperate, and everything that had been simmering between us came to a head.

Evan was faster. His arm shot out, knocking Leon off balance just as the flames around us surged higher, creating a wall of fire that separated us from any hope of escape. The moment felt suspended in time, everything slowing as Evan pushed me back, his eyes wide with a mix of fear and something else I couldn't quite place.

"Run!" he shouted, his voice cracking with urgency. But before I could make a move, Leon was on him, a blur of motion and rage. My heart stopped, the adrenaline surging through my veins as I rushed toward them, but Evan's voice rang in my ears, cutting through the chaos. "Go!"

I couldn't leave him. I wouldn't leave him.

But Leon was a wild animal, thrashing and snarling, his strength fueled by the same desperation I'd seen in his eyes just moments before. I didn't know if it was the fire, the madness, or something else entirely, but it was clear that Evan was holding back. He wasn't fighting Leon in the way he normally would. He was trying to subdue him, to talk him down.

And then it hit me. Leon was just as trapped as we were. In the end, we were all the same, scrambling for survival, consumed by the flames of our own making. And no matter how badly we wanted to run, none of us could.

The air was thick, alive with the sound of crackling wood and the faint groans of a structure straining under its own weight. The heat had become unbearable, the smoke so dense that it was nearly impossible to see more than a few feet in front of us. I could feel the perspiration rolling down my back, slick and cold, even as the fire threatened to devour everything around us. My heart pounded in my chest, and I could hardly tell if it was from the running, the panic, or the adrenaline coursing through my veins. Maybe it was all three.

Evan and I were no longer talking. There was no time. Every second counted now, and as much as I wanted to turn back and make sure everything was okay—check on the others, confirm our safety, or just take a damn breath—I couldn't. Not yet. Not while Leon was still standing.

He was still there, standing like a monument to all the destruction he'd caused, surrounded by flames that danced in the air like a perverse reflection of his madness. He looked unhinged, eyes wild and full of a manic kind of joy that made my stomach churn. This wasn't just about a fire anymore. This was something deeper. Something darker. It was as if he had finally embraced the chaos he'd tried to create.

"You think you can stop this?" Leon's voice sliced through the air, harsh and filled with a kind of sick satisfaction. His grin was wide, almost too wide, as though it could stretch and swallow the world whole.

I steadied myself, gripping the iron beam that still held a faint resemblance to a doorframe. My pulse was erratic, my head a whirlpool of conflicting thoughts. How had it come to this? How had this man—this man who once seemed so methodical, so composed—fallen into this abyss?

But even as I searched for answers, my body knew what I had to do. I had to stop him. I couldn't let him destroy everything.

Evan's breath was steady beside me, his presence grounding, even when the world was so unsteady. I glanced at him, and for a brief moment, I saw something in his eyes that I couldn't quite place. Not fear, exactly—not in the way you would expect—but something else. Something deeper. A resolve. He wasn't just trying to get out of here. He was trying to save something more than just himself. It was like we were bound together in this, our fates tangled in a way I didn't fully understand, but could feel in my bones.

"Ready?" His voice was low, calm despite the chaos swirling around us.

I didn't answer at first. Instead, I took a deep breath, the acrid air burning my lungs as it scraped at my throat. My fingers tingled with the adrenaline, and I pushed myself forward, each step heavier than the last. I didn't think about the fire. I didn't think about anything except Leon and the fact that if we didn't stop him now, we wouldn't get another chance.

We moved together—two people, one purpose—navigating the flames like ghosts in the night. The fire crackled around us, the heat and smoke thickening with each passing moment. Leon was still watching, still waiting for us to make a move. But he didn't seem quite as invincible as before. Something had shifted, something I couldn't quite explain. Maybe it was the weight of the fire, maybe it was the strain of his own plans coming undone, but there was a subtle shift in his posture, a tremor in his hand. It was almost imperceptible, but it was there.

"You think you can change me?" he sneered, his eyes flashing with a maddened brilliance. "I'm already too far gone. There's no saving me."

I almost believed him. There was something chilling in his words, something that made the hairs on the back of my neck stand up. But then Evan's hand found mine, and the warmth of it, despite the chaos, grounded me. It reminded me that no matter how much Leon tried to control this situation, no matter how much fire he had thrown into the world, there was always a way out—always a chance to fight back.

"We've always had a choice, Leon," Evan said, his voice as steady as ever, despite the rising fury in the air. "And this? This isn't it."

With that, we closed the distance between us, and the world seemed to slow, the heat intensifying in an almost surreal way. Every step was a battle, every breath a struggle against the smoke and ash that swirled through the air like an invitation to suffocate. But we kept moving, kept pushing forward, until there was no more distance between us.

It happened so fast I could hardly comprehend it. Leon lunged toward Evan, but this time, there was no hesitation. No second thoughts. Evan was already prepared, his movements a blur, his fist connecting with Leon's jaw in a single, fluid motion. The impact was so hard I could hear it—crackling through the air like the sound of thunder, followed by a muffled groan of pain from Leon.

But Leon wasn't done. Not yet.

Before I could react, he grabbed Evan's arm, twisting it in a move so quick and vicious it made me gasp. The flames around us roared louder, feeding on the tension, the rage, the sheer rawness of what was happening. I watched, frozen, as Leon and Evan grappled, the space between them closing tighter with each passing second.

"Evan!" I shouted, but my voice was drowned out by the sound of cracking wood, the entire structure buckling beneath the weight of its own destruction.

Evan fought back, his movements graceful and precise, like a dancer caught in the flames of a terrible opera. But there was something wrong. He was struggling more than he should have, and I could see it now—the sweat on his brow, the way his breath came in uneven gasps.

It was then that I saw it. The faintest shimmer of a blade in Leon's hand.

I didn't think. I just acted.

With everything I had left, I threw myself into the fray. My hand shot out, and in one desperate motion, I lunged for Leon's arm, trying to break his hold on Evan. But as my fingers closed around his wrist, the world seemed to crack in half, and I was left staring at the blade, the edge catching the firelight, as it came down toward Evan's exposed side.

And then, everything went black.

Chapter 40: Rising from the Ashes

The morning sun was still reluctant to rise, as if it too was hesitant to face the aftermath. The streets of the city, once charred and broken, now bristled with the first signs of recovery. I stood at the window, my fingers brushing against the cool glass as I watched the city breathe again, slowly but surely. The smoke had long since dissipated, leaving only the faintest trace of its scent lingering in the air like a whispered memory. The walls of our home, once shuddering with the crackle of fire and the rush of footsteps, now stood silent, waiting for their next chapter.

Evan's presence behind me was steady, unwavering, like a shield I never knew I needed. He had been my anchor in the storm, and now, in this new quiet, I felt his warmth even more acutely. The rise of the sun cast a soft glow across his face, the shadows of the night retreating in the face of the light. He didn't speak at first, content to let the silence settle between us, the way two people who had fought side by side could communicate without words.

But I knew he was thinking about it all—the destruction, the pain, the victory. He had seen too much to ever be the same, just as I had. We had both been burned, scarred in ways that couldn't be hidden beneath clothes or smiles. But, somehow, we had risen from the ashes of our own lives, holding onto each other with a desperation that was born from survival itself. I turned to face him, watching the way the sunlight danced in his eyes, tracing the lines of his jaw, the shape of his lips. There was a tenderness there that hadn't been present before, an unspoken promise that now we were here, together, and nothing would tear us apart.

"Are you sure you're ready for this?" he asked, his voice a low murmur that sent a ripple through the quiet morning.

I didn't need to ask what he meant. We had talked about it so many times, each conversation weaving its own path toward this moment. The future, the one we had once thought was impossible, was now ours to shape. A life beyond the chaos, beyond the fire. A life built on the trust we had forged and the love we had discovered in the most unlikely of places.

"I think I'm as ready as I'll ever be," I replied, my hand reaching out to touch his, our fingers intertwining. There was a strength in that simple gesture, something that spoke volumes about the battles we had faced and the battles still to come.

Evan's smile was small, but it carried the weight of everything we had endured. "We've been through hell and back," he said, his thumb gently brushing the back of my hand. "But we're here. Together."

I leaned into him, pressing my forehead against his chest, feeling the steady beat of his heart beneath the fabric of his shirt. There was something undeniably comforting in the rhythm of it, something that made me believe that maybe, just maybe, we had finally found our peace. "Together," I echoed, the word tasting sweeter than any promise.

The city, though, was not quite ready to rest. It still hummed with the energy of recovery, of rebuilding, and the echoes of a past that would never be forgotten. People moved through the streets below, their faces determined, as if they were fighting their own battles. In the distance, I could hear the sounds of construction, the clatter of tools, and the murmurs of workers as they rebuilt what had been lost. It was a process that would take time, a slow and steady return to normalcy. But nothing would ever be quite the same. The fires had left a mark, one that could never be erased, no matter how much we tried to move forward.

Still, there was hope in the air now, a palpable shift that had settled over the city in the wake of Leon's capture. His reign of terror was over, his name whispered in fear only by those who hadn't yet realized that the storm had passed. I had no illusions about what was to come, no false sense of security. The world was far from perfect, but at least now we had a fighting chance to rebuild it. And Evan and I? We would face it together, as we always had.

"Do you ever wonder if we've earned this?" I asked, my voice breaking through the quiet like a sudden gust of wind. "This peace?"

Evan's hand slid up to my cheek, his touch gentle but firm. "I think we've earned every moment," he said, his lips brushing my forehead in a soft kiss. "And I think we'll keep earning it. Every single day."

I closed my eyes, letting the weight of his words settle over me, feeling the depth of them sink into my bones. This wasn't the end. This was just the beginning. The fire had burned hot and fierce, but we were still standing, stronger for it. And together, we would rise every time the world tried to knock us down.

The days stretched out like a lazy cat, settling into the warmth of something resembling peace, but still wary of what might disrupt it. I could feel it in the air, a quiet tension—like the earth knew that after every storm, there's always another one brewing on the horizon. The city's pulse was steady, but underneath, I could hear the distant hum of its recovery, its people restless and ready to rise again.

It wasn't easy, though. Even with the fires behind us, there were whispers of what might come next. People were still picking up the pieces of their lives, one broken brick at a time. But each day, the ground felt less unstable, less likely to crack underfoot. And then there was Evan, whose presence was becoming a kind of anchor for me, even when I had moments of doubt.

It was a Thursday afternoon when the first signs of the shift hit. We were walking through the park, the trees that had once been blackened stumps now growing tender leaves, their buds eager for the sunshine. It was funny how nature worked, how it always seemed to find a way to start over, no matter how bad things had been. I found myself thinking that maybe, just maybe, we were doing the same.

Evan's hand brushed mine as we strolled along the winding path, his fingers warm against my skin. It felt like a quiet celebration of the mundane, of all the little things we had been denied. He was speaking to me about some project he had in the works—a new initiative to help with the rebuilding efforts—but I wasn't really listening. I was too busy studying the way his lips moved when he spoke, the way his eyes crinkled when he smiled.

Suddenly, he stopped, pulling me gently to a halt in the middle of the path. His expression shifted, something unreadable passing over his face.

"What's wrong?" I asked, my voice laced with concern.

"I've been thinking," he said, his tone carefully measured. "About what happens next. About... us."

I frowned, unsure of where this was heading. "What about us?"

He exhaled slowly, like he was bracing himself. "I know we've been through a lot. And I know things have changed. But I—" He stopped and looked down at the ground for a moment before meeting my gaze again. "I don't know if I can do this anymore, live like this."

For a split second, the world seemed to tilt. The air between us grew thick with unspoken words, and the park around us fell silent, as if waiting for the next part of the story.

I could feel the blood rush to my face, my heart thundering in my chest. "What do you mean? I thought... I thought we were in this together."

He stepped closer, the heat from his body pressing against mine, but his eyes were distant. "I love you, but I'm not sure I can stay in this city. I don't think I can keep living like this, always looking over my shoulder, waiting for the other shoe to drop. It's not just about the city. It's about what happened here. The fires, the fear, the constant fight. It's... exhausting."

I stared at him, my mind racing to piece together the words. "Evan," I said, my voice faltering. "You can't just—leave. Not after everything. Not now."

He reached out to touch my cheek, his fingers feather-light. "I'm not saying I'm leaving you. I'm just saying that I need to find a way to breathe again. And maybe that means being somewhere else. I don't know yet."

The words stung more than I expected, more than I cared to admit. I had always known Evan was a man who needed space, who could lose himself in his work, in his thoughts. But this felt different, like the man I thought I knew was slipping away, piece by piece, and I had no control over it.

"I don't know what you want me to say," I replied, my voice tight. "But I can't go with you. Not if you're running away from everything we've fought for. I thought we had something real. I thought we were—"

"Don't say it," he interrupted, shaking his head. "This isn't about you, it's about me. I don't want to hurt you, but I need space to figure this out. Please don't make it harder than it already is."

The words hung in the air, like smoke from a fire that had yet to settle. I stood there, motionless, as the truth of what he was saying sank into me. Maybe it wasn't about me at all. Maybe it was about him, about the war he had fought silently in his mind long before the flames ever touched our city.

I wanted to say something more, to beg him not to go, but I couldn't. The words died in my throat, and the park around us seemed to stretch farther, the distance between us widening with each passing second.

"I need to think," I whispered, my voice barely audible. "We both do."

Evan nodded once, his gaze never leaving mine. "I'll be here when you're ready."

But even as he spoke, I knew something had shifted. Not just in him, but in me. I had felt the ache of losing him before, but this—this was different. It was a quiet resignation, a truth we both had to face. That no matter how hard we fought, we might not be able to save each other.

As he walked away, I stayed rooted to the spot, the weight of his absence pressing down on me. The trees, the grass, the path—all of it blurred into the background as I tried to hold onto the pieces of him that were slipping through my fingers.

The days that followed Evan's confession felt like something out of a dream I couldn't quite wake from. I went through the motions—work, the city's slow recovery, the constant hum of life around me—but none of it felt real. Not without him. He was still there, in the quiet spaces between my thoughts, in the coffee cups we used to share, in the places where our fingers used to meet. I hadn't realized how deeply he had rooted himself in my life until now, until the absence of him pressed against me like an open wound.

I found myself wandering through our apartment more often than I'd like to admit, trying to catch pieces of him, like fragments of a dream slipping away with each blink. The kitchen, once a place of easy conversation, was now empty, the counters untouched. His favorite chair by the window was vacant, and the faint smell of his cologne lingered in the fabric, a reminder of what we'd been and what we might never be again.

I wasn't sure when it happened, but one evening I found myself standing in front of the door, my hand resting on the cool brass handle. I had done it a thousand times before—left the apartment, ventured into the world beyond. But tonight felt different. Tonight, I wasn't just walking out; I was walking away from the safety we had built, from the fragile peace we had forged.

The city felt quieter than usual as I stepped outside, the hum of traffic and chatter subdued under a blanket of silence. It was as if the streets knew I was making a choice, and they held their breath, waiting. I wasn't sure where I was going, only that I needed to move, to feel something that wasn't the weight of Evan's absence.

I walked for hours, the city slipping by in a blur of neon lights and late-night faces, until I found myself standing in front of the old bookstore. It was a place I had always loved, a quiet haven where the world seemed to slow down, where time and space ceased to matter. I hadn't been here in months, not since Leon's capture had taken all the air from the room, leaving nothing but the ghosts of what had been.

The bell above the door jingled as I stepped inside, the familiar scent of paper and ink enveloping me. I ran my fingers along the spines of the books, the worn leather and soft cloth soothing in a way I couldn't explain. I didn't know why I came here; perhaps it was the need to find something that still held meaning, to search for a way back to who I had been before the fire, before everything had changed.

The shop was empty, save for the elderly man behind the counter. His glasses were perched precariously on the end of his nose, and he looked up as I approached, his wrinkled face breaking into a knowing smile.

"Back again, are we?" he said, his voice gruff but warm, like an old friend.

I nodded, my throat tight. "Just looking."

He chuckled softly. "You know, you'll never find what you're looking for by wandering the aisles aimlessly. Not that I'd know anything about that." His eyes twinkled with a hint of mischief, and I couldn't help but smile.

I walked further into the store, past the shelves that seemed to sag with the weight of forgotten stories. It wasn't until I reached the back corner that I saw it—the old leather-bound book I had once admired, the one with the faded gold lettering. It was tucked away on the top shelf, almost as if it had been waiting for me.

I pulled it down, the weight of it grounding me in a way I hadn't expected. There was something comforting in the familiarity of it, something that felt like the possibility of rediscovery. As I opened the cover, a small note fell out, yellowed with age. I unfolded it carefully, a strange sense of deja vu settling over me.

The note was brief, written in a scrawl that looked almost frantic. It read: "The past has a way of catching up with you. When it does, be ready."

I stared at the note for a long moment, my heart skipping a beat. It wasn't the first time I had felt the weight of those words—of something unfinished, lurking in the corners of my life, waiting for its moment. The world had been quiet since Evan left, but in that stillness, I couldn't shake the feeling that something was coming.

The shopkeeper's voice interrupted my thoughts. "You look like you've seen a ghost."

I blinked, shaking off the sense of unease that had settled over me. "I'm fine," I said, though my voice betrayed me. "I'll take this one."

He nodded, his gaze lingering on me for a moment before he went back to sorting through the piles of paper. I paid quickly, my fingers brushing against the edge of the note as I tucked it into my coat pocket.

The walk home was different, the air thicker somehow. As I crossed the threshold into the apartment, the silence hit me harder than before, like it was wrapping itself around me, suffocating the space we had shared.

I hadn't realized how desperately I had been searching for some sort of sign, something to guide me through the uncertainty. But the note, the book—it was a sign, wasn't it? The past had a way of catching up with you, and I had the uneasy feeling that mine was about to show up at my doorstep, uninvited and unforgiving.

Just as I set the book down on the table, the doorbell rang. The sound echoed through the apartment, a sharp and sudden intrusion. I froze, my heart thudding in my chest. There was no way I was expecting anyone—not tonight, not with everything so unsettled.

I moved cautiously to the door, my hand trembling as I reached for the handle. When I opened it, the sight that met me was the last thing I expected.

Chapter 41: A New Flame

The wind was sharp that morning, the kind that whips through your coat like it's a secret, whispering messages no one else could hear. I tugged my scarf tighter around my neck, the wool scratching at my skin, and wished I had the sense to bring gloves. Evan had told me it was going to be cold, but somehow I had convinced myself I could outsmart the weather. I was always too confident in my ability to avoid things like discomfort. It's a habit that often catches up with me, but today, I was willing to pay the price if it meant a few extra moments of peace.

He walked beside me, as steady and predictable as the ticking of the clock in my grandmother's kitchen. His hand was warm in mine, as if he could offer me all the heat I needed, as if we were sealed against the world outside our little bubble. The past few weeks had felt like the kind of exhaustion you can only accumulate after trying to do something for the world. It started with the fire, the flickering tragedy that swept through the town like a storm you saw coming but could never avoid. It lingered in the air, even now, despite the cold, despite the attempts to rebuild and renew. We had started the fund for the victims, a small but necessary way to give something back after everything that had been taken. The thought of it consumed me in odd, unsettling ways. The fire had taken so much, and it felt only right to try to restore balance, even if that meant pouring all of myself into this cause.

Evan caught my eye as we passed the local bakery, the scent of freshly baked bread greeting us like an old friend. The windows were fogged up, and the sound of a coffee grinder hummed from inside. I couldn't help but smile, the small pleasures of life sometimes outweighing the heavy things you carry in your heart. "Do you want to stop?" he asked, his voice still rough from the long days we'd spent going through paperwork and planning the next steps. He didn't have to ask twice.

We stepped into the warmth of the bakery, the doorbell chiming overhead, signaling our entrance. The interior was soft with the glow of early morning sunlight streaming through the windows, golden beams landing on the worn wooden floors and the mismatched chairs scattered about. The woman behind the counter, a little older than me with kind eyes and an apron dusted in flour, looked up and grinned when she saw us.

"Well, if it isn't the town's most famous couple," she teased, setting down a tray of croissants. "You've been keeping everyone busy, haven't you?"

I flushed slightly, glancing at Evan. He hadn't noticed. "We're just doing what we can," I said, trying not to let the weight of it all show. But there was no hiding it anymore. The work we'd been doing was exhausting, and despite the small victories—like seeing the first donation come in, or knowing that people were starting to trust the fund—it all felt too heavy some days. It wasn't just the paperwork, the endless phone calls, or even the people who came to us for help. It was the constant undercurrent of grief, of remembering what we had lost and how much more we could lose if we weren't careful.

Evan was leaning against the counter, scanning the display case with a familiarity that made me smile. "What do you recommend, June?" he asked, his voice still gruff, but with a hint of warmth that made me feel like we were, for a moment, just two people trying to live.

June didn't miss a beat. "The cinnamon rolls, no question. They're perfect every time." She slid them onto a small plate, and I could already taste the sugar on my tongue, the promise of warmth after the cold walk.

We sat at a table by the window, the steam from our coffee rising in delicate swirls. The bakery was small but vibrant, and as I looked out at the street, the quiet bustle of the town seemed somehow comforting. People came and went, faces familiar and unknown in equal measure. Life had moved on in the most ordinary of ways, and yet for me, it felt as though we were still in a kind of suspended animation. The fire had changed everything, even the things that had once seemed immovable. And in the midst of that change, Evan and I had found a new rhythm, one that didn't feel like the chaos we had known, but also wasn't quite the life we had imagined.

"Do you think we're doing enough?" I asked him, voice soft against the steady hum of the bakery. He paused, taking a sip of his coffee, and I could see the wheels turning in his mind.

"I don't know," he said finally, his gaze steady on mine. "But we're doing something. And that matters. More than you think."

I wanted to believe him. I did. But the truth was, nothing felt like it could ever truly be enough. Not after the fire, not after everything we had lost. The weight of those memories sat with me, heavy as a stone in my chest. But Evan had always been the practical one. The one who could turn any disaster into a plan, any setback into something to learn from. He was my anchor. I just wasn't sure yet if I was strong enough to hold my own weight.

As if sensing the tension swirling between us, he reached across the table, his fingers brushing mine with an unexpected gentleness. "We're not done yet," he said softly. "But we'll face whatever comes next, together."

His words were a balm, but they didn't quite heal the ache inside me. I nodded, though, not trusting myself to speak. The promise lingered between us, fragile and hopeful, like the light that filtered through the bakery windows. It wasn't everything, but it was enough for today. And today was all I had.

We slipped out of the bakery with our cinnamon rolls in hand, the warmth of the pastries mingling with the chilly bite of the air. Evan held the door open for me, a gesture that should have felt familiar, but today it seemed somehow more intimate, more deliberate. He caught me looking at him, that glint of mischief in his eyes again, as if we were two schoolchildren sneaking moments of rebellion when the world wasn't watching.

"You know, I think you just wanted an excuse to come here," I said, biting into the soft, sticky sweetness of the roll.

"Maybe," he replied, his grin pulling wide, and I couldn't help but feel that he was hiding something behind that playful expression. "But I think it's more about balance, don't you? Too much work and not enough sugar... well, that's a recipe for disaster."

I laughed, more at the thought of him trying to justify his pastry obsession than the actual statement itself. There was an ease in the way we interacted, even after everything that had happened. It wasn't flawless, but it was ours.

We walked in silence for a while, the small town streets stretching out before us in that way that always made me feel both grounded and untethered. The leaves were starting to turn; gold and amber hues dotted the trees, promising the full embrace of autumn soon. But for now, there was still the lingering warmth of summer in the air, clinging to the back of your neck like a memory you can't quite shake.

I felt the weight of Evan's hand brush against mine, and for a brief moment, everything felt quiet again. As if all of the noise—the charity work, the paperwork, the people looking to us for guidance—had softened into a low hum in the background, and all that remained was this space, this connection between us. It wasn't often I allowed myself to indulge in these small moments of serenity, but today, it felt like we had earned it.

"You've been quiet today," Evan finally said, his voice low and thoughtful. It wasn't accusatory, just an observation.

"Just thinking," I replied, turning to look up at him. "About how we got here, you know? How... everything is different now." I wasn't sure if I wanted to go further, but Evan had this way of making me feel like he could handle my thoughts, no matter how heavy they were.

He nodded, that same understanding gaze in his eyes. "I know what you mean." His thumb brushed against the back of my hand. "But I think the difference now is that we're in it together. We're not alone, not anymore."

There was comfort in his words, but also something sharper that made me hesitate. The idea of "together" was becoming complicated. The fire had been a catalyst, a point in time where we had both been forced to confront who we were, who we had been, and what we could become. I wasn't entirely sure yet if the person I was becoming was the one I wanted to be. I felt like I had a foot in both worlds—the old one, where things made sense, and this new one, where uncertainty reigned.

We reached the park and stopped by the fountain. Evan leaned against the stone edge, his expression more serious now. "You've been carrying a lot, haven't you?" It wasn't a question so much as a gentle prompt.

I let out a breath, trying to gather my thoughts, feeling the weight of them pile up in the space between us. "I don't know how to make sense of all of it sometimes. The fire, the fund, the pressure to do it right, to make it count. People are counting on us, Evan. And it feels like... like I could fail them." I let the words tumble out, not realizing how much I'd been bottling up until that moment.

"You won't fail them." His voice was firm, and I could hear the quiet conviction behind it. "And even if we make mistakes, we're still here, still trying. That matters."

I wanted to believe him. I needed to believe him. But in the back of my mind, there was that voice, the one that had always been there, questioning everything I did. What if this wasn't enough? What if, despite all our efforts, we couldn't fix what was broken?

The sun was starting to dip lower, casting long shadows across the park, and I felt the chill of it seeping into my bones. It wasn't just the weather. There was something in the air, a change that had nothing to do with the season.

I stood up straighter, feeling the pull of something, a decision I hadn't even realized I was making. "I'm scared, Evan. Not of failing in the traditional way—of running out of money or not raising enough—but of losing what we've built. What we are." The confession hung in the air between us, too raw to ignore.

Evan studied me, his eyes searching mine as if trying to uncover a part of me I hadn't shown him before. For a moment, I thought he might say something—something reassuring, something perfect—but instead, he stood up and pulled me into a tight hug. His chest was solid, warm against mine, and the scent of him—the woodsy cologne he always wore, the faint musk of his jacket—wrapped around me like a comfort I hadn't known I needed until it was there.

"I'm not going anywhere," he murmured into my hair. "We'll figure it out. But we're in this for the long haul. You and me."

I closed my eyes, letting the sound of his heartbeat against my ear anchor me in that moment. And though I still felt the weight of the unknown pressing against my chest, I also felt something shift—a small, quiet reassurance that maybe, just maybe, we would make it through this. Together.

The days had blurred into weeks, and I was beginning to lose track of time. It wasn't just the weight of our project that threatened to swallow me whole; it was the ever-present undercurrent of fear, the quiet suspicion that we weren't just battling the ghosts of the fire but something much harder to define. The world felt different now, sharper somehow, as though we were all walking in the shadow of something that still hadn't quite materialized.

But life didn't stop. It never did. Every morning, the sun came up, the coffee brewed, the emails piled up, and people continued to ask for help, to seek out answers, to hold out their hands for something we couldn't always give. We were learning that being part of a community wasn't just about offering assistance; it was about showing up, even when you didn't have all the answers. Even when you weren't sure who you were anymore.

It was another evening when I found myself standing in the kitchen, stirring a pot of soup that had grown colder than I'd meant it to. The faint scent of garlic and onions filled the air, mingling with the dampness that always seemed to hang in the house after a long day. Evan had gone out for a run, something he had taken up as a way to clear his head, and I was left in the quiet of our home, alone with my thoughts.

I heard the door open and close, the familiar sound of his sneakers squeaking against the tile floor. Then the weight of his footsteps on the stairs, the soft rhythm of his breathing as he entered the kitchen. He came up behind me, his hands warm as they settled around my waist, his chin resting on my shoulder.

"You've been quiet again," he said, his voice thick with exhaustion. There was a rawness to it that made my stomach tighten. "You sure you're okay?"

I couldn't lie. I didn't want to. Not to him. But the words were harder to say than I had anticipated, as if the simple act of speaking them would unravel the fragile thread of control I had managed to keep taut for weeks. I leaned back into him, grateful for the grounding sensation of his body against mine, even as I felt the walls inside me begin to crack.

"I don't know if I am," I said, the words slipping out like a confession. "There's just so much. So much we've had to do. So many people to help. And yet, I feel like we're all just... barely holding on."

His fingers tightened on my waist, pulling me closer. "You don't have to carry it all, you know. We'll figure it out together."

I closed my eyes, leaning into the warmth of his embrace. "I don't want to let anyone down."

"You won't," he promised, but his voice was quiet, almost as if he were reassuring himself.

The silence stretched between us again, thick and uncomfortable. I wanted to believe him. I wanted to believe that we could make this work, that all of this—this feeling of being stretched too thin, of facing an unrelenting tide of demands—would somehow resolve itself. But there was something gnawing at me, a feeling I couldn't shake, like an itch in the back of my mind that I couldn't reach.

I turned to face him, taking his hands in mine. "What if... what if this isn't enough?" The words fell out before I could stop them, and once they were said, I couldn't take them back.

Evan looked at me with an expression I hadn't quite seen before, something deeper than the usual warmth, something that made the air between us feel charged. He swallowed, then nodded slowly, as if processing my question. "I don't know, Liv. I don't know if it will ever feel like enough. But we're trying, aren't we? We're doing everything we can."

But the more he spoke, the more I felt the weight of it pressing down on me. The desire to fix things, to make it all better, was suffocating. I wasn't sure how much longer I could keep up the charade, the act of pretending everything was fine when underneath it all, I was losing myself bit by bit.

I pulled away, suddenly needing space, feeling too confined by the intimacy of his touch. "Maybe trying isn't enough," I said, the words sharper than I meant them to be. "Maybe we need to be more than just a couple of people with good intentions."

He flinched, and for a brief moment, I regretted the sharpness of my tone. But it was out there now, hanging between us like an uninvited guest.

"Are you saying you don't believe in what we're doing?" he asked, his voice low, barely audible.

"No," I whispered, shaking my head. "I believe in what we're doing, but it feels like we're drowning, Evan. Drowning in all these expectations... and what if we fail? What if we can't do what we set out to do?"

He stood there, frozen for a long moment, before letting out a long, slow breath. His shoulders sagged slightly, as if the weight of my words had hit him in a place he hadn't expected. "I don't know," he said again, and this time, it wasn't reassuring. It wasn't confident. It was raw. "I don't know what happens if we don't make it, Liv. But I do know this—we've already been through hell and back. And whatever happens next, we'll face it together. But I need you to believe that."

I didn't answer him right away. My mind was racing, heart pounding, and before I could stop myself, I reached out and grabbed my phone off the counter, my fingers already typing a message before I'd fully thought it through.

The words flashed on the screen, brief and matter-of-fact: We need to talk.

I hit send before I could second-guess myself.

Evan's eyes flicked to mine, confusion etched in his features. "Who was that?"

But before I could answer, the sharp chime of the doorbell cut through the tension, and the knot in my stomach twisted tighter.

Something had shifted. I wasn't sure what. But I knew, in that instant, that everything was about to change again.

The doorbell rang a second time. Louder this time.

Chapter 42: Eternal Ember

The wind felt like it was whispering secrets as it curled through the gap in the brick wall behind me, its cold fingers brushing against my skin. The city sprawled beneath us, a labyrinth of neon lights and shadowed alleyways. Each flicker in the distance was like a heartbeat, a pulse that matched the thrum of my own. The rooftop, my usual escape, had never felt so distant, so full of unspoken promises. And there, next to me, stood Evan, his silhouette sharp against the darkening sky, the weight of the world between us as palpable as the warmth of his presence.

We didn't speak for a while—didn't need to. The city had a way of stealing words from us, making silence more comforting than any conversation ever could. I studied his profile, the way his jaw tightened when he looked out over the skyline, as if trying to hold onto something intangible. The familiar hum of traffic, the distant wail of sirens, and the occasional shout of a drunk reveler below us—the noise of the world, oblivious to the quiet, stolen moments we shared above it all.

"Can you see it?" Evan finally asked, his voice a low rumble, a warm tremor that slipped through the cold night air. He was talking about the future, of course—he always did, as if he could pull the strings of time, as if we could step into it, hand in hand. I didn't answer immediately, because there was no point. The city was always changing, always becoming something new. And I? I was still trying to figure out where I fit into that picture.

He reached into the pocket of his jacket and pulled something out—small, metallic, and shimmering in the fading light. I barely had time to register the motion before he was beside me, his hand in mine, something cold and unfamiliar pressed against my skin. My breath caught in my throat as I looked down, the sight of the ring dazzling me with its simplicity, the kind of simplicity that spoke volumes.

"Is this...?" My voice was caught somewhere between disbelief and wonder, my heart thumping erratically as I tried to make sense of what was happening. The city, the lights, the rooftop—none of it seemed to matter anymore. Only this, only the weight of the promise slipping onto my finger.

"It's ours," Evan said, his voice steady, but I could hear the tremor in it too, like he was waiting for me to say something, anything, to let him know I felt it too. The change. The shift. Whatever this was between us, it wasn't just a fleeting moment. It wasn't just some passing whim or a promise that could be broken by the first gust of wind. No, this was something more.

I turned my hand, watching the ring catch the last of the sunlight, its gleam a reflection of the fire inside me. It wasn't just a ring, not just a symbol. It was a promise—an eternal ember. One that would burn even in the coldest of nights, in the darkest of days.

"You know what this means?" I asked, finally breaking the silence that had cocooned us, my voice teasing but laced with something deeper, something heavier than I cared to acknowledge. Because Evan wasn't just a person to me. He was the fire, the chaos, the calm—all wrapped in one impossibly perfect package. And I couldn't help but wonder if we had the strength to survive the storm that was bound to come.

He didn't flinch at my words, didn't step back. Instead, he pulled me closer, his hand resting against the small of my back, his thumb brushing across the fabric of my shirt. The heat of his touch burned through me, and I fought the instinct to lean into it. To let the fire consume me.

"Means forever," he said simply, as if that one word could unravel everything. It was enough to make the world tilt on its axis, to make the sound of the city below us fade into something distant, irrelevant. The world could have stopped spinning right then, and I think I would've been okay with it, because in that moment, I understood. We were fire. And fire could never be contained.

But it wasn't just the ring, was it? It wasn't the promise that burned in our veins. It was the weight of everything we'd survived to get here. The battles we fought, the walls we'd built, and the slow, fragile dance of trust that had crept between us like a wild thing, untamed and dangerous. We weren't just two people on a rooftop. We were the aftermath of all we had endured, the fragile threads of a story woven together by fate.

"I never thought it would be this easy," I admitted, my voice barely above a whisper, as if saying the words aloud would somehow make them less real. But the truth was there, and I couldn't deny it. Not anymore.

Evan's eyes softened, the intensity behind them flickering like a candle struggling against a draft. "You think it's easy?" he asked, his words a soft challenge. "You think any of this has been easy?"

I laughed, bitter and low. "Maybe easy wasn't the right word," I said. "But I never thought we'd get here. That we'd be standing here, together, with the city at our feet, a ring on my finger, and the world in our hands. I didn't think we'd get to this part of the story."

"You and me?" Evan asked, his voice so sure, so steady. "We've always been here. We've just been too stubborn to see it."

The wind shifted then, like a signal, and for the first time, I let myself believe it. That we had always been here. That we'd always been a part of this, this fire, this love, this unspoken promise that burned brighter than anything I'd ever known.

And the fire? It wasn't going anywhere. It was just getting started.

It wasn't that the city's lights ever looked any different—it was just that tonight, they seemed to hum louder, to pulse with a rhythm that matched my own. The buildings, tall and jagged, almost seemed to breathe with me. I didn't know if it was the ring on my finger, the heat of Evan's hand on my back, or the fact that in that moment, everything felt oddly still despite the world continuing its dizzying spin around us.

"I don't know how to do this," I said suddenly, and the words fell from my lips as easily as the breeze that ruffled my hair. They were out before I could stop them, hanging in the air like smoke, unexpected but undeniable.

Evan paused, turning to me with that look—the one that always made my heart skip, a mix of curiosity and concern, like he wanted to peel back every layer of me until he could see what made me tick. But instead of the usual reassurance, instead of his hand on my cheek or a quick kiss to silence the anxiety that always seemed to coil inside me, he stepped back. A single step, like he was distancing himself without meaning to.

"What do you mean?" he asked, the softness of his voice a sharp contrast to the sudden distance between us.

I shrugged, feeling the weight of his gaze like an invisible pressure pushing against me. "I mean, this—us. What we're doing. What we're about to do. It feels too... big. And I'm not sure I know how to carry that. I'm not sure I know how to be the kind of person who deserves this."

He didn't speak right away, and I could feel the tension winding tighter, wrapping itself around my chest. I could see his thoughts running through his mind—how he was probably trying to piece together the puzzle of my words, figure out where I was coming from. But I knew him too well. I could feel his hesitation, feel him weighing the decision to either press me or pull back.

Instead of pressing, though, he let out a slow breath, the kind that seemed to release all the tension in his body, and he closed the space between us.

"You think this is too big for you?" he asked, his hands finding mine again, his fingers curling around mine like they were meant to be there. "You think you're too small to carry this?"

I felt my breath catch, and something inside me softened, though I still couldn't explain the knot in my stomach. "I'm not like you," I admitted quietly. "You're so sure. You know what you want. You know what you're doing. Me? I'm just... trying to figure it out as I go. And sometimes, I think I'm not good at it. At us."

Evan's laugh was soft but genuine, a sound that vibrated in my bones in the most unexpected way. "You know," he said, his thumb brushing over the back of my hand, "I think you're selling yourself short. But if you really want to get into it, then maybe we should talk about you being too much like me."

I raised an eyebrow, more out of instinct than anything else. "What?"

He smiled then, his gaze locking with mine in that way that made everything else fade into the background. "You think I'm sure about everything? You think I've got this whole thing figured out? You think I don't lie awake some nights wondering if I'm about to screw it all up? If this ring is too big a promise for me to keep?"

I opened my mouth to say something—maybe to disagree, maybe to offer some kind of reassurance—but the words died before they could take shape. I wasn't used to seeing Evan like this. The mask of confidence was gone, replaced by something more raw, something unspoken but still just as true. It was a reminder that none of us, no matter how sure we appeared on the outside, ever really had it all figured out.

"I don't know what we're doing either," he continued, his voice lower now, more intimate, like we were the only two people in the world. "But I know it feels right. And I know that I'd rather face it with you than face it alone. So, maybe we're not perfect. Maybe we don't have it all figured out. But if there's one thing I do know... it's that I can't imagine doing this with anyone else."

The vulnerability in his words shook me, left me off-kilter. I knew it wasn't meant to be an easy answer, and I knew that part of me had expected him to be the rock I leaned on, the one who always had everything under control. But this? This was something different. This was Evan giving me the truth in its most undiluted form. And the raw honesty of it left me breathless.

I swallowed hard, feeling something shift deep within me. "Evan," I whispered, unsure whether I meant it as a plea, a question, or something else entirely.

His fingers tightened around mine, and he stepped even closer, his forehead brushing against mine. "We're going to get through this," he murmured, as though it was a quiet declaration to the universe. "We've already made it this far, haven't we?"

I nodded slowly, my pulse quickening. Maybe I was more scared than I was letting on, more uncertain about what the future might hold. But there was a certainty in his words that I couldn't ignore. We were already bound by something, something strong and enduring, like the fire that had once threatened to consume us, but now it felt like it was keeping us warm instead.

"And if it's not easy?" I asked, the question slipping out before I could stop it, even though I knew the answer.

"Then we'll make it easy," he replied simply. "We'll do whatever it takes. But together."

In that moment, I didn't need to hear more. The weight of his words, their quiet promise, was enough. Because I knew—deep in my bones—that we were in this together. And that was all that mattered.

The city stretched out before us, its lights like little fires scattered across the night, but even they seemed insignificant next to the heat between us. I leaned into Evan's chest, feeling the steady rise and fall of his breath beneath my cheek. It was hard to believe that a few moments ago, we had been standing here, uncertain, tangled in the words we hadn't known how to say. Now, all that was left was the warmth of his embrace and the ring on my finger, like some promise I still wasn't sure I deserved.

"You're quiet," he murmured, his voice a soft hum in the night air, just shy of a whisper. I hadn't realized how much silence had settled around us until he spoke.

I tilted my head back, eyes tracing the stars above, but they seemed so far away, unreachable in the way that dreams sometimes felt. "I'm thinking," I said, my words slow, careful, as though they might break if I wasn't gentle enough. "Thinking about everything. About how we got here. And about what happens next."

Evan's hand shifted, his thumb brushing lightly over my ring, a reminder that nothing was ever quite as simple as it seemed. "What do you mean, next?"

I let out a small laugh, but there was no humor in it. "Next, like... after the promises. After the rings. After all of this. What happens when the world doesn't stop spinning, when the noise picks up again, when the chaos comes knocking? What happens when we realize that everything we've promised each other is going to be tested?" My words tumbled out faster now, a flood I couldn't control, a torrent of thoughts I hadn't meant to voice. "What if I can't be what you need? What if I fail?"

Evan didn't pull back, didn't flinch. Instead, he held me tighter, as though somehow anchoring me to him, to this moment. "You think I haven't asked myself those same questions?" he asked, his voice low and steady. "You think I haven't stood here, just like you, wondering if I can be the man you deserve? If I can be enough?"

I turned in his arms, meeting his gaze. "But you are enough, Evan. You are." I was surprised by the force of my words, by how true they felt. But there was more—something else I hadn't said yet. "It's me I'm worried about."

Evan's expression softened, his brow furrowing slightly in that familiar way. "And what about you?"

I swallowed hard, the weight of it all pressing against my chest. "What if I'm not enough for me?" I said, my voice barely above a whisper, the words raw and vulnerable. The truth of them hurt more than I had expected. But it was there, lodged deep inside me, this quiet fear that I couldn't shake. That I would reach for something greater and fall short, that the flames we'd built would flicker out, leaving me in the cold.

He didn't answer immediately. Instead, he cupped my face in his hands, his touch tender, gentle, as though I were something fragile that might shatter if he wasn't careful. "I can't promise that life won't get messy. That things won't get hard. But I can promise that no matter what, I'll be here. We'll be here, together. And you don't have to be anything more than you are."

I closed my eyes, letting the warmth of his hands sink into my skin, grounding me in the present, in this moment where the rest of the world felt so far away. It was more than I could have hoped for, more than I could have asked for, but it still wasn't enough. There was something else, something lingering at the edges of my mind, something I couldn't ignore.

I opened my eyes again, searching his face for some sign that he knew what was coming, that he could sense it too. "I know you're here," I said, the words thick with the weight of everything I hadn't said yet. "But I need to know that you'll still be here when the world goes up in flames. Because it will. It always does."

For a moment, Evan didn't speak, his gaze locking onto mine, like he was reading the unspoken parts of me that I hadn't even known existed. And then, slowly, deliberately, he leaned in, pressing his lips against mine in a kiss that was soft at first, then insistent, as if he were trying to burn away all my fears, all my doubts. And for a moment, I let him. Let myself believe that maybe, just maybe, we could survive this. All of it.

But as we pulled away, something shifted in the air. The wind grew colder, sharper, and I felt the hairs on the back of my neck rise, a familiar sense of danger creeping in, like the first signs of a storm. My heart rate spiked, the warmth of the moment slipping through my fingers like sand. Something was wrong. I could feel it.

"Did you hear that?" I whispered, my voice barely above the wind.

Evan stiffened, his eyes narrowing, scanning the rooftops around us, the shadows suddenly seeming darker, more alive. "What do you mean?"

I took a step back, suddenly uneasy, my pulse quickening. The city, once so comforting, now felt like a maze, a place where danger could lurk behind every corner, where the fire I'd trusted so completely could turn on me in an instant.

"I don't know," I said, the words feeling inadequate even as they left my mouth. "But something's not right."

And then, from somewhere in the distance, I heard it. The faint sound of footsteps—too heavy, too deliberate to be just another passerby. My heart lurched. "Evan—"

But before I could finish, the unmistakable sound of a door slamming open echoed from behind us. The world tilted on its axis, and I felt a chill settle in my bones, the kind that had nothing to do with the wind.

The footsteps grew closer. And then, the unmistakable crackle of static filled the air.

"Don't move," a voice barked from the shadows, sharp and cold.

And just like that, the fire that had burned so brightly between us faltered, caught in the wind, threatened to burn out entirely.